T0339934

continued . . .

THE
LONE
WARRIOR

DENISE ROSSETTI

BERKLEY SENSATION, NEW YORK

THE BERKLEY PUBLISHING GROUP
Published by the Penguin Group
Penguin Group (USA) Inc.
375 Hudson Street, New York, New York 10014, USA
Penguin Group (Canada), 90 Eglinton Avenue East, Suite 700, Toronto, Ontario M4P 2Y3, Canada
(a division of Pearson Penguin Canada Inc.)
Penguin Books Ltd., 80 Strand, London WC2R 0RL, England
Penguin Group Ireland, 25 St. Stephen's Green, Dublin 2, Ireland (a division of Penguin Books Ltd.)
Penguin Group (Australia), 250 Camberwell Road, Camberwell, Victoria 3124, Australia
(a division of Pearson Australia Group Pty. Ltd.)
Penguin Books India Pvt. Ltd., 11 Community Centre, Panchsheel Park, New Delhi—110 017, India
Penguin Group (NZ), 67 Apollo Drive, Rosedale, Auckland 0632, New Zealand
(a division of Pearson New Zealand Ltd.)
Penguin Books (South Africa) (Pty.) Ltd., 24 Sturdee Avenue, Rosebank, Johannesburg 2196,
South Africa

Penguin Books Ltd., Registered Offices: 80 Strand, London WC2R 0RL, England

This book is an original publication of The Berkley Publishing Group.

PRINTING HISTORY
Berkley Sensation trade paperback edition / May 2011

Library of Congress Cataloging-in-Publication Data

Rossetti, Denise.
  The lone warrior / Denise Rossetti.—Berkley Sensation trade pbk. ed.
      p. cm.
  ISBN: 978-0-425-24091-5
  1. Female assassins—Fiction. 2. Demonology—Fiction. I. Title.
  PS3618.O8484L66   2011
  813'.6—dc22   2010054170

147204767

Prologue

She was dead, gone from him forever. And all for the life of a puny girl child.

"Show me," said the baron of Lonefell Keep.

Shaking with terror, the midwife placed a small warm bundle in his arms. Reflexively, he tightened his grip and the babe squirmed, mewling. The baron stared down at the skin of her cheek, palest ivory and roses, and examined the slender fingers and long bones. Then he looked for an endless time at the body of the tiny, olive-skinned woman lying twisted among the bloodied sheets. She had been his cousin, and there was a strong resemblance between them.

Finally, he lifted his gaze to the window. Outside, in the barrack square, his sergeant of the guard drilled Lonefell's soldiers. The man had journeyed an unimaginable distance from the far north to join the baron's service. A light breeze fondled his long braids, so fair as to be almost white. Sunlight caressed broad shoulders and long, straight limbs.

A film of ice formed over the baron's heart, for he had been foolish enough to love his pretty young wife.

He thrust the child at the trembling midwife and ripped open the door. His captain stood outside, awaiting his lord's pleasure. With a jerk of his chin, the baron drew the man to him. "Kill the northern barbarian!"

When the man's face went slack with shock, he snarled, "*Now!*"

He strode away without a backward look, dismissing the child from his mind and his life.

After a week, the midwife, nonplussed, named the babe Mehcredi, for that had been her sister's name. Then she handed the infant over to a passing maidservant and departed. The squalling bundle passed from one exasperated maid to another until one more ruthless than the others set the child aside in a distant storeroom. She considered it a politic move, for after all, hadn't the baron made his disinterest clear? In any case, the life of a single girl child was a cheap and easy thing.

Mehcredi would have died, save for the merest chance. A few days later, the keep's laundress was brought to bed of a stillborn son. That in itself was not such an unusual occurrence, but the loss affected the woman strangely. She fell into a deep melancholy, complicated by milk fever. By the time her best friend bethought herself of the abandoned babe, the child was almost too weak to suck.

But suck she did, with an avid desperation, and the washerwoman recovered. But the melancholy lingered like an evil spell. Mehcredi had reached the toddling stage when the woman drowned herself in one of the deep stone tubs in the laundry, her hair floating like weeds among the baron's sheets.

The child grew wild and dirty, scavenging like a little animal, her fingers always clawed, ready to snatch, her strange, light eyes stretched wide. As the seasons passed, she shot up like a sturdy sapling, pale as a snow birch seeking the sun. No one spoke to her, save in passing. No one touched her, save for an absentminded buffet if she were underfoot.

Only fat old Cook noticed the girl, for he loved to see a body eat and Mehcredi inhaled anything he gave her, in any amount, at any time. She haunted the cavernous kitchen, for there it was warm and she could fill the emptiness inside her. But all she did was grow— and grow and grow—her long limbs straight and true, her shoulders square and well set.

The laughter of the castle children excited her almost unbearably, but they interacted according to unwritten rules she had no hope of understanding. On the rare occasions she was permitted to join in, something always went wrong, though she was never able to pin down what it was. Baffled, angry and hurt, she'd stand like a lump while the little ones pointed and complained and the older children jeered.

Chewing her thumb, she lurked in the shadows, a tall, pale wraith, staring, always staring. More than once, she pushed or kicked a smaller child, so she could watch with greedy eyes when it ran to its mother and was comforted. She had to blink back the tears every time, though she could never work out where they came from or why—or even prevent them in the first place. With a defiant sniff, she'd stamp off to the kitchens and swipe a pastry.

By the time she had breasts and a woman's hips, Mehcredi was already taller than most men, monosyllabic and sullen. A few years later, when she stood at Cook's graveside, she was six feet in height, her strange silver eyes shielded by thick, light brown lashes. A tangle of ice-pale hair straggled down her broad back, almost as far as the swell of her buttocks.

Before dawn the following morning, she crept into the baron's study, levered open the lock on his treasure box and took what she thought she was owed simply for surviving. Without a word, she hauled herself onto one of the castle's grain wagons, heading for market in Caracole of the Leaves. By first light, she was long gone.

Mehcredi discovered, rather to her surprise, that she liked Caracole, that city of sea-canals and shining white towers and smiling vice, a far cry from the silence and cold unyielding stone of Lonefell Keep. When she sat idle, watching the summer breeze play chase and kiss with the blue wavelets in the canals, strange thoughts drifted into her head, tantalizing fragments of meaning hovering just beyond her grasp, eluding her by the smallest of margins. Skiffs and barges floated by, the people on board talking, laughing, arguing, or sitting in comfortable silence with their arms around each other.

She'd hoped it might be different here, away from the keep, but it wasn't. She didn't know how to do any of the things other folk did so naturally. When she tried, they looked at her sidelong—or worse, they laughed outright and turned away.

As if life were a cruel game and they had all the pieces, while she'd been robbed of hers before birth.

After a week of increasing frustration, grief and fury, Mehcredi betook herself and the baron's gold to the House of the Assassins. The

Lonefell soldiers made the sign of the Sibling Moons every time the place was mentioned, half in awed admiration, half in horror. If they were impressed, so was she. She thought no more deeply than that, like a child who only comprehends enough of the world to want what it wants.

Those who had the power of life and death controlled the pieces and the board, and therefore the game itself. Or so she reasoned.

1

Death padded in pursuit, slipping through the double shadows without a sound. Like the worst nightmare Mehcredi could imagine, except this was all too horribly real. How much longer could she elude him, the man with the hunter's face? Panting, she glanced over her shoulder at the dark figure pacing behind. As he drifted from one patch of shadow to the next, something pale gleamed where the light of the Sibling Moons tangled in his black hair. Feathers worked into a long braid, and . . . bones?

Were they *finger bones?*

The shock thrilled down her nerves, making her head swim and her vision blur, but her long legs carried her away at a swift, stumbling run, lurching down a narrow alley, deeper into the reeking slum the people of Caracole called the Melting Pot. Turning to fight never entered her head. Gods, she'd barely scraped through the First Circle tests as it was, and her first real commission for the Guild of Assassins had been an unqualified disaster. No, she wouldn't have a chance.

She couldn't hear his footfall, couldn't detect any movement, but his presence behind her was a tangible force. Every cell in her body sensed him with the animal instinct of the hunted—his predatory focus, the grim relish with which he anticipated her death. From her left came the frantic click of claws on the cobbles, a soft whining noise. That damn dog! She might as well wave a flaming torch above her head and be done with it.

"Get lost," she hissed, glancing around for something to throw.

"Scat!" But the little animal only skittered aside, continuing to flank her.

Mehcredi twisted and doubled back. One hand pressed to the stitch in her side, she reeled around a corner and inevitably, there he stood, waiting—pitiless. He wasn't a great deal taller than she was, but much broader. Lithe and strong and graceful, where she was long-boned and clumsy and doomed.

She opened her mouth to shriek, to plead, but long-fingered hands fastened around her throat. As he slowly increased the pressure, digging painfully into the soft flesh under her jaw, the man smiled, lips pulling back from white teeth. The expression gave him an eerie, chilling beauty. He could have been an avenging angel or a handsome demon. Either way, those elegant brutal hands were the sure instruments of her death.

Her fists flailed, punching. When that failed, she raked at his forearms with her nails, but he didn't even flinch. Mehcredi knew she was strong, stronger than any woman she'd ever met, but it made no difference. Black spots formed in her vision, her lungs labored and cramped.

"No," she tried to rasp. "No, please."

From far off, as if down a long tunnel, came the sound of hysterical barking.

The man thrust his face into hers. "*Now you pay,*" he snarled as he sent her down into the dark. "*Assassin.*"

By the bones of Those Before, she was a strange one, this Mehcredi. Walker had never seen a woman like her. Certainly, never one so pale, nor so big. He stared down at her unconscious form, stretched full length in the bottom of the skiff he was poling under the Bridge of Empty Pockets. He flexed his shoulders, still a little surprised by her bulk. But he'd managed well enough in the end, heaving her over his shoulder in the alley and manhandling her into the skiff without tipping it over. Drowning the assassin wasn't part of his plan. Every time she looked like regaining consciousness, he shoved hard fingers into the nerve cluster behind her ear and she slipped away again.

Arriving at his House of Swords, he moored the skiff, hauled her out and dumped her at the foot of the stairs. Then he woke Pounder, whose room was on the ground floor. It took the combined heft of two fit, powerful men to haul her long limp body up the steep flights to the top floor. Once they had her laid out in the narrow bed, Walker unfastened her cloak, discovering it was thickly padded. So was her jerkin and vest. An interesting disguise, part of an assassin's stock in trade. No wonder she'd looked so bulky.

He had the woman down to shirt and trews before heavy breath on the back of his neck recalled him to the presence of his companion.

"Brother's balls," rumbled Pounder, chewing his moustache, battered brows arched in surprise. "She's not bad. Don't look like a murderin' bitch, not really. Who'd a thought it?"

Who indeed?

The woman moaned and rolled her head on the pillow. Her lashes fluttered, revealing a glimpse of strange silver irises. Unnerved, Pounder fell back with a curse, making the sign of the Sibling Moons.

Her white blond hair whispering across his knuckles, Walker used the nerve-pinch to send her under again. The agitation smoothed away, leaving her face unlined and innocent as a sleeping child's, marred only by the ugly necklace of bruises around her white throat. Her body was . . . well, *lush* was the word that came to mind, broad-shouldered and deep-bosomed. Long, strong bones. No wonder they'd found her dead weight so awkward to maneuver.

A murderer for hire.

Walker sent Pounder away before he unlaced her shirt and folded it back to expose one magnificent breast. The left. He had to be able to access her heart.

His fingers itched to slap her awake, to take his blade and carve Dai's full name into the soft swell of flesh. The Ancestors had blessed him; he was light handed, deft. He could make the agony last for hours.

He closed his eyes, seeing Dai convulsing on the tavern floor until his spine cracked, the hideous clotted sounds he'd made as the prettydeath clawed his gullet to ribbons. Gods, poor Dai—merry and wicked, gifted with the charm of a junior angel and the morals of an alley cat. Yet the man was never casual about his blade work. He could have been a swordmaster in his own right, with his own establishment, but he'd chosen to stay at Walker's House of Swords, the gods knew why.

He owed Dai for his loyalty. The assassin owed the man for his pain.

Walker prayed to Those Before for the discipline not to kill her. Then he reached out and spread the fingers of his left hand over Mehcredi's breast and cleavage. He touched only what he needed to touch, even when her nipple stiffened, ruching into a velvety pout as tender and pink as a new rose.

Kneeling by the bed, he concentrated so hard everything faded away save the beating heart beneath his palm and the Magick he drew from deep in the loamy earth, welling up from the *ch'qui* of the planet. One tendril at a time, he willed green spectral shoots out of the rich moist soil and wound them gently around her heart, a cage of Magick to keep her with him, interwoven with guards to prevent her doing further harm to Dai. What he crafted was beautiful, because to do less with what the Ancestors had given him would have been blasphemy. In the end, he let instinct guide him and when he opened his eyes, the thing was done, the delicate fronds of the pattern as pleasing to his aesthetic sense as the graceful, unbreakable strength of the Magick.

Walker laced up her shirt, his fingers a little unsteady. Something deep in his guts ached. He hadn't done a Magick as powerful as that for a long time. Why bother? The Shar were gone, his people no more than ash blown by the hot desert winds. Alone, always and ever.

The dreams were terrible. Or was this death? A succession of horrors to be endured over and over, endlessly?

A cloak of formless evil gathered in the night sky and swooped—smothering her mouth and eyes and nostrils in a blanket of filth, plucking at her nerves with strong, cruel fingers. Mehcredi tried to scream her agony, but no sound emerged. Instead, the Necromancer's thin, sexless voice echoed in her skull. *You failed me, assassin,* it said. *Failure is not acceptable in my service.*

Her soul shrank with horror. Gods, not again, she'd rather die. Every dream visit from the Necromancer had been a leisurely violation, undertaken with casual, lip-smacking glee.

The hunter appeared suddenly, all of a piece, as dream figures do. Immediately, the Necromancer's hideous form shrank, coalescing until it was no more than a greasy spot that oozed away, trickling down a gutter. Mehcredi turned to her nemesis with something very like a sigh of relief, her throat bared and vulnerable. Merciless he might be, but his presence was clean, sharp as a blade, with none of the taint of evil about it. There was the strangest comfort in that. Strong fingers squeezed, choking, hurting.

Writhing, she struggled for air. A painful gasp brought her awake, her eyes snapping open. Above was a low, whitewashed ceiling with a pronounced slope. Wonderingly, she patted her throat with her fingertips. Gods, she was alive! But how—?

She turned her head.

A man sat opposite on a wooden chair placed squarely against the door, his empty hands in plain sight, folded across a flat stomach. His eyes closed, he was so still in the warm light of the lamp he could have been a statue cast in bronze. Mehcredi's gaze darted over high slashing cheekbones, an imperious nose and uncompromising mouth. His body was all lean length, whipcord and muscle, clad conventionally enough in a working man's shirt and trews, soft boots.

Beyond him, on the other side of the door, lay freedom.

Soundlessly, Mehcredi eased herself up on her elbows, her head pounding like a funeral drum. She was lying on a narrow bed, no more than a pallet, in a room not much bigger than a cupboard. Remarkably, there were no ropes, no restraints, nothing to impede her— save the man.

His long legs were stretched before him, ankles crossed. Mehcredi stared longingly at the scabbard hanging from his belt. She ran her tongue over dry lips. If she could grab the weapon before he woke . . .

She lifted her gaze to his face and swallowed a scream.

The man was watching her, his dark gaze unreadable. But then, she'd never been able to fathom what people were thinking, feeling. His eyes were black—as dark as his hair. The lamplight struck bluish gleams from the sable thickness of it, falling soft and straight as rain over his shoulders, two thin braids on either side of his face.

And she knew him.

"The bones." Her voice came out raspy, even huskier than usual. "Where are the bones?"

The hunter regarded her in silence. Unnerved, Mehcredi scrambled as far away as possible, until her shoulder blades were pressed right up against the wall behind the bed. She tucked her legs beneath her.

After an interminable wait, during which her heart banged against her ribs like a trapped bird, he said, "You are Mehcredi the assassin." It wasn't a question.

She raised her chin. "I—" Her voice cracked so badly she had to stop and swallow. The hunter crossed his arms over his chest and the gleam in his eye became more pronounced. "I am a member of the Guild, yes."

"Count yourself fortunate Dai's not dead. Thanks to Erik's quick wits."

She hadn't known the man's name, only that watching him writhe on the tavern floor, his merry handsome face contorted into a mask of excruciating pain, had made her guts heave. At the memory, bile rose in her throat, sour and burning. "H-he's not?" She swallowed again. "Water, I need water."

The hunter went on as if she hadn't spoken. "Though I don't doubt he wishes he was." A pause. "You used prettydeath, assassin."

This time, Mehcredi had no problem recognizing the expression that flashed across his grim features. She'd seen it every day of her life. Revulsion. Disgust.

"What's that?" she whispered. "I swear, I—"

"You didn't know it's absolute agony? That it can take a whole day to die?"

Abruptly, the hunter rose, lethal grace in every line of him. Stalking to the foot of the bed, he raised one arm and pressed his palm against the low ceiling. He leaned in, dominating, his eyes flat and black. "Someone wanted him to suffer. Don't lie to me, *assassin*."

"No." Mehcredi shook her head, panic slowing her wits. "No, I'm not lying. Anyway, it was a mistake. He wasn't supposed—" She broke off on a gasp.

"I know. It was Erik Thorensen you were meant to murder. The singer."

"N-not murder. I had a . . . had a commission."

His lips compressed. "Don't dress it up. Murder, pure and simple."

"The Guild Master calls them commissions."

A dark brow winged up.

Desperately, Mehcredi stumbled on, wishing he would look away, give her even a split second of relief. "He said he'd help me, seeing it was my first, so he gave me . . . gave me—May I have some water? Please?"

"No. Gave you what?"

"The . . . the poison. P-prettydeath."

"And you didn't know what it was? Is that the story?"

She shook her head. "He didn't say. Only that it never failed."

The hunter's hand dropped to the hilt of the long dagger in his belt. He straightened, his lip curling. "Then you must have crawled from beneath a rock. Prettydeath is notorious here, and among all the known worlds."

"I'm not from Caracole, or anywhere near it."

He grunted. "Where, then?"

"Lonefell."

A shrug.

"Beyond the Cressy Plains. In the high hills."

His hard stare shifted to the tangle of her pale hair. "To the north?"

She nodded.

Another grunt. The hunter returned to his seat. "You kidnapped Prue McGuire, didn't you?"

Mehcredi's nerve cracked. "Who are you? What do you *want*?"

Another of those dreadful silences. At last, he said, "My name is Walker and this is my House of Swords. As for what I want?" His lips pulled back from his teeth. "I will see you pay for your crimes, assassin."

"*But what did I do to you?*" she cried, almost sobbing.

"To me? Why, nothing." Again that feral expression, like a tygre crouched for the kill. "But on the floor below is a man who can't make a sound louder than a kitten, though he needs to scream. Your poison stripped the flesh from his throat."

When she opened her mouth, he overrode her. "You kidnapped a woman from The Garden of Nocturnal Delights, an innocent you delivered into the filthy hands of unimaginable evil. Even now—"

When he broke off frowning, his hair shifted on his shoulders like a shawl of midnight silk. "She might be dead. And Erik's likely to get himself killed finding her."

"I don't understand." *Unimaginable evil.* Mehcredi's skin crawled. She searched the hunter's face, but regardless of what he might be feeling, it told her nothing. Faces rarely did.

"Why do you care? What are they to you?"

"Why do I—? It's none of your concern, assassin, but Dai works for me. As for Prue McGuire, she audits my accounts."

Prue. Oh yes, she remembered Prue. Unconsciously, Mehcredi rubbed the bruise on her thigh, wincing. Who'd have thought someone so small would be so fierce? Sister in the sky, the woman had very nearly got away. If it hadn't been for the special cloth saturated with the stupefying drug . . . She owed that to the Guild Master too.

Walker's gaze was fixed on her flexing fingers. The corners of his mouth turned up, very slightly. Did that mean he was amused? Was it safe to relax? "She hurt you, didn't she?" he said. "Good."

Mehcredi blinked. "Why is that good?"

A vertical crease formed between his brows. "Don't be stupid," he said, biting off each word.

"I'm not." Mehcredi chewed her lip, feeling the heat rising in her cheeks.

Half-wit, they used to call her at Lonefell. A casual clout across the ear from the housekeeper. *Get out o' the way, ye great daft lump!* Followed by the muttered aside to a visitor. *She's not all there, ye know.*

But she *was*, she *was* all there. She just didn't like staring eyes and hard, cruel hands—or things she didn't understand, like the human race in general.

Mehcredi forced herself to concentrate. From what she'd seen at the keep, people cared only about those they loved or feared, but it didn't sound as though Prue and Dai were Walker's lovers, or that they scared him. At least, she didn't think so. Which left . . . "These two, they're your, uh, friends?"

Every vestige of expression disappeared from his face and she was back where she'd begun. Clueless.

"Who employed you?" he demanded.

The tremors became so bad, she had to wrap her arms around her torso to stop the shaking. "I'm sure you know," she whispered, staring fixedly at his boots.

"Possibly." A shift in the air told her he was leaning forward again, intent. "Give me a description."

"C-can't."

"Too scared?" Contempt again, the expression familiar.

Mehcredi shook her head, beads of cold sweat springing up around her hairline. The only power in the world she found more discomfiting than the Necromancer stood right in front of her. "A b-black cloud, he came as a black cloud, a shadow. There was nothing to see."

He moved without warning, more swiftly than the eye could follow. Before she could blink, Walker was crouched at her side, the point of a long silvery blade pressed into the pit of her throat. Cold, so very cold.

"You lie." His eyes blazed into hers.

"No, no!" She didn't dare even to swallow.

"Tell me, then. Everything you remember, every detail, no matter how small, every impression."

"A s-servant made the arrangements, told me to c-come to the Pavilion of Clouds and Rain at The Garden of Nocturnal Delights."

The tip of the knife drifted over her skin in a calculated, icy caress. "I know the place. Go on."

"He was there, waiting."

"And?"

"I thought he was wearing a cloak at first." The force of Walker's stare dragged the words out of her. "But he *was* the cloak. When I looked, there was n-nothing inside. Only black. No eyes, nothing."

"The voice. Did he have an accent?"

Mehcredi wet her lips with the point of her tongue. "I'm not very good with voices."

"Don't tempt me, assassin. I'd enjoy carving it out of you." Walker's teeth gleamed white against the bronze of his face. "His accent?"

Oh, gods. She squeezed her eyes shut for a moment, trying to think, to recall. "Like everyone here in the city." She shot him a glance. "Except you."

A muscle in his jaw tightened. "I'm not from Caracole. So, a local accent. What else?"

Mehcredi frowned, her brain spinning with effort. "We keep saying 'he,' but I don't know . . . It was thin and light. Maybe female." A
thought struck her and she grabbed his forearm. "Oh!"

The muscles beneath the linen of his shirt went rigid. How could
the heat of him burn her palm when the blade he held at her throat
was colder than the dark waters of Lonefell tarn?

"What?"

"The servant! Why don't you torture him instead of me?"

Walker eased back. "I intend to." Smoothly, he rose and turned
to the rickety nightstand tucked under the lowest part of the roof.
Sheathing the blade at his waist, he busied himself with a chipped
earthenware jug and a rough cup.

Turning, he thrust the cup at her. "Here."

Greedily, Mehcredi gulped the cool water. Nothing had ever felt
so good.

"Slowly." Strong, warm hands closed over hers and she gasped with
shock. A touch that was not a blow. "Don't choke yourself. I have
plans for you, Mehcredi."

She wiped her mouth with the back of her hand. "Plans?" Her
stomach lurched unpleasantly. "What plans?"

Walker gave her another of those impenetrable stares. "All in good
time. Tell me again, from the very beginning."

"You already know!"

A shrug. "Again," he said inexorably.

Mehcredi gritted her teeth. "But why?"

"There may be something we missed. I'll know if you lie, assassin."

She sprang to her feet, fists clenched. "But I don't know how to
lie!"

"*Sit down.*" He didn't raise his voice, but it cracked like a whip.

2

Mehcredi's knees turned to water. Stunned and shaky, she collapsed on the bed.

"You've had dealings with a necromancer," said Walker. "Very foolish. How did he contact you? Through the servant?"

"He . . . he came to me in my dreams." She couldn't prevent the reminiscent shudder. Phrase by halting phrase, Walker drew the experience out of her, every hideous second of it.

By the end, he looked more like a statue than ever. "He hurt you," he said. "The bastard enjoyed your pain."

Her eyes stung. When she rubbed them, her fingers came away wet. "He touched me with his Magick in places . . . Gods, I can't explain properly." She glanced at Walker's hard face, but there was no help there. "Deep inside . . . *me*. It hurt so bad."

If she hadn't woken, she was sure the agony would have killed her, but for once in her miserable life, she'd been lucky. Thank the Sister for the filthy little stray and its insistence on following her everywhere. She couldn't possibly have slept through those piercing barks, the frantic scrabbling at her door.

"I see. The Necromancer simply frightened you into committing murder." His lip had curled again. Was that what people called a sneer? "What happened to greed?"

"He paid me," she said. "But he kept dropping the fee. I think, I think he wanted to kill me. Or . . . something."

"*Something* most likely," said Walker in a voice like winter at Lone-fell Keep.

Cautiously, Mehcredi swung her feet to the floor. She cleared her throat. "Right," she said, trying not to croak. "I've told you everything I know. I'll be off now."

Walker's dark eyes widened, then narrowed. "You think?"

Folding his arms, he leaned against the wall, all casual menace. "You will remain here. There's someone I have to see, but I'll be back before dawn. Get some sleep." A flash of white teeth. "It's going to be a long day, assassin."

He moved so quickly, Mehcredi was left staring as the door clicked quietly behind him. From outside, she heard the decisive rattle of a strong bolt. Godsdammit! Leaping to her feet, she hurried to the small dusty window set beneath the roof line.

A few seconds later, Walker's shadowy figure emerged from the building and strode toward the water stair on the canal. Cursing, she tugged at the stiff catch, exerting all her strength. With a tired creak, the window opened a scant inch and cool night air flooded into the room. The frame looked sturdy enough. Mehcredi set her shoulder to it and *shoved*. The screech of protesting wood echoed like a clarion call in the hush. Ignoring it, she thrust her upper body out into space.

Innumerable stars twinkled smearily against the night sky, the se-rene silver disk of the Sister dipping toward the horizon on a bank of cloud, the Brother at Her heels.

Below, Walker stepped into a small skiff moored at the foot of the stairs. He paused, his head lifting, staring at her for the space of a single heartbeat. Then he grasped the pole and sculled smoothly away down the canal without a backward look.

When she glanced down, her head swam. No wonder he wasn't concerned. The attic room had to be four flights up, and the wall was sheer—no handholds, convenient pipes or trellises. Knowing it was hopeless, she crossed to the door. But she couldn't shift it. Even the nightstand was useless, empty except for a thick layer of dust, the water jug and the cup.

Dully, Mehcredi sank onto the bed, the night breeze cooling her cheeks and playing with her hair. If she propped herself up with the thin pillow at her back, she could see out the window and straight down to the canal. Still shaking a little, she settled down to watch and wait.

Ye great daft lump!

Could she have made a greater mess of it? Not only poisoning the wrong man, but—Oh, gods. She squeezed her eyes tight shut, but behind them, painted on her eyelids, she saw Dai's body twist and heave, bloody foam flecking his lips. What must it feel like to experience such excruciating, relentless pain? Like having your throat lined with shards of glass? Experimentally, she swallowed, trying to imagine it. She succeeded so well that, for a hideous moment, she thought she might vomit. Curling into a fetal position on the bed, Mehcredi wrapped her arms around herself and rocked.

Sister save her, she should have stayed at Lonefell. At least she knew what to expect there, horrible as it was. Rough, bruising hands, beery laughter and offhand brutality. *C'mere, ye half-wit slut.* There was a limit to the number of hidey-holes big enough to accommodate her, even in a rambling keep. One day, she'd be trapped.

Sister save her, what if it was one of the baron's guards, a man she couldn't fight off, ruthless enough to kill her when he was done?

Gazing blankly at the moonslight glancing off the dark wavelets in the canal, she compared the expression on Walker's face with that of the baron's men. Contempt and anger, nothing subtle, nothing she had to guess at. But—she frowned, grappling with thoughts that slid away like small slippery fish—surely there was some kind of difference?

Walker had said he'd make her pay and she believed him absolutely. Whatever he had in mind was going to hurt. A lot.

But when he'd stared into her eyes, he hadn't been looking at a punching bag or a receptacle for his lust. Drawing a breath, she squared her shoulders. No, he'd seen an assassin, someone who *mattered*. She'd never mattered before, to anyone.

Her stomach still aching, Mehcredi rose and began to pace. Three steps forward, a glance out of the window, turn, three steps back, another glance.

Walker returned with the sunrise, appearing out of the dazzle on the water like a djinn, so she had to squint to make him out. Five interminable minutes later, the door opened though she hadn't heard his footfall in the passage. He'd confined the rippling wealth of his hair at the nape of his neck with a leather tie. It exposed the grim severity of his jaw, highlighting the strong bone structure of his face. If possible, he looked even more formidable.

Mehcredi hurried into speech before her nerve could fail her. "I'm ready," she said. "Beat me, flog me, whatever. I promise I'll leave Cara-cole straight after. You'll never see me again." She'd been beaten often enough. She could take it.

Walker's brows winged up. "It's tempting, but no."

Her heart leaped into her throat. "You mean I'm free to go?"

His mouth curved. "You can try, assassin."

Mehcredi knitted her brows. Clearly, he meant for her to under-stand something. But what? The familiar frustration welled up. Why didn't people say what they meant straight out?

"You'll have to tell me," she said bitterly. "I'm stupid, after all."

His eyes did that widening, narrowing thing again. Then, slowly, his lips pulled back from his teeth. He looked . . . *hungry.* "You're mine," he said. "I Marked you."

Mehcredi's mouth fell open. "*What?*"

Walker indicated her chest with his chin. "Have a look."

Almost light-headed with terror, she turned her back, ripping at the laces of her shirt. She stared down. On the inner slope of her left breast, beneath the curve of smooth, pale flesh, gleamed a pattern of intricate whorls and spirals, like ritual smoke trapped under glass. Ex-cept it wasn't gray or black, but a deep greenish bronze.

Mehcredi patted the sinuous shapes with frantic fingers. No pain. Her skin felt exactly the same, warm and smooth. It wasn't a tattoo. She whirled around. "Damn you! What have you done? What is it?"

"I told you." His eyes glinted. "My Mark. To ensure you are mine for as long as I wish it. Your penance, assassin."

Every vestige of warmth bleached from the gold-tinted ivory of the assassin's skin, leaving her the color of old bone. Grimly entertained, Walker watched her process the implications of the Mark, wonder-ing if she might pass out with terror. No problem, the bed was right behind her.

"You *touched* me!" Her husky contralto, already adversely affected by the brutal way he'd choked her, cracked on an ugly rasp.

"Obviously. To do that, I had to."

Mehcredi scrambled back onto the bed, as far away from him as it was possible to get within the confines of the attic room. "I don't like to be touched," she whispered. "And what do you mean, *yours?*"

"Not what you're thinking."

Walker surveyed her from top to toe, taking his time over it, letting her see his scorn, his indifference. He needed to make his meaning clear because, judging by her face, the assassin was bracing herself to resist a rape. Which didn't say much for her previous associates.

He spoke with quiet deliberation. "Don't flatter yourself. You are not appealing to me in any way whatsoever."

A painful flush scalded Mehcredi's cheeks. He let his insolent gaze wander over her body, as if she were a beast at market. She shook so hard, the bed ropes creaked. Good.

"Your skin is fine enough, I suppose. And your coloring is certainly unusual. Silver eyes are rare in the Isles and unknown in Trinitaria." He made his face bland. "You'd bring good creds in a southern slave market." She really was going to faint. "A novelty item."

"No. Please." Her mouth shaped the words, but no sound emerged.

Abruptly, the game lost its savor. "The Mark ensures you cannot escape."

Her brow creased with puzzlement.

"As for your punishment . . ." He paused for effect, conscious of the fixed intensity of her gaze. "I want you to see what you did at close quarters, to feel the impact of it with every beat of what passes for your heart. You will care for what you damaged."

He pinned her with a steady glare. "If your touch is anything less than tender, the Mark will cause you unimaginable pain. I trust you believe me?"

Mehcredi wet her lips with the tip of a pink tongue. "I don't—I don't understand."

"What, again? You really are stupid, assassin," he said cruelly, and watched her flinch. It was strange though, because he could swear he saw intelligence, shining bright as a blade in those amazing eyes. And something that might have been childlike curiosity, swiftly veiled.

When he leaned forward, she shrank away. "You will be Dai's nursemaid," he said. "You will feed him, wash him—sit by his bed and sing to him, if that's what he wants."

"He's not going to"—again, the tongue swiping across pale pink lips—"die?"

"The healers say not." Gods, he hadn't talked so much in years.

His hand on the latch, Walker turned back to face her. "When Dai doesn't need you, there's plenty of dirty work in the scullery, the laundry, the stable. Go see Serafina in the kitchen, she'll tell you what to do. Not an idle moment, assassin."

Her gaze flicked past him to the unlocked door. Whatever this woman's gifts, subterfuge wasn't among them. Unless she was diabolically clever and the ineptness was an act. But somehow, he didn't think so.

He said, "Dai is on the floor below, third door to the left, the room with the view over the water. I called in. He's conscious, more or less, and he knows you're coming."

After a frozen moment, she nodded. Smiling grimly, Walker closed the door quietly behind him. With his usual soundless step, he went downstairs, out to his favorite spot in the garden, a secluded nook where he'd built a small, irregularly shaped pond. Sitting on a bench in the thin morning sun, he waited, listening to the contented burble of running water. When a touchme bush nuzzled his shoulder, he smiled faintly, brushing his fingers over the silvery blossoms. Their happy chime melded with the sound of the fountain.

Any minute now.

From where he sat, screened by the bushes, he could see straight into the fighting salle, the large, airy space empty at this early hour, its sides open to the garden. A rectangle of darkness appeared at the far end, Mehcredi's vague figure hovering uncertainly in the doorway. *Go ahead*, thought Walker. *Get it over with and stop wasting my time.*

But instead of rushing, the assassin lingered, drifting around the perimeter of the room, her face alight with wonder as she examined the racks of weapons on the walls. The touchme bush tinkled mournfully when Walker moved it gently aside. What would she choose? The practice swords were all either wood or blunted metal, but there were throwing stars, a couple of maces, an entire wall full of quarterstaves. And out of reach, high on the opposite wall, a Trinitarian Janizar's two-hander, consisting of a broad curved blade with a jeweled hilt and a poniard so thin it resembled a meat skewer.

Mehcredi grabbed a quarterstaff and gave it an experimental swish. A huge grin bloomed on her face and she executed a funny little lockstep. When her eyes sparkled like that, she looked nothing like the sullen lump he'd just interrogated. Walker's breath caught in his throat, Pounder's rough bass echoing in his head. *Who'd a thought it?*

The quarterstaff twirled, wobbled and collected the assassin smartly on the shin. "Ow!"

Immediately, she glanced around, guilt and apprehension in every line of her. After a moment or two, she relaxed, dropped the staff and bent right over to roll up the leg of her trews, her rounded bottom hoisted in the air.

Walker frowned. Mehcredi had to be the oddest assassin he'd ever encountered. She was certainly flexible enough, as she'd just demonstrated, but her coordination left everything to be desired. How in the Ancestors' names had she passed the Circle tests? The Assassins' Guild insisted on them.

Gingerly, she limped over to the rack and replaced the quarterstaff. He knew the moment she caught sight of the Trinitarian blades on the wall because she went completely still. She thought for what seemed an endless time, one hand absently massaging the necklace of bruises he'd left on her throat. Then she rose on tiptoes, stretching an arm high over her head.

Her fingertips scrabbled uselessly against the wall, at least a foot too short. Now what, assassin?

Her gaze darted around the salle. Biting her lip, she crossed to the door and peered back down the silent passageway. Apparently satisfied, she flipped the lock. Walker shook his head. Any halfway decent sneak thief would have done that in the first place, let alone a Guild-trained professional.

Mehcredi picked up a heavy wooden bench from under a window and wrestled it over to the wall. Now that was impressive. He didn't know another woman strong enough to do that by herself.

Stepping up easily onto the bench, she examined the curved sword, probably drawn by the glitter of gems if the way she was running her fingers over the hilt was any indication.

A stifled yelp sharpened his attention. Still standing on the bench, Mehcredi glared at her forefinger. Then she wiped it on her shirt and stuck it in her mouth, looking so like a petulant child, he almost smiled. Favoring the curved sword with a last, accusing glower, she turned her attention to the thin wicked dagger. With the utmost caution, she lifted it from the supporting brackets, keeping the point well away from her body.

But once she'd gained the floor, she didn't know what to do with it. She had no sword belt, no scabbard or sheath, only the clothes she stood up in. When she tried to shove the blade into her waistband, she came within a hairsbreadth of disemboweling herself. Walker winced. 'Cestors' bones, didn't she know to put it in her boot? What was the Assassins' Guild teaching these days?

Eventually, she worked it out for herself and slid the evil thing into her left boot. Despite the fact she was right-handed, thought Walker in irritation. Cautiously, she stepped out into the garden, her wary gaze passing straight over the touchme bushes that concealed him. On the other hand, she ignored the obvious, the path down to the water stair. Instead, she sidled to the rear corner of the building and peered around it. With an audible huff of relief, she headed toward the stable and the garden sheds.

Silently, Walker rose and padded after her.

Beyond was a small gate giving out onto the narrow street that ran behind all the buildings facing the canal. As the assassin swung it open, he saw her shoulders lift in a huge sigh.

A sharp bark rent the silence. Mehcredi froze, glaring down at the shaggy mongrel capering around her knees. It was an indeterminate color, something between brown, gray and dirt, with a tail like a tattered flag.

"*Will you shut up?*" she hissed, her voice carrying clear as a deep sweet bell in the still morning air. "And stop following me! This is all your fault!"

Walker very nearly laughed aloud, which was a strange thing in itself. In general, he didn't find life amusing.

Unfazed, the dog continued to prance, its whole attitude one of cheerful adoration. Walker suspected there was a toothy grin hidden somewhere under the hair, although only the tip of a black quivering nose was visible.

With a final furtive glance over her shoulder, the assassin stepped into the street.

She stopped in midstride, as if she'd run into a wall. One hand flapped about in a vague sort of way, while the other clutched at her chest. Mehcredi crumpled, shrinking into herself. Her knees went from under her and she fell back through the open gate, landing hard on her backside in a mud puddle.

Gods! Walker took two rapid strides forward, his hand extended.

But the assassin was making too much noise to be dead, rocking back and forth, moaning and hugging herself. The dog nosed at her face, whining and licking.

Walker exhaled carefully, fading back behind the sweeping branches of a convenient widow's hair tree. The Mark was working as it should. For a second there, he thought he might have miscalculated and killed her. Setting his jaw, he told himself to enjoy the spectacle, and waited. An eternity later, she batted the dog out of the way, uncurled and sat up slowly, tears shining on chalk white cheeks.

"Get out of it, you scrounger," she muttered to the little animal, but without much venom. Slowly, she climbed to her feet and turned to stare at the House of Swords.

Almost in full view save for the foliage of his tree, Walker froze and her gaze passed right over him. Again.

Mehcredi wiped her face on her sleeve and sniffed loudly. Then she tugged ineffectually at her muddy trews. "Ah, shit!" she said with tremendous feeling.

Satisfaction warmed Walker's chest. *The penalty for disobedience. Off you go now, assassin, do as you're told.*

But to his surprise, she spun on her heel, hauled in a huge breath and charged the gate with her head down like a human battering ram.

In the second it took him to reach her, she screamed and went down in the street as if poleaxed. Without ceremony, Walker wrapped his fingers around her upper arm and hoisted her bodily to her feet. "I told you," he snapped, hauling her back through the gate.

Gulping, Mehcredi leaned hard against his arm, her face a ghastly shade of gray.

"Throw up on me," he said, "and I'll make you sorry you were ever born."

Huge silver eyes stared into his. "T-too late." She pressed the back of her hand against her mouth and her next words came out muffled. "I already am—sorry I was born, I mean.

Yanking the shirt away from her skin, she peered inside. Walker averted his gaze from what looked like smooth curves of finest-quality alabaster.

"Gods, what have you *done* to me? What *are* you?"

3

"I was a shaman among my people once, long ago, before I took to the sword."

Walker's mouth shut like a trap, as if he hadn't meant to say even that much.

For the gods' sakes, where had he come from? One minute she'd been alone, save for the bloody dog, but making her escape easily enough. The next, her heart caught fire and exploded in her chest. Before the black spots cleared from her vision, Walker had materialized, seemingly out of thin air, wearing his hunter's face.

"A shaman?" Her bones were still rattling like a snow birch in a winter gale, her left breast burning as if she'd been branded. Mehcredi locked her knees. "Is that like a necromancer?"

"No."

He was angry with her again—or perhaps he'd never stopped.

"Are you a wizard?"

"No." Walker turned and strode toward the building, but because he hadn't released his iron grip on her arm, she was dragged along behind him like a naughty child. Sweet Sister, he was strong, stronger even than the Lonefell blacksmith. He'd lifted her out of the mud as if she weighed next to nothing.

The dog trotted at their heels with the jaunty air of one about to be entertained.

Mehcredi tried to pull free without success. "You *hurt* me!"

Walker slid her a stern glance. "Step outside the gate and you will die, assassin."

Atavistic terror raised all the small hairs on the back of her neck. She didn't doubt him.

The Necromancer had swum into her dreams, descending on her like a foul cloud, his cruel, spectral fingers sinking deep into her body, tweaking and pinching her nerves. The violation had had a malicious intent to it, a kind of hideous relish. Walker's Mark was just as lethal, but somehow, it felt impersonal. Like a tygre lying in wait to cut out the weakest in the herd, it was what its nature made it and no more. Only . . . she wasn't the weakest, was she? Stupid might be stupid, but it had its own stubborn endurance.

Mehcredi hauled in a breath and gritted her teeth.

Walker jerked her to a halt in the room with all the weapons on the walls. He snapped his fingers under her nose. "The dagger. Hand it over."

"What dagger?" She held the obsidian gaze.

He didn't blink. "The one in your boot."

He'd said he was a shaman. Did that mean he was a mind-reader too? No, he must have been watching. It was the only answer that made sense. With a shrug of resignation, she retrieved the blade. Handing it over, she asked, "What do you do in here?"

"It's a fighting salle."

"A what?"

A long pause. Walker's eyes narrowed. "For a trained assassin, you don't know much," he said at last.

He didn't need to know how close she'd come to failing even the First Circle. She raised her chin. "So tell me."

"I am a swordmaster. I train mercenaries, soldiers, guards. Here."

"Oh." He must be good, then. Mehcredi considered, mentally contrasting Walker's uncanny patience with the scathing demeanor of the Guild's Arms Master. *Graceful as a sow in rut,* the man had said, tugging at his sparse hair.

Her heart leaped at the thought of a second chance. A swordmaster with his own establishment. He could hardly be worse than the Arms Master. "Would you train me?"

"Not funny, assassin."

"I'll work hard, I promise."

Strong fingers gripped her jaw, tilting her head at an awkward angle. Walker glared into her face, his eyes so fiercely black, she realized she'd misstepped again. Godsdammit, she hadn't meant to make him angry. Would she never learn?

"You," he said, "have the most extraordinary nerve."

Somewhere around their knees, the dog whined, breaking the tension. Walker grunted, lowering his gaze, and Mehcredi released a shaky breath.

"Out." Pointing a stern finger at the garden, he glared at the dog.

It danced about in indecision. Then it plopped its furry backside down on the nice clean mats and turned a shaggy head toward Mehcredi. It must have eyes because she'd noticed it didn't bump into things.

"Get rid of it," growled Walker. "Or I will."

"It's not mine," she protested.

"You're lying. Again."

"No, no." She grabbed at his sleeve. "He follows me everywhere." She shot the dog a murderous glare, but he grinned back, tongue lolling. "I don't want him, but I can't shake him, the stupid, godsbedamned—" Breathing hard, she broke off. "I think he belongs to the Necromancer."

Walker made a huffing noise, deep in his throat. When his lips curved, she decided it might signify amusement.

"Unlikely." Crouching in a single, lithe movement, he snapped his fingers and the dog padded forward to have his ears rubbed. "Necromancers don't keep pets, only corpses." He glanced up. "Do you feed him?"

"Sometimes." For some unknown reason, heat flushed her cheeks. "Hardly ever."

"There you are then." Walker rose in his graceful, unhurried manner. "You're a meal ticket. A stray's idea of heaven."

Between one breath and the next, his face hardened. "The animal's crawling with bitemes. Put him out."

Mehcredi snapped her fingers the way Walker had done and the dog came to her side as if the gesture were Magick. To her surprise, when she moved toward the outer doors, he trotted along. On impulse, she sank to her knees in the doorway and got a lick on the face and a blast of disgustingly hot doggy breath for her trouble.

"Ack!" She wiped her face with her sleeve. "Run away," she hissed. "I don't want you. Go!"

The dog retreated half a dozen steps. Reaching the shade of a ticklewhisker hedge, he sat and scratched behind one ear. Then he turned two full circles, cast a wary glance around the quiet garden and flopped down, boneless. He yawned, showing surprisingly white teeth.

Feeling strangely warmed, Mehcredi closed the doors and returned to Walker.

"Come." He led her back into the dim hush of the sleeping house. The thick, sable tail of his hair fell past his trim waist. She'd never seen a man with hair so long.

"Why don't you cut your hair? It must take an awful lot of looking after."

One of those all-purpose masculine grunts.

Shoulder to shoulder, they climbed the stairs. "It's pretty," she persisted, "but did you know you're going gray, just here—"

As they reached a landing, she raised her fingers to touch his temple, but he knocked her arm away. "Keep your hands to yourself, assassin!"

Unobtrusively, Mehcredi cradled her aching wrist. "Sorry," she said, striving for dignity. "Where are the bones you wore last night? What sort are they? What are they for? You didn't say."

Walker came to a dead halt. When he turned, his face was expressionless, but Mehcredi found herself backing away nonetheless, until the stair rail pressed hard across the small of her back. Silent and remorseless, he followed until she could feel the warmth of his muscular body all along her front. Funny how she tended to think of him as cold, when his physical presence was hotter than anything she'd ever known.

Slowly, so she would know what was coming, Walker raised his hands and fitted them around her throat. His touch was gentle, caressing even, but she'd never felt more terrified, not even when she'd known he was going to kill her.

"Who I am, what I am, is none of your godsbedamned business," he said softly. "You're a coldhearted bitch, a murderer for hire. Not a particularly good one, I grant you, but nonetheless—"

His touch was waking the bruises on her neck. They throbbed in time with her heart.

"You are not my servant, nor my student," continued that quiet, inexorable voice. "And thanks be to Those Before, you are not my friend. Nor will you be, ever."

He drew even closer, as close as a lover, exerting enough pressure to crack her spine over the stair rail. Absurdly luxuriant in that hard face, inky lashes brushed his high cheekbones. "You are my slave, as surely as if I bought you from a dealer in Trinitaria." Callused fingertips drew idle patterns over her thundering pulse. "Slaves do not ask impertinent questions. Understand?"

She nodded as best she could.

His voice dropped to a sibilant whisper. "What are you, Mehcredi?"

"S-slave. Your slave."

"Good. Do not forget it, even for an instant." For the space of two heartbeats, he leaned even harder into her body. Then he withdrew without haste, leaving her braced against the rail, panting.

He'd already reached the third floor before she caught up with him. Despite his warning, new questions seethed in her brain. Who were Those Before? She'd never heard an oath like that.

She supposed she'd become inured to asking questions. When you found it difficult to decipher expressions, it was often the only way. Ask and be damned with a cuff around the head, a bloodied lip.

Don't ask and be double damned.

Sister save her, she had enough problems at the moment. Mehcredi bit her tongue.

"In here." Walker opened a door and they stepped into a chamber so dim, she had difficulty making out the figure lying stiffly under the bedclothes. She wrinkled her nose, her most primitive sense clamoring, telling her this was a lair where an animal had crawled to die. It wasn't so much the pervasive smell of illness, but something thick and dragging that suffocated the spirit.

Walker walked over to the bed, leaving her at the door as if she'd taken root there. The man on the bed didn't move. With his fingertips, Walker brushed the back of the lax hand that lay on the covers. "Dai?" he said softly. "Dai, I know you're awake."

Silence.

"I caught her. Don't you want to see?" Without turning, the sword-master beckoned Mehcredi forward.

Just a job, the Guild Master had said. *Something even you can cope with, Mehcredi of the First Circle.* He'd lifted his brows, lips slightly pursed. His gaze had reminded her of the fish laid out in glittering rows on slabs in Fish Alley in the Melting Pot, all pale and cold and gelatinous. How she'd yearned to take the Master's spare form and break him over her knee!

Just a job. Nausea still roiled in her belly. Holy Sister, it must be the episode at the gate, because now the sensation had intensified. She was going to faint or throw up, or both. Mehcredi edged back, out into the passage, one hand pressed to the still-tender swell of her left breast.

Walker spun around, his long tail of hair swinging like a whip. He didn't raise his voice. "*Come here.*"

Her reluctant feet scuffing draglines in the nap of an exquisite rug, she advanced a couple of steps.

"Closer." Reaching out, he grasped her wrist and yanked her forward.

No. It had to be a mistake. This wasn't the man.

She remembered all three of the people who'd sat with Erik the Golden that night at the Sailor's Lay—after all, she'd spent the whole evening watching them from the back of the tavern, wrapped in her enveloping cloak. A scruffy boy, a brown-haired woman with bright eyes and a handsome laughing man playing some silly game with the lad—*Dai.* He'd been nowhere near as tall and broad as Erik, her quarry, but striking in his own way, all in black, neat and elegant as a cat. A ruby drop had glistened in his ear like a drop of blood and his face had been alight with the joy of a life lived full-tilt.

By the light of the single lamp, she could see now the man in the bed was slight and gaunt, the skin of his face plastered tight against the bones beneath, his dark hair lying lank against the pillow. His dull gaze fastened on her face, wandered away and returned, narrowing. He frowned, the fingers of one hand plucking at the sheet.

Luckily the bed was a four-poster because she had to grab something for support and she'd rather die than lean on Walker again.

When the Guild Master had handed over the tiny vial, he'd told her prettydeath was a sure thing. *Extraordinarily effective,* he'd said. The bastard.

"Her name is Mehcredi," Walker was saying. "She may be the world's worst assassin, but she's caused enough grief for a dozen Tenth Circle masters."

When Mehcredi flinched, one dark brow winged up.

"She was hired to kill Erik Thorensen, but you got in the way." He glanced over his shoulder at her, his eyes as hard as flint. "Think of her as your body slave. Whatever you want, Dai, she'll do it for you."

Dai's head moved fretfully on the pillow. *No.*

"Yes." Walker folded his arms. "You know I don't have any staff to spare, let alone the creds to pay for a nurse. Be as rough with her as you like. This is her punishment—our justice." The teeth flashed in his dark face. "I've Marked her. She can't escape and she can't hurt you."

He turned to Mehcredi. "Purist Bartelm left this powder to be mixed with water and given every two hours without fail." Walker tapped the lid of a small square box that sat on the polished wood of the dresser. "One spoon, no more, no less."

"Who?"

Walker looked at her in silence for a moment. "Purist Bartelm, the most senior wizard in the Enclave. How long have you been in Caracole?"

In the shadowed room, Dai's eyes were great dark pits in his pale face. Intent. Mehcredi wondered if he had a knife under the pillow. Probably.

"A month and a bit." Suddenly needing to move, she crossed to the dresser, removed the lid of the box and peered inside, uneasily conscious of the flat gaze tracking her from the bed. "Oh, it's all sparkly!" she exclaimed in surprise.

"*Don't touch!*"

"Wasn't going to," she muttered, putting the box down with a snap.

"You were." A vertical crease had appeared between Walker's brows. "There's a special spoon with it. Use that."

The powder was pretty, like dark brown sand glittering with specks of red and bronze. "What's in it?" Lifting it again, she took a cautious sniff. Funny, the stuff might look brown, but it smelled rankly green, like the weeds from the north pasture at home, the one that was always a bit boggy.

"Healall, scaldlily and coolbalm. Plus some Science stuff Bartelm bought from the Technomage Tower. Purist or no, it took him hours of talking to get the local Primus to part with it. That box is worth more than you are, *slave*."

He turned back to Dai. "I'll have food sent up."

Another of those infinitesimal headshakes. Walker ignored it.

"You don't eat until he does, assassin."

Once again, he stepped close so quickly she had no time to evade the crushing grip on her upper arms. He hauled her up an inch so their eyes were level. "Remember, I will *know*. Everything you do, every thought that passes through your devious blond head."

When he let go, her heels hit the floor with a thump. Devious? Walker thought she was *devious*? Mehcredi stared at his retreating back, her mouth open. Not such a daft lump, then. The door swung shut behind him with a quiet snick, the long tail of black hair brushing the rise of a firm backside.

If she didn't have to look at the man in the bed, the warm feeling Walker's words had caused might last a little longer and her insides would have time to settle. Pinning a smile on her lips, she crossed to the windows and threw back the heavy drapes. Outside, the city was waking. Skiffs passed on the canal, weighed down with loads of produce or carrying passengers. The men and women working the poles chaffed at each other good-naturedly, much of the slang still incomprehensible to her ear. Fresh air and sunlight poured into the chamber, gilding the patina of polished woods and the jeweled tones in the rugs.

Mehcredi rubbed the heel of her hand over her chest, while the silence behind her gathered force, a palpable weight on the nape of her neck. Grimly, she ignored it. The skin of her breast still stung as if she'd strayed too close to a flash fire, but it was infinitely better than the dreadful retribution Walker's black glare had promised. Sister be praised, she'd been *lucky*. Really, this wasn't so bad.

Up in the attic, she had a real room with a proper bed in it and a lock on the door. Gods, she'd be able to sleep, and sleep deeply. At Lonefell, she'd snatched catnaps in her succession of hiding places, often moving several times a night.

Even in Caracole, she hadn't done much better. In its own way, the tumbledown inn that was all she could afford was worse than the keep. To judge by the stench wafting up through the broken shutters, it was situated over the top of the ripest open sewer in the Melting Pot. She made a face, remembering. Almost all of the baron's gold had disappeared into the rapacious grasp of the Master of Assassins. For the training, he'd said as he stowed it away, his face completely expressionless. For a moment there, Mehcredi had thought he was trying not to laugh, but she couldn't be sure.

No, she was much better off here—where the Necromancer would have to go through Walker to reach her. The man's grim, silent presence, his strange hunter's Magick, would be more than enough for any practitioner of the Dark Arts. She didn't doubt it for an instant.

The bedclothes rustled. From behind, came a tiny noise, a sort of pained mewl.

Clenching her fists, Mehcredi ignored it. The hollow feeling in her middle was hunger, pure and simple. The kitchen would be somewhere downstairs. She should go and see this Serafina person.

A small object struck her a stinging blow between the shoulder blades and clattered to the floor. Startled, she spun around.

Dai had raised himself on one elbow. His mouth contorted and another of those tortured kitten sounds emerged.

"I d-don't understand."

When he swallowed, wincing, she found she had to do the same. There was a huge lump in her throat.

"What do you want?"

Dai's thin fingers clawed at the covers. Then he pointed.

Mehcredi glanced down. The object that had hit her was a piece of chalk. She scooped it up. "You want this?"

Dai held out his hand, scowling. In the cheerful brutality of the sunlight, she could see that he was indeed the same pretty young man she'd seen in the Sailor's Lay. His eyes weren't dark, as she'd supposed. They were a clear green gold, like a cat's, fringed with thick black lashes, so brilliant they might have been burnished with tears.

Extending her arm to its fullest extent, Mehcredi dropped the chalk into his palm.

Dai snatched up a slate from the nightstand. She knew what it was because the youngest of the keep children carried them to lessons. Dai scribbled something, pressing so hard the chalk squeaked.

A final stab and he thrust the slate at her.

Mehcredi stared down at the scribble, feeling the heat rise in her cheeks. The curse of the fair-skinned. "I can't read." She dropped the useless thing on the bed by his knee.

The force of Dai's glare was so ferocious, she almost put her hands to her face to ensure he hadn't flayed the skin right off her skull. Rage, revulsion, hurt. All her old friends.

His mouth worked. "W-why?"

Thinking about it later, she wasn't sure she heard a sound emerge at all. But she couldn't mistake the shape of the word on his lips.

"I had a commission," she said. "Erik the Golden, the singer. But I made a mistake." She wiped her clammy palms down the sides of her trews. "You drank the prettydeath instead."

Dai waved a hand, brows raised. *And?*

Clearly, something more was expected. But what? Mehcredi dithered.

"Sorry?" she offered.

Dai hurled the slate at her head.

Walker knew Deiter was there, sitting on a boulder in the shade of a big cedderwood. He'd chosen that rock personally and supervised its transport and installation. It might be bench shaped, but it was still hard and cold. Every few seconds, the old reprobate would shift his skinny behind and scratch his ear, or his belly. Then he'd give a gusty sigh. Walker ignored him, flowing through the movements of his martial arts practice, his swords catching the light as they twisted and spun a hairsbreadth from his flesh.

He'd chosen a *nea-kata* from the twenty-second level because he needed the lethal beauty of razor-sharp blades to concentrate his mind. The Purist might be the most powerful wizard Walker had ever known, but he could damn well wait.

Ten minutes later, he laid the two swords aside, his blood humming as it should, all his senses alert. "Well?" he said. "What is it?"

"We have them back." Deiter twinkled up at him. "Erik and Prue."

Walker stared. "Why the hell didn't you say so in the first place?" He reached for the shirt he'd hooked on a branch.

"You were busy," said the old wizard blandly, his eyes wandering over Walker's bare chest. He sighed. "I used to have a body like that."

Meeting a flat black gaze, he hurried on. "Yes, well. Prue's fine, more or less. Erik . . ." He shrugged. "He took on more than he was ready for, the fool. The Necromancer—" Deiter broke off to spit, right into Walker's prized bed of dark roses. "Bastard nearly did for him. Bartelm saved his life in the proverbial nick of time." His mouth twisted amid the wine-stained whiskers. "Pompous git's still going on about it."

He didn't lack for guts, Erik Thorensen. "And the Necromancer?"

"Gone. Maybe dead, maybe not." He raised faded eyes to Walker's. "I need more information. Give me the assassin."

"No."

Bushy brows rose. "Why not?"

"She's mine."

Deiter gave a dirty chuckle. "I see."

"I doubt it." With steady hands, Walker took the soft cloth he'd hung on a bush and wiped down the first sword. His shamanic senses vibrated with the power of the old man's Magick. "I told you everything I got out of her when I came to The Garden. Before dawn, I might add. Remember?"

"So?"

"She was too terrified to lie. I'm not even sure she knows how." He repressed the urge to growl. "I know you, Purist. You're frustrated. You want to play."

"What's wrong with a little screaming? I wouldn't overdo it, I swear. Think of poor Dai."

"I am. She's going to be his body slave, his nurse, for as long as he needs it. Longer, if I see fit."

Deiter stopped fidgeting. With exquisite care, Walker rubbed the second blade until it gleamed, watching the old man's hands out of the corner of his eye. You never knew with wizards.

At last, Deiter said, "You owe me for this, Walker. And lest you think I'm too senile to remember, let me say I know what you are. What you could be. I've known from the instant I clapped eyes on you."

Walker said nothing.

With a muttered curse, the wizard rose, one hand pressed to the small of his back. He glanced toward the canal and the water stair, then back at Walker. "I'll be at The Garden if you change your mind." The twinkle had returned.

"About what?"

"You. The assassin." A snaggletoothed grin. "Especially the assassin."

Walker watched him hobble across the grass and onto the path. "Not likely," he murmured under his breath. "Gods, you'd ruin her."

By the time he realized how odd that sounded, Deiter was out of earshot.

4

Mehcredi stood trembling in the passage outside Dai's door. Twice, she lifted her hand to the latch. Twice, she let it fall to her side. The tray she carried tilted, plates and cups skittering about as if to taunt her with her own stupidity. Serafina the housekeeper would skin her alive if she dropped Dai's lunch.

For some godsbedamned reason, her entire body went into revolt every time she tried to force herself over the threshold. She'd managed it so far, ten days in a row, but the effect seemed to be cumulative. Her head swam and her heart pounded. Sister, if she didn't get hold of herself, she'd faint! She swallowed, breathing hard through her nose, willing the weakness away.

It could be lack of food, she thought darkly. The meals were probably nourishing enough, but hell, she'd never cared for vegetables. Complaining to Walker was a waste of breath. He ignored her.

Serafina had said waspishly, "Nothin' wrong with good, plain vittles. Yer ladyship's gettin' the same as everyone else." When Mehcredi explained she wasn't any kind of nobility, Serafina glared down her sharp nose in silence. Then she pointed an imperious finger at a sink full of crusted pots and hot soapy water.

Mehcredi's stomach grumbled. It had to be part of the torture— the swordmaster intended to starve her until his revenge was complete. Unless, of course, Dai found a way to kill her from flat on his back or Serafina worked her to death.

Morosely, she wiped a sweaty palm on the simple shift she wore. It was modest enough, resembling a large linen sack that hung to below her knees, but already limp and grubby. She'd been up since dawn, first in the kitchen, then in the laundry. Even her blisters had blisters. She'd spent her childhood trying to keep out of the way, but it was no use in Walker's House of Swords. The premises were small compared with a rambling keep, and anyway, Serafina seemed to have more than the usual complement of senses. The bloody woman was a witch.

Mehcredi scowled. If Dai refused his lunch, the housekeeper would have her up beyond midnight, scrubbing floors with a nail-brush or something.

It had been a week before the swordsman could produce more than thin, mewling noises, let alone rise from his bed, but by the third day, Mehcredi knew his body as well as she knew her own. His smooth, muscled limbs left her unmoved, though a part of her knew he was beautiful. On the fourth day, he ripped the sponge from her grasp with a silent snarl and pointed to the door. Even a great daft lump could work out what that meant. *Get out, bitch, and give me my privacy.*

His mind she knew not at all, though he followed her always with his eyes as she lumbered about in sullen silence, scrubbing, sweeping, polishing. The bright unblinking focus unnerved her almost as much as Walker's grim silent presence.

If it weren't for the godsbedamned Mark . . .

She'd tested its power to the absolute limits of her endurance. Four times, she nerved herself to walk through that damned gate and four times, she'd known beyond a shadow of a doubt her heart would explode in a messy shower if she took another step. After the last attempt, late one night, she'd had to retire to her tiny attic room, shaking so hard she stopped twice to rest on the stairs. Gods, no more. Walker had said the Mark would also prevent her from harming Dai. Not that she particularly wanted to, though the man's silent hate-filled stare made her guts cramp. She blew out a gusty breath. With any luck, he'd eaten some of his breakfast.

Before she could lose her nerve, Mehcredi shouldered Dai's door open.

The bed was empty. The swordsman stood with his back turned, hunched over something he held cradled against his chest. He rocked back and forth on his heels.

"Dai?" she whispered. "Dai, are you—?"

His head jerked up and he whirled around so suddenly he nearly pitched over. At the last second, he grabbed the edge of the dresser with one hand; in the other he clutched the neck of a small stringed instrument. His eyes were red-rimmed, his cheeks wet.

Dai's mouth contorted, but only an agonized gargle emerged. A second later, he launched himself forward, reaching for her with clawed fingers, snarling, barely human. The instrument fell unheeded to the floor.

Mehcredi dropped the tray so she could shield her face. Despite his current weakness, Dai was nonetheless male to her female and a master swordsman at the peak of his powers. She had no hope of evading the blow, but at the last moment, he pulled it and what had started out as a punch capable of breaking her jaw became an open-handed slap that rattled her teeth.

Mehcredi's heel caught on the rug and she tripped, landing hard on her back, Dai following her down. Another slap had her seeing stars. Desperately, she gripped his wrist with one hand, her strength equal to his. "Shit! Stop it, stop it! Don't—"

Her flailing hand encountered an object with a jagged edge. A shard from a broken plate. Instinctively, she closed her fingers around it, but the moment she did so, a familiar iron fist closed over her heart and her vision grayed out.

Gods, if she defended herself, she'd die. If she didn't, Dai would kill her.

Their legs thrashed, seeking purchase. Mehcredi kicked out, her foot connecting with something solid. Strings sang a jangled dissonance, accompanied by a decisive crunch, a kind of nasty counterpoint.

Dai froze, poised above her, his chest heaving. The scarlet flush drained from his face, leaving him as pale as paper. Squeezing his eyes shut, he made a noise in his throat—the softest, most heartrending wail she'd ever heard. All the manic strength spilled out of him, his eyes rolled back and he slumped, rolling off Mehcredi to lie beside her on the rug.

Their harsh breath echoed in the silence. Mehcredi uncurled her fingers and released the shard. She turned her head to gaze into Dai's face. Even his lips were gray. They lay full length in the ruins of his lunch, as close as lovers.

"Dai?" Gingerly, she patted his cheek, absently noting the scruff on his jaw. She'd offer to shave him, but he unsettled her so much, she'd never be able to keep her hands steady.

His eyes fluttered open, focused on her face, and narrowed. She shifted away a few inches, then stopped, her heart thumping.

His mouth opened. "*Why?*" No more than a thread of sound.

"I told you," she said, "I had a commiss—"

Dai clamped callused fingers across her lips. He shook his head. *Shut up.*

"Why . . . Do . . . You . . . Hate . . . Me?" Although he wrestled with each word as if it were a deadly foe, all that came out was a travesty of human speech, a scratchy, agonized rasp.

Mehcredi's throat closed in sympathy. "I don't." Unable to hold that burning gaze, she dropped her eyes and pushed the remains of a cup about with one finger. "I made a mistake, that's all. The prettydeath was meant for Erik the Golden. I didn't know—" For some reason, she had to break off and swallow hard. "I didn't know how awful it was. How much it would hurt."

But Dai had stopped listening. Frowning, he was gathering up the pieces of the instrument, picking splinters out of the rug.

"Here, I can do that."

When he curled his lip like a truculent dog and knocked her hand out of the way, she sat nonplussed. Now what? Was making conversation part of her duties? Sitting up, she worked her tender jaw. Ow, ow. She still had all her teeth, but she'd been fortunate, because clearly, Dai was feeling a great deal better.

She shot him a doubtful glance, wondering if he was bored. She would be. "Um. Can you play it?"

His brows shot up, so she guessed she'd surprised him somehow. Another glare and he levered himself carefully to his feet, swaying a little.

Mehcredi sighed, knowing she'd missed something obvious. With her luck, next time he lost his temper, he'd be strong enough to kill her outright. Godsdammit, she had to work out what had set him off, and quickly. Her brain spinning, she rose and went to the dresser to mix a dose of the special medicine.

"Here." She held out the tumbler of polished wood.

Dai sank to the side of the bed and swallowed the mixture, one painful sip at a time. Wincing, Mehcredi watched his throat bob.

His throat . . . "You used to play. And sing. That's it, isn't it?"

His features smoothing into a mask she couldn't read, Dai shrugged. With a flick of his wrist, he flipped the empty tumbler in her general direction. She had to lunge sideways, but she managed to snag it before it hit the floor.

Still deep in thought, she filled it with water from the jug and passed it back. "Like Erik?"

His mouth tipped up at one corner. Was that a smile? He shook his head. *No.* He made a downward motion with one hand. *Not as good.* The hand descended to knee level. *Nowhere near as good.*

A tiny spark of warmth bloomed behind Mehcredi's breastbone. This was real communication, the give-and-take of conversation— sort of. "No wonder you were crying."

Dai froze, his jaw setting so hard she could see the hinge bones knot.

Shit.

"It's all right. I would, anyone would." She knew she was babbling, but something about his fisted hands and rigid shoulders yanked the words out of her. "I understand . . . At least, I think I do . . . About the pain, I mean, and not being able to talk."

In a smooth rush that reminded her of Walker, Dai surged up from the bed and seized her arm in a steely grip. Hauling her to the door, he thrust her out into the passageway with such force she stumbled three or four paces before she could regain her balance. The door slammed, so fiercely the walls vibrated. The ensuing silence rang in her ears, broken by a metallic click that sounded for all the world like a warrior arming a crossbow, but it was only Dai locking the door.

Mehcredi leaned her forehead against the wall, cursing under her breath. Why did she even try? *Ye great daft lump.* She'd never understand, never get it right. Her head bowed, she trudged down the stairs.

Dai hadn't swallowed a thing, not one spoonful of his minced meat and vegetables. So there'd be no food for Mehcredi until supper time. Worse, how was she to tell Serafina about the broken plates, the wasted meal? That deserved a beating. She cringed at the thought, though only Walker had really laid hands on her. No one else at the House of Swords had tried to punish her with the pain she deserved, but surely it was just a question of time? It was all small cruelties, and though she'd been accustomed to them all her life, they'd never been so pointed, so piercing.

In fact, violence would come as a relief. Whenever she had to pass through the salle, the men and women practicing with blunted swords stopped, lowered their weapons as one, and stared. Her skin prickling, she'd put her head down and trot past as quickly as possible. People jostled her in the passageways, on the stairs. Once, a small woman who looked like she was made of iron and whipcord caught her with a sly elbow to the midsection that nearly sent her reeling off the third-floor landing. If it hadn't been for the grizzled veteran called Pounder, she might have broken her neck.

His meaty hand had caught her upper arm and hauled her back to safety. Cold brown eyes under shaggy brows had raked her up and down. "Ye got work to do, lass?"

Rubbing her arm, she'd nodded. "Yes, lots. I have to—"

Pounder had turned on his heel and left her standing.

Every night, she waited 'til after midnight before slinking out to the small bathhouse. It was worth losing sleep to soak in one of the deep stone tubs, though more than once she nearly slid right under the surface when she nodded off. There was a small cupboard filled with standard medical supplies too. She'd already worked her way through the best part of a jar of healall, slathering it over the purplish blotches marring the pale flesh of her throat. The gods knew what would happen if Serafina missed it.

Bending to dry a leg, Mehcredi stared determinedly at her toes—anything to avoid a glimpse of the smooth white breast flesh he'd desecrated. Sister save her, a shaman's Mark! She shivered, though it wasn't with cold. The slightest touch still set off the strangest reaction, part burn, part tingle, part pain, part . . . something else. She hated it. The soft flesh would tighten almost unbearably—and not only on the Marked breast. The right side would draw up too, until both nipples had ruched up into pink velvety points, so sensitive she couldn't stand even to brush them with her fingertips.

Every time she passed Walker, in the cool passageways, in the garden, the salle, she felt compelled to stare at his hands, wondering. Like the rest of him, they were beautifully proportioned, strong and graceful. Ah gods, he'd *touched* her! Not casually, not violently, but with a deeper intimacy than she'd ever known. Wrapping her arms around herself, she hunched over, waiting it out, this unfamiliar rush of sensation. Behind her eyelids, she seemed to see the pads of his fingers creating the swirling patterns, slipping lightly, so very lightly, over warm resilient satin, never pausing, never doubting, a flowing stream of Magick caressing the outer layer of skin, sinking deep into the flesh beneath . . .

Gods! Mehcredi twisted the thin towel so hard it creaked with the strain. Not that the swordmaster lowered himself to speak to her. His dark eyes might flick over her, but his expression never changed, not that she could discern, even though she'd made such a thorough study of his features they were graven on her soul. If she closed her eyes now, she could see him, standing by the bed looking down at Dai, a crease between his straight black brows.

Oh yes, everyone in Walker's House of Swords loved Dai. Without exception, they detested her for what she'd done to him. There wasn't a single one of them, or in all of Caracole for that matter, who didn't find the swordmaster's forbearance as inexplicable as it was misguided. Or so Serafina informed her, as if Mehcredi were too stupid to work it out for herself, finishing with an emphatic sniff. But then she'd turn away, dabbing at her eyes with her apron, and Mehcredi came to think the housekeeper really did love Dai, like she said.

On the whole, Lonefell might be preferable. And she couldn't believe she'd had the thought.

Sighing, Mehcredi obliterated all traces of her presence, wiping over the bath and hanging up her towel. How she loathed everything about bloody Walker's Sister-forsaken House of Swords!

Well, not everything.

He was waiting for her in the quiet peace of the garden, sitting bolt upright on the bench near Walker's rose beds.

"Get down from there, you filthy little beast."

The Sister and the Brother shone high in the night sky. In the moonslight, she watched the shaggy head turn to glance at the greasy packet of scraps in her hand. Nimbly, he hopped down, tail waving in happy expectation. Mehcredi coughed. Not even the heady perfume of dark roses could mask the almost visible miasma of filthy canine.

It had taken her a full five minutes to parcel up the disgusting bits of gristle and fat and the same amount of time to scour the stink off her hands with harsh soap. The scraps lasted approximately ten seconds.

"Gods, you're a scrounger," she murmured, a smile tugging at her lips. "No manners. Fine food should be savored, you know."

The tilt of the dog's head intimated that manners were a luxury he couldn't afford and was there any more? Strange, she had no difficulty reading his expression, even through the hair.

"No," she said. "That's all. And I should go. I have to be up before dawn."

But when the little animal settled at her feet and laid his head on her ankle, she continued to sit, enjoying the night scents of Walker's garden. Tilting her head, she stared up at the silver blue serenity of the Sister, the martial red of the Brother in determined persuit. A flitter buzzed past, a mechanical insect silhouetted against the faces of the Sibling Moons. There'd be Technomages on board, bound for the gods knew where. She'd never seen a Technomage.

The sea breeze from the canal danced by, carrying with it a swarm of ripe glowspores. Enchanted, Mehcredi watched them float past, sparkling and winking. The slightest touch and they burst, releasing a cloud of fragrant dust. One of them brushed the dog's ear. He sneezed, shaking his head, and she laughed, but softly. Why did they do that? How she wished she knew! Somewhere a touchme bush tinkled a cheerful harmony.

"Walker has a gift," Serafina had told her, her wrinkled face intent. Apparently, even the most unlikely plants grew as if he'd bewitched them, and in his spare time, he designed gardens for aristocratic clients, most of whom wanted him to give up his House of Swords and work for them, but he wouldn't. "He's a man of honor," said Serafina, with a dark look. "Loyal. Did you scrub the second-floor privy?"

Ow! Dislodging the dog, Mehcredi bent to scratch her ankle. When she lifted her hand, blood smeared her fingertip, dark in the moonslight. "You little shit." She glared at him. "Keep your damn bitemes to yourself."

Grumbling, she rose. Completely unabashed, the dog accompanied her down the winding path to the kitchen door. She blocked further progress with her leg. "You can't come in, scrounger," she said. "Gods, no. Serafina would kill me." A shiver ran up her spine as if dark eyes tracked her from the shadows. "Not to mention Walker."

The dog knew. He didn't whine when she shut the door in his face.

Safely in her room, she stripped naked and checked, but there were no more of the disgusting little bloodsuckers. Meditatively, she sat on the bed and scratched the bite. What must it be like to be infested with the horrible things? Poor dog.

Walker had intended to stop her before she entered the bathhouse, but then he'd had second thoughts. An unwashed assassin was as much a punishment for him and everyone else in the House of Swords as it would be for Mehcredi. He'd always been fastidious, what of it?

"You're wasting your time," he murmured to the dog, sitting hopefully at his feet. Swiftly, he bent, grasping the animal's jaw with strong fingers. "Dig anywhere in my garden, and I'll bury you in the hole myself." He pushed the fall of coarse hair out of the animal's eyes with his other hand. Held the dark-bright stare. "Understand?"

The dog whined.

"Good." Walker wiped his palms on his trews. Gods, the creature stank. He should have Pounder take it back to the Melting Pot and let it go. Except it would almost certainly come back and Pounder was too soft to kill it. Lightly, he caressed the hilt of the long dagger at his waist.

'Cestors' bones, the dog was the assassin's problem. He let his hand drop, lips curving without humor. Let her deal with it—if she had the balls.

She'd been such a long time in the bath, he'd already completed an entire mediation cycle, not that it had been particularly effective. Why he was waiting for her to finish, he didn't rightly know. Everything about the godsbedamned woman was a problem.

Dai had a young man's resilience. He was improving daily. Soon, he wouldn't need a nursemaid. Every other day, Purist Deiter sent a message demanding to see her, by turns wheedling and threatening.

What the fuck was he to do about Mehcredi the assassin?

Cross-legged, Walker settled with his back to the smooth trunk of a purplemist tree.

5

As always, the *ch'qui* of the planet flowed deep and true, a balm to Walker's soul. Keeping a wary eye on the bathhouse door, he dropped quickly into a state of relaxed readiness, opening himself to the springing, green essence of his world, letting it soothe all the empty places inside that ached still and would forever ache.

Because he would always be the last of the Shar. No one left to sing the Songs so integral to the spiritual life of his people, not a single voice to chant his own Song of Birth and Life, to weave the strands of his soul with those of the Ancestors, a never-ending tapestry of intertwined lives that reached back to the dawn of time. His desert tribe was gone, every man, woman and child wiped from the face of the earth, of no more consequence than a nest of bitemes. All due to the greed and overweening ambition of Pasha Ghuis Gremani Giral of the Trinitarian Republic, and his fucking diablomen.

No one to speak his language, to say his name out loud. Only the vengeance that was all he had to give to the Shar'd'iloned't'Hywil, to those he'd loved and lost. His offering and his atonement.

The night he'd opened the first of the Trinitarian diablomen from neck to groin, he finally slept deep, almost to dawn, without the dreams of spraying blood and shattered bone, the guttural chants of the dark wizards calling their demons. Worse though, much worse, were the creatures' eldritch howls, the green acrid fog that alternately cloaked and revealed their hideous forms. Pincers and mandibles, skinny shanks and horned toes, segmented limbs and spittle-slick tusks. Even now, the memory of the fundamental *wrongness* of them made his guts lurch.

When it came to the second kill, he allowed the diabloman to see him, to know and fear his fate. The man had stared at the finger bones threaded into Walker's long braids. "Barbarian," he sneered. "Move aside or—"

The last words he spoke.

Now, fifteen years later, Pasha Giral, architect of the entire atrocity, was dead, murdered by his pet assassin, if rumor was true. Walker ground his teeth, realized he was doing it and stopped. Nearly over. With Giral's escape, only one of the bastards remained, the fifteenth diabloman, Nerajyb Nyzarl, a great greasy bull of a man, too indolent to stray from the fleshpots—and the safety—of the High Palace of the Grand Pasha.

He'd worked his way through the demon masters, stalking them one by one, planning with meticulous care—it was no easy thing to destroy a man bound body and soul to a devil—even less so if you wanted to draw out the agony, gaze into their eyes while they pissed themselves with terror.

And if the executioner's ice had entered his heart and frozen it from the inside out, who was there left to know or care? There were times he wondered if there was anything left of his soul at all, every last particle consumed by the Shar's vengeance, and he himself was nothing but an empty husk that walked and talked and went through the motions.

It wouldn't be easy to reach Nyzarl, but he'd find a way. Soon, soon, once Mehcredi had completed her penance. Walker had to lean hard on his discipline to prevent himself from shifting with annoyance. A complication he didn't need. He maintained his straight-backed posture, but the hand that had rested open on his thigh curled slowly into a fist.

The door of the bathhouse clicked open. The dog catapulted off the bench where he'd been lying and trotted over to frolic around the assassin's legs. ". . . filthy little beast," he heard her say, her voice somehow different in the dark, warm as Trinitarian brandy, its huskiness just as potent.

Walker came to his feet, every sense alert. You could learn a great deal about an adversary from their first, unguarded reaction. But once again, she failed to even glance in his direction, though he was standing in plain sight and the Sibling Moons were high.

Conscious of the oddest thread of disappointment, he studied her, taking his time. She looked different, posed in a bright fall of moonslight, her pale skin glowing like a temple statue come to life. All she wore was a loose shift that left her arms and legs bare and skimmed over the shape beneath, her silver blond hair twisted up into a careless knot on the top of her head. Wisps of it escaped to brush her cheeks and caress the column of her throat. It exposed the elegant severity of her jawline and the tender nape of her neck, giving what he knew to be an erroneous impression of vulnerability. Walker's lip curled. Under the puppy fat, Mehcredi the assassin was what Rose would call handsome rather than merely pretty. As the owner of The Garden of Nocturnal Delights, the best courtesan house in Caracole, her judgment in such matters could not be faulted. Godsdammit, he didn't doubt any normal, red-blooded man would deem Mehcredi eminently fuckable, if a little strange. *Plenty to hold on to,* he thought sourly, suppressing a snarl. The dog glanced up from devouring a noisome little pile of scraps, but the assassin continued to gaze up at the moons, oblivious.

She laughed suddenly for no reason, a deep, joyous gurgle, unexpectedly sensuous in the soft night air, and the faintest ripple of response traveled over the sensitive skin of his scrotum, like the slow, gelid swirl of water trapped under ice. Walker blinked, genuinely astonished.

Still human after all. Father's balls, who'd have thought it? He hadn't been with a woman in . . . How long? He frowned, trying to recall. More than a year.

That part of him, the sexual part, the lonely youth who craved warmth and connection, had closed down, slowly but inexorably, over the years of his vengeance. He gave a wry smile in the dark. Too fastidious for his own good, because quick fumbles in the dark left him cold. On the other hand, lengthy entanglements were something he couldn't afford.

It was easier—cleaner—to remain his own contained, enigmatic self. If it got too bad, he had his own hand.

Another few moments of communing with nature and the assassin rose with a sigh, closing the door in the dog's hopeful face.

Walker stretched, feeling joints pop and muscles sing. Thanks be to the Ancestors for the discipline of the *nea-kata* that kept him supple and balanced, mentally and physically. Every morning at dawn, he practiced, flowing from one movement to the next, making each element as close to perfect as possible for a mere mortal, his homage to the Ancestors.

Stripped to a loin pouch, he'd offer all that he was, the morning breeze off the water caressing his sweaty skin, the lush, short grass cool under his bare soles, the only spectators the small hopping birds. These last few days, of course, he could add the assassin to his audience, peering from behind the kitchen door, where she thought he couldn't see her.

Idly, he wondered what she made of it and whether she'd be there again on the morrow. She hadn't missed a day in a week so far. Then he decided he didn't care and went in to bed.

Though her bones ached with tiredness, Mehcredi slept badly, so anxious she'd miss him it seemed she woke every hour. It was still dark when she dragged herself down to the kitchen, but that didn't matter, she'd come to know the place like the back of her hand. Deftly, she raked over the coals in the big wood-fired stove that was Serafina's pride and joy, and put on a kettle for a tisane.

Walker arrived early. How she knew he was there, she wasn't sure, only that a ghostly sensation prickled over her skin and gave her goose bumps. Her grip tightened on the stoneware cup, warm and rough against her palms. Creeping to the door, she eased it open a crack.

Bathed in the cool gray light of dawn, the swordmaster had his back to her, removing his shirt. Soundlessly, Mehcredi let out a long breath. Light and shadow flirted with the hollows and planes of his body, pooling in the smooth indents that paralleled the groove of his spine, gleaming across the strong horizontal bone structure that gave his shoulders their width. The male body wasn't new to her—the baron's men had no use for modesty. When they bathed, which wasn't an especially frequent occurrence, they did so in the deep tarn above the keep. There they splashed and wrestled in the freezing water like frisky warhounds, obscenities echoing back and forth in the chill mountain air.

She'd seen plenty of male flesh, but by the Sister, she'd never seen skin like Walker's, bronze satin sliding sweetly over long strong bones and shapely swells of muscle. The keep guards were hairy, some of them as thickly rugged on the back as the front. But though she stared at the swordmaster until her eyes ached, all she could see was a mouthwatering expanse of smooth skin, his only blemishes four wicked scars—she'd counted. For some insane reason, they made her want to weep. The worst of them was a set of five parallel gouges curving over his left hip, disappearing under the waistband of his trews. They looked like claw marks.

Mehcredi's fingers tightened on the cup. What had hurt him so badly? A direwolf? A tygre? Had he cried out in rage and pain? Had he killed it? She snorted quietly. Of course he had.

The first time she'd seen him perform this strange ritual, he'd worn nothing more than a leather pouch that cradled his genitals, leaving his taut buttocks bare, so that her wide-eyed gaze swept unimpeded— except for the thin leather strip at his waist—all the way up the hard luxurious glory of him, from strong bare feet to long thighs and high muscular buttocks, a trim waist and broad shoulders.

She'd come down early that particular morning, because Serafina had charged her with starting the porridge and she'd wanted to take her time, get something right for once. Catching sight of him through the small window, the jug she held had slipped from her lax fingers. Fortunately, she caught it, ignoring the milk that splashed and dripped over her legs and feet.

You'd think he was dancing—until you saw the swords. Entranced, she leaned against the wall and watched him flow through a series of intricate, fluid movements. Bronze-clad muscles expanded and contracted, the swords flashed and arced, and the end result was a poem of such grace, power and control that it made her yearn for something beyond her grasp.

His features were more relaxed than she'd ever seen them, tranquil, with a purity she hadn't noticed before. Perhaps this too was a part of his shaman's Magick. The Mark over her heart surged with heat and she trembled all over.

She'd spent the week struggling through the unfamiliar feelings, thinking about him, about that strong, perfect body. Watching now, mourning the appearance of the trews, her lips curved in a wry smile. This had to be sexual attraction. *Desire.* She wasn't prepared to call it lust, didn't want to associate this lovely warm tingle with the rutting that was all she'd known of relations between men and women.

The swordmaster was . . . clean, as beautiful as one of his blades. Wistfully, she watched him spin and bend, the long black tail of hair whipping about as he turned, his strong bare feet landing with precision on the short turf. The wicked razor-sharp edges whirled hungrily all around his body. Godsdammit, how was it he still had all his limbs?

Here it came, the slow, graceful pattern that meant he was about to finish. Mehcredi set the cup down on the floor, her brow furrowed with concentration as she copied his movements. Right arm over the head, sweep down in a balletic arc to the left hip, rock back on the left heel, raise the right foot—Oh, shit. She wobbled and the posture collapsed.

Hell, she couldn't get anything right. Might as well be back at Lonefell. *Half-wit slut,* sneered Taso, swaggering out of memory like a bad dream, eyes bright with cruel hunger. *Lucky ye don' keep yer brains in yer cunt.*

She shuddered. Walker wasn't anything like Taso.

"It's called the *nea-kata.*"

Mehcredi's eyes flashed open and she jerked, one foot kicking the cup. It rolled into the wall with an audible clink.

Slowly, she raised her eyes to meet the swordmaster's long-lidded gaze as he stood in the doorway. "Sorry," she meant to say, but what came out of her mouth was, "Teach me. Please."

"No." Walker didn't even blink. Stepping aside, he picked up his shirt.

Mehcredi's chest went tight. "I can watch though?"

He shrugged. "Makes no difference to me."

Facts snapped together in Mehcredi's head. The man was a hunter, the most skilled she'd ever met. His senses were far keener than hers.

"That's not right," she said triumphantly. "You knew I was here, right from that very first day. And it does make a difference, because now you're wearing trews." She waved a hand in the general direction of his groin. "Instead of that little pouch thing."

Walker froze. His lips went thin and sooty lashes swept down, concealing his eyes. The hint of a flush bloomed on his high cheekbones.

A reaction! Mehcredi caught the chuckle before it could bubble out of her throat. She might not be very bright, but she had a feeling laughing at the swordmaster's expense was an exceptionally bad idea.

"The porridge is burning," he said.

By the time she rushed to the stove, he'd disappeared in the direction of the bathhouse.

Mehcredi suspected she'd ruined everything with Dai. Each day, she stood outside his door, breathing hard, her belly aching, trying to force herself over the threshold. There were times she could swear there was an invisible barrier, as thick as glue. If it hadn't been for the swordmaster and his godsbedamned Mark . . . Every time the swordsman fought to swallow, her own throat closed and she couldn't breathe or think.

Reminding herself she'd survived worse—a little voice in her head sneered, *Really? And what might that be?*—she knocked, shouldered the door open and maneuvered herself and the lunch tray inside. To her surprise, Dai wasn't alone. A skinny boy sat cross-legged on a chair opposite the swordsman, frowning down at the small table drawn up between them.

He twisted around, raising a belligerent chin. "You're t' fookin' assassin," he said, in the strangest accent she'd ever heard.

Mehcredi shrugged, avoiding Dai's knowing, ironic gaze. She began unloading her tray, putting the covered dishes on the dresser. "Who are you?"

"Florien. From T' Garden." His chest expanded. "Rose an' Prue sent me with stuff fer Walker."

"Really?" Questions crowded in her mind, so many, she didn't know where to begin. "Is Erik all right? I heard the Necromancer hurt him. And what about Prue, how—?"

"They're fine now." The boy scowled, a messy lock of hair falling into his eyes. "No thanks t' you."

"Is the . . . the Necromancer dead?" Mehcredi barreled on, her heart drumming so hard she could feel it in her throat. Gods, she had to know. "Did Walker kill him?"

"What are ye, daft? Didn't ye hear?"

Mehcredi flinched as if the boy had slapped her. "No," she whispered.

Florien went on, ignoring her. "Prue done fer him. Wit' a shovel. Only . . ." The savage grin fading, he picked up what looked like the shell of a nut from the table and jiggled it in his palm. "They ain't found a body yet."

"Shit." Knees shaking with the visceral memory of terror, she leaned back against the wall, grateful for the support.

"Yah," agreed the boy. "That's about right." He exchanged glances with Dai, and after a moment, the swordsman nodded. Florien's grin returned, full force. "Want t' play?"

"Play? Play what?"

"T' shell game."

Intrigued, Mehcredi drew closer. "How does it work?"

They were both smiling now, but their eyes glittered. "Is t' hand quicker than t' eye? Dai never gets it."

The swordsman grunted his displeasure, but when he punched Florien lightly on the arm, the boy glowed.

"I'll give ye one fer free." He held up a small black bead for her inspection, then placed it under one of the three shells and swiveled them about, his hands a blur. "Where is it, assassin?"

Mehcredi chuckled. "Why, it's there." She pointed to the shell in the middle.

Florien turned to the silent swordsman. "Dai?"

He tapped the shell on the right, curling his lip at her, just as he always did.

His face a careful blank, the boy lifted the center shell to reveal the bead.

"Luck," rasped Dai painfully, leaning forward. "Again."

"Nah," said Florien, all serious purpose. "Not without a bet."

"I don't have any money," said Mehcredi.

"What do ye have?"

Her shoulders slumped. "Nothing." Nothing at all, no skills, no future, no one to care.

"Lunch," said the boy with decision, favoring the dishes with a longing gaze. "I'll play ye fer lunch."

"But that's Dai's," said Mehcredi, shocked.

Florien stared. "So where's yours?"

"Serafina's rules. I only eat if he does." She shrugged. "I don't care."

"But that's—"

Dai tapped the lad's bony knee. "Not . . . hungry." The swordsman waved a hand. *Go ahead.*

"Wait, wait." Mehcredi tugged at her braid. "If I lose, Florien, you get Dai's lunch, but if I win . . ." She pulled in a breath. "You eat half of it, Dai. At least."

Dai shot her a startled glance, then he shrugged. *All right.*

"Best of three," said Florien briskly. "Ready?"

Mehcredi nodded, her brow furrowed with concentration.

"That one." The shell lifted and there was the bead. Florien snorted, nimble fingers flying once more.

"That one." This time, she got silence and a flat stare.

"That one."

"Fookin' 'ell." Florien's hands dropped to his lap. "Three outa fookin' three. No one does that, not t' me."

6

Dai sat frozen. Slowly, his lips tucked up at the corners and his shoulders began to shake. After a stunned second, it dawned on Mehcredi he was laughing. Without a sound, true, but for the first time since she'd come to the House of Swords, she recognized the handsome merry man she'd seen that night in the Sailor's Lay.

"Let's go outside," she said impulsively. "Dai, you'd like that, wouldn't you?"

"Yah." Florien hopped out of the chair. "He would." When he tugged at Dai's shoulder, the swordsman rolled his eyes, but he nodded.

Between them, they levered Dai to his feet, his arms over their shoulders. The boy was all bony angles and lanky limbs, shooting up in the first growth spurt of adolescence. Still a hand span taller, the swordsman was trying to spare Florien's meager frame his full weight. Idiot. With a grunt, Mehcredi slipped an arm around Dai's trim waist, getting a good grip.

By the time they reached the door of the salle, Dai was pale to the lips, sweat beading his brow. But he shook his head fiercely when they reached the beds of dark roses, so they struggled on, across a delicately arched bridge that spanned a pond and gave out on a velvety sward of moss-grass the deepest green Mehcredi had ever seen. Tall flowers like yellow trumpets grew in clumps along the waterline, interspersed with bending sprays of a feathery plant dotted with violet stars. Reflections shimmered, tangling with those of passing clouds, high above. Water gurgled and a touchme bush tinkled happily somewhere nearby. It was perfect, like a small gem of a room in a lovely house, exquisitely furnished, but outdoors.

For some godsbedamned reason, her eyes stung with tears.

"This do?" panted Florien, as Dai spread himself out on the grass with a grateful sigh.

"I'll go back for the tray," said Mehcredi.

"Me too." Florien leaped to his feet, his eyes brightening. "All right, Dai?"

The swordsman raised a finger. *Wait.* Extracting a small pad of paper and a pencil from his pocket, he scribbled a note. Folding it over, he thrust it at Mehcredi. "Serafina," he husked. "Picnic." Then he waved her away. *Go.*

Mehcredi went, the boy at her heels. The moment they were over the bridge, she handed the note to Florien. "What's it say?"

"How t' fook should I know?" The boy shoved it back toward her.

Mehcredi stopped dead. "You can't read? Truly? I thought everyone—" She broke off. "Except me, that is."

"Not if ye were born in a slum."

She bent her head, fretting at the edge of the note with her thumbnail. "Dai can hardly talk." Bile burned in her throat. She had to swallow hard before she could go on. "Because of me."

The lad snorted. "'Course he can. A bit, anyway. Just don' wanna talk to ye." He caught sight of her face. "Yah, well. You find Serafina. I'll go up fer t' tray."

The glint in his eye reminded her of the little boys caught sticky-fingered in Cook's pantry, a lifetime ago. "No, you won't." She tucked the note into his grubby fist. "She should be in the kitchen."

"T' kitchen? Why didn't you say so?" Florien trotted away.

Walker had a small office on the second floor of the House of Swords. He didn't care for paperwork, but it was an unavoidable part of making a living, so he set the hours aside, gritted his teeth and applied himself. The room was Spartan—a desk, an upright chair and a set of cupboards for his files.

Today was the first time he'd felt it wasn't big enough.

His hands laid flat on the desk, he gazed coldly at Purist Deiter. "*What* did you just say?"

"You heard me." The old wizard clasped his hands together over his small paunch. "Have you ever died?"

Walker stared him down.

"Ah," said Deiter, smirking. "Right again. Gotta love being me." He rummaged around inside the battered satchel slung over one shoulder. "What happened? Did you see the wild desert gods of the Shar?"

Walker's eyes narrowed. "What do you know of the Shar, old man?"

Deiter shrugged. "Enough to imagine Giral's death made you very happy." With a satisfied grunt, he extracted a long tube made of stout leather. "Did you celebrate? Go out and get drunk?" His fading eyes brightening, he gave the tube an obscene waggle. "Or, the gods forbid, laid?"

Before Walker could reply, the wizard shook his head, the three plaits of his beard dancing together like grizzled snakes. "Of course not." He snorted. "You'd have to give up control for the split second it took you to come."

Walker schooled his face to forbidding indifference. 'Cestors' bones, his brain seethed with questions. Leaning back in his chair, he breathed in, deep and even. Once, twice. That was better. "Tell me how Giral died. Exactly."

"He fought a duel with his own assassin." Deiter gave a dry, nasty chuckle. "But the other man had an unfair advantage—a prettydeath blade. Apparently, it took the Ambassador-Pasha the whole night to die."

A tygre snarl rumbled in Walker's throat. Prettydeath—the tool of assassins the world over. Mehcredi's weapon of choice.

The Purist sat up straight and suddenly, the air thrummed with Magick. "I've answered your question, shaman. Now answer mine. *Did you see your gods?*"

The first lines of his Song.

Welderyn'd'haraleen't'Lenquisquilirian, babe twice blessed with life and love.

First Mother's breath to sing his Song, First Father's touch on his downy head.

Like all newborns, he'd drawn his first breath as he was pulled from his mother's body. But when the shaman laid him against her breast, he'd uttered a single choked cry and fallen silent. Frantic, the man had worked on the tiny body, his prayers resounding in the incense-laden air of the birthing tent. To no avail.

His mother, Shar warrior that she'd been, always paused at this point in the story to regain her composure. "Twice blessed, Welderyn," she'd say. The Shar were not a demonstrative people, but one time—he'd been about six, he thought—she'd hugged him in front of everybody.

The shaman had pretty well given up when the baby's cloudy, slate-colored eyes snapped open, staring at something over the man's shoulder. The walls of the tent had rippled, though there was no breeze, and the shaman gasped, strangled by the backwash of power. As he toppled forward, eyes rolling up in his head, Welderyn had sucked in a breath and wailed his displeasure, loud and clear.

Or so he'd been told. He certainly had no recollection—of the First Ancestors or anything else.

"No gods," he said to Deiter. "Or not that I recall."

He frowned down at the ledger lying open on the desk before him. All through his childhood and adolescence, he'd had dreams . . . Not many, to be sure, and like all dreams, vivid in patches, but overall, maddeningly vague. A round, motherly face crowned with a coronet of dark braids woven with flowers bright as stars, eyes so dark he could fall into them and never find the way back. An enormous masculine palm cradling a cedderwood nut-corn; the corn splitting, a tree springing forth, branches reaching for the sky, a canopy of green for the entire world; the *ch'qui* suffusing his soul, his flesh, until every nerve ending quivered, burning with the energy of life itself.

And he'd wake, convinced there was something he'd been born to do—or more accurately, a task he'd been saved to undertake. Until Giral and his diablomen had fallen upon the Shar'd'iloned't'Hywil, he'd searched for it in vain, but from that terrible day on, he'd comprehended his destiny only too well.

No, the old Purist didn't need to know about the vengeance of the Shar. Nor that Welderyn'd'haraleen't'Lenquisquilirian had not heard his true name spoken aloud for fifteen years.

He raised a brow. "It's an odd question, Deiter, even for you. Why do you ask?"

The wizard stood, slapping the leather tube down across the ledger book Prue had drawn up so meticulously. "Here. Let me show you." Fumbling a little, he drew forth a thick, creamy sheet of parchment, expensive stuff. As he unrolled it, he said, "Do you know what this is?"

"A five-pointed star, a pentacle." Walker studied the glowing colors, the fine brushstrokes, and his brow creased. "Very pretty." He looked up into sharp old eyes. "So what?"

The old man sighed. "I don't suppose you've got a wine jug anywhere about?"

"There's a water carafe behind you on the shelf."

"Bah!" Deiter's lip curled. "You'll kill me. Forget it."

He tugged at his beard, collecting his thoughts. "I had a vision," he said at last. "Of a great evil, greater than anything the worlds have ever known, all-encompassing, universal, swallowing everything light and good. Even the gods can't—" He broke off, his face gray.

"I've got it," said Walker, watching cold sweat pop on the wizard's brow. "Go on."

"Wouldn't leave me alone, godsdammit, like I was poisoned. Thought I'd never stop puking my guts up 'til I—Anyway, I saw the Pattern—this one, a Great Pentacle. With four Sides: Fire, Air, Earth and Water."

"I hate to break it to you, Purist, but a pentacle has five sides."

Deiter shot him a glare from under bushy brows. "Godsdammit, man, I can bloody count! If I may be allowed to finish?"

"I doubt I could stop you," Walker said dryly.

"No," agreed the wizard. "You couldn't. Where was I?" He pinched the bridge of his nose. "Ah, yes. The Lord and the Lady haven't seen fit to inform me who the fucking fifth Side is, but—"

"Who?"

"Hmm. What?"

"You're talking about lines in a geometric figure. What do you mean *who*?"

Deiter glared. "It's a construct, you fool, a metaphor."

"Feel free to leave any time, Purist. I have plenty to do." Walker picked up the ink brush and turned it over in his fingers.

The wizard went on as if he hadn't spoken. "Each Side represents an element and for each element, the gods have chosen . . . someone to gift with power." He snorted. "Whether they want it or not."

Walker raised a brow, a cold tide spreading low in his gut. But he said nothing.

"Cenda nearly died of a fever. It took her child, but in return, the Lord and the Lady gave her the power of Fire."

"Erik got Air," said Walker slowly. When Deiter shot him a glance, he shrugged. "I saw him in action, remember?" Ah yes, big Erik in a fury had been something to behold. An angry Air wizard tended to be hard on loose crockery.

"So you did."

Walker waited.

Deiter took a turn about the room, shabby robes swishing. He came to an abrupt halt. "You're Earth."

"Yes."

Something flashed in the old wizard's eyes. It could have been surprise. "You don't deny it?"

"If I didn't know the source of my power, I wouldn't be a shaman. Who's Water?"

Deiter collapsed into a chair with a huff of exasperation. "Don't fucking know. But it's someone close, I can feel it."

Walker folded his lips together. They stared at each other in silence. A scent-laden breeze drifted in the window, flirting with the corners of the parchment on the desk, bringing with it distant sounds, shouts and splashes. Children skylarking in the blue waters of the canal.

"No," said Walker at last, very quietly. "I won't do it." Everything inside him went still and watchful. Ready. He flexed his fingers.

But all Deiter said was, "Why not?"

"Your gods are not mine, Purist."

"The Shar worship their ancestors, don't they?"

"An oversimplification," Walker said stiffly.

Deiter waved it off. "No offense intended. Anyway, don't you see? They're all the same, only the names change. The Lord and the Lady, the Brother and the Sister."

First Mother, First Father. Likely the old reprobate was right. Not that it mattered. It wasn't that Walker didn't believe in evil—he did, unconditionally. Who better, after all? But evil was made of blood and mud and shit and stink, not pretty pictures. He dealt with it his own way, one monster at a time. This Pentacle thing had storybook quest written all over it, a stalwart band of brothers riding shoulder to shoulder, off to save the world. 'Cestors save him from wide-eyed idealism!

"We need you." Deiter's lip lifted, exposing wine-stained teeth in what was doubtless intended to be a winning smile.

"I am not in the habit of repeating myself, Purist." People he barely knew and certainly didn't trust. Like Deiter, for instance.

The wizard nodded at the hand Walker had spread over the parchment to prevent it fluttering away. "Look."

With a muttered curse, Walker snatched his fingers away. The godsbedamned thing was alive!

Minuscule salamanders burned all down one Side, capering about in a fiery dance, though the creamy surface remained unmarred. Tiny clouds shot with rainbows scudded around the entire shape, coming to rest above the second Side. He thought he could hear them singing, a faraway chorus like distilled joy. But the third Side—

He'd forgotten how to breathe.

The *ch'qui* suffused the page, creating a trench no wider than his thumb, full of dark, fragrant soil, so rich and deep he could smell it, like Concordian chocolat. Threads of green sprang forth, growing while he watched, tangling and twining, the essence of life and birth and joy. Blossoms no bigger than pinheads burst open into tiny stars, releasing an intoxicating perfume.

Walker lifted his gaze. "Amazing," he said, meaning it.

Deiter stared, unblinking. "But the answer's still no."

"Good-bye, Purist." He pushed the parchment aside and drew the ledger closer.

"For now." The old man rose with a grunt, and retrieved the Pentacle. "One day," he said as he turned toward the door, "there'll be no more demons left to kill. What will you do then, retire and grow pretty fl—" He froze, staring out the window at the garden below. His throat moved, producing a gobbling noise like a scrawny old fowl surprised by a housewife with a cleaver.

Two strides and Walker was at his shoulder, following his gaze.

The swordmaster's mouth fell open, the scene below seared into his retinas.

Wearing only a soaking shift, every line of her lush body clearly displayed in the sunlight, Mehcredi the assassin stood thigh deep in the crystal-clear water of his special contemplation pool, holding that filthy dog by the scruff of its neck. The skinny boy that Prue had taken in at The Garden was with her. He scrubbed at the animal with a big bar of rough soap, his industry producing a thick scurf of bubbly foam. Even from up here, Walker could *feel* the daffydillies wilting, the shy little water plants choking and dying.

Dai reclined against the trunk of the venerable cedderwood that shaded the area, the remains of what was clearly a lavish picnic scattered about on the grass. His face was alight with laughter, though he had a protective hand covering his throat. They were all laughing, 'Cestors take them. As Walker stared in horror and disbelief, the boy compounded the disaster by losing the soap in the water. Completely uninhibited, Mehcredi threw her head back, laughing from the belly like a man. The action lifted her glorious breasts, pushing them hard against wet, semitransparent cloth.

Gods.

He could see every swirling line of his Mark, the pout of pink nipples pebbled by the cool of the water. Even though he curled his hands into fists, every nerve beneath the skin remembered the heft of her breast, the trusting satiny weight of it cradled in his palm. Worse, the shift delineated the curve of her waist, the swell of womanly hips. Unable to help himself, Walker tracked downward over the slight curve of her belly, tracing the drape of material to the sweet space between strong slim thighs. Fuck, even the rise of her mons was visible, but no pubic hair. Or none that he could see.

And he'd thought that part of him was dead. Shit! The breath rasped in his lungs.

Lips smacked noisily right next to his ear. "Yum, yum," said Deiter, amid hoarse chuckles. "You should see your face."

Walker snapped his jaw shut so hard it hurt. Whirling, he shoved past the wizard, leaping down the stairs three at a time.

Behind him, he could hear Deiter's mad cackling, broken at intervals by racking coughs. With any luck, his own amusement would carry the old bastard off, but in the meantime—Walker ground his teeth—he was going to make the assassin sorry she was ever born.

Some streetwise instinct of self-preservation made the boy spin around to face him, but Mehcredi remained oblivious. It wasn't until she'd clamped the wriggling dog firmly under one arm that she noticed Florien's curious immobility. She turned her head and some of the humor faded from her expression. "Oh," she said. "It's you."

"Mehcredi." The effort of self-control cost him so dearly, all Walker could produce was a menacing whisper. "What the fuck do you think you're doing?" He never swore aloud.

Her brow knitted. "Washing the dog," she said, as if to a senile uncle.

"In my pool. With"—Walker forced the word out—"soap."

"You said yourself he was filthy." With one hand, she grasped the dog's dripping jaw and pushed his head up, looking into miserable brown eyes. "And he had bitemes, poor thing."

"Out."

Clad only in a pair of drawers, the boy scrambled onto the grass and hunkered down next to Dai, shivering. The swordsman's expression remained grave, though he kept rubbing one thumb across his lips and his eyes danced.

Mehcredi gave him a dismissive wave. "Just a minute." Before Walker could stop her, she bent and dunked the dog all the way under the water.

"*Now!*"

This time, she did jump. "He needed rinsing," she said resentfully.

Walker set his hands on his hips and shot her a flat black glare.

7

"No, wait. Get the soap," gritted Walker, his head ringing with the assault on the *ch'qui* of his garden, his scrotum tightening with every breath the assassin took. She was so pale, she could have been sculpted of marble. But only the most expensive stone, the top grade that came from the Grand Pasha's private mines in Trinitaria, would come close to replicating the fine-grained beauty of her skin, the glow and luster of life. Long, supple muscle ran smooth beneath it, strong and yet ineffably female.

Mehcredi grumbled under her breath, but she dropped to her knees and felt around with her hands. The dog paddled past, cast her a glance that showed a thin rim of white and hauled himself out onto the grass near Walker. There he stopped, setting all four feet. The swordmaster fixed the animal with a gimlet eye. "*Don't.*"

The dog cocked an ear, then trotted over the bridge toward the approaching figure of the Purist Deiter. A foot away, he shook vigorously, water spraying in all directions.

"Aaargh!" The wizard recoiled, brushing frantically at his robes.

"Serves you right," snarled Walker. Bending, he whipped a checkered tablecloth off the grass, scattering plates and utensils. "Cover yourself." He shoved it toward the assassin.

Four pairs of eyes regarded him with varying degrees of wariness—five if he counted the dog. Ignoring them, Walker went to one knee by the pond, feeling the grass cool and damp beneath his palm, the rich deep soil below, the huge healing strength of the *ch'qui,* infinite because there was an entire world of it.

He'd flown into a rage over a body of water the size of a large bath. This was ridiculous. *He* was ridiculous.

The daffydillies might wilt, but godsdammit, his pool would recover from a little soap. 'Cestors save him, he'd lost control. A man famous for his icy calm under pressure, his impenetrable reserve. The incarnation of Shar vengeance and he'd raised his voice, shouted—

His gaze zeroed in on the assassin and narrowed, thoughts skittering about inside his skull like bitemes on a hot griddle. She'd passed the tablecloth to the boy, gods damn her, which meant he mustn't permit his stare to drop below her neck. She was shivering, lips paler than ever. *Why aren't you the way you're supposed to be?* he thought savagely. *This is all your fault.*

As if she'd heard his thought, Mehcredi tilted her head to one side, her silvery eyes huge. "Sorry," she said. "But I thought you wanted—"

"You have no idea of what I want." Walker ripped the shirt off over his head, balled it up and threw it at her.

"I know." Her hands closed hard on the garment, but she made no move to put it on, frowning. "You have to *tell* me, you see," she said. "I'm stupid, I don't always understand, so you have to—"

"You are *not* stupid!" Walker breathed carefully through his nose. "Don't pretend with me, assassin. It won't work."

"I'm not pretending." Her features went stiff with offense, but she rubbed the soft fabric against her throat, blotting up the drips.

Dai was shaking his head. Beckoning Walker closer, he grasped the hand the swordmaster offered and hauled himself to his feet. "She . . . meant . . . well," he rasped, pulling a small pad of paper from a pocket.

"But it was my idea." Mehcredi raised a hand as if to touch Walker's arm, then thought better of it. She stuck her chin out. "All of it."

"Nah," said the boy through chattering teeth. "T'weren't just you. Me too."

Dai dug Walker in the ribs and handed him a note. *I asked S. for picnic,* it said in a slashing scrawl. *Dog washing mutual idea.*

'Cestors' bones, they were *defending* her. How had she done it? But then—she seemed to be trying to shield them too, in her own strange way.

Godsdammit, what did they think he was going to do to her?

"Allow me to help you with that, my dear." With a snaggletoothed grin, Deiter stepped past him, reaching for the shirt.

Walker clamped iron fingers around the old man's wrist. "Don't touch her!"

Deiter swore. At every point of contact between them, Walker's flesh burned with Magick, so much so that it took every ounce of discipline he possessed not to jerk away. Instead, he released the wizard as slowly as possible and turned to Mehcredi. "Go to your room," he said coldly. "When you've changed, return to your duties."

"But Dai should—"

"I'll take care of Dai. And you, lad—" The boy scowled up at him from under an unruly black fringe. He'd struggled into his trews, standing with one hand hidden behind his back. A slum rat if ever he'd seen one, blade at the ready.

"Florien, isn't it?" Gods, if he had a mind to, he could count the child's ribs.

A nod.

"Where are you from?"

"Sybaris." His lips barely parted, the word grudgingly given.

"Your parents? Family?"

A shake this time. "Cenda," the boy said after a pause. "I guess. Mebbe Erik." A frown. "An' I work fer Prue, fer 'em all." He squared skinny shoulders.

Deiter snorted. "Boy's a guttersnipe. But Cenda insisted on bringing him. The gods know why."

Florien curled a lip, though Walker noted the trembling hands, the pulse beating in his thin neck. The child was terrified, as well he might be. "Wouldn't work fer ye, old man. Not iffen ye paid me."

But he had balls. Fleetingly, Walker saw another face, a girl with hair as black as his own and a wheedling grin. *C'mon, big brother, I'm tall enough now. Teach me quarterstaff. Mam won't know, I swear.*

Casually, he stepped between Deiter and the boy. "Get Dai to show you the basics, without the knife, mind. When he says you're ready, come to me."

Florien's mouth dropped open. Then he flushed a deep scarlet, eyes as black as Walker's own sparkling like polished jet.

"No," Mehcredi said immediately. "Dai's not up to anything like that."

Walker ignored her. "Dai?"

A nod and a smile. *Sure.*

"Good." Walker turned on his heel and headed back toward his accounts.

Her skin still flushed with warmth after another stolen bath, Mehcredi lit the stub of a candle, lowered herself to the edge of her bed and stared at the swordmaster's shirt. The moment he'd disappeared into the building, she'd stopped using it as a makeshift towel. And once she gained her room, she draped it carefully over the back of the single chair to dry.

She was trembling now, with the oddest mixture of excitement and trepidation. All day she'd been thinking of that piece of linen, a secret pleasure that filled her with glee, naughty as a child with stolen candy.

Biting her lip, she reached out to finger a dangling cuff. It wasn't a good shirt, she'd done enough laundry to know that, just something he chose for rough work. The fabric was worn and soft, with a couple of neat darns. One of the laces was frayed at the end. Not a garment he was likely to miss.

Letting out a gusty breath, she rose and spread it out over the bed, patting and twitching it into place as if it were a fine satin quilt. Then she jammed the back of the chair under the doorknob, as she did every night. Without giving herself time to think, she reefed the shift over her head and flung it to the floor.

Her heart banged about behind her ribs, the sonorous beat so loud it echoed in her ears.

Now. Sweet Sister, *now*!

Before she lost her nerve, Mehcredi grabbed the shirt, squeezed her eyes shut and slid into it the way she slipped under the deep water of her bath, fumbling her arms into the sleeves. Walker was broader across the shoulders and the chest and the cut of the garment was loose, so it slithered down over breasts, hips and buttocks without hindrance, a whispered caress that finished midthigh.

It smelled of man—not just any man—of *him*, his skin, his body, his uncompromising masculinity. As if he'd put his arms around her and drawn her close, her nose buried against the soft skin behind his ear. The sensation was more overpowering than she'd anticipated, so much so that she swayed where she stood. When she raised an arm to brace herself against the low ceiling, the soft linen shifted, sliding against the sensitive skin under her arm, brushing the shaman's Mark on her breast, the curve of her stomach.

Silvery heat flared low in her belly, so bright and clenching, she doubled over, stumbled and fell back on the bed with a choked cry. Pressing the heel of her hand against the mound of her sex made it worse, even more intense. *Gods.* Every swirling line of the Mark on her breast tingled. The tender flesh swelled, the skin tightening. Her nipples ached as if compressed between hard fingers. Shaking, she stroked fingertips over the fabric, tracing every line of the Mark beneath. If she closed her eyes, she could imagine it was the sword-master, hunter's face intent, Magick flowing from his fingers, soaking into her skin in the wake of his skilled touch. With his other hand, he'd cradle the breast, pulling the skin taut with a thumb to create his canvas.

He'd only done it because he had to, she knew that, and he'd probably been disgusted, but for these few moments, all her senses wrapped up by the fabric that had touched his skin, she'd allow herself the fantasy.

The soft folds between her legs were wet and swollen, puffy with lust. She might be a half-wit slut, but she wasn't completely ignorant. Because lust was all it was, pure and simple. Or not so pure. The half-formed chuckle morphed into a long groan. She knew what she was about to do, knew how stupid it was, but she'd never felt so . . . so . . . lit up. She almost expected the heat to be visible through her skin, a luminescent glow like a fire blazing behind a screen.

If there was one thing she'd learned at Lonefell, it was the comfort her own body could give her. The only names she knew for what she did were ugly or childish, or both—frigging, beating off, jerking off. Taso called that soft, sensitive place a *cunt*, spitting out the word as if it tasted foul in his mouth. But when she lay hunched in some hidey-hole at the keep, cold and miserable and unable to sleep, stroking it helped. The fingers of one hand busy, she'd achieve release, the other fist shoved in her mouth to stifle her cries. Afterward, she'd drift off, telling herself it didn't matter, that at least one person cared enough to gift her with pleasure—even if it was she herself.

Mehcredi fixed her gaze on the square of night sky framed by the window under the eaves, but what she saw was the swordmaster dancing with his swords on the green grass, his near-nude body so brutally male the impact of its beauty made her heart ache. He wore what she'd come to think of as his *inward* face, all his attention focused within, hard with concentration. Try as she might, even in her mind's eye, she couldn't change that expression to something softer. She tried to imagine how he'd look if he cared about the woman he was fucking, but it was beyond her. She couldn't even make her mental image smile.

Her eyes stung. Godsdammit, she'd take what she could get, pathetic though it might be.

Inhaling deeply, she filled her lungs with dark spice, allowing one hand to drift down, down, over ribs and belly, to the satin skin on the inside of her thigh. Back up, the hem of the shirt riding on her wrist. The muscles in her legs went slack and her thighs lolled open. With her fingertips, she furrowed through sparse curls, quivering when she encountered wet flesh.

He was wrapped around her, his body a welcome weight holding her down. His muscled forearm brushed the tender skin of her inner thigh, the touch of his fingers on her most secret place arrogantly confident. His command of her body was absolute. He understood the import of every gasp, every quiver. He was going to make her feel good, so good . . .

Mehcredi threw her head back when he circled a finger around the sucking entrance to her body and slid it deep inside. With his other hand, he plucked at a nipple, rolling it between his fingers, pinching to an exquisite point that hovered between pleasure and pain.

"Please," she whimpered to the silent room, lifting her hips in yearning. "Oh, please."

He took pity on her, adding another finger, and finally, finally, strumming the little bump of hot aching flesh at the apex of her cleft with his thumb. How so much sensation could be concentrated in such a small area she had no idea, but Walker knew.

Tension grew unbearably, a solid wall of heat behind her pubic bone.

Usually, she experienced release as a whiplash of uncoil and recoil, but this time—with him—it was different.

It began as a bud, tightly furled, hard and new. Rapidly, it grew and blossomed, putting out tendrils of heat that twined around the base of her spine, spiraling up and up until she was light-headed with pleasure, writhing beneath him, almost frightened. Every line of the Mark flexed like a living thing, strong as the first growth of spring, but all she felt was an excruciatingly pleasurable tingle, as if her skin were enclosed in a net woven of silky rose petals. She could swear the Mark was expanding, cradling both breasts, brushing the nerve-rich flesh of her nipples, gentle but completely inexorable.

Every muscle in her body went rigid, panic and arousal combined. She couldn't, she couldn't—Someone groaned, so deep it had to be him.

"Ah, Mehcredi," he murmured, the strange accent more marked than usual.

With the last fragment of her sanity, Mehcredi turned her head and bit the pillow.

Everything dissolved. White lightning flashed across the inside of her eyelids. As she shuddered and arched, the earth spun, trees grew tall as the sky, spreading their branches in canopies that covered the world, withered, died and sprang forth again. More silvery flashes, slowly dissipating, until they became simple spasms of pleasure and then no more than the reminiscent twitching of exhausted nerve and muscle.

She clamped her eyelids shut, riding it out, moaning and gasping into the pillow.

When she opened her eyes, an eon later, the stars in the window were watery smears. She could smell herself, her body sheened with sweat, thighs shiny with her own juices. Every muscle ached.

Sniffing, she wiped her eyes and removed the shirt. Carefully, she hung it over the back of the chair and wiped herself down with a corner of the threadbare sheet. Her knees felt like water, the pulse still drumming in her ears.

That had been . . . She swallowed hard. Sweet Sister, she'd thought she was going to die—and she hadn't cared.

Tears dripped down her cheek and off her chin, hot and salty. She'd felt . . . exalted, as though her passion was holy and beautiful, a force of Nature. But now, she sat in a bare little room in the House of Swords, sweat pooling in the small of her back, the muscles of her legs protesting because she'd frigged herself into a stupor like the half-wit slut she was.

All the breath whooshed out of her, as effectively as if she'd tumbled down all four flights of stairs and landed in a heap at Walker's feet in the front hall. Was it part of his shaman's Magick, of his justice, to punish her like this? To make her feel small and dirty?

Rolling over, she picked up a shard of mirror from the rickety nightstand. She had a broken-backed hairbrush too, both rescued from the trash heap. The mirror was shaped like a long, narrow triangle that came to a nasty point, lethal as a poniard. From the moment she'd seen it, she'd thought it might make a useful weapon. She still thought so. Tilting it, she stared into her own eyes, a stormy gray luminous with tears. Her nose was pink, so were her cheeks.

Well, shit. What was done was done. Mehcredi set her jaw. A daft lump she might be, but small and dirty she wasn't. Her lips twisted in a wry smile. Certainly not small.

She poured herself a cup of water from the chipped jug and drank it slowly, thinking. Walker wasn't interested in her body, in fucking. He'd made that clear enough from the outset. *You are not appealing to me in any way whatsoever,* he'd said, his voice deep, each word spaced for emphasis. So it followed he would have no knowledge of her stupid sluttish fantasies.

They were all her own. Her gaze traveled to the shirt. With a wistful smile, she wrapped her arms around her middle. All her own. It was tempting, but she wouldn't sleep in the shirt, or even with it. If she did, it would end up smelling like her and she'd lose this tiny stolen piece of an impossible dream.

She'd never met anyone like the swordmaster, could never have imagined such a man might exist. But then, she had so little experience. Perhaps there were men like him all over the world?

No, not possible. She wasn't the only one who thought he was amazing. Wait a minute. Mehcredi corrugated her brow, thinking. Had she seen anyone laugh in Walker's presence? Or even giggle? She didn't think so. Serafina had made her loyalties clear from the very beginning, so had the ex-mercenary called Pounder, the man who'd prevented her from falling down the stairs, but they hadn't claimed friendship with the swordmaster—respect maybe, but not friendship. When she'd asked Walker if Prue and Dai were his friends, he hadn't answered.

Normal people tended to *cluster*, she knew that much. Resolutely, she set aside the grief that came with the thought. Nothing to be done. People had families, or barrack mates. They made connections, took food together, laughed and fought and argued. Even the revolting Taso had an equally revolting father, a senile bundle of rags he referred to as the Old One.

Who was in the swordmaster's cluster? Dai perhaps? She made a mental note to ask the man.

There wasn't a person in the world who wasn't a mystery to her, but none so intriguing as Walker. He'd been angry with her today, even though the dog needed washing, as he'd pointed out himself a few days ago. Mehcredi puzzled her way through the encounter in the garden, trying to recall every nuance. If she separated his words from his actions . . .

She should have been frightened—Florien certainly had been—and yet it hadn't been so. She'd been wet and cold and Walker had given her his shirt. Taking hold of an empty sleeve, she pleated the linen between her fingers. He'd promised the boy training.

With an irritated snort, she let the sleeve drop.

If the boy could learn, why couldn't she? But what could she offer in exchange? Because that was how the world worked. *Ye don't get somethin' fer nothin'*, Cook used to say. All she had was her physical self—another pair of hands, a strong back, a cunt. She grimaced, thinking of Taso's disgusting tongue licking over the shape of the word. Surely there must be other terms for that part of her? She made a second mental note. Ask Dai.

Wistfully, she thought of Walker flowing from one movement of the *nea-kata* to the next, graceful as a widow's hair tree dancing with the wind, and just as strong.

Sweet Sister, everything about the swordmaster fascinated her. Questions trembled on her tongue. Where was he from? How did his shaman's Magick work? How did he get those scars? What was he thinking when he studied her with that black, dispassionate gaze?

His face, his hands, his body—oh gods, the acres and acres of bronze skin. She *ached* with the need to touch and be touched in return. This yearning wasn't a new sensation, it had been part and parcel of her existence for as long as she could remember. She'd lost count of the nights spent rocking to and fro, curled into herself, numb with misery and longing. *Skin hunger*, she called it, painful as the gut cramps of starvation.

Grabbing the broken brush, she dragged it through her hair, the teeth scraping across her scalp, bringing the blood to the surface, helping her think.

She knew the difference between his *inward* face and his hunter's face. She wasn't sure how, but she did. There was a more relaxed expression too, when he sat in the afternoons, talking quietly with Dai.

Mentally, Mehcredi reviewed every conversation they'd ever had, right from the first terrifying moment. Her eyes rounded. Word for word, she'd spoken more with the swordmaster than with anyone else in her entire life, even Cook. Little wonder she was obsessed. She knew him not at all and yet she knew him best.

8

When she entered the next morning with Dai's breakfast, Mehcredi found him stamping into his boots. "What are you doing?" she asked.

The swordsman shrugged. "Living," he whispered. "Going . . . on." His Adam's apple bobbed as he swallowed. Wincing, he massaged his throat.

"Dai—" She broke off, her mouth working. The words hurt, like hard-edged stones, digging into the soft flesh of her tongue and palate. "Sorry, so sorry. I . . ." Gasping, she ran out of air, her chest heaving.

Dai turned to stare into her eyes, a brow raised. "What, again?" A heavy flush bloomed on his cheeks as a cough wracked his body. When it receded, he was whiter than the sheets on the unmade bed. But he persisted. "*Still?*"

Mehcredi sank down on the bed, her brain spinning. What did *sorry* mean, truly? Her stomach ached. The silence stretched, broken only by the harsh whistle of Dai's breath and the distant calls of the skiffmen on the canal.

At last, she said slowly, feeling her way, "I wish I hadn't done it, that I could turn back time and undo it all. Even though the Necromancer would kill me." She risked a glance from under her lashes, but she could find no clue in his expression. Of course.

"When you hurt, I do too." She raised a hand before he could speak. "I know it's nothing compared with . . . but I feel . . . I feel . . ." She shook her head, unable to express her distress in anything as inadequate as words. His pain was like a foul ague that infected her as well—how, she had no idea. "Awful," she whispered.

Dai gave her his back, turning away to pour himself a cup of water.

"Medicine," said Mehcredi absently. He added the requisite spoonful of sparkly powder.

Sip by sip, he drank it down, finally turning to watch her over the rim of the cup.

"Does it help, that stuff?" she asked, unable to bear the silence.

Dai nodded, setting the cup aside. "It's called guilt," he rasped.

"Guilt? What I feel?"

A nod.

"Oh." Mehcredi fiddled with the hem of her shift. *Guilt.* "Thank you. That's good to know."

"You," said Dai, "are the . . . strangest person . . . I've ever met."

"I'm from Lonefell."

His mouth curved, very slightly. "Not . . . what I meant." He sank into a chair and extended his legs, feet crossed at the ankles. His eyes gleamed green gold, very bright. "Tell."

"What? About Lonefell."

"No . . . you."

"Me?" Her voice cracked with surprise. Mehcredi shut her sagging jaw. "You sure?"

Nod.

"Uh, all right then." She wriggled up the bed, curling her legs beneath her. Her cheeks heated, a corresponding wave of warmth suffusing her entire body. "I had one friend," she started slowly. "Cook. At least . . ." She frowned, remembering. "I think I did. Anyway, he used to—"

Half an hour later, she'd barely drawn a breath, so giddy with the luxury of an audience that words tumbled out of her in a torrent, her hands waving as she described Taso with his wet mouth and lewd talk, the keep children laughing behind their hands, the cavernous kitchen and cruel winters, Cook and his pastries, her clever little hidey-holes, the narrow escapes. Through it all, Dai's catlike eyes remained fixed on her face, though she thought the hard line of his lips had softened a little.

"And then . . ." She faltered, everything crashing back, the weight of what she'd done falling over in a suffocating tide. "The Guild Master sent me to the Necromancer." Her shoulders hunched. "Sorry."

Dai waved a hand. "Stop. Let me . . . think."

All the joy leaking out of her, Mehcredi rose to tidy the bed.

"You've grown," said that travesty of a voice from behind her.

"No." She gave the pillow an angry thump. "I've lost weight. All my clothes are loose."

"Nu-uh." He tapped the left side of his chest. "Here."

Mehcredi straightened, staring. Dai closed one eye in a deliberate wink, flipped one hand in a casual salute and walked out the door. Her knees going out from under her, she sat down so hard that the bed ropes creaked.

If he hurried, he'd have time to prune the first bed of dark roses before dinner. As the skiff bearing Rose and Florien disappeared around a bend in the canal, Walker turned away, heading for the garden shed and his tools. The precision and repetitive nature of the task would soothe his soul. He looked forward to it. And the roses would be grateful too.

But as he rounded his favorite venerable cedderwood tree, he slowed to a reluctant halt. The assassin sat on a bench shaded by touchme bushes, bent almost double, her head clutched in her hands. The dog, now marginally lighter in color, lay curled up on the grass at her feet.

"Why aren't you at work?" he asked coldly and her head jerked up to reveal eyes no longer silver, but dark as storm clouds, her lashes clumpy with moisture. Strange, he would have expected them to be as pale as her hair, but they were a light brown. Brows too. The framing gave her eyes an impact that resonated deep in a man's chest, all the more effective because he could swear she was unaware of it—almost.

Her lips twisted, taking on a bitter line he hadn't seen before. "I went up to clear away the tea things and Dai threw me out. Told me to fuck off." Her voice dropped. "I thought we were doing better this week. Silly me." The touchme bush chimed its distress, feathery fronds bending to brush across her cheek in an effort to comfort.

"You're upsetting my garden, assassin."

"What?"

"Never mind. Go find something to do. Anything." Deliberately filling his mind with roses, Walker stepped back onto the path.

A noisy sniff came from behind him.

Godsdammit. He turned. "It's not you," he said, reaching up to soothe a quivering touchme blossom. "It's Rose."

"Who?"

"Rosarina from The Garden of Nocturnal Delights. The Dark Rose. The incredibly beautiful woman who just spent the last hour with Dai."

"Oh." The assassin thought for a moment. "Long dark hair, strange eyes, great tits. That the one?"

Walker bit the inside of his cheek. Hadn't Dai said that Mehcredi was hands down, the weirdest woman he'd ever met? "That's her," he agreed. "Dai's had a crush on her since he was a lad." And why he was telling her this he had no idea.

"Does she love him back?" Mehcredi grinned and he blinked, taken aback by the way her face lit up. "That would be nice."

Walker shrugged. "Only in a way. She's fond of him, but like a sister. What you did hit her hard. She loved how he used to make her laugh."

Mehcredi couldn't conceal the flinch, though her pain gave him less satisfaction than it should.

"Rose has everything—beauty, charm, brains. See those blooms?" He indicated the bed of roses, each fist-size bloom a satiny purple so dark it might as well be black. Their rich spicy perfume pervaded the air. "They're dark roses. I bred them specifically for her. There isn't a man in Caracole who doesn't want Rosarina."

"Poor Dai." Mehcredi snagged him with her shining gaze, so he made a point of staring back without blinking. "Does that include you?"

"Me?"

"Do you want her too? You made those flowers for her." She watched him so intently, a little tendril of unease unfurled in his gut. No, oh no, she couldn't, she didn't—Not possible, not after what he'd done to her.

"I'm human," he said, showing his teeth. "Though you may not think so."

But the assassin remained unfazed. "You've got scars," she said calmly. "I see them every morning, remember?"

He didn't know why he hadn't put a stop to it long since. Willing the heat not to rise in his cheeks, he said, "Well, that's over. As of now, your invitation is rescinded."

She didn't move, not an inch, but Walker had the unnerving sensation of witnessing an internal collapse, all the life draining out of her as surely as if he'd failed to protect her and the Necromancer had pierced her to the heart with his death Magick.

"Please," she whispered, a thread of sound.

She rose and took a shaky step forward, standing nearly as tall as he, close as a lover, closer even. No one invaded Walker's personal space, his air of chilly reserve made it impossible, which was exactly how he liked it. He couldn't fathom why he was allowing it now, but the depth of misery in the assassin's expression hooked him and held him immobile. Her rapid breath puffed warm and moist against his jaw as she grabbed his forearm.

"I need, I need . . ." She seemed to lose her nerve, a pink tongue creeping out to moisten her lower lip. "T-teach me. *Please.*"

Without haste, Walker gripped her wrist, quite gently, and removed her hand from his sleeve. A small choked sound caught in her throat and from somewhere down at knee level, the dog whimpered. The swordmaster forced her chin up with his fist and studied her eyes. "Dai says you're sorry. That true, assassin?"

Gulping, she nodded.

"Not good enough." Walker shifted his hold, wrapping hard fingers around her jaw. "Give me words."

"I didn't . . . didn't understand at first. What it means to hurt someone that way." She swallowed, the skin of her throat moving smooth and warm beneath his palm. "How it hurts us both. I wish— gods, I *wish* I hadn't done it." Without warning, she sagged in his grip, so he had to steady her with the other hand on her waist. "But I did."

"You're sorry because you were caught."

"Well, yes. I mean no." Confusion swam in her eyes. "I d-don't know what you want me to say."

"How old are you, Mehcredi?" he said softly.

She blinked. "Don't know that either."

She wasn't lying, he was certain. Dispassionately, he noted the un-blemished quality of her skin, like ivory velvet, the smooth brow and firm chin. There were weary shadows beneath her eyes, but no lines. Mid-twenties at the most. So young—too young to embark on a life-time of guilt and piercing regret.

"I could kill you a hundred different ways. Slow, fast, screaming, silent. Shall I teach you all that? Is that what you want, to be a better assassin?"

Her tremors had ramped up into long rippling shudders. If he hadn't been holding her so firmly, her teeth would have chattered. She tried to shake her head, but he refused to permit the movement.

He leaned in, close enough to kiss—or to bite. "Well?"

Very slowly, her eyes on his, she wrapped her fingers around his wrist and tugged cautiously. An unpleasant twist in his gut, Walker released her. He'd been gripping hard enough to leave bruises on that pale perfect skin.

"I think," she whispered at last, "you might be my last chance."

"Chance? Chance for what?"

She was thinking so hard he could almost hear the effort, whirring and clicking like a Technomage machine. "I'm not sure. To be nor-mal? To know . . . things . . . Not to be ignorant." Her lashes swept down, then up. "*Stupid.*"

"Everyone does stupid things." He fought the urge to blink, to blot out her pleading expression, just for an instant. "You're not exempt." *Unfortunately, neither am I.*

Her respiration had become rapid and shallow, a pulse beating in the soft pit of her throat. But she lifted her chin. "Teach me the *nea-kata.* Please."

"Why?"

He'd expected her to hesitate again, to stammer, but she surprised him. "I want what it gives you," she said steadily.

"And what do you think that is?"

The breath whistled out of her on a long sigh. "Peace."

When he didn't reply, she hurried into speech. "There's something in your face that's, that's . . ." Two vertical lines appeared between her brows. "Like you've gone away somewhere beautiful, but you're still here and you're beautiful too and—" She broke off, color rising in her cheeks. "I'm being stupid again."

Walker grunted, torn between darkest unease and reluctant amusement. "It's concentration that you see. The swords don't forgive."

"But you wouldn't start a beginner with blades," she said shrewdly.

No, he wouldn't. Though he hadn't taught first-level *nea-kata* for years. Dai and Pounder did that, so Walker could concentrate on those sufficiently gifted—or bloody-minded—to survive his brutally demanding brand of tuition.

Strange though, despite his impatience with anything less than perfection, a part of him rejoiced in passing on his skills, in teaching. Until Giral and his diablomen descended on the Shar, he'd never known a time when he wasn't the oldest—the big brother, the one in charge. He'd been so serious about his responsibilities—looking back from an adult perspective, he was pretty certain he'd usually overdone it. Brennard and Owen used to gang up on him like a pair of angry puppies, but even with the typical sibling arguments and scuffles, the bond between them ran deep and true. They'd been growing into fine warriors, his brothers, fit to be initiated at the Spring of Shiloh, but that possibility was long gone, faded into the mist of might-have-beens. Because he'd failed them, hadn't he?

And Amae, the little sister he'd adored.

The old pain twisted in Walker's chest and he had to wait a moment to catch his breath. He hadn't found her body, nor those of two other girls. The Trinitarians had taken them for torture and rape at worst, slavery at best. But he'd taught Amae to fight, and gods, she'd been fearless! She would have fought to the death, he had no doubt of it. Nonetheless, he spent five years in fruitless searching. It took a further three to completely extinguish the stubborn ember of hope.

He'd trekked alone through the desert then, to Shiloh. At the sacred Spring, he'd sung Amae's Song, and for a short period, he lost his mind once more to the grief, as fresh as if the blood of the slain still trickled from the wounds, wet and warm and smelling of sweet copper.

His rage had made him careless. A few weeks later, he'd underestimated both diabloman and demon. Reflexively, he laid a palm over the claw marks on his hip. They weren't especially deep, but the wounds had taken fifteen months of festering to heal properly. They still ached when he was tired.

Not now. Walker inhaled the purple ebony scent of his dark roses, letting the *ch'qui* of the perfume obliterate the remembered stench of dark Magick, demon fog and spilled guts.

The assassin stared hopefully into his face, almost vibrating with tension. Gods, she was young. So very, very *hungry.* Passion and yearning shone in her eyes, still overlaid with that sense of wonder she hadn't managed to lose. The Ancestors didn't give the gift of intellectual curiosity to everyone. *Like you've gone away somewhere beautiful, but you're still here,* she'd whispered. It wasn't such a bad summation.

Amae's face had sparkled with an expression very like that, though her eyes and hair had been as dark as his own. Standing side by side, the two women would be a study in obsidian and marble.

Don't, whispered the voice of good sense. *By the seven million Songs of the Ancestors, don't do it.*

If anyone needed to learn control, it was Mehcredi the assassin. The discipline of the *nea-kata* would give her that at least. Whether it brought the gift of peace in its wake was a different matter.

Walker stepped away from her. "Stand still," he growled when she would have spoken, and she subsided, grumbling under her breath.

He took his time, studying the big body from heels to top of shining head. "You think you're strong enough?"

Mehcredi drew herself up. "I'm stronger than most men."

"I was referring to mental strength, but yes, you've lost some of the puppy fat, put on a bit of muscle." Physically, she had the potential to be the most formidable woman he'd ever trained. "But you're clumsy."

Her head drooped, though he caught the faint curve of a triumphant smile. "I know."

"Impulsive."

"I try, honestly I do, but I—" A sigh. "Yes."

"I won't tolerate half measures, Mehcredi."

She stared at him, frowning.

"The *nea-kata* isn't a fad. It's not even a martial art, though that's part of it. It's a spiritual practice. Be very careful before you decide. Do you understand?"

"No." Her face lit up as if a sun had risen inside her. "You'll do it?" She took a pace forward, putting out a hand. "Oh, Walker, thank—"

"Now you *are* being stupid," he snarled. "You're going to hate me, more than you do now, if that's possible." *Which will be an excellent thing.* "Dai says you've done enough penance as far as he's concerned. I disagree." He favored her with a thin smile, brimful of menace, and was gratified to see her breath hitch. "Are you sure, assassin?"

She swallowed hard. "Yes."

"Tomorrow at dawn, then. Usual place." He strode away, feeling the prickle of her stare between his shoulder blades. The placid mirror surface of his contemplation pool jogged his memory. He turned. "Assassin?"

"Yes."

"Where's that shirt of mine?"

She sank down onto the bench, extending a pale leg to scratch the dog's belly with her toes. "In the laundry," she said, and bent down to ruffle the animal's ears.

9

"Here." Walker thrust a bundle of clothing into her hands. "We're much of a size. Change."

Mehcredi retired behind the screen of a ticklewhisker bush. Goose bumps rose on her skin as she stripped. There was a shirt, and the loose drawstring pants were no problem, though she had to roll the legs up a few times. Wondering if they were his, she buried her nose in a worn sleeve, but all she could smell was soap and sunshine. The third item, a wide strip of heavy linen with reinforced eyelets and sturdy laces, was a real puzzle. As she turned it over in her hands, she called, "What am I supposed to do with this belt thing?"

A short pause, then Walker's voice said, "It's a breastband."

Oh, she'd heard of them. Well, that seemed sensible in the circumstances. It took her a couple of tries, but eventually, she wriggled herself into the thing and tied it off firmly. Experimentally, she flexed her shoulders. Oh yes, a breastband was an excellent idea. She slipped the shirt on over her head.

When she emerged, the swordmaster was gazing at something in the middle distance, as self-contained as ever.

"Where on earth did you get a breastband?" Mehcredi asked, grinning.

"Move over there," he said, waving toward an area of closely clipped grass. "First posture."

"Yes, but what about the—?"

Walker turned to face her, and though his expression didn't change, she had the sense he'd stiffened. "I don't respond to impertinent questions," he said softly. "Much less from a student."

Shit, not again. "I didn't mean it that way."

"I will have respect, assassin. Or your lessons finish before they begin."

Gods no. Sweet Sister, she was so close! "I'm sorry," she babbled. "I have a problem." She squeezed her eyes shut. "Problems."

"You think?" His long-lidded gaze burned into hers.

"I need to . . . explain something." She wet her lips. "But it's hard."

"Go on."

She got it out all in one breath. "I can't tell what you're thinking."

A black brow arched. "No reason you should."

Mehcredi tried again. "I'm not . . . normal."

The swordmaster continued to stare, unblinking. The silence grew like a living thing.

"I don't know how to *be* with people," she plowed on. "I don't get jokes. I ask stupid questions, and then . . . everyone stops talking and *looks* at me."

Walker made a *huh* sound, deep in his throat.

"See?" Mehcredi waved her hands in frustration. "What does that mean?" Tears of rage stung her eyes and she averted her face, refusing to let him see. "All I know is that you don't like me."

"What was your first clue?" The deep voice was very dry.

"Don't be silly," she said. "Gods, you tried to kill me!" A high-pitched giggle bubbled in her throat, but she gulped it down. Unconsciously, she pressed her hand to the curve of her breast, compressed behind a firm shield of fabric. "And you Marked me with your Magick. As a punishment."

"Do you blame me?"

She shook her head. "I understand now," she whispered. "Why you did it."

The sleepy twitter of an early-morning bird broke the silence.

"We're wasting time," said Walker.

In her agitation, Mehcredi took a step forward. "But this is important!"

"To you perhaps." He released a long breath. "All right, if it's plain speaking you want?" Both brows went up this time.

"If you're asking me, I . . . guess so."

"Very well." He folded his arms. "You, assassin, have no tact, no manners and, apparently, no finer feelings. Physically, you have potential, and I believe you possess a perfectly adequate brain—not that you appear to use it."

Mehcredi's mouth fell open. The blighting words washed right over her—she'd heard them all before, and worse. Tears welled up, trembled on her lashes and spilled over. "Then I'm not a great daft lump?"

"Who called you that?" he asked sharply. "Your parents?"

"Don't have parents. Never did."

"Family? Brothers and sisters?"

"No."

He frowned. "Who brought you up then?"

Mehcredi wiped the tears away with the backs of her hands, relief coursing through her, heady and sweet. She was going to learn the *nea-kata*, she really was. "I did," she said absently.

The swordmaster was looking at her so strangely. "How old were you? At the beginning?"

She shrugged. "Oh, quite little, I think. I could walk though."

"Come here." Walker drew her over to the grass. "Sit." He pointed.

Bemused, but willing, she sank down and he settled cross-legged in front of her. "We'll start the lessons tomorrow," he said. "For now, I need to know about my student." He held up a hand. "Just the highlights."

Unlike Dai, the swordmaster asked questions, shrewd and sometimes difficult to answer. She had to think, and think hard. Sunlight grew and swelled, spilling over the trees and bushes, burnishing foliage to a blinding green.

"This Taso," he said at last. "Did he catch you?"

"Oh yes." Mehcredi grinned. "But I kneed him in the balls and broke his finger." Amusement fled. "He said he'd be back, with his friends. That was one of the reasons I ran."

She risked a glance. Walker's face was stony, his jaw tight.

For the first time in her life, Mehcredi found the nerve to ask straight out. "Are you angry?"

He shot her a fathomless glance. His lips barely moved. "Yes, but not with you." In a single lithe movement, he rose. "Anything else is none of your business."

As he walked away, she studied the tail of his hair, as thick as her wrist and blacker than the night sky. Gods, she loved the way it fell, bisecting the broad expanse of linen shirt, just brushing the taut curve where his ass began.

If the swordmaster was aware that Mehcredi watched him all the way back to the salle, he gave no indication of it.

Deep in the Trinitarian Republic, an itinerant scribe set up his shingle in the shade of the north wall of the Grand Pasha's palace. Beneath a snowy head cloth, he wore spectacles mended with tape and a mildly anxious expression. His throat had the flabby look of one who'd lost weight quickly and recently. Behind him, huddled up against the huge roughly hewn blocks of masonry, sat a figure concealed by all-enveloping black robes. As he put together a shabby traveling desk and laid out parchment, ink block and brushes, the scribe ignored his companion, despite the rocking and muttering. More than one passerby averted his eyes, making the sign of the Trimagistos, the briefest touch to forehead, heart and groin.

The open square baked in the afternoon sun, mangy dogs dozed and pedestrians sauntered, the light linen of summer robes swishing about their calves. Nothing much happened until a matched set of eight male slaves, oiled and gleaming, rounded a corner and trotted toward the tall gates. Knees lifting smartly, all in step, they bore on their muscular shoulders an ornate sedan chair. As it drew level with the scribe, the gauzy curtains parted and a large hand emerged holding a knobby cane. A barked command, a vicious blow on the nearest back and the chair came to a halt, the slaves shuffling their bare horny feet in the dust.

The little scribe came to his feet and bowed so low his nose nearly collided with his knees.

A small female slave, dressed economically in a few strategic swathes of cloth, leaped out of the conveyance and hastened to unfold a set of steps. That accomplished, she held up a trembling hand to support the weight of the huge man who emerged. The scribe glanced over from under his lashes. It would be more than his life was worth to be caught staring. Clad in robes of dazzling white, relieved only by a midnight blue head cloth, the man was not so much fat as simply enormous, broad and beefy as well as tall. His heavy jaw gleamed with sweat.

"How may I be of assistance, Pasha?" murmured the scribe. "My talents, meager though they be, are at your disposal."

The man poked the scribe in the shoulder with the point of his cane. "Who are you, one-name?" he rumbled. "You're new."

"Hantan, I am called, Pasha. I have come on pilgrimage to the Tri-Lobed Temple, as all men must do at least once before they die."

"What's that?" A stab of the cane indicated the bundle of black robes.

The scribe's lips thinned. "My sister Dotty, mighty lord. She's not right in the head, but what's a man to do?" He spread his hands.

A grunt. "Couldn't sell her, hmm?"

"Regrettably not, Pasha."

The big man fingered a fleshy lower lip. "Hmpf."

Without another word, he clambered back into his sedan chair, the slaves staggering under the weight. As he was carried past the Janizars on the gate, they snapped to attention, hands falling to the hilts of their wickedly curved blades.

The scribe perched on the rickety stool behind his desk. "Know who that was, Dotty?" he said to his sister.

The black bundle emitted a string of numbers, fingers writhing as she counted.

"That," said the Necromancer, with tremendous satisfaction, "was Nerajyb Nyzarl, the Grand Pasha's senior diabloman." His mild blue eyes rested thoughtfully on the palace towers, reaching white and narrow into the blinding azure of the sky. "How very fortuitous."

"Diabloman," said Dotty suddenly, briefly channeling the Technomage Primus she'd once been. "May also be defined as demon master, but there are no empirical studies of demons and therefore no proof of their existence."

"If I offer your sorry carcass to Nerajyb Nyzarl, you'll find out, won't you?"

"Dead," she said. "Dead. Good. Be dead."

"Not yet, my dear," said the Necromancer. "You're still too useful, I'm afraid."

Dotty keened, a high and eerie sound.

"By Shaitan, will you shut up!" He hopped off his stool to administer a swift, satisfying kick.

With a startled squeak, Dotty resumed counting.

"Are you Walker's friend?" asked Mehcredi as she emptied a drawer of shirts. The healers had pronounced Dai as whole as he would ever be and he was moving out of what she now knew to be Walker's room and back into his own.

Dai gave a soft snort. "Doesn't have friends."

"I thought everyone had friends." She retrieved an errant sock.

"Too cold, too scary. Never . . . smiles."

Mehcredi thought of the deep pool of silence that seemed to surround the swordmaster. When he passed through a crowd, people melted away without seeming to realize they'd done so. She'd seen it. "But you, ah, like him?"

Dai shrugged. "Got my back. I got his."

"Loyalty's a part of friendship?"

The swordsman stopped stuffing garments into a duffel bag to shoot her an interested glance.

"There has to be more?"

Dai nodded.

"So how do you know if someone's your friend?"

He'd developed the habit of speaking in short bursts, presumably to spare his throat. Mehcredi wasn't brave enough to ask how much it still hurt.

"They . . . take care of each other." Pause to cough. "Laugh together, know . . . each other's secrets."

"Oh."

When Dai bent to roll up the magnificent rug, she hurried over to help him. "Rose's," he said. "Loan."

"Is Rose your friend?"

A shadow crossed Dai's face.

"Sorry," said Mehcredi immediately. Shit, that was stupid. Hadn't

Walker said the swordsman fancied himself in love with the oh-so-beautiful Rosarina?

"Dai?"

"Hmm?" He buckled the straps around a duffel, securing them with vicious jerks.

"Would you tell me a secret? Just a little one, about you?"

She tried not to flush as he studied her face for a long time, but her stomach pitched with nerves. Then the corners of his lips tucked up and his shoulders moved in a *what-the-hell* shrug. "Was a . . . virgin 'til . . . nineteen."

Mehcredi's eyes went wide. "That's a secret?"

Dai inclined his head, then gestured. *Now you.*

Shit, she hadn't thought that far ahead because she hadn't expected—Right. Squaring her shoulders, she got it out before her nerve failed her. "I'm a terrible assassin."

Without missing a beat, Dai said, "Is that . . . a secret?"

Mehcredi dithered, pleating the fabric of her shift with nervous fingers. Something warm bubbled up inside her, fizzing until her head swam with it. "You made a joke."

When he smirked, her own smile grew so wide her cheeks bunched up. "I must be bad at it because you're still here, that's it, isn't it?"

She didn't wait for a further response. "Gods, that *is* funny." The giddy feeling exploded out of her in gales of giggles. Wrapping her arms around her middle, Mehcredi laughed until she couldn't see straight.

When she finally wiped the tears from her eyes, the swordsman was leaning against the wall watching her, a small smile on his lips. "Tell you . . . another . . . secret."

"What?"

"I'm the best . . . card player . . . in the Isles."

"Really?"

She got a blandly wicked smile. "I cheat. Teaching boy . . . teach you too. Move room first."

Stuffed too full of joy for speech, Mehcredi grabbed the duffel and took off down the stairs two at a time.

∞

Memorizing the numbers and symbols on Dai's battered pack of cards wasn't too difficult, though it took Mehcredi a couple of hands and the rough side of Florien's gutter tongue before she figured out the actual purpose of the game. After that, the various strategies became clear enough, so much so that a few days later, she raked in the biggest heap of dried beans, while man and boy cursed and glowered.

"I won!" she caroled, dancing about the room. "I won!"

"Enough with . . . nice," rasped Dai, reaching for another pack. "Cheating now."

Learning how to cheat turned out to be as difficult as the *nea-kata*, and for similar reasons. *Control,* growled Walker every morning. *Concentrate, woman.*

"It all shows on yer face," snapped Florien as he arranged his pile of dried beans. "Gotta control yer feelings, see?"

Feelings.

Sister in the sky, these days she was bursting with the damn things, as if she'd lost a layer of skin and all her nerve endings were exposed to the unforgiving air. Every night, she promised herself she wouldn't do it, but the temptation was beyond her to resist. Pulse pounding, she'd bury her face in Walker's shirt, inhaling the man-smell in deep gulps. The next few moments varied, depending on what sort of day it had been. Most often the tears flowed hot and salty, but sometimes she rubbed the fabric against her cheek, smiling. She hadn't used the shirt to find release again. The experience had been so strange, so powerful, that whenever she thought of it she shuddered all over. Such an extremity of pleasure. Next time she might die and while it wouldn't be a bad way to go, dead was nonetheless dead. Life had become a thing of color and interest, two steps forward and one step back.

She'd never been so happy—nor so angry and confused.

Mehcredi's world shrank to the House of Swords, the swordmaster at its center, but at the same time, it had never been so large, so enormous with marvelous possibility.

10

The disciplined beauty of the *nea-kata* drew her in and frustrated her beyond measure. "It's too hard!" she wailed to Walker. "I can't!"

"No problem," he said. "Give up and stop wasting my time."

Every muscle complaining, Mehcredi scowled. Serafina had been stricken with a blinding headache, so she'd had to struggle with all the wet, heavy sheets by herself. "No!"

"Then do it again—the bridge of clouds—and this time, keep your elbow higher." He lifted her arm into position with impersonal fingers. In fact, he touched her often, but always fleetingly.

With sweaty palms, she gripped the short wooden staff that was all he'd allow her and thought longingly of murdering her tormentor. Except that she didn't want him to die. She wanted, she wanted . . . Oh, she wanted to dangle him over a chasm and only pull him up when he agreed to be her slave. Or, even better, she'd feed him a Magick potion that turned his stern features all puppy-soft and adoring. Then she'd laugh and kick him down the stairs.

"Your form must be perfect, every motion automatic," said that quiet, inexorable voice. "Clear your mind, center yourself and start again. All the way from first posture to tenth."

Grimly, she began, feeling floaty with exhaustion. But partway through, the floatiness morphed into something else, a lightness of being she'd never experienced before, a rightness where everything almost made sense.

When she finished, Walker unfolded his arms and said only, "Better."

Mehcredi's knees shook. Casually, she lowered her staff and leaned against the wall, dizzy with relief and pride.

That was the first glimpse.

After that, she took to sneaking off to quiet corners of the garden to practice. Inevitably, the dog would appear from somewhere and flop down in the shade to watch. He was a surprisingly restful companion.

Mehcredi discovered the hardest part of the _nea-kata_ wasn't control, it was letting go. As the days passed, a measure of peace stole into her soul. The first fragments came so shyly, she didn't recognize them at first. The sensations were fleeting, but in those precious moments, she glimpsed something of such ineffable beauty that tears streaked her cheeks. Once or twice, she even found the quiet place at her very center.

One morning, Walker took her to the fighting salle, gave her a blunted practice sword and said, "The first level, every posture. Do it."

Her heart banged about so hard, she couldn't ground. Her thoughts swooped and skittered like demons on crazyspice.

Walker's hand closed over hers on the hilt, his palm and fingers rough with the calluses of a professional swordsman, but warm. "You've worked hard, assassin," he said. "Show me."

Mehcredi swallowed, expelled a long gusty breath and steadied.

Then she flowed into the first posture.

She emerged as if from a dream to see the swordmaster standing in the middle of the floor, hands on hips.

"Well done," he said, and she knew she glowed. "Third and sixth postures need improvement, but the rest was quite good."

"Wrong," rasped a voice. Dai stood at the door, grinning. "For a beginner . . . was bloody marvelous. Praise . . . where it's due, man."

He grabbed a wooden practice sword and flourished it. "Defend yourself, assassin." Eyes gleaming, he advanced the length of the salle.

"Uh," she said, backpedaling in alarm. "What the hell are you doing, Dai?"

"Just a taste," said Dai in a rough croon. "See what you're . . . made of." And he struck at her throat, the movement so swift it was a blur.

She barely got her blade up in time. The impact ricocheted up her arm to the shoulder. "Dai. Stop, stop, I can't—"

"Tygre crouching," snapped Walker, seemingly in her ear. Panic freezing her mental processes, Mehcredi did the only thing left, flowing into the posture.

Crack!

She stepped sideways. Dai came on, his teeth bared in a wild grin.

"Spreading fan," called Walker.

Dai's blade slid down hers and glanced off. Mehcredi danced away, knuckles stinging.

"Keep your wrist steady." The swordmaster was a shadow at the periphery of her vision. "Horse's tail. *Now!*"

But she was too slow and Dai caught her with a blow that rattled her ribs. "You're dead." He gave her a nasty smile.

"That hurt!" She glared.

Dai said nothing, attacking in a ruthless flurry that forced her backward, defending frantically.

"Bridge of clouds!"

She must have got her elbow at the right angle because Dai parried and then misstepped. Before she knew she was going to do it, Mehcredi bent her knees, ducked under his guard and poked him under the breastbone with the blunt tip of her weapon.

"Fuck!" Dai skipped out of the way.

Suddenly, Walker was between them, a solid wall of muscle. "Stop," he said. "Now."

Mehcredi pushed forward, gritting her teeth. "I'll kill him, I swear."

Rubbing his chest, Dai gave a whispery laugh. "What, again?"

"Enough!" Walker turned a cool gaze on the swordsman. "Got it out of your system?" he asked mildly.

"I guess." Dai lowered his wooden blade, chest heaving, face pale. "Good test though." He sank onto the bench under the window.

Shock, rage and hurt combined to rob Mehcredi of breath. Like a fool, she'd thought Dai was her friend. She fought off the familiar feelings of despair. She wouldn't give up, she *wouldn't*. "Test?" she managed.

Dai glanced at the swordmaster's impassive face. "Tell her."

A short pause, and Walker said, "We didn't plan this, Mehcredi, but he's right, it was an excellent test and you did well."

"I did?" She must be staring like a half-wit.

"There's only so much about swordplay that can be taught." She had the sense Walker was choosing his words with care. "For some, the *nea-kata* will never be more than a form of spiritual and physical exercise. Not you."

"Reflexes," husked Dai. "Excellent."

Mehcredi addressed Walker. "But I'm clumsy, you said so yourself!"

"Not when you stop thinking and let the *nea-kata* take you. Your instincts are good."

"How good?"

Another lengthy pause, and Walker said, "Train hard enough and you could make a living at it." When she opened her mouth, he frowned her down. "One day. Possibly."

Dai pushed himself to his feet and laid his blade on the bench. Without a word, he walked quietly out of the salle and down the path toward the water stair.

Mehcredi stared after him, aching all over. She pressed the heel of her hand against the firm restraint of the breastband as if the pressure would help hold her together.

"You thought he'd forgiven and forgotten, didn't you?"

She nodded, gulping. "How . . . how did you know?"

Walker shrugged. "It's written all over your face."

There it was again. Feelings, faces. Well, *shit!* Why did she get to be the open book?

"Nothing's written on yours," she said resentfully.

Walker plucked the practice sword from her unresisting grasp. "Good." He turned to slot it into the rack.

Her fingers itched with the urge to grab the tail of his hair in both hands and yank it like a bellpull, but then he said, apparently to the wall, "Give Dai time. His whole life has changed because of you."

Mehcredi gnawed on a thumbnail. If she tried to speak about it she'd either scream or burst into tears. Instead, she asked, "Are we going on?"

When he glanced over his shoulder, one brow raised in inquiry, she waved a hand, encompassing the salle and the gleaming weapons on the walls. "With, ah, all these?" She straightened her spine, her heart thudding with excitement and hope. Walker fighting with the quarterstaff was all lethal grace, brute force and cracking blows. Gods, how she wanted that, to be complete like him, a thing of beauty and power.

"We'd better. Right now, you only know enough to be dangerous."

She blew out an unobtrusive breath of relief, her whole being yearning to touch his shoulder, to thank him, but she was held inside her crystal prison, separate, *different*—and it wasn't possible.

"Usual time tomorrow, assassin."

When she didn't move, Walker frowned. "Surely you have floors to scrub?"

Mehcredi stared, caught up in an astonishing discovery. His eyes weren't black as she'd supposed. This close, even shielded by those extravagant lashes, she could see they were deepest, darkest, richest brown, and if she tilted her head . . . like . . . that, the light revealed fugitive gleams of gold. *How pretty,* she thought, but for once she managed to shut her mouth before the words escaped.

"What?" said Walker, and he sounded as if he might be annoyed. Everything was normal.

"Please," she said. "Please don't call me that. I'm not an assassin anymore, truly I'm not."

The swordmaster studied her face for the longest time, while she wondered glumly what particular stupidity was written there for him to read.

"Tomorrow, Mehcredi," he said at last, leaving her standing in the middle of the floor.

⌒∞⌒

"You sent for me, mighty lord?"

Nerajyb Nyzarl clicked his fingers and a slave sidled out from behind a pierced and fretted screen. The same girl as before, thought the Necromancer, no more than a child really, her breasts just budded. "Sherbet," growled the diabloman. The slave bowed and whisked herself away.

Nyzarl's shrewd deep-set eyes returned to the shrinking figure of the little scribe. "Hmpf," he grunted and then lapsed into silence, thick fingers drumming on his thigh.

Get on with it, you fat fool. The Necromancer schooled his features into a suitably obsequious expression. Galling, that's what it was, waiting on the pleasure of a slug like this. But by Shaitan, power rolled off the man in dark heady waves. The Necromancer's nostrils dilated with pleasure. He could sense Nyzarl's demon, concealed by a fold in the fabric of reality, slavering and starving, hating its master with its whole black heart—or whatever passed for such an organ in that place.

"I am to be three-named," said Nyzarl abruptly, as if he'd come to a decision.

The scribe dropped awkwardly to one knee. "My most humble congratulations, Pasha," he murmured to the pattern on the tiled floor. "Richly deserved, if I may say so?"

"You think the honor overdue, do you, scribe?"

"Ah." The Necromancer dithered, and hated it.

The other man stared, enjoying his discomfiture.

"It is not my place to think at all, mighty lord," he said at last. "Only to serve to the best of my humble abilities."

"Humble is right."

The girl slave returned to kneel at her master's elbow, infinitely more graceful than the scribe. The diabloman lifted the chased goblet from the tray she proffered. Its sides were misty with condensation.

The Necromancer ran a tongue over parched lips and purpose firmed within him. Nyzarl had been one among a number of possibilities. Now he was the only one. Imagining the heavy spice of the man's death energy, he smiled on the inside. Not that it would be easy, not with the demon. He'd need Dotty, after all, the Dark Lord take her.

The diabloman broke into his musings. "Can you write in cipher, one-name?"

"Of course, Pasha." He bowed once more, his hips paining him. He'd gulped the death energy of the original scribe in a single draft, but Hantan had been in his sixties and not particularly healthy at that. It had helped, but not enough. How old was the diabloman? Forty? Forty-five at the outside?

The goblet whizzed by his ear and bounced off the wall with a clang, its contents spraying across the floor.

The Necromancer looked up in time to see Nyzarl backhand the slave, sending her sprawling across the floor. "Melted!" he snarled. "Get another."

Reminding the Necromancer of nothing so much as a beaten dog, the girl scrambled to her feet, snatched up the goblet and ran from the room, a hand over her mouth. She hadn't made a sound.

Unpredictable as well as a hair-trigger temper. This just got better and better.

"The title comes with an estate on the southern border."

Despite himself, the Necromancer's eyes widened. Perfect— Shaitan, it was perfect!

Fleeing south to Trinitaria had been the obvious course. He'd had the forethought to secret not only cash, but the Technomage's drawings and research results, in a concealed drawer in his office. But a night passage in a swift galley across the Three-Pronged Strait didn't come cheap. Nor did food and lodgings for two. Nonetheless, he'd contrived. Given he'd been too weak to wield his Dark Magick, he flattered himself he'd accomplished the murders with aplomb, if not with a certain flair. He'd forgotten how much artistry could be invested in knife work.

Not bad for a man his age—first an elderly flower seller, too feeble to resist, though she'd had a few creds and her death energy to offer. After that, a dockworker, drunk and vomiting his guts up in an alley in the souk and then—Hantan, the scribe. This last was truly a stroke of genius, even if he did say so himself. Appropriating the trappings of the man's livelihood had made all the difference, given him a reason to exist in Trinitarian society.

Once established, he'd drifted farther south, hauling Dotty along with him, a piece of baggage that muttered and mumbled and rocked back and forth. Thank the Dark Lord, the average Trinitarian paid zero attention to a female unless he needed to be fed or fucked. Gradually, the conviction stole over him that he was moving south for a reason. He began to dream, the same vision repeated over and over—a formless presence, nothing he could discern; many voices screaming in concert; strange high-pitched whining noises, and best of all, the sparkle and pop of souls winking out. He'd wake trembling, covered in sweat, a hand shoved under the waistband of his trews, hungering.

He obtained maps, puzzled over them. What called to him had to be infinitely far away, deep in the southern desert. When he passed his fingertips over the area on the creased parchment, they tingled.

"The south, my lord?" he asked carefully.

Nyzarl removed his head cloth and ran his fingers through a head of shiny black curls. No gray, the Necromancer noted. The diabloman was propped up on a lavish daybed, supported by embroidered pillows.

"Used to be Shar country," he said. "Wiped 'em out myself, the savages. Years ago."

"The Grand Pasha, blessed be his name, is wise in his recognition of service."

"As am I." Nyzarl turned his head to watch the girl return. With her, carrying the tray, was a pretty young man wearing a loincloth. The youth knelt by his master, while the girl crouched to wipe up the spill. Blood trickled from the corner of her mouth and dripped down her neck, but she didn't raise a hand to it.

"Every slave's a spy," Nyzarl rumbled. The smooth circular motion of the girl's cloth on the floor paused for an instant, then resumed. "I do not tolerate spies."

"My discretion is absolute, Pasha," said the Necromancer. "I can assure you of that."

"Hmpf." Another narrow glance. "Let's make sure, shall we?" Another click of the fingers. "Girl."

The slave's olive skin went a pasty green gray, but she rose and crossed the room dutifully enough. The young man moved hastily aside, the slave tattoo showing dark and vivid on his cheek. Idly, the Necromancer wondered where the girl wore hers. Somewhere inconspicuous, no doubt. Grabbing a fistful of hair, Nyzarl tugged her down to land hard on her knees by his side. Uttering a string of guttural syllables, he sketched a shape in the air with his free hand, spreading his fingers wide, then closing them slowly.

The Necromancer peered, fascinated. Acrid green fog flowed swiftly into the room, through what he could only call an aperture. He wrinkled his nose at the stench. *Faugh.*

The girl moaned, low and soft. Despairing. "Master, no, please—"

"Shut your mouth and I may yet find a use for you."

The misty green substance coalesced into a tall, narrow shape. As it drew together, the Necromancer was able to discern a long narrow lipless face, attenuated limbs and black-tipped talons. The creature was completely naked, its hide a muddy brown, hard and warty. It had four arms, segmented with what looked like more than the usual number of elbows, each bearing a wicked spur. Its legs were spindle-shanked and knock-kneed and a thin spiked tail lashed behind it. No more than usual size, a limp phallus swung between its legs, but the organ was barbed, the wicked spines presently lying snug against its length.

Interestingly enough, the demon's huge round black eyes were fixed not on the slave, but on the master. They literally glowed with hatred.

It took a lurching step forward, out of the mist, then halted as if it had run into a wall. Nyzarl was speaking again, a harsh rapid tumble of noise, so hard-edged and angular it sounded painful, as if he had a mouthful of thorns. The only syllables the Necromancer could distinguish from the guttural mumble sounded something like Xotclic.

Indifferent to the creature's furious attention, the diabloman paused and drew a steadying breath. "Demon, I conjure you to my will by right of your True Name," he said formally.

The thin-lipped mouth opened. "Sss?" Though technically, the Necromancer thought, watching carefully, the demon had no lips, only a set of opposing horny plates.

"I have a treat for you." The slave girl had sagged, her knees gone from under her, her body weight hanging from the diabloman's grip on her braid. "No real damage, but you may add your own sauce."

"Sss."

Gods, the thing was so ugly, it was beautiful. He wanted it more than breath.

11

Xotclic paused in its progress toward the girl and shot the Necromancer a penetrating glance over one bony shoulder. Immediately, he dropped his gaze. *I'm a scribe, nothing more than a terrified scribe. See? I'm shaking, going to piss my trews.*

When Nyzarl released the girl's hair, the demon seized it in one clawed hand. Then it pressed its sunken chest against the girl's back and nuzzled its horny mouth into her neck. A thin forked tongue flickered out and licked up the blood from beneath the girl's ear.

With a noise like a stricken puppy, she froze.

The demon moved around to face her, and as it did so, it began to change, slowly at first and then more rapidly. The emaciated body morphed into a strong broad frame, the horrible narrow head became a mature handsome face with a pugnacious jaw.

The girl's eyes widened until the whites showed all around. Clearly, she knew this person. "No," she whispered. "Gods, no." Even with the demon flickering in and out behind the simulacrum, there was a clear resemblance between them. Her father, perhaps?

This must be the sauce. There was a straightforward, uncomplicated cruelty to it he had to admire. Most ingenious.

When the forked tongue flickered out of her father's mouth to scoop up the blood on her chin, the girl's eyes rolled up. Urine pattered down her legs to drip on the floor. Undeterred, the demon licked until every trace of blood was gone.

Over their heads, Nyzarl pinned the scribe with a hard stare. "There are things worse than death."

"Oh yes, my lord, I know," said the Necromancer, with perfect truth. "It would be my honor to work for you." With some difficulty, he prostrated himself on the floor and banged his forehead three times on the tiles.

Walker noticed the slip of paper straightaway, a pale square lying on the floor, a foot inside the door. He contemplated it for a moment, then squatted to pick it up. Balanced comfortably on his heels in the way of his people, he unfolded it with steady fingers.

Yes!

Nyzarl's name leaped off the page, one word in a block of script, below which sat the modest sigil of Caracole's spymaster, known as the Left Hand of the Queen. The Left Hand answered only to the reigning monarch, the office so secret that no one knew who he was—not even Uyeda, who was Queen Sikara's Right Hand and her chief executive officer. The arrangement took the concept of separation of powers to a unique level, but it worked with perfect, ruthless efficiency.

Walker had received notes like this before, written in the anonymous, well-formed hand of a clerk. To be precise—he'd had missives concerning diablomen six, nine, eleven and thirteen. Times, dates, places, names—the information was a gift he'd taken and used with relish. His lips drew back from his teeth in a hunter's grin.

He returned to the paper. So Nerajyb Nyzarl was about to leave the shelter of the tripartite palace? Thanks be to the Ancestors. He read on. Even better, the bastard would be vulnerable, traveling south to take up a new estate near—

The note crinkled softly as Walker crushed it in his fist. Cold sweat sprang up on his brow, the back of his neck. 'Cestors' bones, he hadn't been back there in years, not since he'd sung the Song of Death for Amae. His throat went dry, as raw as if the last anguished note had just left his lips.

He *couldn't.*

But he would. As he tripped the mechanism to the secret drawer in his dresser, a low menacing noise filled the air, a kind of rumbling purr. When he straightened, a long box of polished cedderwood in his hands, he caught a glimpse of his face in the mirror. His eyes were wild and his teeth gleamed very white.

Gods, he not only sounded like a direwolf, he resembled one too.

Not displeased, Walker lifted the lid and stared down at his trophies. The bleached finger bones shone a shocking white—fourteen digits, fourteen diablomen. His lip curled in a hard sneer. Barbaric no doubt, but then Commander-Pasha Ghuis Gremani Giral had decreed the Shar to be no more than animals, vermin to be exterminated.

Plans clicking in an orderly procession through his brain, he began selecting items and shoving them in a battered pack. He wouldn't need to be gone long—two, perhaps three, weeks. Dai was very nearly back to full strength. Between them, he and Pounder could run the House of Swords without much trouble. They'd done it often enough before. He'd ask Rose if he could borrow her gardener. The elderly woman was no artist, but she was conscientious and thorough. No problem.

His long fingers stilled on the Trinitarian head cloth he was folding. Mehcredi the assassin.

Well, shit.

Walker tossed the head cloth onto the bed and crossed the room to stare out the window at the beauty of his garden, but there was little comfort to be found there.

His responsibility, in every possible way. The Mark tied Mehcredi to the House of Swords—and to him, though she didn't know that.

She was brash and ignorant and on the way to becoming the most gifted swordswoman he'd ever known. The potential of her shone so bright it dazzled. It was there in the happy silver of her gaze, in her strength and beauty on the practice floor, even in the devotion of that godsbedamned dog. The physical changes were indescribable. Mehcredi didn't hunch into herself anymore. She stood tall and strong and proud, every muscle smoothly delineated, her hair a long shining fall like a river of ice speaking to the sun.

Walker growled under his breath.

The other week, he'd walked in on Dai teaching the assassin and the slum boy how to cheat at cards. They'd been laughing—*laughing*! Yesterday, he'd discovered the man showing her his favorite defensive move, quarterstaff a blur of motion as he demonstrated under her admiring gaze.

Mehcredi might have endeared herself to Dai, but Walker wasn't such an easy touch. The assassin's penance wasn't over yet. By the Ancestors, a lifetime under his control wouldn't be enough.

He cursed aloud, his voice bouncing off the walls in the quiet room.

Fuck it all to the icy hells, why hadn't he seen it before? He *couldn't* let her go, even if he wished to. Freedom would be her death warrant. Vividly, he recalled Deiter's face, the wizard's callous greed. Remove the Mark, and even with Dai's protection, by the time he got back, the old wizard would have her. The hair rose on the nape of his neck. There wouldn't be enough sense left in her skull to fill a teaspoon.

Walker's chest went tight with something that felt like anger but might have been regret. He pinched the bridge of his nose, seething. Godsdammit, he'd spent all the years of his adult life avoiding entanglements, and now look what he'd done. Vaguely, he wondered if the Ancestors were amused. Too dangerous to leave her, too risky to take her. A woman who looked like Mehcredi, who *acted* like Mehcredi, in Trinitaria? He suppressed a shudder.

But he'd be there, wouldn't he? Him, not Deiter. He'd cow her into obedience, frighten her so thoroughly she wouldn't dare set a foot out of line. He'd keep her safe. Because the assassin—and her penance—belonged to him.

Shit, shit, *shit*!

❧

The moment they reached the dock at the far end of the Melting Pot, Walker pulled Mehcredi behind a couple of tall barrels. "Tell me again," he said. "Who are you?"

Her head turned toward him, though he could see nothing of her face behind the dark veils, not even her bright eyes. He'd chosen them for that very purpose.

"I'm a Trinitarian woman," she murmured, obediently enough, though he could sense her positively vibrating with excitement beneath yards of black fabric. "Oh, is that our ship? I've never seen a ship. It's not as big as I expected."

He ignored the question. "I am a blade for hire, no questions asked, Trinitarian style. Whose woman are you?"

"Um, your woman?" Was that a smile in her voice?

"That's right. How much are you worth to me?"

"Less than an old horse."

"Good. Slouch a bit, you're too damn tall. Anyway, you're supposed to be frightened of me. Of any man."

She slumped a little, the all-enveloping robes rustling around her. "That better? Oh look, they're putting out a ramp. Is that what they call a gangplank?"

"So if I slap you around in public, or do this"—Walker grabbed a handful of ass cheek and squeezed; Mehcredi yelped—"what do you do?"

"Uh, uh . . ." She didn't move away, but she was breathing hard; he could see her breasts rise and fall beneath the robe. "I take it." A pause. "Without ripping your balls off and shoving them down your throat."

"Very good." With a thin smile, Walker opened his fingers, ignoring the instinctive desire to shake the tingles out. "Remember, every female in Trinitaria is property. Your wishes mean nothing, you have no rights and you are worth very little in monetary terms."

He twitched his robes into place. "If something happens to me, try to disguise yourself as a man, because otherwise you'll be prey. Right now, you are mine to do with as I will."

She might have muttered, "What else is new?" but a couple of burly laborers pushed past them to roll the barrels away and the words got lost in the rumble of wooden staves on the cobbles.

"Come on," said Walker, setting off toward the *Spicy Venture*. "Two steps behind me at all times, and for the gods' sakes, at least try to *look* servile."

A small mongrel trotted out from behind a stack of bales and cocked its leg on the lowest one. The words "Best Silk Rugs, Produce of Trinitaria," were stenciled on the heavy canvas. As it hastened to catch up with the Trinitarian couple, the bundle of robes that was the woman fell a few paces behind, as was proper. The dog dived under her skirts and disappeared from view.

❧

"Little scrounger," murmured Mehcredi without surprise. A warm, wet tongue swiped her behind the knee. What had Dai said? Friends were loyal. *He's got my back. I got his.*

Excitement fizzed and bubbled in her blood. The veil was infuriating, reducing the vividness of sky and sea to a monotone gray, but still . . . She sniffed the crisp salt in the air, the tarry odor of wet rope and ripe fish and rotting piles. The dock was alive with shouting scurrying figures—sailors, laborers, traders, beggars, a woman with a tray of dubious-looking snacks. Flocks of shiny white birds swooped and called in high-pitched voices.

With a cracking boom that hurt the ears, a starship sprang into the blue from somewhere beyond the horizon. The bone-shaking roar swelled, then diminished as it streaked westward. *Offworld,* thought Mehcredi, her brain scrambling to process the enormity of the concept. Different skies, new worlds, other peoples. One day, sweet Sister, one day she'd go, she swore it. Hell, even a kid like Florien had seen more than she had, though Caracole and the House of Swords sounded far preferable to Sybaris, where he came from, a world ruled entirely by Technomages.

"Head down," hissed Walker.

Damn. Mehcredi bent her knees and dropped her shoulders as they climbed the gangplank. She did her best to shuffle, her head still spinning.

This morning, instead of the usual dawn session with the *nea-kata,* Walker had sent her back to her attic room with a roll of black clothing and a bag of soft scuffed leather. "Get dressed, then pack," he ordered. "You're coming with me."

When she opened her mouth, he snapped, "Answers later. Pack now."

To her delight, the bag contained a serviceable sword belt, scabbards and two blades—one a long dagger with a plain black hilt, the other a dainty knife about four inches long. In addition, there were a couple of light shirts, her old boots and trews, her padded cloak and vest.

When Walker met her at the water stair, dressed in the flowing robes and head cloth of a Trinitarian male, she gaped. With his bronze skin and hooded black eyes, he looked as if he'd walked straight out of a souk. Belted about his waist, he wore the exotic sword set she'd last seen on the walls of the fighting salle—the curved blade she'd cut herself with and the wicked poniard she'd tried to steal.

A single glance raked her from head to heels. "Good, you'll do." He hustled her into a waiting craft and instructed the skiffman to take them to the Melting Pot. It wasn't until they were past the first bend that it hit her.

In a panic, she pressed both hands to her breast, to the Mark. The pain, where was the crushing pain? Why hadn't her heart exploded?

"Relax," said Walker. "As long as you're with me, there's no problem."

Shakily, she sat back. "Where are we going?" she asked when she recovered sufficient breath to speak.

"Trinitaria. I've booked passage on a spice ship across the Three-Pronged Strait." After a moment, he waved a hand before her face. "Mehcredi?"

She blinked. "Yes?"

A black brow quirked. "Speechless?"

She nodded.

"By the First Father, a miracle. I'll tell you more once we're underway, but to get on board you have to be convincing as a Trinitarian female, do you understand?"

Bemused, she'd shaken her head, so Walker had spent the rest of the short trip talking, explaining, grilling her when he was finished. Then he did it all over again.

Now she peered down at the oily water sliding between the dock and the wooden sides of the vessel and swallowed. It was a long way down.

A normal person would be completely disconcerted by the turn of events. Why wasn't she?

She'd go wherever the swordmaster led and be content to have it so. How very odd. The simplest explanation was that he'd bewitched her, stolen her will with his Magick. But that wasn't it. Surely she'd feel . . . different? And she hadn't gone suddenly mad either, she knew that—a half-wit in her own way, yes, maybe, but she could still think straight.

Gingerly, she poked at her own feelings. Beneath the trepidation and the puzzlement, lay a deep core of calm. After all, she'd spent the last months trying to atone for what she'd done, to please him. Nothing in her life had thrilled her so deeply as his measured praise. Walker's quiet presence had become the strongest, most dependable thing in her universe. She couldn't give him up, not yet. Gods, she might not understand him, might not be able to read his face, but she wasn't the only one. He was a difficult man to understand, harder to like, even Dai said so.

Beneath the veil, her lips curved in a slow smile. She trusted Walker. It might not be particularly clever, she was still a daft lump, but she couldn't help it. From the moment he'd wrapped his hands around her throat, life had glittered with challenge and terror and excitement. What else did she have to do anyway? Go back to Lonefell? She'd rather die.

More to the point, he hadn't lied to her, not once, not ever. And he'd chosen *her*—Mehcredi the assassin. No, not the assassin, he'd chosen Mehcredi of Lonefell to go with him on an adventure. She longed to wrap her arms around herself and dance a jig. An adventure. *Together.*

As they reached the deck, she suppressed the urge to grab his arm and swing on it like a child.

"I am Wajar," said Walker, fixing the nearest barefoot sailor with his usual hard stare. "My accommodations, yes?" His voice sounded different, oily and proud all at the same time.

With a barely concealed sneer, the man waved at a dark hatchway. "Aft," he grunted.

Partway down the narrow passage, they ran into a harried-looking boy of about fifteen, clutching a sheaf of papers. "You're Wajar? Says here, passage for one across the Three-Pronged Strait, two days, one night." He shot a wide-eyed glance at Mehcredi. "What about? Um . . . her?"

Walker shrugged. "No matter. Floor is soft enough."

The youth moistened a thumb and flipped through the pages. "Right. Well." He appeared to come to some sort of decision. "Only one other passenger on this run so we can, uh, upgrade you. Second left."

With another wary, fascinated glance, he edged past. Was that pity in his eyes? It was hard to tell, what with the gloom and the veil and all her usual problems.

The room—she supposed it was a cabin—was narrow. Two bunk beds hung suspended on chains from the ceiling, one above the other. A lamp was bolted to the opposite wall and a wooden chair had been jammed into the far corner. Above it, a small round window begrimed with salt let in a fitful light. That was all. But there was a lock on the door. Walker shot the bolt.

Immediately, Mehcredi pulled the veils off and threw them aside. She clawed at her braids, shaking them free. "Gods, that's better! Would you really make me sleep on the floor?"

Walker's hard mouth twitched. "You could have had the blanket," he said gravely.

With a sneeze, the dog emerged from beneath her robes and the swordmaster's jaw knotted. "No," he said. "Hell, no." He shot a measuring glance from the dog, now leaning against Mehcredi's leg with his tongue lolled out in a canine grin, to the porthole and back again.

"Please." She wet her lips. "He's clean, I promise. No bitemes."

"That's not the point." Walker stepped forward and the dog bounced to his feet, tail waving. "We're still anchored. It's a short swim."

Something in Mehcredi's head went *snick*! She heard it distinctly. Without knowing how she got there, she found herself standing breast to breast with the swordmaster, her fingers digging into his biceps. They were almost nose to nose. "He's my friend—the only one I've got!" She shook him for emphasis, but it was like trying to shift a cedderwood.

Walker said quietly, "It's dangerous where we're going, even for dogs. If he's truly your friend, put him out the window. He's a survivor."

Stubbornly, Mehcredi shook her head. "I'll look after him. I promise."

Walker's midnight eyes studied her features, one by one. After an endless time, he cupped her cheek in his callused palm.

"You've finally learned to care, assassin." One thumb brushed across her cheekbone in an unconscious caress. "I don't recommend it." His mouth twisted and the warmth of the touch fell away.

"Are you angry?" Mehcredi pressed shaking fingers to the spot.

Before he could reply, a huge rumble emerged from the bowels of the vessel. Every timber creaked in protest as the ship shuddered from bow to stern. "We're weighing anchor," he said. "Do you want to watch?"

But Mehcredi had already twisted her hair into a knot and grabbed her veils. Exhilarated, she hurried to the door, only to feel hard fingers lock onto her elbow and spin her back into Walker's chest.

"Behind me at all times, woman. Remember?"

"Are you angry?" she asked again.

Walker shook his head, his face even more hawklike in the frame of the head cloth. "I will be if you or that misbegotten mongrel gets us killed."

"What are we doing in Trinitaria? You didn't say."

He set his back to the door and fixed her with a level gaze. "I have a man to kill, that's all you need to know for the moment."

With a finger under her chin, he closed her sagging jaw. "Come on."

12

They stayed on deck until the dark shadow of Caracole disappeared below the horizon. The dog found a spot out of the way of traffic and dozed off, whimpering occasionally in his sleep. The sun shone, the water hissed merrily along the hull, creaming into a long frothing wake—the kind of day that made you glad to be alive. Unfortunately, the veils itched as if they were infested with bitemes. Mehcredi longed to rip the godsbedamned things off and let the wind snatch them away.

Slim dark shapes sped along beneath the water, riding a bow wave that curved like a traveling wall of blue glass. When one, then two, then three, broke through, she gasped aloud. Gossamer wings, wider than the creatures were long, spread to catch the wind. Where sunlight hit the streamlined bodies, they sparkled with rainbow iridescence.

"Skimwings," said Walker's voice in her ear.

To speak would have spoiled it. Mehcredi hung out over the rail, only peripherally conscious of the strong fist that gripped the back of her robe and kept her safe.

"Greetings," said a voice from behind. "Calm seas today, thank Trimagistos."

Mehcredi spun around, but Walker didn't move, and she realized he'd known the man was there.

The captain had set aside a small area for passengers forward, with a small sail rigged for shade, a couple of chairs and a rug on the deck. Upended, a half barrel served as a makeshift table. The sailors gave the space a wide berth, their weathered faces dark with dislike.

A small man, his swarthy face soft and round beneath a red- and white-striped head cloth, sat bolt upright in one of the chairs. He shrugged, smiling. "I confess I'm not a good sailor. Please." Indicating a carafe and a couple of cups, he sighed. "Do join me. I long to hear a voice from home."

"My thanks." With a nod, the swordmaster took the other seat. A hard hand on her shoulder pressed Mehcredi to her knees beside him. "I am Wajar."

"Vartan Vezil." The little man's chest expanded as he pronounced both the names. "You are returning home?"

Walker gave a curt nod. "I have completed my task in the Isles." Negligently, he caressed the hilt of the curved sword. "And you?"

Vezil's gaze dropped to follow the motion. "I've just come from the court of she-devil. Thanks to the Three my tour of duty is over." He made a complicated gesture that traveled from forehead to chest to groin. "Faugh, the eunuch stink of it." Turning his head to the side, he hawked and spat.

Suddenly, his voice changed, grew sharp. "What are you waiting for, woman?"

Mehcredi started.

Walker nudged her leg with a casual toe. "Serve," he said. "And be quick about it."

Biting her lip, she poured two cups of chilled wine. Her mouth was parched. But when she offered a cup to Walker, he frowned. "Not me."

Flushing, she turned to Vezil.

"What's wrong with her?" said the little man, frowning.

Walker's mouth shut like a trap. "Nothing."

Vezil stared at her hands, the only part of her exposed. "Not Trinitarian," he said with certainty. "Too pale. Wife or slave?"

Walker's eyes flickered, and for the first time ever, Mehcredi had a flash of genuine insight. The swordmaster was weighing his options and he didn't care for either one.

"Slave," he said, his lips barely moving.

"Hmm." Vezil's stare felt sharp enough to penetrate the veils. Mehcredi's skin crawled. "Looks exotic. Had her long?"

"A few months."

"Stand up straight, girl," said Vezil. "Let me look at you."

Startled, Mehcredi shot a glance at Walker and received the slightest nod in return. Very well. She'd show the little worm. Taking her time, she straightened her spine, squaring her shoulders and pulling in a deep breath. She took a calculated step sideways, knowing she was looming, blocking the Trinitarian's sun, intending to do it.

"Oh yes." Far from being intimidated, Vezil's eyes brightened. His tongue crept out to wet his lips. "She a strong ride?"

Walker gave a noncommittal grunt.

"It's been too long." Vezil lifted his cup in a toast and drank deeply. "Ah." He smacked his lips. "Send her to me tonight, will you?"

For the space of a few heartbeats, the world stopped turning on its axis. Then common sense returned and Mehcredi had to bite the inside of her cheek to stop the chuckle. She had to be a foot taller than this shrimp. Gods, she could snap his spine over her knee. With a grin beneath the concealment of the veil, she waited for Walker to wipe Vezil from the face of the earth.

Sails flapped, water gurgled and rushed, hurrying on its way past. Sailors' voices rumbled in the distance. *No.* Gods, no, he wouldn't, he couldn't—

"I have not yet had my fill," said the swordmaster calmly.

Vezil set his cup down with a clink. "I don't understand." A frown creased his brow. "You're a one-name. What's the problem?"

"This," gritted Walker, "is the problem."

In a single smooth movement, he rose, grasped Mehcredi around the waist and swung her into his body, her back to the Trinitarian. The other hand flipped up her veil. Before she could blink, the swordmaster's hard mouth descended on hers.

"Mmpf," she said as their teeth clinked. Her fingers clutched spasmodically at his shoulders. She couldn't breathe. This was a kiss, this . . . this *invasion*? Godsdammit, she was going to pass out for lack of air. She stiffened, pulling back.

Walker's fingers flexed against her cheek in an unmistakable signal, the pressure of his lips eased and she could breathe again, more or less. Sweet Sister, this was what he'd meant, a public exhibition. Deliberately, she relaxed, grounding and centering the way he'd taught her in the fighting salle, and he gathered her close again, one palm stroking up and down her spine, the way you'd soothe a nervous cat. She'd promised not to feed him his own balls, except that standing in the circle of his arms on the sunlit deck, breathing him in, she had not the slightest urge to do him harm. His body was so hard, her breasts were mashed against a wall of unyielding muscle, and gods, he was *hot*, his spicy smell filling her head and making it swim. Every nerve in her body quivering, she pressed closer, tilting her head to offer a better angle. The hilt of his sword pushed into her belly.

Beyond that, she didn't know what to do, so she softened her mouth and let him take the lead. He'd taught her everything, she thought muzzily, had given her the discipline and peace of the *neakata*. Walker had reshaped her life, he could teach her this too. Her head fell back against his arm.

The swordmaster murmured something encouraging into her mouth and his hand slid down to grasp a buttock and pull her nearer, if that were possible. His lips gentled on hers, brushing to and fro across the cushion of her lower lip. Enthralled, Mehcredi turned her head to follow, but the fingers on her jaw held her still.

To her astonishment, his tongue prodded at the seam of her lips. *What?* Then he licked, a hot wet flick across sensitive skin, and her knees went from under her. Without fuss, Walker took her weight as she sagged. But he didn't stop. He nibbled on her lower lip, making her moan, then slipped his tongue right inside her mouth.

Mehcredi's eyes flew open. She hadn't even been aware she'd closed them. At this range, all she could see were Walker's magnificent lashes, black as ink, fanned across his cheekbone.

Concentrate, Mehcredi, said his remembered voice in her head.

All very well, but this wasn't swordplay and what should she do with her tongue?

Suddenly, she was looking straight into his eyes, so close, drowning in the rich dark brown of them, the pretty gold flecks.

A pause, a blink, and he withdrew, no more than half an inch.

"Wa—"

"Sshh." His thumb brushed her lips, his whisper so soft, the sound was no more than a breath in her mouth. "Shut your eyes."

Behind her, the Trinitarian spoke sharply, his tone huffy with offense, but her head was swimming and the words made no sense.

Obediently, her lashes fluttered down. Warm and wet and confident, Walker's tongue swept once, twice, over her lower lip. He paused, waiting.

Oh. Tentatively, Mehcredi returned the caress. Gods, his lips were smooth and soft. How extraordinary for a man so hard.

Walker slid his tongue over hers, but when she tried to reciprocate, he captured it, suckling gently on the tip. Mehcredi gurgled. Slowly, he raised one hand, brushing his knuckles up over her ribs. Giving her time to grow accustomed to his touch, she realized dimly.

When his fingers trailed over the Mark, she cried out, the sound muffled by the swordmaster's mouth.

The Magick pattern flexed and caught fire, her nipples flaring with almost painful sensation. The world, the ship, the Trinitarian, the deck beneath her feet—everything went away. She'd felt this sensation of impending dissolution before, and been terrified. But this time, she had so much more than an empty shirt to hold on to; she had the real thing—*Walker*, solid and strong and infinitely reassuring. He wouldn't let her fall, he'd never let her fall.

Mehcredi released all coherent thought, abandoning herself to instinct. Nothing existed except Walker, his mouth, his hands, the hard body pressed against hers, the long unmistakable shape of an erection nudging her hip.

It could have been a lifetime, it could have been mere seconds, but finally he pulled back. Mehcredi stood, eyes closed and face upturned, shaking with reaction. Random aftershocks tingled up and down her spine, chased over her ribs, her breasts, the soft flesh between her legs. Slowly, the swordmaster's fingers slid away from her cheek. Shifting his palm to the back of her head, he urged her closer, until she could tuck her face into the curve between his neck and his shoulder and hide. She was beyond grateful.

"Now, *two-name*," he said, and the chill in his voice slid down her spine like a sliver of ice, strangely thrilling. "Is there any part of 'mine' you don't understand?"

"I'll report you," huffed Vezil, cheeks blotchy with outrage.

Walker laughed. The first time she'd heard the sound, but he definitely wasn't amused.

Mehcredi nuzzled closer, inhaling deeply. She'd be content to stay right here for the rest of her life, she thought vaguely.

"I won't forget this, Wajar." Footsteps receded across the decking.

"He's gone." Walker gave her a little shake. "Wake up, Mehcredi."

Reluctantly, she peeled herself away.

"You kiss like a novice," he said.

The last wisps of pleasure dissipated as if they'd never been. "What did you expect?" She yanked her veil into place, grateful for the concealment.

Walker settled back in a chair and stretched out his legs. He pointed to a spot on the rug by his side. "Come and sit at my feet like a good slave."

Grumbling under her breath, Mehcredi sank down in a billow of fusty black. The dog sighed and padded over to nudge her hand with his nose. Automatically, she scratched behind one inside-out ear.

"Vezil could be a problem," he said softly. "Less indulgent masters whip their slaves."

He had to be joking. With an effort, Mehcredi pushed even the possibility of it to the back of her mind. "I couldn't have been that bad at the kissing. He was convinced."

Walker lifted his face into the wind. Mehcredi watched it toy with the edges of his head cloth. It had come from Trinitaria, that bundle of warm air, a place even more alien than the familiar world that continued to hold her at arm's length. She shivered, all the excitement leaking out of her.

"You did improve," he said.

Mehcredi regarded him thoughtfully. "Really?"

The swordmaster didn't answer, just stared out to sea. Very gradually, she allowed herself to lean closer, until she was slumped against the side of his chair. With a rattling sigh, she exhaled, the thunder of her pulse slowing a little. Sweet Sister, she hadn't realized how tense she'd been. A huge yawn caught her unawares.

"Sleep if you want."

"I thought"—she swallowed another yawn—"you wanted to talk?"

"That's best kept for later." Barely there, his fingers brushed the back of her head. Perhaps she'd imagined it. "Too many ears on deck."

"Mmm." Half drugged with the comfort of it all, Mehcredi laid her cheek against a powerful thigh. No one to see her, no one to judge, save the swordmaster, and she was pretty sure she knew what he thought. Sails filled and flapped, the dog snuffled peacefully at her feet. Nice.

She drifted off.

His leg had gone numb, but something about Mehcredi's confiding weight and the soft regularity of her respiration pinned him in the chair, watching the sun sink low and the surface of the water turn opaque, oily and mysterious. Walker didn't much care for the sea; his spirit yearned toward the distant coastline, to the *ch'qui*, to the deep solid earth and growing things. But passage from Caracole to Belizare, the busy port across the Three-Pronged Strait, shaved a good week off travel time to Trinitaria. A galley would have been even faster, but that he refused to contemplate. Once experienced, the reek of a Trinitarian slave galley was unforgettable—an unholy mixture of unwashed bodies, piss and utter despair.

He'd pick up employment as a caravan guard in Belizare easily enough. Merchants heading inland for the capital of Trimegrace could always use another sword on the journey south. The Grand Pasha appeared to have little grasp of everyday economic realities. Under his gods-centered but eccentric rule, bands of masterless men roamed the trade routes, preying on the caravans.

Finding a van master to employ him would be no problem—except for the assassin. His fingers slid under the veil to the nape of her neck and cupped it. As a wife, Trinitarian custom gave her some protection, however meager. No man wanted to raise another's bastard. But as a slave, he might have to fight to prove his ownership, many times over. He ground his teeth. Only the presence of the sailors had prevented him from tossing Vezil overboard for the krakenfish and the jarracudas. Arrogant little shit. *Two-name.* A grim smile flitted over his features. He should have let Mehcredi have her head, though it would hardly have been fair. He'd have enjoyed watching her make mincemeat of the man.

If only she wasn't so pale, but the beautiful ivory of her skin, her height and athletic frame—all of them fairly screamed *foreigner*. No

Trinitarian would breed children upon a foreign female. They were exotic, for enjoyment only. He squeezed his eyes shut, focusing on the sparkly darkness on the inside of his eyelids, but he wasn't quick enough. Mehcredi stood in his contemplation pool, guilty but unrepentant, the fabric of her shift plastered to every contour of her magnificent body. Automatically, Walker spread his thighs to accommodate the surge of his cock.

Exotic? Gods, yes.

But innocent, untried. He licked his lips. They still burned. Gods, such a gorgeous uncomplicated response. How could any man resist it? She'd all but come undone in his arms, as if she'd been waiting all her life for his kiss, his arms to hold her close. Safe.

Should have left her to take her chances with Deiter, he thought with a snarl. But if he were honest, he'd known almost from the beginning he couldn't throw her to the old direwolf. A heavy rope of bound silk, the thickness of her braid slid smoothly across his knuckles, while his thumb brushed rhythmically over the vulnerable spot where skull met neck, the unobtrusive area where a Trinitarian master would place his tattoo. Spoiling the appearance of a bed slave with the usual ink on the cheekbone would reduce her value.

What little he knew of Mehcredi's life said her earliest memories were of abandonment. Worse, the pattern had been repeated many times over, and yet she retained that bright-eyed sense of wonder, a desire for life and learning so powerful it transcended her fears. Amazing.

She murmured, shifting in her sleep, and one hand came to rest against his shin, a loose curl of fingers over hard bone. Nearly as big as his, broad palms, long fingers, short nails. Capable.

And against the dark of his robe, white as the upturned face of a nightpearl blossom.

Walker's thoughts ran on, sorting and sifting various strategies. The slave thing was too dangerous—'Cestors save him, it was all too dangerous. She needed another disguise, but what? He drummed his fingers on one knee.

The *Spicy Venture* heeled into the wind and the mainsail boomed like a drum as the helmsman adjusted their course. The sound stirred him out of his reverie. He looked down and froze, shocked into immobility.

Mehcredi the assassin leaned comfortably into his leg, deeply relaxed and completely unconscious, holding on to him as if he were all that kept the nightmares away. None of that was news. The unwelcome jolt came from what *he* was doing.

Welderyn'd'haraleen't'Lenquisquilirian, last warrior of the Shar, an ice-cold hunter dedicated to vengeance, sat—oh-so-tenderly—caressing the back of a woman's neck. 'Cestors' bones! The stroking—gods, the *fondling*—that was bad enough, but the worst part—the absolute worst—was that he'd done it automatically, instinctively.

He snatched his hand away as if her skin had combusted beneath his fingers. The kissing must have temporarily disordered his brain, regardless of the necessity for it.

Mehcredi murmured something indistinguishable, her breath warm and moist on his thigh even through layers of fabric.

Walker's ordered world spun, then steadied. Breathing hard through his nose, he stared down at the assassin's sleeping form. Then he recalled the deaths of his brothers, his mother, his tribe, one by one, in excruciating, vivid detail, every scream, every sickening thud of metal and mandible against vulnerable flesh, every crack of bone and snap of sinew.

Unseeing, he stared at the silver sickle of the Sister, rising over the curve of the planet's shoulder. His task was clear, as it had always been. Mehcredi was a peripheral consideration, a nuisance if he were to be brutally frank. Except—

He refused to glance down, acutely aware of her weight pressed against him.

Fuck it all to the seven hells, she *trusted* him. And he, unutterable fool that he was, had done nothing to disabuse her. Oh no, he thought caustically, far from it. You thought you were so bloody clever, didn't you, *swordmaster?* Being tough, riding her hard, giving her the discipline and structure she's always needed. Letting her earn the forgiveness she craves.

Something deep inside him wanted to twist and howl, but he held on to it with iron control, one hand gripping the hilt of the Janizar's sword so hard the metal dug into his palm.

From the first, he'd assumed such extraordinary innocence must be a cover for cunning. No one could be so . . . direct, so transparent. But Mehcredi knew nothing of subterfuge, she was as clear as a mountain spring, every thought and feeling shown on her face, in those striking silver eyes. Walker's chest squeezed, remembering the tilt of her head as she concentrated on his voice, the quick glances at his body when she thought he wasn't looking, the brightness of her smile when the realization dawned that he wasn't leaving her behind.

Well, fuck it all to the seven icy hells.

He'd ignored what his gut had been telling him all along, and this—this godsawful, godsbedamned mess—was the result. Mehcredi the assassin was as deeply imprinted on him as the little dog was on her. Who else did she have, after all? Who else cared? Walker tried to remember the last time he'd misstepped so comprehensively and came up empty.

Unless you counted surviving the massacre of everyone he'd ever known or loved. Amae's laugh sounded in his head, no longer quicksilver, the way it had been in life, but harsh and mocking like the call of a corpsebird.

His course was set. He could keep Mehcredi safe—probably—but only if she did exactly as she was told. The puppy love didn't matter, if that's what it was. She'd grow out of it soon enough, and if she didn't, the moment she saw what he really was, the infatuation would be over.

"Wake up, slave." He nudged her with his knee, then bent to shake her shoulder.

"Mmpf?"

Walker stood, leaving her to flounder. "Come below. We have to talk."

Below. In a cabin so narrow they couldn't pass each other without brushing shoulders.

Mehcredi wobbled to her feet, yawning hugely under the veil. When the deck tilted, she grabbed his arm as if she'd been doing it all her life.

Father's balls!

With a muttered curse, Walker shook her off and headed for the hatchway. It was going to be a long night.

13

In Belizare, Walker took a chamber for them in the souk, two floors above a bar that was little more than a dark slit in a stucco wall. The sun beat down into the narrow street, creating a sharp line of demarcation between deep wells of shadow and blinding reflections off sheer whitewashed walls and flat roofs. Faded canvas awnings in dusty shades of orange and umber struggled to provide shade for stall after stall, where everything from strangely shaped fruit and vegetables to leather sandals to miserable songbirds drooping in wire cages was on sale. The smell was indescribable, an almost palpable blow to the nose, a mélange of baked dust, rotting fruit and incense.

Sister save her, it was hot! Not the moist subtropical heat of Caracole, but something hard and dry like the bleached bones of a fallen desert idol. The moment they gained the privacy of the room, Mehcredi ripped the veil off and hurled the enveloping robes into the farthest corner.

Walker gave her another of those cool raking glances, grunted and shook his head.

"What? No one stopped us on the way." She put her hands on her hips. "I was good. I even kept my hands in my sleeves, the way you said."

"So you did, but you forgot to walk behind."

The flush on her cheeks made her feel even hotter. "There were so many people. I was frightened I'd lose you."

"Mehcredi."

She stared at her boots.

"Look at me."

Scowling, she lifted her gaze.

"You will not lose me, nor I you. I guarantee it."

He wouldn't say it if it wasn't true. The way the thought steadied her was eerily like the peace of the *nea-kata*.

She inhaled deeply, about to ask the question burning in the back of her brain, but he forestalled her. "I have arrangements to make," he said. "Swear to me you won't leave this chamber, not for any reason."

"No problem." Mehcredi pulled a face. "I don't think I like Trinitaria." It was such an alien hard-edged place, with none of the elegant charm of Caracole. As for Lonefell—her lips twisted—the grimness of the baron's icebound keep was a world away.

Eyes wide, Mehcredi perched on the end of the ramshackle bed, peering down at daily life in Belizare through a shuttered window. Despite her light trews and loose shirt, sweat gathered under her hair, in the small of her back. The dog retreated under the bed, a panting miserable bundle of fur.

Below, four men, obviously soldiers of some kind, swaggered into the narrow thoroughfare. They wore the same type of curved sword as Walker, but with plain serviceable grips. The crowds melted away before them and reformed behind, fluid as blue water in the wake of the *Spicy Venture*. The souk was full of robed bodies, women as well as men, but Mehcredi searched in vain for a bare female face.

She wasn't watching for him, really she wasn't, but when she caught sight of his tall lean figure, she leaned forward with a gasp, startled by the extent of her relief. A small bundle tucked under one arm, the swordmaster haggled with a food vendor, the old man's hands flying as they spoke. Mehcredi grinned. Some things were universal. She'd seen exactly the same pantomime in the Melting Pot. No doubt the stallholder was the sole support of a dozen ailing grandchildren.

She pressed the heel of her hand to her pounding heart. The kiss on the deck of the *Spicy Venture* had been a revelation, not only turning her world upside down, but giving it a brisk shake as well. She'd never been—well, *inside* a kiss before. How could she have known? It had been totally amazing. A whole new area of human experience, as intriguing as swordplay and the *nea-kata*, as exciting and challenging, but this was something normal people did. She suspected they did it a lot. Gods, after a single taste, she would too, if she could.

Which brought her neatly to the problem—and the solution.

Mehcredi swallowed hard, firming her resolve. Godsdammit, she was going to do this, ask for what she needed. She had to know, had to learn. Last night, lying in the top bunk, listening to Walker's even breath beneath her, she'd tamped down her excitement, forced herself to think the plan through, examine every angle. From her point of view, it made perfect sense, but unfortunately, her thought processes weren't the same as other people's. Since her arrival at the House of Swords, that had become clearer than ever. Sighing, she worried at a thumbnail.

But from the beginning, the swordmaster had seen *her*—Mehcredi—not a half-wit, but a person as real as he was. He hadn't liked her much, true, but there'd been no beatings, no casual violence, no cruelty. Walker was unique—such a wonderful combination. For a start, she trusted him. He was an excellent teacher when he put his mind to it, stern and patient all at once. He pushed her to do her best. Her breath hitched. And gods, he was beautiful. Unconsciously, she pressed a hand against the Mark. She wanted him so badly.

Even better, he wanted her. Her eyes half closed with pleasure, she hugged the knowledge to herself. During that mind-altering, world-shaking kiss, she'd felt the hard evidence pressed against her. Mehcredi stifled a giggle. She'd aroused Walker, she, Mehcredi of Lonefell. Gods, it was a marvellous thought.

But by the time the prearranged knock came at the door, she was pacing back and forth across the dusty floorboards. As she lifted the heavy wooden bar, she sucked in a deep, steadying breath. She'd persuaded him to teach her the *nea-kata*, hadn't she? And look how well that had turned out. This was just a little more . . . personal, but perfectly reasonable. He'd see it, she was sure. Sweet Sister, she was scared!

Walker strode past her without a word of greeting and tossed the bundle onto the bed. He turned. "I got work on a caravan. We join them tomorrow on the spice road south. Everything all right?"

"Oh yes. Here." She poured him a cup of tepid water from the jug and handed it over. "Walker?"

He drained the cup and wiped his mouth with the back of his hand. "What?"

"I want to talk to you."

A pause. Dark brows rose. "Go ahead. I doubt I could stop you."

She wasn't so sure about that. "Um." Well, she had to start somewhere. She took the plunge. "You know how you taught me the *nea-kata?*"

"I trust you did some practice while I was gone," he said dryly. "Yes, so?"

"I wanted to . . . to say thanks. It's good, it helps."

She was pretty certain surprise flashed across his features. But he merely nodded, busying himself unbuckling his sword belt.

"I had an idea."

He drew the curved sword from its scabbard and squinted critically along the bright edge.

Mehcredi grabbed his arm. "I need you to listen!"

Walker glanced down at the hand on his sleeve and back up at her face. He'd gone perfectly still. "Don't touch me, assassin," he said, his voice very soft.

Little sparks went off in her head, like firecrackers, one after the other. Boom, boom, boom. "I. Am. Not. An. Assassin," she got out through clenched teeth.

"True." The muscle beneath her fingers relaxed a trifle. "Very well, what is this idea?"

"Forget it," she muttered, turning away to gaze out the window. She gripped her hands together and concentrated on breathing. In, out. In, out.

After a couple of minutes of strained silence, he muttered something under his breath. It sounded like a curse, but unlike all the other men she'd known, the swordmaster didn't swear much, save for the strange oaths he refused to explain. "Godsdammit, woman, you're thinking so loudly, they can hear you at the Grand Pasha's palace. Whatever it is, say it."

Mehcredi fixed her eyes on a tattered awning swinging in the evening breeze off the sea. "I know I wasn't very good at the . . . the kissing. I haven't done it before."

She turned, her stomach jumping with excitement and nerves. The sensation was very like launching herself off a cliff. Would the sword-master let her fall or catch her before she hit the ground? She met his hard gaze. "It's a good idea," she said, "really it is."

He folded his arms, frowning. "Yes?" he said.

Mehcredi jumped, right out into space. Advancing until they were almost nose to nose, she forced her trembling lips into a grin, right in that handsome unsmiling face. "You taught me everything I know about anything," she said. Pause for breath. "And I trust you and we need kissing for the disguise. Teach me how to do it properly."

When he didn't react, save for an indrawn breath, she threw caution to the winds, sliding her hands up over his shoulders. "I liked it. Can we do it some more?"

Walker's hands came up to clamp over her wrists like manacles, but he hadn't pushed her away. Her heart lifting, Mehcredi took another half pace forward, pressing her hips into his, feeling the hardness of his thighs against hers, a stirring beneath the fabric of his trews. Raising her chin, she spoke into the warm skin below his ear. "Show me. Teach me everything men and women do."

She swallowed hard, wanting desperately to be clear, so he couldn't misunderstand. Men liked to be crude, didn't they? The baron's men certainly did. Gathering all her courage, she whispered, "You can fuck me if you like."

Walker exploded. In a single surge, he flung Mehcredi away from him and onto the bed, so hard that it listed to one side as a leg gave way under her weight. "Are you fucking *insane?*" he roared, his eyes blazing.

The dog jumped about at his feet, emitting sharp yips of excitement. "And you shut up!" It subsided, panting.

Sprawled against the wall, Mehcredi stared at his furious face, her mind wiped clean by the shock. "No," she said, with as much dignity as she could muster, "I may be stupid, but I'm not insane."

"I didn't mean—" Walker broke off and pinched the bridge of his nose. "Gods give me strength."

"I thought about it carefully." She sat up. "I know I'm not pretty, but I didn't think you'd mind. Or at least not very much."

"Didn't think I'd—" The swordmaster blinked at her, his high cheekbones flushed.

"You got hard when you kissed me. I felt it." She got to her feet and dusted herself off. "All men like sex, I know that much."

The flush intensified. "That was mechanics. Mehcredi, this is out of the question."

"I don't see why." To her intense interest, when she took a pace toward him, he retreated. "I've got a packet of mothermeknot and I drink a cup every morning. No babies, no matter what we do."

Walker pulled off his head cloth and tugged viciously at his hair. "No."

"But—"

"*No!*" The flimsy walls rattled.

They stared at each other.

Wrong again. *Ye great daft lump.* Biting her lip, Mehcredi returned to contemplation of the ragged awning across the way. "I'm sorry I'm so . . . funny looking," she said to it. "I know you wouldn't say no to Rose."

Iron fingers sank into her arm and spun her around so fast she stumbled. "You are *not* funny looking." Walker steadied her. "And you damn well know it."

When she shook her head dumbly, he gave her a little shake. "I don't want Rose. I never have."

"Am I—?" She wet her lips. "Am I pretty? Even a little bit?"

For answer, he slid his hands around her throat, his thumbs brushing under her jaw. She could feel calluses and, remarkably, the faintest tremor in his fingers. "No," he said slowly, and she wanted to hunch over the hurt, wrap her arms about herself for comfort.

"Pretty doesn't come close." A pause while his brows drew together. "Some might say—" He cleared his throat. "Magnificent."

He never lied. All the hurt melted in a heady rush of pleasure. "Truly?" she whispered.

"Do you know what the lads call you at the House of Swords?" Walker's eyes gleamed.

Bereft of speech, she shook her head.

"The Ice Goddess. Florien's keeping a book on who thaws you out. He thinks I don't know."

Mehcredi goggled. "Who's favorite?" she croaked.

Walker made a chuffing sound that could have signified amusement. "Dai."

"But that's silly!"

"Indeed?" A brow rose. "I thought you liked him."

"I do, but I don't want Dai, I want you!" she said impatiently, and just like that they were back where they'd begun.

He released her so abruptly, she staggered. "Well, you can't have me."

"Why not? You just said I'm pretty enough. At least, I think you did." With a flourish, she produced her trump card. "You're a man. You got hard."

Walker shook his head as if besieged by a swarm of bitemes. "I am not having this conversation." He bit off every word with an almost perceptible snap.

What an odd thing to say. Her brow knitted. "Of course you are."

His chest rose and fell as he sucked in two deep breaths. "Mehcredi, people generally do as I tell them."

"That's because they're scared."

He gave her a not-smile loaded with teeth. "As you should be."

She took a moment to think about it. "You were so cold, so angry," she said slowly. "At first, I was sure you were going to kill me." She raised her eyes to his. "But you didn't."

"Mehcredi—"

"Let me finish. I don't understand what you did or how you did it or even why," she said, working it out as she went along. "Everything was so awful I thought I'd die, but now—I think I might be happy. It's—" She broke off, searching for words, her lips curving into a tremulous smile, tears stinging her eyes.

The swordmaster cleared his throat. "Good?"

She nodded, light-headed with the burst of realization, his features no more than a bronzed blur. Happy—who'd have thought it?

"That's as may be, but here in Trinitaria you will be guided by me. Hesitate and you'll get us both killed. Agreed?"

Mehcredi grinned, her blood fizzing. If she knew how, she'd dance around the shabby room. "I'll be the best slave ever, I promise. All I need to know is how to kiss like one?" She sashayed a little closer.

But Walker gave her his back as he retrieved the bundle from the bed. "No need." He thrust it into her hands. "Because after tonight, you won't be a woman, let alone a slave."

When she stared, he said, "Open it."

Inside, was a dark blue head cloth, a canvas vest with a number of pockets, a pair of gold-rimmed spectacles with dark lenses and a strange oval object with a shiny black skin that gave off an astringent smell.

"I don't understand."

"You're no actor, Mehcredi. It wouldn't matter what I taught you, you'll never convince a Trinitarian you're a slave, or even a wife. You'll be better off as a man."

"A man?"

"'Cestors' bones, you're near as tall as me. You can hold a sword or a staff like you mean it. Deepen your voice a bit—or better yet, say nothing—and you'll pass for a boy, my companion, my apprentice." He touched her shoulder. "Surely you'd prefer that?"

"Yes, oh yes," she said absently. Oh gods, to be able to stride out, free of the enveloping robes. But she wouldn't forget about the kissing. She held up what had to be a fruit. "What's this then?"

"A blengo." He drew the long dagger from his belt and, with a deft twist, opened the fruit at one end. Seizing an earthenware cup, he squeezed and chocolat-colored fluid streamed out. "The juice stains the skin and the pulp is very nutritious, though it's rather an acquired taste."

Carefully, he measured a few drops into a cracked bowl and added a cup of water. "Roll up your sleeves and come here."

By the time she'd soaked to his satisfaction, the murky brew had turned her hands and forearms a golden brown, almost as dark as his.

"The Siblings are up," he said, glancing out the window at the moons. "Get dressed and we'll go eat."

Mehcredi glowered at the bundle of black on the end of the bed. "I thought I was a man."

"I came with a female slave, I need to be seen with that slave. We'll do your face and hair later, dress you as a man and be gone before dawn. In the meantime, think of a name you'll remember to answer to."

She stopped him as they went out the door. "Magnificent?" she said. "You did say magnificent?"

Walker gave her the expressionless stare she'd grown to dislike with every fiber of her being. "On occasion," he said severely. "When you do what you're told."

The bar was deep and narrow, with a low arched doorway opening to the souk and another giving onto a small yard shaded by what looked like a piece of old sail. A skinny slave boy clad in a dirty loincloth poked desultorily at a covered pan on a brazier. It wasn't crowded, half a dozen men lounged on low stools, two of them hunched over a stained table, throwing dice. The air was thick with the last of the day's heat, the bitter dregs of thin Trinitarian beer mixing not unpleasantly with the scent of grilled meat and hot peppers.

Good. He wouldn't have to take Mehcredi out into the market. Out of the corner of his eye, Walker checked her posture. He sighed. She'd hunched herself up like an old woman, but she was still taller than every man in the room save himself. Her head swung from side to side, scanning. His chest tightened with exasperation and something that might have been pity. Behind the veil, her silver eyes would be bright with interest, lips parted softly as she drank it all in. He knew that expression. Part child, all woman.

He needed to get a grip.

"There." He pointed to the darkest corner and she sank obediently to the floor. "Do not move. Do not speak."

As she gave a jerky nod, that damned dog sidled around the corner and settled beside her. By the First Father, how could one small animal look so downright shifty? It might as well wear a sign around its scruffy neck that said, "Up to no good."

Hastily, Mehcredi flipped the edge of her robe over it until only the tip of a quivering black nose was visible. Though he couldn't see it, Walker had an uneasy feeling her expression mirrored the dog's—*up to no good.*

The skinny man behind the bar wiped his hands on a grubby towel and said, "What'll it be?"

"Beer," grunted Walker, allowing a hint of Shar to flavor his speech, conscious of the silence spreading behind him. "And a bowl of what-ever's cooking." After so many years, the intonation felt strange on his tongue, like a ghostly presence. The hair rose on the back of his neck, as if the spectral forms of his Ancestors stood behind him, rank after serried rank.

A shouted order for the boy in the yard and the man returned to swiping his rag over the pitted wooden surface of the bar. "Southerner, are ye?"

With satisfaction, he noted the sidelong glance at the Janizar's sword. It had to be abundantly clear Walker was not a member of the Grand Pasha's elite guard, and that he never had been. Which meant he'd obtained the weapon some other way. Giving the barkeep a cold-eyed stare that said, "Cross me if you dare," he watched slightly alarmed speculation flicker across the man's swarthy features.

Aloud, he said, "Heading home. Might join a caravan."

"Fancy yerself a guard, yes?" said a different, gruffer voice.

Taking his time, Walker turned to face the man who'd come to lounge at his elbow. The smell of stale sweat poured off him, rank and sour. He was short and burly, his head cloth wrapped around his skull turban style. Hard physical labor had thickened his frame and made him look older than he undoubtedly was. A dockworker perhaps. Drunk enough to be friendly, one drink short of truculence.

"Something like that," Walker said evenly.

He got a sloppy, gap-toothed grin. "Sword's mighty fine, friend." The man bumped their shoulders together. "Lemme see it?"

"Kassan—" the barkeep broke in. "Not here." He shook his head.

The sullen boy banged an earthenware bowl full of stew down on the bar and slouched back to his post by the brazier. Walker collected the food, together with his beer. "Maybe later." Calmly, he returned to the corner where he'd left Mehcredi.

A short pause and the rumble of conversation resumed, the dice clicking as they tumbled across the table.

"That man's staring at you," whispered Mehcredi. "Looks angry."

"Don't worry about it." Apart from a couple of curious, semi-covetous glances, the men were ignoring her, but the more she spoke, the more they chanced unwelcome attention.

"Yes, but—"

"No speaking unless I ask a question." He dug into the food with the only utensil provided, a narrow slab of hard bread. The meat was sinewy and tough, but it was filling, sweet and sour with strange Trinitarian spices. "You don't eat 'til I'm finished."

He stretched out his legs, while she sat and simmered beside him. Irresistibly drawn by the scent of food, the dog crept out from under her skirts, slinking on his belly. His ragged tail thumped the floor in a hopeful rhythm.

Funnily enough, it wasn't Mehcredi who brought them undone, or even the unlovely Kassan, but the slave boy and the dog.

14

Walker ordered a second helping and made a pretence of eating before handing the remains to Mehcredi. Grumbling under her breath, she turned her face to the wall and fumbled about under the veil. In the end, she gave up trying to use the bread as a spoon and resorted to fingers. Every few moments, she dropped a morsel for the dog. Finished, she relaxed against Walker's leg with a long sigh, licking the grease off her fingers. He caught a glimpse of the pink curl of her tongue, neat as a cat.

Propelled by a slap over the head from the barkeep, the slave slouched over to collect the empty dish. But as he turned away, his foot caught in Mehcredi's robe and he shot out a hand to steady himself, grabbing her shoulder. The whole disaster had an awful inevitability. Under Walker's appalled gaze, everything happened in slow motion, as if the participants were mired in treacle. And yet, even though he leaped immediately to his feet, he was too late to stop it.

The boy's weight pushed Mehcredi nearly to the floor. Hearing her cry of surprise, the dog barked his defiance, bristling. The slave swore, swung his leg back and connected hard with the animal's ribs, which elicited a sharp yelp followed by a positive fusillade of barking. Mehcredi growled, surging up from the floor in a dusty billow of retribution. He had to admit, her movements were a miracle of efficiency. A second later, the slave boy was spread-eagled against the wall, Mehcredi's hand at his throat, the point of her blade hovering half an inch from his quivering eyeball.

An instant's silence, as if the entire Republic of Trinitaria pulled in a shocked breath at such presumption from a female. All hell broke loose.

Even in the dim light, the Janizar's sword flashed like a living thing. Barely in time, Walker interposed himself between Mehcredi and half a dozen outraged Trinitarians, the barkeep and Kassan dead-heating in the front row.

"Release him!" he snapped at her over his shoulder. "Now!" A breath later, the slave boy hurtled past to crash heavily onto the gamblers' table, sending beer, dice and coins spraying in all directions.

With a happy roar, Kassan snatched an ale jug from the bar and hurtled forward, his small dark eyes focused primarily on Mehcredi.

Walker's guts cramped with terror, the sensation so alien that he froze, and Kassan caught him a glancing blow that rattled his teeth.

The barkeep dived past him, snarling, "Fuckin' bitch, kill ye—"

The venomous words cut off with a meaty thunk. Walker heard a single high-pitched bark, Mehcredi's screech of triumph. After that, he was released somehow, able to move, all fire and ice and familiar patterns coming smooth as silk. He used the flat of the blade, his fists and his boots, nothing barred beyond the killing blows. Not that he cared, but a tavern brawl was one thing, slicing his opponents to gobbets and thereby drawing the attention of the authorities another.

Peripherally, he was conscious of Mehcredi seizing a stool and breaking it over someone's head. Then she set her back to his as if to the manner born. He could sense her dancing back and forth, jabbing and striking, swearing continuously under her breath. Must be the slave boy again. Well, she'd already shown she could cope with him.

He'd have to break her of the cursing, he thought, sinking his boot into the softness of one man's belly and intercepting Kassan's knobby fist as it traveled past his ear. No one was getting through him to reach her, not while he lived. Swearing was a waste of breath, destroyed the concentration. Grasping his sword by the hilt, he clipped Kassan neatly on the chin.

The man swayed, eyes rolling. "Uh," he grunted. "G-good . . . fi . . . ght." A wobbly smile and he hit the floor with a crash.

Silence fell.

Walker lowered his sword. "You all right?" He turned.

She hadn't had time to remove the veil, but she was hefting a stool leg like a quarterstaff, her chest rising and falling like a runner's. The slave boy slumped against the wall, clutching his belly, his face puke green. The dog was nowhere to be seen.

"Yes. What about—"

Walker wrapped iron fingers around her arm and hauled her up the stairs. He thrust her into their room and whirled to drop the heavy bar across the door. His heart thundering in his ears, he ripped a strip off the bed cover and dunked it in the blengo juice.

She was talking, but the words went by in a tiresome jumble of noise. Urgency clawed at his chest. How much time did they have? Ten minutes? Five? No more.

"Come here."

"But what are—"

"*Come here!*"

'Cestors be thanked, she came. Working rapidly, he pulled off the veil and smeared the brown stuff all over her pale, perfect skin, over her face and neck.

"Get the robes off and put a head cloth on." Fortunately, he hadn't unpacked. Seizing Mehcredi's bag, he began shoving things in all anyhow. "Make sure you cover your hair."

"We're leaving?" Her brow creased and little furrows appeared in the dye. He'd have to do it again the moment they were settled somewhere safe. "But how?"

He allowed himself a soundless chuckle. "How do you think? The window." He tossed the two packs out into the night, hearing the soft thumps as they landed on the awning below.

Swiftly, he knotted the remains of the coverlet to the leg of the bed and threw the rest over the sill. "Grab this and lower yourself. When you let go, the kitchen awning's directly underneath. Slide down it."

"Oh." Mehcredi peered down. "Right. What about—"

"I'll be fine." Voices rumbled below, feet hit the stairs, the building shook. "Go, go."

"But the dog's—"

"He can look after himself. Godsdammit, woman, *move!*"

Mehcredi gave a funny little gasp. Then she sank her fingers into his hair and jerked his head down, pressing a clumsy kiss against his mouth. In a single movement, she tore herself away, seized the make-shift rope and flung herself out of the window. He heard a muffled thump and a sharp exclamation.

Walker winced, but when he checked, she was perfectly safe, standing in the yard, gazing upward, her eyes shining weirdly out of her brown face. She had one hand on that rounded ass, rubbing. He pressed the back of his hand against his tingling lips. She'd wasted valuable seconds on that kiss.

The door shuddered under a heavy blow. "Southern scum! Forty creds fer damages ye owe me." The barkeep.

Walker slung one leg over the sill. Thank all the gods he hadn't given a name.

Another rattling thump, the rising rumble of other voices. Was that Kassan?

"The woman will do if ye don't have the cash." The slave boy's voice rose in protest, followed by the sound of a slap and a sharp cry.

Walker snarled. Then he smiled, slow and grim. By the bones of Those Before, it would serve the man right if he handed her over. Mehcredi would have his balls on toast—with the slave boy as an appetizer.

After which, of course, she'd be tortured to death. All amusement gone, he considered the door, now vibrating under a steady pounding. The rusty hinges creaked.

Walker pulled his leg back into the room. Then he dug deep, tracing the flow of *ch'qui* down through the foundations of the building, all the way to the baked heart of the earth. When he pressed his palm against the door, the raw blind energy of the planet's life, the rush of green sap, made him stagger. Uncaring, it used him as a conduit, surging into dry dusty wood that sucked it up the way a desert drank rain. All around the edges of the door, tender green shoots appeared, bursting so fast out of the old wood they writhed like snakes, twining and intertwining, forming what amounted to a thicket.

"Walker? Are you coming?" Mehcredi's voice floated up from below. It had a quaver in it.

His pulse still thrumming with reaction, the swordmaster lowered himself to the furthest extent of the rope and let himself drop. Rolling with the fall, he scooped up his pack.

"Now what?" panted Mehcredi.

"Now we run like hell."

Tail waving like a tattered flag, the dog caught up with them before they reached the first corner.

⌒⧫⌒

Mehcredi had never run so far, so fast, in her life. Down the twisted alleys, she and Walker had fled flat out, then dropped to a jog-trot, then run again, through the souk, through a quieter residential area where large houses loomed behind high walls of plastered sun-dried brick and finally, into a poorer quarter that smelled of manure and dust and spices.

"This is the waggoners' district," said the swordmaster. He gestured at an arch in a mud-brick wall. It was fitted with a set of swinging doors. From beyond it, came the rumble of masculine voices, an occasional shout and crash and a reedy thread of music played on some out-of-tune wind instrument. "This is a waggoners' tavern. The only women here are the lowest sort of whores, so tell me again, who are you?"

"I'm your cousin's boy, Meck," she recited, still breathless. "You took me on as a favor to him, even though I'm a half-breed he got on some foreign slave. You think I'm soft, whereas I'm so scared of you I can barely speak, let alone hold my head up." With a sigh of relief, she dropped the pack at her feet and straightened her shoulders, delighting in the firm feel of the sword belt around her waist, the freedom of the trews. "I've got weak eyes, which is why I have the shaded spectacles."

"Good." He eyed her critically. "Hunch your shoulders more and don't swing your hips."

Beyond the archway, the area opened up into a courtyard, with stables down one side and a sprawling ramble of rooms on the other. Despite the lateness of the hour, lights streamed out of open doors and Walker had no difficulty obtaining a key from the surly gatekeeper. Feeling very clever, her heart pitter-pattering with excitement, Mehcredi took care to hang her head and keep to the shadows. The dog quartered the yard back and forth in a businesslike manner, loftily ignoring the baleful glare of a black-and-white tom perched on top of a barrel.

She'd been frightened, she didn't mind admitting it. Standing helpless in the yard, staring up at that godsbedamned window while angry men beat down the door to get at Walker—that had been the worst moment. What would she do without him? The prospect was literally inconceivable, more than her mind could encompass. Her heart squeezed. Sister save her, she wouldn't need to worry, because his Mark would kill her the moment he ceased to breathe. Uneasily, she rubbed the heel of her hand over the spot.

The thing with the dog had been all her fault. *Shit.* The flock of flutterbyes currently resident in her belly took an abrupt right-angled turn. But on the whole—she trailed Walker into yet another shabby chamber—she didn't think she'd done too badly. Now that it was over, she'd almost enjoyed the fight. Her nerves sang with the remembered rush.

The slave boy had been hopeless. She gave a fierce grin, reliving that perfect jab in the gut. By all the gods, she'd got something right for once. Competence was a heady, unaccustomed glow behind her breastbone. Anyhow, it served him right, the little shit. The names he'd called her took her right back to Lonefell. Cunt, whore, slut.

There were two dusty pallets, slung on sagging bed ropes, and a rickety table. That was all.

"Stay here," ordered Walker, the door swinging shut behind him.

A few moments later, he returned, carrying a chipped jug and a widemouthed mug.

Mehcredi stiffened her spine, taking comfort from the press of a furry body against her calf. Best to get it over with. "I'm sorry," she said. "About the fight, I mean."

Walker turned, dagger in one hand, one of those strange black fruits in the other. "I should never have brought you."

"Oh no." She took an eager step forward. "I'm glad you did." A grin bloomed on her face, she couldn't help it. "I've never had an adventure before."

The swordmaster's lips went thin. Somehow, he seemed to grow, looming over her, all lean and bronzed. And shit, he was angry again.

"Is that what you think this is?" His voice rose. "Some lighthearted frolic? Nerajyb Nyzarl has a demon."

He tossed the blengo onto the nearest pallet so he could wrap his fingers around her throat. He forced her head up so she couldn't avoid his eyes, blazing like fiery coals. "I've seen a demon turn a man inside out like an old sock and suck his guts like a noodle dinner."

"A demon?" Mehcredi's stomach lurched. She stared into those pitiless eyes, her brain spinning. "What do you mean? He's a diabloman? You want to kill a *diabloman*?"

Walker released her so abruptly she stumbled. "Yes."

"B-but . . . *how*?"

"Same way I killed the other fourteen." Scooping up the blengo, he struck the top off with a single vicious slash. "You're still too pale, *Meck*. And do something with the shirt unless you want it dyed too." He busied himself squeezing juice into the jug.

Her fingers trembled so badly, it took forever to unpick the knot in the laces. *Diablomen?* But everyone knew—*Fourteen* of them? Still in a fog, she dithered. The back of her neck must still be as white as the Sister. She glanced down. Not to mention her chest. How far down did the stain need to go? And then there was the mass of her hair. In the end, she let the shirt slip right off her shoulders, clutching it to the upper swell of her breasts, exposing the first graceful swooping curves of Walker's shaman Mark. The air brushed against her skin in a pleasant caress. A wave of gooseflesh ran up her spine. Her nipples stiffened.

Walker ripped the sleeve out of her robe. "Right," he said, turning toward her. "Hold st—"

Truly, she was learning all the time. Who'd have thought a man's gaze could make you feel like you'd stood too close to the fire? The Mark burned worst of all.

"What are you thinking?" she asked.

"You don't want to know."

"Yes, I do." She looked him in the eye. "And you promised you'd tell me, remember?"

Walker's mouth tucked up at the corners. "You look decidedly odd." Strong fingers spread over the back of her skull, pushing her head down.

Mehcredi suppressed the urge to arch into the touch the way the dog did when she rubbed behind his ears.

"Like one of Serafina's chocolat and cream cakes, but a trifle, ah, underdone. Don't move now."

Damp and cool, the rag whispered over the back of her neck. Carefully, he wiped over the shell of her ears, covering one finger to delve into the whorls and curves. When Mehcredi wriggled, he slapped her casually on the rump. "Be still. This is delicate work."

It was strangely intimate, sensing his strong body so close, hearing the quiet rhythm of his respiration while he performed this very personal service. Eyes half closed with pleasure, Mehcredi hummed under her breath, tilting her head as he directed. Oh, it was beyond good to be touched, to be stroked like this. She'd had no idea. He could paint her brown all over if he liked. Oh, gods. Once the thought appeared, she wasn't able to banish it. *All over.* When she pressed her thighs together, her secret place burned hot and slick. Tingles coiled at the base of her spine, before breaking loose to skitter across her quivering belly and up over her ribs.

"Close your eyes and lift your chin."

Was his breath coming faster? It was hard to tell.

With exquisite care, he smoothed over her forehead, tracing each eyebrow with a firm gentle thumb. When his fingertips moved over her eyelids, light as a flutterbye's wing, she had to swallow hard to banish the foolish prickle of tears. Casually, she crossed her arms over her breasts, pressing against her stinging nipples. It didn't help.

"That's better," said his deep voice. "Not so streaky. Open your mouth a little."

When he ran a slow thumb over her lower lip, she had to lock her knees to keep from staggering. Despite herself, she made a small choked noise.

He stopped. "You all right?"

If she opened her eyes, the Magick would stop. "Yes," she said into the darkness behind her eyelids.

The swab moved down to the pit of her throat, paused, then glided across her collarbones. Her breasts tightened, yearning toward his touch.

"That'll do, I think," he said and she could have wept.

"It's over?"

"Not quite." He moved behind her, a wall of muscled warmth an inch from her spine. "Sorry about this." Firmly, he gripped her braid. She felt a sharp tug against her scalp, and suddenly, the oddest sensation of lightness.

Mehcredi's eyes flew open. She whirled around, clapping a hand to the back of her head.

The swordmaster stood before her, blade in one hand, the shining length of her plait dangling from the other. He cleared his throat. "There's too much of it to dye."

The silence stretched. Mehcredi sank onto the bed, and the dog came to lay his head against her knee. She shrugged, digging her fingers into the animal's ruff. "It'll grow back. Just feels strange, that's all."

"Wrap this around your shoulders." Walker thrust the old robe at her. "You know," he said, as if thinking aloud, jug in hand, "you're not like any woman I ever met." He tilted the jug and cold liquid trickled into her hair.

"No, I don't suppose I am," she said, sagging a little. Gloomily, she bit her lip, too depressed to enjoy the sensation of hard fingers massaging her scalp, working the juice well in. What sort of women did he prefer? She wasn't sure, except they'd be intelligent, poised—and undoubtedly lovely.

He was thorough, but it didn't take long. "Here." He pressed a comb carved of some dark shiny wood into her hand.

"No mirror." She passed it back. "I'll just mess it up."

Walker gave an annoyed grunt, but he nudged her chin up with one fist and wielded the comb, his brow knitted with concentration.

"There," he said at last, stepping back. "With the glasses, you'll pass."

Mehcredi ignored this. "Why do you want to kill this Nyz-whatever man?"

He stiffened. "Nerajyb Nyzarl."

"Yes, fine. So why kill him?"

He shot her a narrow-eyed glance. "Don't you ever give up?"

She took a moment to consider it, wishing she could see his face, but he had his back to her, emptying the jug out the window. "If I gave up I'd be dead by now." She shrugged again. "I'm not dead. So answer the question."

"It's necessary." Setting the jug down, he turned off the lamp, plunging the chamber into darkness. "Go to sleep." The bed ropes creaked as he stretched out his lean length.

Biting her lip, she fumbled her boots off, unbuckled her sword belt and laid it aside. With a scuffle and a scrape, the dog settled under the bed. Why was it necessary? Her mind racing, she tried to imagine what a demon might look like and failed. She'd come to believe Walker could do anything, but *this*? Gods, a diabloman! Was it even possible? But if he said he'd done it, it must be.

So many questions trembled on her tongue that she clapped a hand over her mouth lest they escape. She shifted restlessly on the pallet, aggravated on so many levels that her skin itched.

"Mehcredi?" His voice came out of the darkness.

"What?" she asked, her pulse kicking into a gallop.

"Tell me you brought the breastband."

"I brought the breastband." She sat up. "Why?"

"Good." The bed ropes creaked as he rolled over, giving her his broad back. "From now on, wear it."

When the Necromancer returned to the tent, he found Dotty crouched over an odd assemblage of wires and glass. In the uncertain light of the cheap tallow candles, she held the object so close to her nose her eyes were practically crossed. With trembling fingers, she turned it over and over, crooning and stroking.

He brightened. "Nearly finished?"

But the former Technomage Primus of Sybaris continued to squint at the apparatus, her blue gray eyes clouded, an unhappy droop to her mouth. "Need a . . . a . . . *thing*," she muttered, rocking back and forth.

Shaitan take the silly bitch, her brains grew more addled with every passing day. How much longer before the device was complete? More to the point, was she still mentally capable of the work? The scribe's crazy sister had ceased to be amusing. Every time their so-called lord and master—hah!—laid eyes on her, he swore on the Trimagistos and poked the dusty, shambling bundle with his cane. Sometimes Dotty noticed, whereupon she shrieked like a kettle on the boil and scuttled away, her hands flapping in futile defense, but other times she remained oblivious, no matter how savage Nyzarl's jabs became.

"What?" he asked. "What do you need? And it had better be the last."

Finding the strange materials she required as Nyzarl and his entourage traveled southward through an increasingly arid and sparsely populated landscape had taxed his ingenuity to the utmost. He'd scavenged and bartered and bargained. From a shopkeeper in the last outpost of a town, he'd stolen, though he'd really only done it for the challenge.

Funnily enough, money wasn't a problem. Nerajyb Nyzarl had been surprisingly generous with his personal scribe. It seemed he had a hankering for immortality—in ink and parchment. A biography of all things, an overinflated retelling of what felt like every stupefying, vomit-inducing, useless act of his fat, miserable life. What with controlling the urge to stave off the mind-numbing boredom by popping Nyzarl's eyeball with the sharp end of the ink brush, the Necromancer figured he was earning every cred.

"See here?" The Technomage indicated a socket-like spot that looked no different from a number of others. Her tongue crept out, sly and pink, and she shot him a weirdly knowing glance. "I need a male part. It slots . . . right . . . in . . . here." Repeatedly, she jabbed a fingertip in the concave depression. Then she gave a lewd, high-pitched giggle.

15

A wave of revulsion rolled down the Necromancer's spine. By Shaitan, the old bitch had gone beyond disgusting. He ground his teeth. If the trap had worked that first time, he wouldn't be stuck with her now. The whole scheme had been a thing of beauty, baited with the silly little null witch—gods, what an abomination *she* was!—but the air wizard had slipped through his fingers. The man hadn't even had the decency to die, and as for the null witch—

The Necromancer pressed cautious fingertips against a spot on the side of his skull. His head still ached when he grew tired. Completely against his will, memory shoved an unpleasantly vivid image toward him—Prue McGuire advancing, blue green eyes ablaze in her pale face, swinging a gardener's spade with all her compact strength—a fucking *spade*! One day. His lips drew back from his teeth. One day . . . Her screams would never end, he swore it by all that was unholy.

The candles guttered, the temperature in the tent dropping ten degrees in as many seconds. Dotty whimpered, hunching down until she resembled nothing as much as a bundle of dirty laundry.

Gods, every time he thought of Erik the Golden! That big body, so strong and smooth-limbed and physically adept, such a magnificent envelope to house his own Dark Powers. Physically, Nerajyb Nyzarl wasn't much of a substitute, not if one aspired to male beauty, though presumably there was muscle hidden somewhere beneath the lard. Nonetheless, the diabloman had a number of advantages to offer. First, there was the wealth and power conferred by the favor of the

Grand Pasha, nicely topped off by the gift of the estate in the south. The Necromancer licked his lips. The south—where he sensed the weight of some vast presence, utterly alien. It couldn't be coincidence, it *couldn't*.

No longer did he have the power to kill with nothing more than a thought, to pinch nerves and arteries between his spectral fingers, but he and the razor-sharp edge of his blade had managed to make the last murder last a good long time. Crouched in the back room behind an apothecary's shabby shop front, he'd dipped his hands to the wrist in blood and pain, drawing sigils on the dusty floor to net the man's agonized soul with bonds of power.

He'd done what he could with the apothecary, riding the old fool's death hard, as if it were an unruly horse. The Dark Lord had been with him then, vouchsafing him a glimpse of carnage in some hillside village, people running this way and that, shouting, falling in midstride as if felled by crossbow bolts, whereupon they writhed and shrieked like souls in torment. Fascinating. Because there were no bolts, no weapons of any kind, only a strange, shrill, whistling sound, and dark clouds scudding across the indifferent faces of the Sibling Moons.

Instinctively, he'd grasped at the energy released by so many deaths. With the ease of long practice, he let the power buoy him up, and he'd seen it, etched against the stars—the Pattern.

Not as clear as the last time, but still so fucking pretty he wanted to spit. A five-pointed star, a Pentacle, complex and yet perfect. Complete in itself. Drawn despite himself, he'd drifted closer, peering, his breath coming short.

Fortunately, he was always wary. Without warning, a fireball bloomed above the Pentacle like an improbable flower. A whoosh of angry air and it was hurtling toward him, a tail of flame streaming behind with the speed of its passage. He'd barely escaped unsinged. In fact, his retreat had been so precipitate, he'd regained his senses sprawled across the apothecary's doorsill, his cheek resting in a puddle of congealed blood.

He'd recognize the distinctive flavor of the fire witch's fury anywhere. And clearly, although the air wizard was so newly come to his Magick he barely qualified as a novice, Erik Thorensen knew his enemy. The Necromancer's mouth twisted. Shaitan take them, that degree of cooperation did not augur well. As for that old bastard, Deiter—Something in the Necromancer's chest clenched, hurting him. He pressed his palm to the spot. It felt like a warning.

"A power source," said a decisive voice at his elbow, shattering his reverie. Dotty smoothed a steady hand over the graying tangle of her hair like the Technomage of old, her level gaze clear and cold and clever. "Did you realize we don't have one?"

"No." The Necromancer's fingers flexed involuntarily, despite the stiffness in his knuckles. He glanced down at his hands, at the wrinkled mottled skin. He was still stronger than she—perhaps. But if he throttled her now, he'd be left stranded, an old man in an old man's body. "It's your problem, *Technomage*. Solve it."

"I can't." He caught the shadow of a flinch. "I mean, I think I can do it, but only with you—using death energy."

"Ah." The Necromancer regarded her with interest. "How many?"

"Two, if they're young and strong." Little by little, her face collapsed in on itself, as if all the teeth were dissolving in her gums. "Two, two, two," she warbled. "Who are the two? Two by two is four, four by two is—"

"Give me that." The Necromancer took the apparatus out of her hands and placed it carefully in the padded, wooden box he'd purchased especially for the purpose. Then he drew his arm back and cracked the Technomage across the face. "Nyzarl wants to feed you to his demon, did you know that?"

Dotty gibbered, fingers splayed across the reddening mark on her cheekbone. As she scuttled toward the dubious safety of a shadowed corner, not for the first time, the Necromancer considered Xotclic and the interesting problem of its True Name.

He'd been thinking about the demon pretty well continuously from the moment he'd first laid eyes on Nyzarl. Possession of a demon was what defined a diabloman. If he could take all that was Nerajyb Nyzarl's—his body, his demon, his wealth and status—it wouldn't matter if the gods shat Pentacles all over the sky, let alone how many witches and wizards Deiter rallied to the cause.

He'd be as near to a god as made no difference, not only their equal but more, Shaitan's heir maybe. No—he smiled, suffused with fierce pleasure—an usurper, Shaitan Himself.

But without Xotclic's True Name, there was no chance, it was all piss in the wind. Infinitely worse, he'd be trapped in this decaying jar of flesh until the final indignity when it failed him utterly. A cold shudder raised the hair all down his spine, a wave of atavistic terror that took him by surprise, though on reflection, it shouldn't have. The Dark Lord had His own way of dealing with incompetents and upstarts.

The Necromancer sank down onto his blankets. With shaking hands, he removed his spectacles and set them aside, massaging his aching eyes. Once again, he set himself to think. He was a scholar, he'd held the office of Queen's Knowledge. Logic, intellect and experience, they were all on his side.

If only he weren't so godsbedamned tired . . .

No, there was a way. There had to be.

Walker woke, suddenly and completely as he always did. But the regular rhythm of his breath didn't change. He listened to the quality of the silence a moment before rolling over and opening his eyes. Sun poured in through the open window. The little room was empty.

He never slept that soundly, let alone in the presence of another. By the Ancestors, he'd wring her silly neck. Swiftly, he donned his boots and crossed to the door, wrenching it open. He stopped dead, his eyes narrowed.

On the far side of the courtyard, a slim youth stood with his back to Walker, chatting amiably with a wizened old man holding a rake. The boy's hip-shot stance was casually masculine. He leaned against the stable wall, his shoulders straight and square, his waist trim, one hand dug casually into the pocket of his trews. His head was bare, the nut brown hair with the slightest tendency to curl at the nape of his neck. A scruffy little dog sniffed at the old man's horny toes where they protruded from his rope sandals.

Walker blinked and the picture shifted, coming into sharper focus. He hissed. The fabric of her trews pulled tight across that luscious heart-shaped ass. As he watched, Mehcredi turned her head, pushing the tinted spectacles farther up her nose.

Why the fuck had he been fool enough to think they'd get away with it? Yes, the assassin was a tall woman, lush and well made, with good strong bones, but godsdammit, the fineness of her wrists, the pure, sweet line of her jaw, the mouthwatering curve of her backside— How could any man with balls not look at her and . . . *know*?

He was halfway across the courtyard before he realized what he was doing, impelled by a driving compulsion to grab her and hustle her back to the dock and onto a ship bound for Caracole..After which he'd shake her until her teeth rattled. An *adventure*? 'Cestors give him strength!

"Meck," he said sharply and she jumped. "What in the seven icy hells are you playing at?"

A single, wide-eyed glance from behind the tinted spectacles and her head dropped. "Wajar. Um, sorry." Her voice came out husky, a tone deeper than usual. "I was only . . ." She trailed off, scuffing in the dust with the toe of one boot.

"Don't be too hard on the lad." The old man spat into the straw. "He were just lookin' at the horses."

Walker slapped her across the back of the head, pulling the blow at the last second.

"Ow," said Mehcredi, rubbing the spot.

"He has chores," Walker growled. "Lazy little shit."

"Ah well," said the old man, his grin exposing three yellowed teeth in an expanse of gum. "We was all boys once, yes? He weren't no trouble."

"Hmpf." Walker gave Mehcredi a shove to get her moving, then nodded a curt farewell to the old man.

The moment the door closed behind them, Mehcredi whipped off the glasses. "Did you see?" She grinned, her eyes shining. "He didn't have a clue."

"He's probably half blind."

Her face fell. "He is not!" She set her hands on her hips. "And even if he was, the stable slave wasn't, or the van master."

Walker's guts clenched. "Who?"

"The stable sl—"

"The van master. You spoke with him?"

"Only a few words. I mumbled a lot."

"Was he tall and lean, clean-shaven, with a scar on his lip and a gold earring?"

"No, he had a beard." Mehcredi looked puzzled. "Why?"

Walker released a breath. "Then it wasn't Delal Dinari." Reaching for the Janizar's sword, he buckled it on. "I signed on with him as a caravan guard, remember? He's a hard man to fool." He ground his teeth, hating what he was going to say, disappointment and fury a seething mass in his belly. Gods, what a fool he'd been! "We should get back to the dock. You'll be better off taking your chances with Deiter. I can ask Dai to—"

"Walker." Stepping right up to him, she gripped his shoulder. "Don't. I can do it, I promise. I'll be good."

Abruptly, his head was full of Amae, her skinny fingers clutching his arm, black eyes snapping with determination. *C'mon, brother, teach me the blade. I'll try so hard, I promise. You'll be proud of me.*

And he had been. How many trained Trinitarian pikemen had she killed before they got her? Two? Three? Not bad for a slip of girl.

Right on cue, Mehcredi said, "I'll do you proud, I swear."

Standing a prudent three yards behind his demon, Nerajyb Nyzarl had turned his head to watch as they carried Amae's limp body away, and he'd licked his lips.

With a shudder, he dragged himself back to the present. Mehcredi's face was luminous with her intensity. "I'll swear on anything you like," she was saying.

"One chance," he said harshly. "Fool Delal Dinari this morning and we stay. Fail, and—" He shrugged. "I should be able to get us away more or less in one piece."

"You'll help me?"

"What do you think? Of course."

A sparkling smile bloomed. Releasing him, she danced over to her pack and scooped it up. "Let's go, *Wajar*." She shoved the spectacles onto her nose and clapped him on the shoulder.

An hour later, seated cross-legged on a rug in the shade of Dinari's van, Walker sipped at bitterbrew in a tiny enameled bowl. Trinitaria floated on the godsbedamned stuff, all negotiations required pints of it, but he'd never much cared for the taste. Thankfully, his apprentice was too insignificant to warrant such consideration. Leaning against a wheel moodily chewing a thumbnail, Meck was the perfect picture of surly adolescence, with a touch of cowed apprehension thrown in for good measure. He'd hardly credited his eyes at first, until the nagging sense of familiarity gelled into recognition. Florien, gods, she was Florien to the life.

By the First Father, he had to admit it was clever. The head cloth obscured the line of her jaw and the delicacy of her neck, while the swell of those glorious tits had been ruthlessly suppressed by the breastband beneath the folds of the loose shirt. Did it hurt, being bound like that?

"The greatest threat is here . . . and here."

With an inward curse, he wrenched his attention back to Dinari. The van master leaned over the map on the low table between them. Tracing the curving route Trinitarians called the Spice Trail, he tapped decisively. "Trimagistos take them, I think the bastards are breeding in the Stony Hills. They must be. We kill enough every trip, but still they come, like evil djinns."

His hard gaze lifted. "Which is why I'm supplementing my own guards with men like you." A one-name, masterless and mercenary.

Walker allowed himself to look grimly amused. He gave a curt nod.

"You ride?"

Walker lifted a cool brow. "Of course." The Shar had no use for horses, but he'd learned, the same way he'd mastered everything he needed to avenge his people.

Dinari flicked a glance at Mehcredi's slouching figure. "What about the boy?"

"Meck? A little." She'd said she liked horses. He hoped to the gods it was true.

Meck gazed sullenly into the middle distance, apparently absorbed by the cursing, sweating waggoners wrestling reluctant vanbeasts into harness.

"You should teach him. Boy!" The van master beckoned.

Because he was looking for it, Walker saw her eyes widen fractionally behind the tinted lenses. She turned. "Yeah?" A beat while she stared at Dinari's boots. "Uh, I mean, yessir." Perfectly done.

"You and your master are in the third last van. Take the packs and go get settled."

She glanced at Walker for confirmation.

"You deaf, lad?" The van master waved a hand. "Get on with it."

"Yessir." Slinging the packs over her shoulder, she shambled off.

"He'd better earn his keep," said Dinari, looking thoughtful. "Boys that age eat their own weight every meal."

"He will," said Walker. "Or he'll feel the flat of my hand." He placed the cup on the table and rose. "That all?"

Dinari folded his hands over his flat belly. The scar on his lip shone very white against the swarthiness of his skin. "Watch him," he said, his voice cold and hard. "It's a long lonely way to Trimegrace and I don't want trouble. Understood?"

'Cestors' bones! Walker narrowed his eyes, one hand falling to the hilt of the Janizar's sword. "He might be a lazy little shit, but Meck's under my protection. I'll kill any man who touches him."

"See that you don't have to." The van master nodded a dismissal.

The vans were all much the same, basic sturdy wooden trays on six wheels, each with its own canvas roof stretched over semicircular hoops and a seat for the driver at the front. By the time he got to the third from the end, all that was visible of Mehcredi were the soles of her boots and that mouthwatering rump as she fussed about with their packs. The dog was curled up in the shade underneath.

Walker climbed up beside her, pulling the canvas flap closed behind him. "Move over." The heat in the enclosed space struck him like a fist. Beads of sweat popped out on his brow, trickled from his armpits down his ribs.

She shot him a sassy grin. "He didn't have a clue."

"The idea's so shocking it didn't occur to him." When she tried to speak, he frowned her down. "Which is the way we have to keep it."

Mehcredi nodded, then wrinkled her nose. "It smells like someone's boots died in here."

Walker snorted, looking at the other four packs already there, the pile of tattered bedrolls dim lumps in the shadows. "Probably did."

"Bet there are bed bitemes. Is this where we sleep? It's revolting."

"Not necessarily. Some waggoners sleep around the campfire, some under their vans."

"Thank the Sister."

He lowered his voice. "This is a man's world. Get used to it. There'll be pissing and farting and dirty talk. You're just a lad. They'll try to make you squirm, even rough you up a bit." He hesitated for an instant. Shit, she needed to know. "Or worse, if they're desperate enough."

Her breath hitched. Bright eyes peered at him over the tops of the spectacles. "But you'll stop them." There wasn't a trace of uncertainty in her tone.

"I can't if I'm busy elsewhere. Toughen up, Meck, my boy."

Her full lips went tight. "I can do that. I've done it before, and with my bare hands too."

"Mehcredi." Lightly, he touched her hand. "Don't hesitate. Sex between men is strictly forbidden by the Trimagistos, though it's probably more common here than in Caracole, where no one cares. If you have to gut someone, go ahead. I'll make it right with Dinari."

The suddenness of her smile caught him under the ribs like a blow. "You're sweet, you know that?"

For the first time in his life, Walker stumbled over his words. "N-no." He pulled himself together and growled, "Sweet, my ass."

Mehcredi chuckled, deep in her throat like a man. "That too." Removing the spectacles, she placed them on top of her pack.

Before he could respond, she turned toward him, took his face between her hands and pressed her lips to his.

Walker froze, clamping his fingers around her wrists. "Stop," he mumbled, but she'd learned. Gods, how she'd learned.

She didn't take control, instead she gave it to him. "Please," she whispered, her lips parting like a shy blossom opening to greet the dawn, just as soft, just as silky. Her tongue brushed his, then retreated. Her head fell back like a rain-soaked flower on a stem. "Show . . ." A tiny lick. ". . . me . . ." Hot and untried and delicious. ". . . please."

16

All Walker's concentration, his rational powers, spilled dark and heavy and stupid into his loins, his cock hardening so swiftly it made him light-headed.

There was a reason—a million and one reasons—that made this insanely risky. He had to pull away, abandon her, reject her like everyone else in her miserable life, right now, this second. She was tough, he knew she was, she'd be fine, but oh gods, the scent of her called to him with the same clarion call as the *ch'qui*, everything primal and instinctive—*right*.

She smelled divine—of slick, feminine desire, the promise of ease for the pounding weight of his cock, of comfort and arms to hold him. As they sank to the floor of the wagon, she arched against him, soft where he was hard, yielding where he needed to thrust, but oh so strong where he needed strength.

A perfect match. Carnal and innocent all at once.

Innocent. Shit, *brand new*.

His brain spinning, Walker reached down to brace himself on the floor so he could peel himself away, but Mehcredi whimpered, squirming beneath him. His fingers brushed the curve of her breast, the Mark searing into his palm like a brand, her nipple thrusting out as hard as a pebble.

Magick shot through him on ruthless runners of green fire, growing with astonishing speed, twining up and down his spine, the sensation of rising sap so vivid it aroused him to the point of pain. All he could do was growl into her mouth and hang on to the last remnants of his sanity. Dimly, he was aware of her soft sweet tongue, the hand buried deep in his hair. She was gasping even as she kissed him, tilting her head for a better fit. One leg was hooked over the back of his calf, pressing him into the cradle of her pelvis.

With a superhuman effort, Walker lifted his hand away from the warm, enticing weight of her breast. "Mehcredi," he mumbled into her mouth, "no more." But the only response was an impatient wriggle and a mewl.

'Cestors save him, she was so direct, so disastrously honest. He managed to pull back a fraction, lips curving in a rueful smile against hers, his chest tight with a ridiculous tenderness.

"Enough," he said firmly, sitting up. He did some rapid mental calculations. If the assassin was in her mid-twenties as he'd surmised, there was well over a decade between them. He winced.

Mehcredi stared up at him in the gloom, her pupils so dilated, only a silver rim showed all around. She let out a shaky breath. "That was amazing. Is kissing always like that?"

"No," said Walker, resisting the temptation to elaborate.

"What are you thinking? Are you angry?"

"I should be." Instead, he felt . . . bleak. The infatuation was ripening nicely, just as he'd foreseen and not only did he feel helpless to stop it, he was making his own contribution to the impending disaster. "Don't do that again. Ever. You hear me?"

"Did ye fix Twister's harness?" said a loud rough voice, seemingly in his ear.

Mehcredi closed her mouth with a snap, snatched up the spectacles and straightened her head cloth.

"What do ye think?" said a different, younger voice, male. A callused hand grabbed the canvas flap, one thumbnail completely black. "'Course I did. Not lettin' the old bugger get away from me again."

By the time a lanky waggoner clambered over the backboard, Meck was seated cross-legged in the darkest corner rummaging in his pack, while his master watched him with a decidedly grim expression.

The waggoner turned out to be Abad, his huskier companion, Taryk. Abad was a genial soul, chatting amiably enough as he retrieved a mess of straps and buckles from a shabby box full of odds and ends. Walker suspected the surlier, sweatier Taryk was the source of the odor in the van.

That settled it. They'd sleep outdoors.

"Van master's up front," said Abad. "Guard chief'll be with him."

Walker nodded his thanks. The waggoner waved a casual farewell and disappeared with Taryk and the mended tack.

"You wanted to know what I'm thinking?" he said, his voice low and hard. "You scare the hell out of me, Mehcredi, for so many reasons I can't count them. We were lucky. A few minutes the other way—" He glared at her.

Her mouth quirked. "They'll decide I'm your kept boy. You said as much yourself." She shrugged. "I don't mind being your property." She had the nerve to send him a roguish twinkle.

Walker ran his hands through his hair. "Will you get it through your fool head? This is dangerous, as in tortured and executed danger-ous. Do you understand me?"

He waited until she nodded, gulping. Then he opened his pack. "Here." He tossed the bundle of leather in her direction.

Fielding it neatly, Mehcredi untangled it with careful fingers. "What is it?"

"A forearm harness for your dagger. I got it yesterday."

Despite the gloom and the stain on her face, he could see her flush of pleasure. But when she moved toward him, he held her off with an upraised hand. Her color deepening, she froze. Her head dropped and she turned away.

By the time dusk was drawing down, Mehcredi had given up anxious excitement in favor of terminal boredom. Dropping the last peeled tuber into the sloshing bucket between her feet, she flexed her wrin-kled, aching fingers. By the Sister, she might as well have stayed in Serafina's kitchen back at the House of Swords.

Walker, on the other hand, had received his assignment from the guard chief, together with a rangy bay horse with one white sock. He'd had no compunction about volunteering Meck as a kitchen hand ei-ther, damn him. With a final admonitory glare that even she could decipher—*Behave yourself or else*—he'd trotted off to spend the day circling the long train of wagons. Each time she glimpsed him, sitting straight and supple on his mount, her insides squirmed in the strangest way and her heart thudded, strong hard beats separated by several long seconds. They hurt—and they didn't. His robes looked dustier on every circuit, while he ignored the caravan completely, his gaze quartering the landscape between the distant dun-colored hills and the stunted bushes by the roadside.

Now she perched on the driver's seat next to the taciturn cook as he guided the chow van down the rutted trail. The plate-size hoofs of the shaggy vanbeasts churned up choking clouds of dust, strongly flavored with herbivore flatulence on a grand scale. Faugh.

Dinari called something from out in front, the command repeated down the line. Cook tugged the reins, swearing under his breath, and the van swung around to take its place in the circle.

Camp. Thank the Sister. Without waiting for permission, Mehcredi jumped down, stumbling on unexpectedly stiff legs.

"Where ye goin', boy?" Cook glowered down at her from under bushy brows. "There's supper still t' get."

Mehcredi scowled, stuffing her hands in her pockets. "Name's Meck," she muttered. "Gotta check Wajar don't need me."

When Cook grunted his reluctant assent, she fled in the direction of the horse string. It wasn't until she met the swordmaster's flat gaze that she realized how badly she'd needed to see him. The breath whistled out of her on a long sigh and her shoulders relaxed.

"I left you with Cook." Walker removed the saddle and the bay tossed its head. Without thinking, Mehcredi laid a soothing palm on the animal's twitching neck. "What are you doing here? And watch him, the bastard bites."

"He's all right." She bestowed an absent pat. "I like horses. How much longer to Trimegrace?"

"Two days, maybe three. You stick with Cook when I'm not around. Make yourself useful."

It was frightening how much she longed to creep into his arms and rest her head on his shoulder. Gods, the skin hunger was insidious, like a feverish illness. He'd taken pity on her, given her a glimpse of heaven, of human contact and caring, and now she craved it like a crazyspice addict.

The kissing, whispered a sly voice in her head. *It was good, but you want more. Look at the pit of his throat, all brown and smooth. You can see the pulse beating there. He might like it if you nuzzle in, you never know. Do you think his nipples are as sensitive as yours? What if you set your mouth to the hard muscle of his belly, would he shudder, get hard? And his ass, gods so tight and high and fine. What if—*

In desperation, she blurted, "Where are we sleeping?"

Walker paused, grooming brush in hand. "Out there." He indicated the dark shapes of the hills with a tilt of his head. "I'll have sentry duty anyway."

Another guard trotted in and swung down with a narrow sidelong glance. "Fill this." Walker shoved a bucket into her midriff. "Water's in the barrel over there. Then get back to Cook. Report to me after supper. Got it?"

"Yeah." With genuine ill-grace, Mehcredi did as she was told.

The dog caught up with her halfway back to the chow van, his step so sprightly it was immediately apparent he hadn't traveled on his own four feet. Mehcredi bent for a quick pat. "And he said *I* was a lazy little shit. Huh!"

The dog said nothing at all, but when they reached the chow van, he settled well out of range of Cook's big boots, nose on his paws, eyes bright.

Under Cook's monosyllabic direction, Mehcredi chopped, stirred and stoked the fires. Then she slopped ladlefuls of highly spiced stew onto rough trenchers made of hard-baked bread for a seemingly endless procession of hard-eyed dirty men. Several directed jocular comments at her, she dropped her head and mumbled until the ones farther down in the line complained and they shuffled on.

Hard fingers grasped her wrist and she looked up, startled. "By the Three," said a wiry guard in his forties, "what sweet morsel do we have here?" His thin smile revealed crooked teeth, the canines glinting gold in the flare of the torches.

Mehcredi lifted a truculent lip. "Keep yer fuckin' hands to yerself." A jerk of the ladle and boiling stew splashed over the man's knuckles.

He snatched his hand back. "Fuck! Why you little—"

Abad stood at his elbow. "Letafa, don't," he said urgently. "The boy's—"

"With me." Walker loomed out of the darkness. Not a muscle in his face moved.

Letafa tilted his chin. "Who the fuck are you?"

"Wajar."

Letafa's gaze dropped to Walker's sword. Then it returned more slowly to his face. He rose on the balls of his feet, and all at once, tension crackled in the air.

Unperturbed, Walker smiled, the effect chilling. "Meck can take care of himself," he said calmly. "Look."

Letafa whirled around. Mehcredi met his eye, trying to copy the menace of Walker's smile, the blade in her fist shining with a baleful glitter.

Someone gave a crack of laughter. "Hey, Letafa," a voice called out of the darkness. "Looks like ye're outmatched. Leastways, 'til the next cathouse." Abad guffawed and slapped his knee while Letafa glared.

"Come on." Walker waited only for her to dish up two meals, then hustled her off beyond the glare of the torches. "Over here." He led the way toward a stand of scrubby vegetation a hundred yards from the camp. Their packs were already there, shoved into a hollow under an arching root.

The swordmaster squatted comfortably on his heels, devouring stew in a series of rapid efficient bites. "Where's that damn dog?" he said, wiping his mouth with the back of his hand.

"Scrounging, I guess. He'll turn up when there's no one left to beg from."

"Keep him with you." Walker rose, a dark shape against the stars. "I got the early shift but I won't be far. Sound carries out here at night. Yell, and I'll hear you." He faded into the darkness without a sound. His voice drifted back to her. "Back the hour before midnight." A rustle, and then nothing save the night breeze playing in the branches and the rumble of masculine voices in the distance.

The sickle of the Sister drifted across the face of the stars, the red disk of the Brother in hot pursuit. The temperature had dropped. Shivering, Mehcredi fished the hated robes out of her pack and wrapped herself up until she was no more than a black bundle in the black night. Setting her back to a tree trunk, she tilted her head back and stared, feeling very small.

Was that smear of light a starship, streaking off to another world, one among an infinity? She squinted. Perhaps it was a falling star, and she should make a wish. Sleepily, she canvassed the options, but apart from getting out of Trinitaria in one piece, all her wishes had but a single name. She sighed. Once, just once, to lie in his arms and hear his cool deep voice murmur extravagant praises—who cared if he lied? Her eyes stung.

When a cold nose touched her hand, she yelped, and got an apologetic lick in response. Lifting her arm, she allowed the solid little body to snuggle close. "Keep your bitemes to yourself, you disgusting little scrounger," she said severely, sinking her fingers into the coarse fur.

When she scratched, the dog groaned with pleasure. "You always come back to me. Why is that, hmm?"

During the first bewildering weeks at the House of Swords, exasperated beyond measure, she'd asked Florien. She didn't want a dog, she didn't need a dog. Godsdammit, the stupid mutt had led the swordmaster straight to her!

"He loves ye," the boy had said, his voice husky and uncertain with the first intimations of adolescence. "Wit' everythin' he's got."

Mehcredi had scrubbed even harder at the big pot in the sink. "But why?"

"Ye saved him frum somethin' awful, dincha?"

Her mouth had fallen open. "The Necromancer was going to— Never mind." She shuddered. "How do you know?"

Florien shrugged, ducking his head so she couldn't see his eyes. "Some dogs is real bright. He knows. An' ye feed him. That counts for lots."

Now a thought occurred to her. "What's your name?" she asked her furry companion. With a canine sigh of contentment, the dog laid his head on her hip bone. "Scrounger?" His ears pricked and she saw the white of an eye.

Mehcredi grinned, ridiculously pleased. "Suits you."

Walker passed through the night, his steps soundless, no more than a moving patch of darkness among the double-edged shadows cast by the Sibling Moons. The true desert, the rocky arid home of the Shar, was still miles away, but if he breathed deeply, the distinctive salty odor of mannaplant filled his nose. The gift of his Ancestors. How could he have forgotten it?

He paused, listening, every sense alert. A couple of fires still burned inside the circle of vans, a few more dotted the perimeter. Three or four dark silhouettes tilted a bottle, threw the dice. From far away, the desolate howl of a direwolf echoed across the landscape. A vanbeast lowed, harness clinked.

Walker frowned. They were only a day out of Belizare. Why were scavengers like direwolves venturing so close?

With a predator's care, he approached the grove where he'd left Mehcredi. Out of habit, he ensured he was upwind. Nonetheless, he was greeted by a low, threatening growl. A stifled exclamation, and a shadow detached itself from the base of a tree to reveal his assassin, eyes wide, blade at the ready.

He stepped out of the dark. "It's me." Hunkering down, he stroked the dog's head. "Good work." To Mehcredi, he said, "Did you sleep?"

A shoulder hunched. "Dozed."

"Cold?"

"A little."

Well, shit, why hadn't he thought of it? She wouldn't have a clue how to make a fire. He should have done it before he left her.

Her teeth gleamed in a swift smile as she rubbed her hip. "The ground's hard."

"That it is." But when he pulled her to her feet, she came easily enough. Ah, youth. "Wait while I get us settled."

There were a few stray bunches of feathergrass dotted about. They'd do.

Deliberately, he grounded himself, reaching out with his shamanic senses. Yes, there! The feathergrasses were hardy and persistent, eking out a precarious existence in the leached soil. Walker fed them *ch'qui* until they burgeoned, the stems multiplying so rapidly they hissed and slithered as they grew, tangling into a thick, springy mat, longer and wider than any bedroll.

At his elbow, the assassin squeaked with surprise.

When he finally paused for breath, she said in a hushed voice, "Did you do that with, uh, Magick?"

His blood singing, Walker reached above his head and grabbed a branch. "Yes, and here's more." His tingling body the conduit, he wove the *ch'qui* through the branches, bending, thickening and interlacing them into a serviceable bower. By the time it was finished, only a few stray moonbeams made their way through to gild the tips of the feathergrass stems with silver.

No more than a few days away from his garden, but gods, how he'd missed this! Like the *nea-kata*, the surging life force of his world centered him, giving him back the equilibrium he needed to function on a day-to-day basis. Some days, it was all that kept him hanging on.

Nerves still thrumming with power, his balls drawn up tight with it, he gathered the kindling for a small fire and dug out his tinderbox.

As the first flames spread and the air in the confined space warmed, Mehcredi removed her robes and spread them over the feathergrass mattress. Sinking down, she shot him a cautious glance from under her lashes, then held her hands out to the fire. "Thanks."

Comfortably cross-legged, Walker allowed himself to reflect on the day, sorting and discarding impressions, memories, images. As was his custom, he was dispassionate, setting aside what was messy and weak—regret, self-pity, fear and guilt. All his old friends, sealed away where they couldn't grin and chatter like the picked-clean skulls of those he'd loved.

Sometimes it worked. Other times, it didn't.

It was a relief to concentrate on Mehcredi's elegant profile as she gazed into the heart of the tiny fire. Her eyelids drooped, but she sat stiffly, jerking upright every time she dozed.

"Tired?" he murmured.

She huffed out a funny little sound midway between a yawn and a laugh. "Gods, yes."

Praise where it was due. "You did well today. Kept your head with Letafa."

Her lips trembled, and for a horrifying moment, he thought she might cry. But First Father be thanked, she regained control, ducking her head. He heard a long quivering breath, then another.

"Sorry about . . . what happened in the van."

"So you should be." He fed the fire another handful of twigs. "We won't speak of it again. Go to sleep."

"What about you?"

"I have some thinking to do." He should fade away into the darkness and run through a couple of high-level *nea-katas* to settle his mind and reacquaint himself with his duty, his vengeance. He fingered one of the braids at his temple, feeling somehow . . . jangled. Why couldn't he hate her? It would be so much simpler. This entire debacle sprang from her attempt to poison Erik Thorensen. Welderyn'd'haraleen't'Lenquisquilirian hadn't had the slightest doubt about his destiny since the first diabloman gurgled and died, spitted on his blade. He'd been certain no distraction could deflect him from his purpose, but now?

Damn her, how had she got him so tangled in her stupid, wide-eyed hero worship? Why was he so fucking soft with her? He snorted to himself in derision. *Hard* was more like it. But his Ancestors and his people had shaped him, made him a warrior all the way to the marrow of his bones. He couldn't help but respect courage—and what extraordinary courage she possessed, bloody-minded enough to persist with joy and wonder in the face of years of neglect and misery. He at least had been greatly loved, and had loved in return. Despite the horror and death that rode over the hill with Ghuis Gremani Giral and his demon army, he'd been lucky. He'd had a *place*.

She was shivering again, the little fool. "Here," he said brusquely, pushing her down with a hand on her shoulder. "Stretch out." He extended the edge of his robe like a wing, and she crept gratefully into its shelter.

What he hadn't intended was for her to curl up with her poor shorn head on his thigh, but being Mehcredi, she did it anyway. When she sighed with contentment, he hesitated for a second and was lost.

So he continued to sit, cursing himself for a fool, trying like hell to ground and listening to the crackle and pop of the fire.

He was dozing when she turned her head, blinking up at him. A tired smile curved her lips. "You need to know," she whispered. "You're my only chance. I can't give you up, not yet." She patted his knee.

"What?" he said, stupid as a plowboy.

"I picked the wrong moment." She covered a yawn with her hand. "You were right." Another yawn. "Risky. Mmm." She snuggled closer.

Walker clenched his jaw so hard, his molars hurt. The fire hissed, as if with scorn. "S-soft," it crackled in his head. "Soft."

And then, oddly enough, his name, over and over. "Walker." Hiss, pop. "Walker." A pause. "Sscenda. It'ss Cenda."

17

Walker blinked. Streamers of flame danced, long and curling, like a woman's fiery tresses. A face formed, flickering in and out of existence, a straight nose, the turn of a long graceful neck.

'Cestors' bones.

Mehcredi raised her head. "Is that—?" Her voice cracked with disbelief.

Walker shoved a small branch into the heart of the fire. It caught and flared up. "Cenda?"

"Yess. Lissten. Message . . . Deiter." The cadence and power of the voice rose and fell with the flames.

"What Magick is this?" he said sharply.

Fiery lips curved with satisfaction, the image firming enough to be completely recognizable. "Sscrying by fire. Be better . . . practiss."

The dog gave a single sharp bark and fell silent.

"Sweet Sister in the sky." Beside him, Mehcredi made the sign of the Sibling Moons.

"Takess power. Can't hold—Lissten . . . great evil in the south . . . the desert. Deiter wants . . . find it."

"That would be Nerajyb Nyzarl." A growl rumbled in his chest. "He's as good as dead."

"No. Forget . . . him." Sparks shot out of the fire as Cenda shook her head. "Monstrous . . . not human. Huge, killing . . . hundreds." The fire witch began to dwindle, the flames sinking. "Deiter . . . needs . . . *lissten . . .*"

Walker leaned forward. "Cenda? Cenda, come back!"

Mehcredi fed the greedy flames a handful of bark and the fire shot up on a draft of air as if someone had taken a bellows to it.

Cenda reappeared, floating in the flames. "Thankss," she said to an unseen presence behind her. Erik and his air Magick, he'd bet his House of Swords on it.

"Deiter has a bargain." She cocked her head, her gaze shifting off to one side, though she looked straight through Mehcredi as if she wasn't there. Then she nodded in response to some unseen comment or instruction. "Locate . . . evil, find out what . . . is and he will give you . . . the last . . . Sshar."

Everything inside Walker contracted to a single point of old pain and fury, hard-edged as a black diamond. "Nonsense. I am the last of the Shar."

Cenda shook her fiery head, her hair whipping around her. With a soft roar, the fire flared, illuminating Mehcredi's expression of open-mouthed fascination, then died down so the shadows swooped back like spread-winged birds.

"Not sso. There's a woman."

Walker curled his lip. "The old man's senile. They're all dead. Fuck, I should know."

Gods, the endless searching, watching the veiled figures of respectable women in the souk, the naked faces of the whores, all the time hoping, hoping . . . Forcing himself to attend slave auctions and smile as if he enjoyed it, every dark-haired female on the block making his heart pound and his gorge rise. In the long years before the bitter certainty of Amae's death grew in his heart like a canker, he could never decide whether he longed to see her up there, on sale to the highest bidder, or whether he dreaded it.

Cenda glanced at the same spot to her right. A beat later, she said, "He only just found her."

"No." Pain and rage sucked all the breath out of his lungs, leaving nothing but a venomous whisper behind. "A name, give me a fucking name!"

Even in the flames, Cenda's discomfort was clear to see. Another sidelong glance, presumably at Deiter. "Walker, I'm . . . ssorry.

He says . . ." She glared at the old man, her lips twisting. "Tell him how . . . desstroy . . . the evil. Then . . . you get . . . name."

"*No!*" Lashing out with his foot, Walker kicked the fire, scattering coals and embers in all directions. After that, everything went black for a few seconds, but the greatest darkness was the yawning empty pit that had been his soul.

He came back to himself on his hands and knees, breathing like a blown horse, every muscle in his body clenched and rigid. His jaw hurt.

"Walker?" A hand touched his hair, fleetingly. "Who are the Shar? Your family?"

He sat back on his heels. "My people," he said dully. "The Shar'd'iloned't'Hywil."

"Oh." A second's pause. "Sorry, I've never heard of them."

Giant hands were squeezing his chest, compressing it unbearably. "Their name has not been spoken in fifteen years." He pulled in a difficult shallow breath. "Neither has mine."

"Walker is not your name?"

He forced himself to glance at her puzzled face. "I am Welderyn'd-'haraleen't'Lenquisquilirian."

She regarded him more doubtfully still. "That's, um, quite a mouthful."

"Shar names are long." *Name the child, shape the life,* went the Ancestors' proverb. "There are"—he caught himself—"*were* layers of meaning."

Everything inside was leached and dry, his body a shell, like the hollowed-out trunk of some great dead cedderwood. A strong wind, the slightest touch, and he'd topple, shatter to dust. It couldn't be true, it *couldn't*.

"You're shaking." Kneeling before him, Mehcredi pulled the edges of his robe together over his chest, fussing over him as if he were a little boy.

With a wordless growl, he knocked her hands away.

Undeterred, she shuffled even closer, reaching out to rub her palms up and down his biceps, her brow knitted with concern. "What happened to them?" Her voice was hushed and quavery. "It was something awful, wasn't it?"

He gave a mirthless bark of laughter. "Ghuis Gremani Giral happened, with his army. There'd been rain, the wadis were full of wildflowers." He'd forgotten that, the vivid carpet of fragile blooms. So much *ch'qui*, and his blood running hot, with spring and the festival and the girls with their pert breasts and sidelong glances.

When he paused, a thread of sound whispered out of the darkness. "Go on."

"We came together to sing the Songs of Spring, all the family bands. A time to give thanks, for first pairings and life bondings. He knew we'd be there, the bastard, Giral knew."

Her breath puffed warm and rapid against his throat. "But *why*? You weren't hurting him."

"Ah, but we had. The Grand Pasha deeded Giral an estate, but he neglected to mention the southern part was Shar land, the gift of the Ancestors. *Ours*." He bared his teeth. "The Shar are warriors. What do you think we did, assassin?"

"Merciful Sister, you fought, didn't you?"

"We stampeded Giral's vanbeasts, stole his horses, burned his fences, and we laughed as we did it. We thought he was slow and foolish, a foreigner. I was a shaman then and the *ch'qui* was strong within me. When his miners raped the earth, I collapsed their tunnels. I was the stupid one, so proud."

Mehcredi's fingers tightened on his arms. She made a small encouraging noise.

"We made the Great Pasha look small. Hell, we didn't even kill anyone, though we made it clear we could have. So he . . . he—" His tongue stuck to the roof his mouth. "He came with a company of pikemen. And diablomen."

"Fifteen," breathed Mehcredi. "You said fifteen."

"Twenty-three. We killed eight. Do you know what demons look like, Mehcredi? Do you have any idea?"

"Tell me."

When she winced, he realized he had both her hands crushed in his. He dropped them and rose, turning his back on her. "No." He wouldn't sully her mind with the images. The furrows on his hip ached, a gut-wrenching reminder. "They're not meant to be here," he said at last. "They pervert the *ch'qui*. Not just evil—*wrong*."

"The what?" She touched his back, her palm rubbing hesitantly up and down his spine.

"Shit, never mind."

But when he jerked away, she only stepped closer, insisting, a wave of warmth against him in the chill desert night. "Walker, I don't understand."

Here it came. He could almost hear the clicks as the pieces fell into place in that quick clever mind.

"Weren't you there? If this Giral man had everyone killed, why aren't you dead too?"

He closed his eyes in agony, his head swimming, remembering the hideous sodden weight of the corpses piled on top of him in the wadi, the reek of old blood, the fecal stink and the bitemes buzzing. "I don't know." Sour bile burned in the back of his throat. "Bad luck? Leave it, Mehcredi." His eyes had been crusted shut with something unspeakable. He'd been forced to claw them open. And when he had—

Vaguely, he wondered if he was going to heave his guts up, all over her boots.

A rustle, and she was right in front of him, both fists buried in his robes. She rose on her toes, which was enough to put them eye to eye. "Don't say that!" She tried to shake him. "There was a reason." Another ineffectual shake. "Look at who you are, what you've done."

"You think?" He went to pry her off, but gods, her fingers were like ice. He wrapped his own around them. "I've avenged my people, but apart from that—" He shrugged.

"No, no!" In her urgency, she pressed closer, her strong supple body molded to his, close as a lover. "Walker, you're the best thing that ever happened to me. And I can't be the only one."

He curled his lip. "I'm efficient," he said. "I'll give you that. Especially with the body count." Unable to help himself, he tightened his grip on hers. "I'll do my best not to add you to it, I swear."

Even in the dappled moonslight, he saw her brow wrinkle. "There's only one left, isn't there?" she said slowly. "This Nyz man. And you'll kill him soon, the same way you killed the others."

"Your confidence in me is touching."

"So what will you do when it's finished?"

"Finished?"

"Your vengeance. Over. Complete. You'll have your life back then."

The ground shifting beneath his feet, the stars winking out, one by one. Over, it would all be over, the defining purpose of his life. 'Cestors' bones, *what fucking life?* The blood roared in his ears, like a sandstorm striding across the desert, blowing everything flat, scouring all the landmarks, obliterating the familiar trails and tracks.

"I hadn't—" he croaked. "Hadn't . . . thought. Fuck." Every moment, waking or sleeping, his vengeance woven in his blood and bone. His reason for living, the justification for his survival when all those he'd loved had—

Gone, all of it, gone. His vision grayed out.

Dimly, he was aware he swayed. Automatically, he reached for the reassuring force of the *ch'qui,* but even as he did so, the assassin slipped both arms around his waist and shoved her shoulder under his arm, propping him up with her remarkable strength.

"It's all right," she muttered into his neck. "I've got you. You're safe. I'm here." The sort of nonsense a mother might murmur over a child with a skinned knee. So stupid, so inappropriate, so completely Mehcredi.

How long had it been since someone held him, offered to kiss his hurts and make them better? His mind couldn't encompass it, but his body knew what to do. He opened his mouth to say, "Get off," but the words died stillborn. Instead, he gave himself to the embrace, burying his face in her hair, his nose full of the scent of warm clean scalp and blengo juice.

Just one second, a single instant out of his entire fucking empty life. "Shut up," he muttered thickly.

With a shaky laugh, Mehcredi raised her head and rubbed her cheek against his. Walker took her face in both hands and sank into her mouth like a man dying of thirst. She tasted sweet, yet earthy, deeply refreshing, like the Spring of Shiloh, sacred to his people.

Gods, so good.

The roaring in his ears rushed back, filling his head. He had the strangest sensation of falling, as if the world had taken a smart step sideways, the *ch'qui* morphing into something entirely different, unfamiliar yet darkly thrilling.

Skin, he had to have skin, pale and warm and perfect. Almost before the thought was complete, his hands were under her shirt, a satin weight nuzzling into his palm. She arched under him, whimpering. Luxuriating, Walker skimmed his fingers up over the knots of her spine, then back down to her waist and under the trews, learning the shape of that superb ass, the first curves, the intriguing dip of the dimples either side of her tailbone.

Mehcredi's tongue met his stroke for stroke, clumsy still, but eager and, oh gods, so generous.

Walker tore his lips away from hers, licking down under her jaw, nibbling the long muscle down to her shoulder as her head fell back in surrender. His balls pulled up so high and swollen they hurt, the tender skin tight with lust and *ch'qui* combined, while his cock was a pulling, throbbing weight demanding to thrust and rut and spill.

Without ceremony, he pushed the shirt aside. The Mark on her breast glowed greenish black in the moonslight, pulsing for him. Rising out of the center of the design, dark against the smooth white flesh, her nipple stood stiff and distended, all crinkled delicious velvet. Growling, he licked around a spiral line, then a delectable sweeping curve, vaguely aware of a deep gasping somewhere in the vicinity.

He rolled fully over her, hips already moving in a primal rhythm, one hand hooked beneath her knee, splaying her wide. He reached down to rip open his trews, but before he could do so, her shaking fingers fumbled over his length, gripped and *squeezed*, the pressure perfect—dreadfully, catastrophically perfect.

His cheek pressed against the silky flesh he'd Marked, Walker ground his teeth together so hard the enamel cracked. The *ch'qui* sizzled and burned up and down his spine, in his balls, his cock, his ass, Magick reaching deep inside to finger every place that made him a man and a shaman. The power of the impending orgasm made his eyes water, sucked all the breath from his lungs.

No, no, no. He fought it, with every fiber of his being, every shred of discipline he possessed. He was a shaman and a warrior, a fully adult male, not a randy youth. It felt like holding off an earthquake, his balls boiling with urgency, the skin of his cock ready to split.

It cost him years of his life to bite back the roar of pain and frustration. What emerged was a sound so strangled it didn't even qualify as a groan. He shuddered, hissing bloodcurdling oaths in every language he knew, especially Shar.

Strong fingers yanked his head up by the hair. "Shit," she said. "Walker, c'mon, c'mon!" Mehcredi patted his cheek, none too gently. "Sorry. I'm sorry, all right? I didn't know, I swear." She fumbled around behind his ear. What was she doing? Feeling for a pulse? Then she was off again with more of the senseless babble. "I never meant . . ."

"Stop . . . that." Grabbing her hand, he raised his head. They were sprawled full length on the mat of feathergrass, the assassin crushed beneath him, tears sparkling on her lashes, her lips swollen. *He'd made her cry?* 'Cestors, he had no recollection of bearing her down to the ground, none whatsoever.

"Are you all right?" he said brusquely, heart still hammering. Gingerly, he levered himself into a sitting position, and her hands dropped away. Thank the gods for the darkness. Even the back of his neck felt hot.

"Of course." She sucked in a hurried breath. "But I hurt you and I never meant to, truly." Her eyes squeezed shut tight. "Sweet Sister, what an unmitigated idiot."

Walker stared, blinking, sucking in huge gulps of air.

Mehcredi's mouth continued moving, a stream of self-recriminations and apologies sailing past his ear. Whatever she thought she'd done, it really bothered her. With the greatest of care, he pressed the heel of his hand against his cock. The first *nea-kata*, the first posture, center, ground . . . *Shit!*

She lay there, those gorgeous tits quivering slightly with every anxious breath. The dark stain stopped just above her cleavage like some weird tide line. In contrast, her breasts gleamed pure and snowy, like nightpearl flowers in the moonlight.

"Hurt me?" he said through gritted teeth, averting his gaze to scowl at the dog, who grinned back as if he knew.

"Well, you made an awful noise. I had no idea a man's—" She broke off, biting her lip, and he was certain her face was scarlet, though it was too dark to see. "That you were so, um, sensitive."

For a moment, he was tempted. Leave her in ignorance and no more advances, her guilt would preserve him from temptation. His famous icy reserve wasn't doing much of a job, let alone his self-control.

You're the best thing that ever happened to me, she'd said with absolute conviction. He wanted to throw his head back and howl the irony of it to the moons.

For whatever reason, he couldn't lie to her about this, not even by omission. He just . . . couldn't. It wasn't fair. "You didn't hurt me," he said heavily. Fortunately, embarrassment and shame were having a salutary effect where he needed it most.

"But then why—?"

Walker turned away to snag his pack. "You touched me and I was . . . aroused. That's all."

"*Really?*"

How, in the names of the honored Ancestors, had she escaped Lonefell if not completely innocent, then relatively unscathed?

"Yes." He busied himself digging for his spare shirt so he didn't have to look at her. "Perfectly normal." Except that it hadn't been. It had been the most profound, the most amazing—Godsdammit, if he got inside her, he might actually die, but a small, insidious voice whispered the experience would be worth an eternity as ash blowing across the endless sand.

With a considerable effort, he cut the thought off cold. "Mehcredi," he said, "are you a virgin? The truth now."

18

A silence, then Mehcredi sat up and drew the shirt closed over those sweet tits. Walker told himself he was grateful. "You couldn't tell?" she said.

Amae had been a virgin when they took her, he could swear to it. But he refused to think of his sister that way, of the inevitable rape, the brutal violation. She'd been such a sprite, slender and slim and strong. 'Cestors grant her mercy, death had come swiftly. He'd never see her again, never stand witness as she put some poor bastard through the Test of the Battle Maiden. The old wizard was fucking with him. He had to be.

And that thought took care of any lingering remnants of lust.

"I guessed," Walker said. "How in the gods' names did you manage it?"

Her knuckles whitened on the shirt. "I fought like hell." She snorted. "It helps to be a big lump. And I had a lot of hiding places."

Ah yes, she'd mentioned a man. A man with friends.

"Taso, wasn't it?"

She tilted her head. "You remember?"

Walker rather thought he'd like to meet Taso. And his friends. He gave her a wolfish smile. "He wouldn't stand a chance against you now, armed or not."

"Gods, yes!" Her answering grin flashed wide and white. "I'd hand him his head." A roll of the shoulders. "Feels good."

"So, how much experience have you had, Mehcredi?"

"With . . . sex?"

"Yes."

Her head was bent over her laces, but she answered readily enough. "I watched the stallions cover the mares and I know what a naked man looks like. I've seen people fucking."

"You have?"

She chuckled. "Are you shocked? I spent a lot of time hiding in the stables. Nedward, the blacksmith, used to take the scullery maids there. He did it standing up. Used to grunt a lot." Her face darkened.

"One of Taso's friends?"

Her eyes widened. "How did you know?"

"Another lucky guess." When he reached out to take both her hands in his, it took all his control not to crush her fingers. "Listen to me, sex is a lot more than rutting in a barn. Or it should be."

"I know, that's why I—"

"Listen, damn you! I'm only going to say this once. First times are special."

"Yes, but—"

"Mehcredi," he said through gritted teeth. "Shut. Up." He cleared his throat. "Don't throw it away. The right man's out there for you, young and strong and clean. Hell, my House of Swords is full of warriors like that."

She regarded him with fascination. Her lips twitched. "Do you know what you sound like? Like—"

Walker snatched his hands away. "Like your dear old auntie. Yes, I know." The heat in his cheeks galled him. Thank the gods for the dark. "But that doesn't make it any less true. Mehcredi"—he leaned forward—"let it go."

But all she did was stare. His fingers itched to shake her until her teeth rattled. Fuck, whatever it took. "Chasing me is stupid," he said coolly, deliberately. "You're making a fool of yourself."

Even in the gloom, her flinch was perceptible. So was the recoil. Well, good, that was what he wanted.

Her silvery gaze studied his face, one feature at a time, the force of her concentration as palpable as a touch. "I thought you . . . wanted me."

"I'm male and you've shown you're willing." He shrugged. "I do, just not enough." The only lie he'd ever told her.

"Enough? What does that mean? What are you thinking?" she said, suddenly, fiercely. Strong fingers dug into his forearm. "Tell me."

He shook her off. "Not enough to make you a convenience, to forgo my honor. It's for your own good, Mehcredi."

Godsdammit, a fatal error.

She reared back, her lips thin. For a long moment, she glared into his face. "I get it," she said. "*Finally*. Sorry for being so slow. I'll take care of it myself."

"Take care—?" Something fluttered in his belly. "What's that supposed to mean?"

"There are towns on the route, aren't there? Dinari said so. I'll find someone." She chuckled, though there was more pain than humor in the sound. "You're looking appalled, right?" She peered. "Yes, you are. Don't worry. I'll dress as a woman, take my time."

When he opened his mouth, she held up a finger. "Give me some credit. I'll be sensible, I won't rush it." She sent him a travesty of a smile. "If the House of Swords is full of good men, I should be able to find one in all of Trinitaria, don't you think?"

Hard cruel hands on her soft flesh, leering faces, disease, brutality, indifference. His lungs contracted. "You're bluffing."

"Try me."

"You can't go out *looking* for it. I won't permit it." That was better, more commanding, colder.

She raised an eyebrow. "How did you plan to stop me?"

With a dreadful sense of foreboding, he recognized her expression. The steely resolve of a true warrior. And 'Cestors help him, he'd taught it to her.

"All right then. I'll wait 'til Trimegrace. It's a big city. I'm not a complete idiot, no matter what you think."

He leaped to his feet, the clean shirt bunched in one fist. "There," he snarled, "you are completely wrong. And not about the city."

Without a backward look, he stepped out of the bower and strode off, heading out into the desert, needing space and the chill earthy smell of the rocky landscape more than his next breath. But his footfalls, as always, were silent.

Hands on hips, the Necromancer stood in the center of the rutted track that wound its way through the gates of Nerajyb Nyzarl's new estate. He turned a full circle, tugging at his lower lip. It would do, he conceded. Very well, in fact.

The main building, only two stories high, sprawled across a small rise, looking down over the rocky valley and across to the dusty hills in the far distance. The Necromancer had to admit he was surprised—on more than one count. He'd imagined the desert as an ocean of dunes, rolling all the way to the horizon under a pitiless sun. The sun was pitiless all right, but it shone on an arid landscape of gravel and scree, crisscrossed by wadis and dotted with clumps of hardy mannaplants and stands of feathergrass. The few small trees visible were bent almost horizontal, sporting narrow gray green leaves and gnarled trunks.

It was a relief to turn his gaze to the house, surrounded by verdant green. Three wells drew sweet water from far below and Ghuis Gremani Giral had lavished it on lawns and flower beds and fountains and purplemist trees. He could hear the quiet splashing even from here, outside the wall. Smaller buildings clustered about gave the impression Nyzarl's mansion had pupped—stables, guard barracks, quarters for guests and huts for slaves. Everything was constructed of mud brick, plastered an eye-aching white.

By Shaitan, the ass-end of the universe, but he'd put up with it for the short term. He needed privacy to deal with Nyzarl. As for whatever lurked out there in the desert . . . He ran his tongue over parched lips. Ally or enemy, he'd find it and learn it the way he was learning Xotclic the demon. Then he'd bend it to his will, make it his pet, his slave. No such thing as coincidence. Everything had conspired to bring him here, to the perfect place.

"Hantan." An impertinent hand tugged at his sleeve.

It was the little slave girl, hollows beneath her eyes like great dark bruises.

The Necromancer rounded on her with a snarl. "Don't touch me."

"He's ready. My lord is ready. He says come at once." Another tug. *"Please."*

It wouldn't do to keep Nyzarl waiting. Besides, Xotclic might be there. He took a steadying breath. He'd made Dotty triple-check everything, then do it again and again. Until she cried.

Tonight, if all went well. His chest ached, a horrible heavy feeling as if the chambers of his heart were full of tar. Gods, it had to be soon, *soon*.

But only if Xotclic took the bait.

Puffing a little, he followed the slave girl up the slope to the mansion and past the hard-eyed stare of the two guards on duty at the ornamental gates. Immense in his snowy robes, Nerajyb Nyzarl sprawled in a huge chair of woven cane, set like a throne in a courtyard shaded by two immense purplemist trees and cooled by a miniature waterfall trickling down over carefully placed rocks and into an artificial grotto. Small black fish darted about in the water while larger golden shapes nosed about the roots of the feathery water plants.

The Necromancer allowed himself a single flash of nostalgia for Caracole and its blue canals. Then he put the foolishness aside. He had a trap to set.

He prostrated himself on the grass. "My lord?"

Nyzarl's eyes narrowed. "You come to me without your tools?"

"The parchments and ink are indoors, mighty lord. Such precious things must be kept in the cool. The merest step. May I send one of these"—he waved a hand at the three slaves in attendance—"to fetch them? I had hoped your lordship would discuss with me whether he wished to continue with his military or diplomatic, ah, exploits, next."

The Necromancer held his breath. Had he overdone it?

But apparently that was impossible. With a grunt, Nyzarl jerked his head at the nearest slave, a tall graceful boy with broad shoulders and a high rounded ass.

Nodding and bowing, the Necromancer inched closer to the path. Nyzarl droned on and a few minutes later, the lad reappeared, his arms full, rolls of parchment balanced on top of the scribe's portable writing desk.

Now!

He extended a foot.

A startled cry and the desk went flying, ink bottles arcing across the grass, sheets of parchment fluttering like broken-backed birds.

"Oh no!" fluted the Necromancer. Frantically he dived across the lawn, managing to snag one page before it landed in the water. Others were not so lucky. Ink ran and smeared before they sank out of sight, and the little back fish gathered to nibble the soggy mess.

"Our work," he wailed, righting an ink bottle with shaking fingers. "All our work. Oh my lord."

"Help him!" roared the diabloman, and the others leaped to do his bidding. But the tall boy stood frozen, his face ashen.

Nyzarl rose, his fleshy face flushed with rage. "You stupid little fucker!" Spittle flew from his lips.

"S-sorry." The boy fell on his face as if his legs had been cut from under him. "My lord, pl—"

Nyzarl stooped, grabbed the slave by the throat and lifted him one-handed until his toes brushed the grass.

Impressive, thought the Necromancer, busily smoothing parchment and moaning. When he heard the familiar garbled syllables and smelled the stench of the green fog, he smiled to himself.

The boy began to scream, short and shrill, but he tuned the sounds out, forcing himself to concentrate. Gathering his Dark Magick, he formed his will into a narrow beam, sharp as a rapier. He thrust. *I know what you want.*

The weight of the demon's attention felt like burning coals on the back of his neck, but he didn't look up.

I can set you free.

The crunch of bone had an inquiring tone to it, if such a thing were possible. The slave shrieked once and fell silent.

The Necromancer drew a deep breath and opened himself. *See? I hide nothing from you. Not like him. Your master.* He invested the last two words with all the mental scorn of which he was capable.

The touch of the demon's mind was hideous, even for the Necromancer. Not because it was evil—he was well accustomed to evil—but because it was *wrong.* Dislocated and set adrift, the moorings of his sanity writhed like worms. He bit his tongue until it bled.

"Get on with it, Xotclic," growled the diabloman. "Take the carrion back with you if you want."

The demon's contempt for Nyzarl burned like acid across the Necromancer's brain.

How little he knows, he whispered silently. *How little he respects you.*

But I know the boy cannot exist in your world. All that sweet blood and terror. Gone.

The pain of maintaining the contact was sending him cross-eyed. Unable to help himself, he clutched at his temples.

"What the fuck's wrong with you, Hantan?" barked Nyzarl.

"M-migraine, my lord," he moaned truthfully. "If you c-could give m-me a moment."

"Day's gone to shit anyhow. Get out of my sight, the lot of you. You too, Xotclic."

Tonight, thought the Necromancer with the last of his strength. *We will bargain, you and I.*

The demon's laughter ricocheted around inside his skull, a distorted echo, vast and abrasive. By Shaitan, the very timbre of it was like a scouring pad, another couple of seconds and his brains would be reduced to the consistency of thin gruel. It hurt, gods it hurt!

Then—mercifully—Xotclic let the slave boy's broken body flop to the ground and departed without a backward glance. Except mercy had nothing to do with it. The creature had its orders.

Though it galled, the Necromancer had to accept the assistance of the little slave girl to get down the hill to his quarters.

A firm hand in the small of her back, he thrust Dotty past the guard on the door and into the brightly lit bedchamber. Two steps later, she stopped dead, emitting a sudden high-pitched giggle fit for a five-year-old. Nerajyb Nyzarl raised his head, his eyes slitted with pleasure as the little slave girl worked the muscles of his bull-like neck. He lay facedown on a padded bench covered with white towels, completely nude, glistening with oil and supremely unconcerned.

"I sent for you, not her." He flapped a big hand in a dismissive gesture.

The Necromancer promptly fell on his face. "Forgive my presumption, mighty lord," he said to the rug on the floor. "I have nothing to offer as apology for this afternoon's, ah, disaster save my worthless life and that of my sister."

When he risked a glance upward, the diabloman was looking thoughtful. He reminded the Necromancer of nothing so much as a beached leviathan, his strength in big bones and hard muscle beneath the blubber. His shoulders and ribcage were massive, his buttocks broad and hairy. In fact, he was furred all over, as far as the Necromancer could see, his jaw dark with beard, a coarse black pelt all down his back. Gods, what a barbarian.

"Her veil," grunted Nyzarl. "Off."

The Necromancer climbed painfully to his feet and did as his master bid. The Technomage Primus of Sybaris blinked in the light of the torches like an idiot child, her faded eyes fixed wistfully on Nyzarl's body.

The diabloman grimaced. "By the Three, not much of an apology."

The Necromancer hung his head. "I had hoped, my lord, that I might still be of use to you. I have nothing beyond this."

Nyzarl sighed, as if much put upon. "She'll do, I suppose. Xotclic isn't fussy, but for the gods' sakes, man, cover her up. And you—" Reaching back, he pinched the slave girl's thigh with his powerful fingers. "Get on with it." A stifled gasp and she shifted her attention to his shoulders.

The first step accomplished. Releasing a careful breath, the Necromancer flipped Dotty's veil back into place and thrust her into a shadowed corner. Reaching into his robes, he withdrew a box containing parchment, ink and brushes. With some difficulty, he sank cross-legged to the floor at the diabloman's feet, the low table bearing refreshments at his elbow. Perfect.

Averting his eyes from the sight of the hairy wrinkled pouch lying slack between the other man's open thighs, he coughed discreetly. "A suggestion, my lord?"

"Hmpf?"

"A fresh chapter. An account of your victory over the demon." He infused his voice with sly admiration. "You must have been immensely strong for one so young. I cannot imagine the courage and learning it must have required."

The story came in fits and starts, punctuated by grunts when the little slave's clever fingers unkinked a knot. If the silences were any indication, the diabloman found it surprisingly difficult to tell. The Necromancer's brows rose. He'd never had much respect for Trinitarian Magick, thinking it all flourish and no subtlety. But while he remained convinced it was more blunt instrument than rapier, the training Nyzarl described was both rigorous and breathtakingly cruel, devised to strip every last vestige of human feeling from the apprentice demon masters.

Enthralled despite himself, the Necromancer took notes in earnest, his brush whisking over the creamy parchment. No one noticed him extract a twist of paper from his box and empty the powder it contained into the diabloman's cup of chilled wine.

The words slowed to a trickle as Nyzarl approached the culmination of his evil apprenticeship. The summoning and enslavement of a demon was the blackest of any Dark Magick known in Trinitaria. It required the aspiring diabloman to sacrifice a life—and not just any life, but that most dear to him.

The diabloman ground to a halt, gulping for breath, his back sheened with sweat and oil. He snapped his fingers. "Wine." The slave took a sip from the cup before placing it in his hands.

The Necromancer's lips curved in a serene and satisfied smile. Such precautions were completely useless. He'd been feeding the diabloman a harmless compound of herbs for a week now. Despite his addiction to fatty foods and strong drink, it would do nothing but improve his already robust health—until the second portion of the mixture met the first. It had taken some juggling, but he'd ensured only the boy tasters had shared the original compound. Not that the girl mattered, but she massaged her master every evening and the man was far too dangerous to be afforded even the slightest warning.

Refreshed, Nyzarl resumed his tale, word by gritted word. The diabloman's choice had fallen upon his youngest brother, whom he truly loved, the boy idolizing him in return. But ambition burned like a fire within him. Besides, in the face of all his sire's dire predictions, he'd finally discovered something at which he truly excelled.

Tears streaming down his face, sobs shaking his deep chest, he'd tied the boy down and subjected him to the hours of systematic torture demanded by the ritual. The hardest thing he'd ever done. Every time he glimpsed the agony and confusion on the lad's beloved, distorted features, he wavered. Eventually, despite his mentor's disapproval, he'd thrown a cover over the head. After that, he'd managed to keep his hands steady, though his tears continued to drip as readily as the blood.

Irresistibly drawn by the delicious pain of both tortured and torturer, Xotclic had slit the curtain of the void with a curious claw and thereby damned itself to servitude.

Nyzarl's voice slowed, slurring as the drug took effect.

By Shaitan, not yet!

19

Leaping to his feet, the Necromancer shoved Dotty forward, sending her sprawling across the floor. At her bleat of surprise, the diabloman lifted his heavy head and blinked.

"Hmpf," he said. His eyes fell closed.

"Summon your demon, lord," urged the Necromancer. "Dotty's not much I know, but surely it is always hungry?"

"True . . . enough." Nyzarl spoke the creature's name in a slow halting mumble.

When the final syllable was out and green fog billowed across the floor, the Necromancer almost fainted with relief. But this was only the first step. Far greater danger lay ahead. Taloned hands grasped the sides of the mist and *pulled*. The demon lurched out into existence, impossibly alien.

"Take her," the diabloman choked. "Take . . ." He stared at his hand in puzzlement, his heavy brows drawn together. "Wha'? . . . Mmpf . . ." Spittle ran down his chin.

The little slave girl made a noise like a frightened kitten, but the Technomage tore off her veil and stared, eyes narrowed with interest.

This was it. The Necromancer drew what Dark Magick he retained about him like a tattered cloak. "Xotclic."

The hideous head swung toward him, then away to focus on the prone figure of the diabloman. A hissing grunt that conveyed both comprehension and bone-deep satisfaction. The demon advanced on the bed, claws sinking deep into the pile of the rugs.

"N-n-no," gurgled Nyzarl, and fell silent, his pupils shrinking to pinpricks of horror.

"*Xotclic,*" said the Necromancer sharply. "Wait. I have something better to offer."

The demon's mouth opened—and opened, and opened—revealing a forked tongue and most of the mottled tract of its gullet. When it roared its displeasure, the building shuddered, as if all its fundamental molecules had been rearranged. For all the Necromancer knew, they had.

The moment the horny plates shut with a snap, he said, "Remember? I said we'd bargain."

Xotclic swung its tail, embedding the barbs in the fleshy part of the diabloman's thigh. He didn't move, though he blinked frantically. Crossing its legs at the ankles, the demon leaned a bony elbow in the small of Nyzarl's back, leaned against the bed and tilted its head. "Ss?"

The Necromancer almost smiled. The thing had nerve, he'd give it that. A worthy foe. "I propose," he said, "a partnership—of equals."

One last throw of the dice. Delving deep, he scraped up every vestige of the power he'd been hoarding, the death throes of the apothecary, Hantan's final scream, even the old flower seller. Shit, this used to be so easy! Shaking with effort, he stretched out a spectral hand to the slave, wrapped his fingers around a couple of ribs and squeezed, ever so gently. In the old days, he would have thrust bone and muscle aside to grip her heart, but now, godsdammit, he hadn't the strength.

Immediately, she clutched her chest, her face turning a horrible putty color.

Easy. Easy now. Slowly, the Necromancer drew her forward, step by stumbling step, until her forehead was pressed against the demon's leathery sunken chest. Sweat popping on his brow, he released his hold, even managing a thin calm smile.

Casually, Xotclic slung one of its arms around the girl's neck and snapped it. Her body slipped to the floor to drape over one clawed foot.

"Your True Name," said the Necromancer hoarsely. "Give it to me and I will give you mine."

Silence.

By Shaitan, what the fuck was it thinking? Did it think at all? He'd gambled everything on its intelligence.

Peripherally, he was aware of the Technomage at his elbow, muttering under her breath as a brush whisked across parchment. He was seized by an insane desire to laugh, but he forced it back. "Well?" he demanded. "You'll be free in this world. Masterless."

Ah, now he had its full attention. The huge dark orbs were like liquid, incongruously beautiful in that repulsive visage. Something else swam behind its face, an echo of someone he'd once known, once desired.

Resolutely, he continued, "I'll give you more than you've ever dreamed—more power, more Magick, more lives."

Xotclic retrieved its tail and blood welled from the deep gouge in Nyzarl's thigh. The Necromancer winced. "And more deaths, but not that one."

Tail lashing, a grating rumble issued from the demon's chest. Its maw opened. "You can have his soul," said the Necromancer hastily, "or whatever passes for it. But I need his body."

The demon slouched around to the head of the table and lifted Nyzarl's chin with a taloned finger. For a long moment, it stared down into the diabloman's terrified eyes.

The Necromancer snatched up a towel and wadded it against the wound. Shit, it was going to hurt like Shaitan's bitch, but hell, it would be worth it. "The drug I gave him won't last much longer," he lied. "Decide."

Xotclic patted Nyzarl's cheek. "Ss," it said.

"You'll do it?"

"Ss."

Oh, thank Shaitan. He had to close his eyes for a second to regain his equilibrium.

"Ss?"

He blinked, only to see the demon staring at him, its head twisted at an impossible angle over one spiky shoulder.

"Ah yes," he said. "How to go about it? I thought . . . we might exchange one syllable at a time, very slowly. We don't want any unpleasantness, do we?"

"Ss."

Was it laughing at him? He couldn't be sure. Abruptly, he rounded on the Technomage. "Get the equipment. Check it all again." He dug his fingers into her shoulder, watching sanity waver back and forth in her faded eyes. "Everything has to be perfect, Dotty. Do you understand me? Because if anything goes wrong, I'll give you to Xotclic, I swear."

She made another bleating noise, threw the demon a last terrified glance over her shoulder and scuttled off.

"Right," said the Necromancer. Crossing the room in defiance of every human instinct was one of the hardest things he'd ever done. His hindbrain writhed, shrieking at him to *run, run*! Carefully avoiding the spikes, he laid a trembling hand on one scaly forearm and very nearly snatched it back. Shaitan! How could something be oily and freezing at the same time?

He bared his teeth in a rictus of a smile. "Let us begin. As a gesture of good faith, I will start, but we will finish together, or not at all."

"Ss."

Show me how you ride, the swordmaster had said. At Lonefell, she'd ridden bareback in the summer, up in the high pasture where no one could see. Saddles she knew nothing about.

He secured a mount for her, an elderly broad-backed mare with a sleepy disposition and an accommodating nature, boosted "Meck" into the saddle and walked him around and around the moving caravan in ever-decreasing circles. Finally, he tied the mare to Abad's van. The dog favored her with a toothy grin as he leaped up to scramble over the backboard, but all Walker said was, "You'll do." Then he'd cantered off for his shift as advance scout.

There'd been so little expression on his face, he might have been sculpted out of bronze. His hunter's face, hooded eyes cold and calm. Mehcredi wondered . . . Gods, how she wondered.

She frowned, thinking back. It's not what he says, she told herself firmly, it's what he *does*. That's the only coin you understand.

Sister save her, all the pain he kept locked up inside him—only someone as unperceptive as she could have missed it. On the other hand . . . She shifted in the saddle as the mare plodded on. To be the only survivor of the massacre of all your kin—that was truly tragic. She thought of his deep voice saying softly in the dark, *Do you know what demons look like?* and shivered in the sun.

Awful beyond her comprehension. Her fingers tightened on the reins. Poor Walker. No, not Walker. What was it? A long liquid run of sound, beautiful in its own way, but incomprehensible. Welderyn . . . something, something. She must ask him to repeat it, slowly.

At Lonefell, gossip had run on greased wheels. People adored it, she knew that much about human nature. If even a single person knew Walker was the last of his people and why, it would be nigh on impossible to keep such a deliciously dreadful story secret.

But she'd heard not the slightest hint of it.

This private, quiet man had trusted her with something no one else knew, a torment wrenched from deep within his soul. Sister in the sky, *her*, Mehcredi of Lonefell. A small sweet glow warmed her insides. She'd never had a secret to keep before, never had a . . . a . . . What *was* Walker, precisely? A friend? A teacher?

Not a lover though.

Scowling, she fingered her lower lip, remembering, and the gods-bedamned feelings started up again. She wasn't sure precisely how to describe them, but they made her so restless if she hadn't been perched so high above the ground she would have had to wriggle to relieve her frustration.

But she had only to close her eyes to feel his weight pressing her into the bed of feathergrass, their bodies sealed together from neck to knee. She knew he was made of muscle—gods, she'd watched him perform the *nea-kata* shirtless every morning for weeks—but she wasn't used to feeling so weak and small, so very feminine. Not only was he damned heavy, but oddly enough, she liked it. In fact, she'd liked it so much, she'd arched up against him, frantic for more. And when it was granted to her and skin met skin, she'd thought she might die of wanting whatever came next.

Despite herself, a disgustingly kittenish sound escaped her lips. One of the mare's ears flicked back, but her steady gait didn't falter. Somewhat heartened by this tacit show of support, Mehcredi gripped the saddle and ground herself down, grumbling under her breath.

It didn't help. In fact, it made her breath hitch and the liquid burn between her thighs intensify. Surreptitiously, she pressed one arm over her breasts. Imprisoned within the confines of the breastband, they tingled with the strangest sort of ache, with the physical memory of his lips and tongue moving over her skin, while his weight held her helpless, so strong, so hot—gods, so *knowing.*

Her secret flesh had flowered for him, slick with her body's honey, yearning so desperately that her thighs had fallen open and she'd reached for what instinct told her she needed.

The scowl deepened.

Shit, she'd ruined it. Brought all the lovely, breathless, soaring flight of mutual desire crashing to the ground. Stupid, *stupid.*

But nonetheless, she, Mehcredi, had aroused him, given him pleasure, the evidence of it hot and rigid in her hand. Gods, he'd been thick, much thicker than she expected. Longer too. The memory made her insides squirm like a puppy being petted.

She hadn't known. How could she? All she'd seen of Nedward and his scullery maid were the pale hairy moons of his bum bunching as he drove upward again and again and the girl's plump white calves wrapped around his waist. When he'd come, he'd just frozen with a final grunt and squeezed the poor girl even harder. The moment it was over, he'd laced up his trews, slapped the girl on the flank and walked back to the forge whistling. The maid had stood staring after him, her face red and her lip quivering

I do want you, Walker said, his voice flat and cold. *Just not enough to make you a convenience.*

Unlike Nedward, let alone Taso.

Mehcredi sagged in the saddle and all the minor twinges associated with the unaccustomed exercise coalesced into a clamoring whole-body ache. The reminiscent tingles, the physical memory of joy, everything dissolved, leaving her miserable and heavy. Exactly like last night, except that now she was baking in the desert sun and covered in dust.

"Hey, Meck?"

She glowered at Abad. The waggoner swayed easily with the lurching movement of the van, reins held negligently in one big brown hand. "How ye doin' over there, lad?"

How was she doing? "Like shit," she muttered. "Thanks for askin'."

Abad reached under the wooden seat and fished out a stoppered bottle. "Thirsty?"

Without waiting for a reply, he tossed it with a flip of the wrist. Mehcredi had to bend and twist to snag it out of the air, nearly unseating herself in the process. Her heart thundering, she cursed Abad even as she wrenched the cork out and tilted it to her lips. Warm, flat water, nectar of the gods. Swishing it around her mouth, she spat to one side, then drank deep.

"Needed that." She tossed the bottle back and the waggoner caught it neatly enough.

Abad grinned, brown eyes twinkling. "How's your ass?"

She glanced sharply at his face, but she couldn't see anything to alarm her. "Fuckin' hurts," she said cautiously.

"Ye can come up here if ye like."

Mehcredi studied him from under her lashes. The waggoner had a pleasant enough face, swarthy like most of his countrymen. Under the head cloth, dark greasy curls tumbled around his ears. Looked safe enough—unless he was the sort who liked boys. Mentally, she contrasted his expression with that of the man with the gold teeth. What was his name? That's right, Letafa.

To her, Abad's face appeared a perfect blank, though his hands were relaxed on the reins. She wanted to hiss with frustration. Why the invitation? Perhaps he was bored? Only one way to find out.

"Are you bored?"

He shrugged. "Could use the company, but please yerself, lad."

Lad? She grinned to herself. He couldn't be much older than she was.

"All right." Urging her mount a little closer, she reached out, grabbed the side of the van and freed one foot from its stirrup. A graceless heave, an undignified scramble and she arrived in a cursing sweaty heap on the seat next to the waggoner. The mare rolled an eye at her as if to say good riddance.

Ow, ow, *ow*. Mehcredi eased from one buttock to the other. The hard wooden seat was no softer than the godsbedamned saddle.

"Not much of a rider, are ye?" said Abad mildly.

A grunt sufficed for answer. There were definitely advantages to being male.

"So," said the waggoner, elaborately casual. "Wajar any good with that fancy sword?"

Her shiver was entirely genuine. "The best I've ever seen."

"What about you?"

"He's teaching me." She shrugged. "I can hold my own." A wry grin tugged at her lips. Of course she could, against a man like Abad at any rate. Walker could slice her to ribbons with his eyes closed. But this line of questioning was dangerous. Hastily, she said, "Are the beasts yours? Do they have names?"

It seemed they were and they did. Nothing loath, the waggoner described each plodding beast, describing its every virtue, vice and ailment in detail. After a couple of miles, Mehcredi relaxed enough to rub the ache out of her thighs. She'd met Abad's sort before—a man who loved the sound of his own voice, thanks be to the Sister. All she need do was insert the occasional murmur of interest and he rambled on and on, the wheels creaking as the sandy track unrolled beneath them.

She'd never be the same, she knew that. Not after last night. Blankly, she gazed out at the sparse grayish vegetation. For the first time in her life, she'd seen *inside* another person, seen a soul laid bare—Walker's agony and guilt, his driving need to avenge his people in blood and pain. Then he'd shown her his pleasure and he'd shown her his Magick.

Her breath caught. How could it have slipped her mind? With his beauty and his tragedy, the swordmaster had driven every other thought clean out of her head. A woman had risen up out of the fire, disembodied, and spoken from the Sister knew how far away. Caracole it seemed like.

And Walker, Walker had—Abruptly, the stunted trees blurred into a long gray splodge. He'd used his Magick to ensure her comfort. Such beautiful Magick too, of green and growing things. It had seemed to her the trees bent to his will with joyous abandon, the feathergrass swishing around his boots like an affectionate cat.

She'd been privileged to see it. Her hand stole to the Mark on her breast. Perhaps to wear it too. And yet—she braced her feet against the floor as the van lurched in and out of a pothole—Walker was a man of such stark contrasts. His Magick bloomed with life and light, but his soul was shadowed in death and darkness.

"Is he a good master then?"

She started. "What?"

"Wajar," said Abad. "Looks like a hard man."

"I'd die for him," growled Mehcredi, realizing with a kind of dull shock that it was true.

By the time she recovered herself, the waggoner was speaking of his two wives, both of whom he clearly adored. He hadn't meant to offer for the second, but he'd been so taken with her sweet eyes and lissome form, he couldn't help himself. A good vanbeast the dowry had cost him, but the little sweetheart was worth twice that. When he smiled, in a sheepish kind of way, he was very nearly good-looking.

"They do well together, my girls," he said fondly. "No fighting. And next year, there'll be two more mouths to feed." Though he reddened, his chest swelled with pride. "Don't like to do such a long trip, but Dinari's a good master and, well, extra creds are always handy when a man's got a family."

Well, well, love and honor did exist in Trinitaria. Who'd have thought it? Mehcredi cast a sidelong look at her companion as he rummaged about under the seat to produce a shabby box, which he opened to reveal a couple of rather squashed manda fruits and several greasy packets.

"Here, lad."

When she investigated, suddenly ravenous, the packet proved to contain a cold savory noodle cake. "Thanks," she mumbled, her mouth full.

As if by Magick, a cold nose materialized in the vicinity of her neck, the dog peering over her shoulder, his panting breath hot against her ear. Mehcredi chuckled. "Scrounger."

Her heart lifted a little as she broke off a piece of cake for him. At least she still had one friend.

You're bluffing, Walker had said in a voice like ice.

And she had been—at first. But he'd made her so mad she couldn't see straight, let alone control the stupidity that fell out of her mouth. She'd had all night to think about it too, to flay herself with useless regrets and recriminations. Godsdammit, she couldn't have made a bigger mess of everything if she'd tried! It had taken her hours to drop off, her mind a seething mass of confusion and wonder. Her sleep had been restless, her dreams nightmares of frustration in which she was running and running, desperate to get . . . somewhere, but when she'd looked down she discovered her feet were rooted to the ground, brambles curling around her ankles.

Walker had shaken her awake with a firm hand on her shoulder, not long after dawn. She'd opened her mouth, ready to say she hadn't meant it, would never—But then she'd seen his face and the words had died stillborn. Not only his hunter's face, but colder than winter iron in Lonefell. She hadn't seen that expression since the night he'd caught her in the Melting Pot and she'd known with absolute certainty he was going to kill her.

Bastard. Double-dyed bastard.

A harsh honk interrupted her thoughts. Three large birds passed over their heads and disappeared toward the distant hills. Abad leaned over the side of the van and spat. Then he made the sign of the Three. "Corpsebirds," he growled. "Hate 'em." From farther around the bend came the bellow of a vanbeast.

Abad really did have a nice face, even frowning as he was now. He gave her hope. There'd be decent men in Trimegrace, there must be. Perhaps a merchant or a well-to-do tradesman, young and clean, with eyes as dark as Concordian chocolat and high cheekbones and long black hair, as soft and straight as rain . . .

The sigh came all the way from her boots. Who did she think she was fool—?

Hoofs thundered from up ahead, approaching at breakneck speed. Men shouted. What the—

Mehcredi leaped onto the seat and rose to her tiptoes.

Walker pulled his horse up on its haunches at the lead van. He leaned over the animal's shoulder, speaking urgently to Dinari, gesturing down the track, the Janizar's sword flashing in the sun.

"Fuck," groaned Abad. "Knew it. Fuckin' bandits, mark my words."

Walker wheeled his horse and raced off again, back the way he'd come, followed by another three men. More dashed toward the horse string on foot.

"Shit! No, Meck, don't—" The waggoner stretched out a hand, but too late.

Mehcredi landed on the startled mare all anyhow, but she managed to settle her feet in the stirrups before kicking her mount into a jarring trot. Bouncing like a sack of taters, blade naked in her hand, she set off in dogged pursuit of the man she knew best in the whole world, the man who *was* her whole world.

20

By the time they hit the bend in the trail, the horse had slowed to a stolid walk and no amount of kicking and swearing would induce her to speed up. Then the wind changed, bringing with it a heavy abattoir reek. The mare snorted, reared and tipped Mehcredi off into the dust.

Painfully, she rose on one elbow, feeling as if a mountain had leaned down and thumped her between the shoulder blades. She blinked, horror overwhelming the aches.

The derelicts had once been caravans, drawn up in a defensive circle. For the rest, it was a butcher's shop from a nightmare. Bodies lay scattered about, limbs contorted, clouds of bitemes buzzing over the carnage. A few vanbeasts struggled feebly in the traces, lowing with distress. Not more than ten feet away, a man stared at her with black sunken eyes, his mouth stretched wide in a rictus of terror, his chest a gaping ruin, black with clotted blood and white with shards of bone. He could have been any age from twenty to sixty, but it was no longer possible to judge.

One hand clapped over her nose and mouth, Mehcredi lurched to her feet. *Walker.* She could see him quite clearly about fifty yards off, in grim conversation with the van master, but for some reason, she knew she wouldn't last another second without feeling the warmth of his flesh under her fingers. Touching him was imperative.

From her left, something called, a low harsh bray. She whirled. Five hulking birds with bare leathery necks and cruel beaks sat in an untidy row on a branch, glaring at her. When one of them shifted its perch, a strip of something pale flapped, tangled in a black claw. Corpsebirds.

Mehcredi's stomach rebelled. Stumbling behind a boulder, she sank to her knees and was briefly and violently ill.

A firm hand clasped the back of her neck. "Breathe," said Walker. "That's it." Sliding his arm around her waist, he hoisted her to her feet. Gratefully, she leaned into his shoulder. "Better?"

When she nodded, gulping, he handed her his water bottle.

"Idiot," he said without heat. "You should have stayed put. You haven't seen death at close quarters before, have you?"

"Yes, but only . . . properly laid out."

His palm traveled up and down her spine in a comforting, matter-of-fact caress. "Battlefields are ugly." His brows contracted, the lines around his mouth deepening. "There's no sign of the enemy. They all died the same way, as if their chests just . . . exploded."

She could only shake her head, wordless, and press closer.

"C'mon, Meck, lad." Someone slapped her on the back. Abad, looking pale and grim. "Don't be such a girl." But he lifted a fold of his head cloth to his nose.

Walker released her immediately. "Go back," he said. "We'll take care of this." He glanced around, his lips thin. "There's something . . ." He shook his head.

It took the rest of the day to collect the bodies and make a pyre. Dinari ordered the caravan to pull off onto the stony plain, half a mile distant, well upwind of the greasy smoke.

Mehcredi helped Cook prepare the evening meal, but no one ate much and conversation around the campfires was subdued. Lying on another of Walker's feathergrass mats in the lee of a big boulder with the dog's head draped over her ankles, she gazed up at the silvery blue disk of the Sister hanging low in the arch of the sky. The Brother, three times Her size, flared an angry crimson, dominating the zenith. Far off, direwolves howled on the hunt, desolate and desperate, and the wind fingered her hair, a sly cool touch. The small hairs rose all over her body.

Scrounger sat up, a growl rumbling in his throat. Gradually, she became aware of another noise, threaded through the wind, a low rhythmic chanting near as desolate as the direwolf song. Through the double-edged shadows, she made out a dark form among the boulders a little way distant.

With a huff of regret, she abandoned her warm cocoon of blankets and walked slowly toward him, pebbles rattling beneath her feet. Walker didn't move that she could see, but the chanting stopped.

"What are you doing?"

For a moment, she thought he wasn't going to answer, then he turned his head, his hair shifting in a dark curtain across his shoulders. A long pause, as if he searched for something in her face. "It's called the Song of Life."

"For the dead?"

He shrugged. "There's no one else to sing it for them."

Anger swept over her, springing out of ambush from the gods knew where. "Not much bloody use is it?" Her voice rose. "They're still dead. Torn to pieces, like so much meat. Gods, left for the corpsebirds and the direwolves."

A strong arm drew her into his warmth. "Sshh." He stroked her hair. "What do you believe, Mehcredi?"

"Believe? About what?"

"About life and death and why we're here." She caught the flash of a thin smile. "The big questions."

"I don't—I never thought about it." Feeling calmer, she settled more comfortably against him. *I believe in you,* she thought and congratulated herself for having the wits to keep her stupid mouth shut. "What about you?"

"The Shar believe in the great cycle—birth, life, death, rebirth. The gift of our Ancestors." Hard fingers lifted her chin, directing her gaze to the stars. "Look up. We're part of that, of everything that is."

Mehcredi snorted. "Sure. No more than bitemes matter to him." She jerked her head toward the dog, her eyes stinging with tears. "In the end, all we are is meat. Blood and bone and muscle and guts, like—" She choked.

Taking her shoulders, Walker turned her to face him. "True enough." He cradled her cheek in one palm, his thumb brushing to and fro across her cheekbone. "But there's more. Yes, we are of the earth and like our Ancestors we return to the earth, but, Mehcredi—"

Utterly intent, he gazed deep into her eyes. "You are made of starstuff, right down to the blood and bone and muscle and guts. So am I, so are we all. Just as pure, just as beautiful, just as real." She thought his smile was tender as well as wry, and rather wistfully, hoped she'd got it right. "The choice is yours. Live your life in the mud or shine like the stars."

Slowly, giving him time to pull away, she lifted a shaking hand and slid her fingers into the silk of his hair. It whispered over her knuckles, cool as water, while his skull curved warm and hard against her palm. He didn't move. "What did you choose?" she whispered.

His short laugh stirred the curls on her forehead. "I don't know. I may never know, not 'til I join my Ancestors."

"But isn't vengeance—" She broke off, conscious that every muscle in his body had gone rigid.

After a long tense moment, he relaxed and she let out a cautious breath.

"I cannot allow them to live," he said, every word clipped.

"Yes," she said shakily. "Yes, I can see that."

He set her at arm's length. "Go on, go back to the fire. You need your sleep."

Rubbing the small of her back, she said, "I ache all over."

The ghost of a smile. "I imagine you do."

"Walker?"

"Yes?"

"Say your name for me again, your real name."

She heard him take a deep breath. "Welderyn'd'haraleen't'Lenqui-squilirian."

"It's awfully long. Pretty though," she added hastily.

"Welderyn will do," he said gravely.

"Mmm. Welderyn?"

"Yes?"

"Can we stay like this a little longer? It's nice, just being held." She met his eyes. "That's all, I swear." Her heart thumped hard. Once, twice.

At last he nodded and held out his arms. With a sob of relief, she went into them and they closed hard around her.

❧

The Necromancer cracked his shin on a footstool. Swearing, he reeled back and immediately tripped over his own big feet. Or, to be more accurate, Nerajyb Nyzarl's feet. He wiggled the diabloman's bare toes, regarding their hairiness with fascination.

His head ached as if a troop of Shaitan's imps danced a victory jig inside it, the wound in the back of his thigh throbbed and he'd discovered that Nyzarl had a bad knee and a back molar that needed attention, but these were truly minor inconveniences.

Directly behind him, Dotty emitted a shrill giggle. Turning carefully, he stretched out an arm that felt impossibly long and grabbed a towel from the massage table. Slinging it around his hips, he glared at her. "Shut your—" he growled, and stopped, startled.

His own voice echoed in his ears, no longer the querulous tones of an old man, but virile and mature. He smiled. "Pack the equipment away," he went on, enjoying every commanding syllable. "We may need it again. Break anything and I'll flog you myself."

"Of course," she said huffily, her hands deft with the complex assemblage of wires and glass and metal.

On the other side of the room, Xotclic watched with interest, the limp body of a slave slung over each shoulder, the stable boy dangling by his ankle from one clawed hand. The Technomage had been wrong, the energy of two deaths hadn't been enough. If it hadn't been for the demon . . .

He'd been helpless, suspended in agony between his own body and that of the diabloman, oblivion beckoning with an icy finger. If he could have screamed, babbled, begged—*anything*—he would have done so. But he was nowhere, nothing, a tiny frantic mote, shrieking its terror into the suffocating never-ending dark. He thought he heard a sly laugh, pitiless and deeply amused, the flap of leathery wings.

Dotty had panicked, damn the useless bitch. As he'd watched in horror, trapped in the reservoir she'd made, the intelligence of the Technomage she'd once been faded from her eyes and her lips went loose, her chin quivering. Wringing her hands, she'd bleated, "Oh no, oh no. Oh, what shall we do? Do, do, do." Then she'd started to giggle, over and over, like a kettle going on and off the boil.

But the demon had lurched out the door, returning a few minutes later with the struggling form of a husky stable boy. A clawed foot spearing the lad's chest, it held him down until Dotty snapped out of her hysteria and connected him to the apparatus. In the nick of time too.

The Necromancer released a quiet breath as he watched the Technomage place the equipment in its padded box, her touch as tender as a mother's.

In the demon's place, he would have taken the opportunity to end the partnership, there and then, without a second thought. He shot a glance at Xotclic from under thick stubby lashes—delightful to see everything without the need for spectacles. As far as he could ascertain, the demon was entertained. Perhaps he constituted an amusement, or the creature had other plans . . . Well, he would be on his guard. Xotclic was but a tool, after all.

He flicked a glance at the husk of his abandoned body, drooling silently into the rug, and his guts heaved. "I'm going to bathe," he announced. Nyzarl's personal hygiene left a great deal to be desired. And he needed to dress the thigh wound before it could fester.

At the door, he forced himself to take a last look at the plump bespectacled body with its mild face and silly fringe of fluffy white hair. There lay everything he'd been, a feeble chrysalis for the primal force he was now. The Queen's Knowledge, librarian, archivist and scholar—*old man*—was truly dead.

"They're all yours," he said to Xotclic, "except her." He indicated Dotty, still fluttering over her box. "If I wish you to hurt her, I'll say so, all right?"

"Ss." Dropping the three corpses in the corner, the demon stalked over to the body of the erstwhile Queen's Knowledge and sank into an ungainly squat. The Necromancer blinked. Were its legs folding *backward*, and in more than one place? Almost gently, it grasped the slack chin, raising it to peer into the face. Was that what passed for a smile on its lipless mouth?

Despite himself, despite all the logic of his fine intellect, bile rose in the Necromancer's throat. Gods save him, the thing on the floor might be no more than an envelope, but he couldn't watch. "If it's going to be . . . messy," he said, "I'd prefer you went outside."

Xotclic reared back and hissed, the forked tongue flickering. Involuntarily, Nyzarl's body took a smart step backward. Oh, so the man had been a coward into the bargain. Grimly, the Necromancer forced himself to meet the creature's eyes. "Very well," he said evenly. "Do as you please. You've earned it, after all."

"Ss."

"We will speak tomorrow."

"Ss."

"Dotty, get back to your quarters." The Necromancer watched her scuttle off. Without a backward look, he set off down the passage, trailing one hand along the wall for balance.

Determinedly, he promised himself he was going to enjoy exploring every inch of this wondrous new flesh, especially the heavy genitals swinging between his thick thighs. By Shaitan, the man was hung like a bull. He'd think of all the pleasures age had wrested from him—youth and strength, and, oh gods, the welcome spur of lust. Girls, boys, separately, together. Fuck, yes! He licked his lips, feeling the responsive ripple in his groin. Delightful.

And tomorrow, he'd tour the estate, speak with Nyzarl's—*his*—steward. He wouldn't mind betting the fellow had been bleeding the place dry, because that's what he'd do in the steward's place. He growled, just for the pleasure of hearing the powerful, masculine sound.

A nobleman's house didn't run without staff. He'd have to replace the three—no, four—dead slaves. That was a nuisance, but there was a ramshackle village about a quarter of a mile away, no doubt sprung up to service the estate. He'd make do.

He paused at the entrance to the bathhouse and gazed about with pleasure at the intricate geometric patterns of mirrors interspersed among small blue tiles, the deep marble tub with its soaps and lotions laid out ready. The little slave girl had all in readiness for her master's bath, a hidden furnace keeping the water piping hot.

It wasn't until after he'd sluiced his wound with healall and submerged himself up to the chin that the image he'd been keeping at bay sprang out of some dark recess of his brain: Xotclic the demon hooking a talon into the Necromancer's glasses, removing them as gently as a lover. From behind the faded blue eyes, owlish in their nakedness, Nerajyb Nyzarl's soul screamed without ceasing.

Not long after dawn on the following day, the rutted ribbon of the Spice Trail began to widen. Paving stones appeared and the occasional splash of green by the side of the track. The wind changed and the vanbeasts' shaggy ears swiveled forward. When they picked up the pace, the whole caravan surged forward as one.

From his driver's seat, Abad grinned across at Mehcredi, her aching thighs still clamped around the mare's broad barrel. "They can smell the water."

"Water?" She gazed around. "Where?"

Abad jerked his chin at a misty smudge on the horizon. "Miles off yet, but it's the Son right enough."

"The what?"

"Ye're the strangest lad I ever met." The waggoner wiped the sweat from his brow with a fold of his head cloth. "Don't ye know nothin'?"

She dropped her head. "Didn't have much schoolin'."

"Trimegrace sits where the three rivers meet—the Father, the Son and the Bastard. Not but what I'd call the Bastard a river. It's either a trickle or a flood and always at the wrong season." He chuckled. "Well named."

Mehcredi lapsed into silence, gazing at the first poor farms with their skinny livestock and meager crops. Walker had spoken a total of ten words to her today, possibly less. With his straight black brows drawn together, it wasn't difficult to tell he was preoccupied, and, she suspected, worried. She shot a glance at his straight back, swaying easily to the rhythm of his horse. He was deep in discussion with Dinari. They'd be talking about yesterday—those horrible wounds and the absence of a single bandit corpse. In fact, there was no evidence to show men had been there at all.

Cautiously, she kicked the mare in the ribs, urging the animal forward until she was within earshot.

"You seen anything like it before?" Dinari growled.

"No. You?"

"Fuck, no." The rings on the van master's fingers glinted as he rubbed his chin. "I'd better go to the Janizars the moment we're settled in the city." His thin face grew hard. "Not that anything will be done. Bandits are beneath the Grand Pasha's notice." He grimaced. "Too fuckin' holy, yes?"

But Walker only grunted, dropping back to ride by Mehcredi's side. "What is it, boy?"

She stared at her horse's ears. "It wasn't bandits, was it?" she said, very low.

"No," he said, equally quietly.

They slowed to a walk. "The evil that Cenda spoke about . . ." She trailed off uncertainly.

"Go on."

She looked at him out of the corner of her eye. "Could you feel um, anything?"

A brow rose. "What makes you think I should?"

At that, she stared. "You're a shaman!"

Walker frowned at her. "Keep your voice down." After a beat, he said, "The *ch'qui* was still . . . distorted. Which means it was powerful."

"Whatever it was."

"Yes." He gathered up the reins. "Dinari will pay me off tonight. I'll get us a decent lodging—with a bathhouse. We'll talk then."

He cantered away.

The bathhouse at the Three Rivers Inn was larger than Walker had expected, with a small cold pool in addition to the two hot tubs. He even took the opportunity to shave, though like all his people, he had so little body hair it was hardly necessary.

As he scraped away with the razor, his thoughts darted about like the tiny silvery fish that lived in the Spring of Shiloh, the ones that no one, not even the most skilled hunter, could catch. Where they came from, no one knew, but he had no difficulty in working out the origins of this unwelcome confusion of mind.

There was Mehcredi the assassin for a start, but she was his own very personal problem.

With a grimace, he returned to the puzzle of the massacre on the road. He'd already heard the crazy rumors flying around the souks—a djinn roaring in on the hot desert wind, death under its dark wings. Looked like Deiter might be right, curse him, though what of his lies about what-might-be? But how could he ignore even the smallest chance of finding a kinswoman? Gods, his head hurt.

Grimly, he stalked over to the nearest bath and sank beneath the steaming water. Out in the stables, by the light of the Sibling Moons, he'd completed not only the twenty-third *nea-kata*, but the twenty-fourth. The little dog his only witness, every movement had been precise, controlled. As close to perfection as the gods permitted a mortal.

He'd reaffirmed his purpose, dwelling unflinchingly on the memory of Nyzarl shouting orders to his demon, torturing himself with visions of the diabloman's heavy-jawed face, glutinous with satisfaction as he surveyed the carnage. Nothing in this life would prevent him from completing the sacred duty the Ancestors had set him, not the old wizard and the nameless evil he feared, nor the assassin with her huge bright eyes and her foolish trust.

And yet . . .

Mehcredi intruded at every turn. Godsdammit all to hell, she had a Magick of her own. One moment his mind would be ticking over as it should, making plans about routes and horses and provisions, the next all he could see was her crestfallen face as he'd left her in their chamber with a bucket of warm water.

"But I'm *filthy*!" she'd wailed.

"I know." He cleared his throat. "But you can't go to the bathhouse. It's men only."

She'd kicked the bucket so hard water slopped over the tiled floor. As she hopped about on one foot, swearing, he hadn't been even remotely tempted to laugh.

At the most inappropriate times, he'd flash onto visions of the things they'd done together, out in the desert dark, the fresh green scent of crushed feathergrass rising around them. He'd been a randy lad once, but that had been a lifetime ago. He had no desire to revisit his adolescence. But oh gods, the piquant contrast between her breasts—the right creamy and un-Marked, topped with a crest like a pale pink summerberry, the smooth flesh of the left proudly bearing the swirling brand of his Magick, the dark lines caging the innocent sweetness of the nipple.

Fuck, his mouth watered every time. He'd even found himself trying to decide which he preferred.

It was asinine.

21

Deliberately, Walker chose a coarse sponge, sat up and scrubbed with vigor. His body was his own to control, as was his mind. A Shar warrior did not buckle under pressure, not even when problems beset him like so many corpsebirds, each squawking for its share of attention.

The door opened to admit a corpulent merchant and his clerk. Walker nodded curtly in response to their greeting and ignored them thereafter.

Welderyn'd'haraleen't'Lenquisquilirian would honor his name. Bestowed by the Elders at the initiation that came with puberty, Shar names were long, involved and descriptive, an integral part of Shar culture. *Name the child, shape the life.*

A short literal translation would be something like Sheltering Branches, though entwined through the lilting syllables was the sense of a great green canopy stretching protective arms across the sky.

Walker allowed himself to slide completely beneath the surface of the water.

The spirit of it, though—that was another matter, and infinitely more complicated. The Ancestors had gifted him with Magick, made him a shaman so he could be the guardian of his people, their shelter and their refuge. And though the Elders had recognized that innate talent in him as a youth, they hadn't known how catastrophically he would fail.

Without warning, his guts cramped and he emerged, gasping, slicking his hair back with both hands.

At his elbow, someone coughed politely. "Room for another?" said the clerk, gesturing at the huge square tub. In the other bath, the fat merchant lolled in solitary splendor, jowls shiny with sweat and water. "I'm finished." Walker glanced up and froze.

Here was Mehcredi's *someone decent*. About thirty, neat dark hair, only the slightest thickening about his waist, clean soft hands, no scars. There was no cruelty, no slyness in the fellow's face, only a dawning embarrassment as another man raked his nakedness up and down.

"It's yours," Walker snarled, water streaming off bronze skin as he rose.

"Uh, right. Thanks," said the clerk, but Walker didn't hear him.

Father's balls, he'd been lounging about taking his ease like some godsbedamned pasha while all she had was a bucket and a washcloth. Worse, she would have finished long since. What was she doing right now? A cold void opened up under his breastbone. Fuck, fuck, *fuck!* Swiftly, he blotted his hair dry, tying it back into a long dripping tail. Then he scrambled into his clothes and took the stairs two at a time.

The room was empty, the covers on the two narrow beds firmly tucked. Her pack lay partly open on one of them.

Whirling, he charged downstairs to the bar. A dozen men glanced up with varying degrees of interest. Shit, no Mehcredi.

"My companion," Walker growled at the barkeep. "The boy. Where is he?"

But the man only shrugged. "Haven't seen 'im."

"Meck, is it?" said another voice.

A tall stooped man in a blue head cloth stood at his elbow.

Walker cleared his throat, subduing the impulse to wrap his fingers around the man's throat and choke the information out of him. "Yes," he said hoarsely. "My apprentice."

"Bright lad," said the tall man, his faded brown eyes lighting up. "No shyness about him at all. We had an interesting chat."

"You did? About what?"

"The palace, the city. He asked excellent questions."

"I bet he did," Walker said sourly.

The other man cocked a brow. "You're training him for the sword?"

"Yes. Where did he go?"

But the man said slowly, "I know boys, used to be a teacher. He's a clever one, your Meck."

The words *could do better* hung in the air. Walker gritted his teeth. "Believe me, I know. *Where did he go?*"

"Oh." A rather wobbly smile. "Only around the corner to the Tygre's Den. He wanted a decent place to eat and it's cheap and clean."

Gods, was she insane? A muttered word of thanks and Walker strode down the street in the direction indicated.

Trimegrace was a beautiful city, the jewel in Trinitaria's crown, with buildings constructed of well-dressed seastone in every shade from purest white to sandy pink, and hanging gardens tumbling luxuriantly from roofs and balconies shaded by fretwork screens. Walker curled his lip. To one desert-bred, such a waste of water was downright obscene. But if it meant the Grand Pasha could gaze down upon his city from the towers of the Tri-Lobed Temple and rest his eyes on greenery, what the hell did it matter if the crops withered in the ground and his people starved?

The Three Rivers Inn was centrally located only two blocks from a popular souk, a clean well-lit area full of dining establishments ranging from outdoor cafes to expensive restaurants. It was one of the reasons he'd chosen it—that and some stupid desire to let her rest in comfort before the rest of it. An *adventure*, she'd said, eyes shining. After the charnel house they'd encountered on the road, he wondered if she still thought it so.

It took him no more than a single sweeping glance to locate his quarry, seated at a small outdoor table under an awning, an ornate brazier on a stand keeping off the night chill. Despite the tinted spectacles and the carefully arranged head cloth, Mehcredi's elegant profile showed in relief, so clean and pure it could have been stamped on a coin. Beneath her chair lounged a small scruffy dog and next to her—

Walker inhaled sharply and his lips drew back in a snarl. What the fuck did she think she was doing? *I'll take care of it myself,* she'd said, but he'd thought she'd try it dressed as a woman. She was going to get herself killed, the stupid little fool.

Because she'd caught herself a three-name, for sure, a perfect little lordling from the rings on his manicured fingers to the silk of his flowing robes with the understated embroidery down the front. Even in this part of the city, the man had to be slumming it, yet he looked— Walker frowned, so ferociously that the waiter who'd been about to approach him veered off to unfold already ironed napkins and refold them into fancy shapes.

The Trinitarian was everything he could have wanted for her, everything he'd promised her if only she'd wait. *Young and strong and clean*. His eyes were a trifle close together and his nose long and thin, but like the clerk, all Walker could see was *ordinary*. A Trinitarian, yes, with all the inherent bastardry of the race, but not a bad man.

Mehcredi leaned back, one arm thrown casually over the back of the spindly chair, those endless legs stretched out before her, a handsome youth on his first visit to the capital. The Trinitarian spoke rapidly, his features animated and intent, while she listened, a faint smile curving her pretty lips.

Walker narrowed his eyes, every instinct clamoring. No matter how innocuous the man seemed, one hunter recognized another. The Trinitarian's gaze flickered from Mehcredi's mouth to the open collar of her shirt, to her thighs in the snug trews. Naturally, the assassin was oblivious. His lips thinning with impatience, the man did it again, his posture a flagrant indication of what he desired.

No reaction.

If Walker hadn't been so furious, he might have laughed at the other man's discomfiture. But the instant the Trinitarian decided a direct approach might succeed where subtlety failed, all the turbulent thoughts coalesced into a flare of pure icy rage. The scene shifted into sharp-edged focus, one of those moments burned so deeply into memory, he knew he'd be able to recall it in every detail on his deathbed—if he lived long enough to have one.

All the essentials crystallized. The assassin bore his Mark, she was his to punish, his to pleasure. Her life belonged to him. Therefore he would not permit her to throw it away for any reason whatsoever, let alone rank stupidity.

He wasn't aware of moving, but when the Trinitarian reached out to place a casual hand on Mehcredi's knee, Walker caught his elbow in a crushing grip. "I wouldn't," he said, and watched the blood drain from the man's face.

"Walker, what the—"

"Shut up, *Meck*."

From under the table, the dog whined, sensing the tension.

"Who—?" spluttered the man. "Who do you think you are?"

"I am Wajar and this"—Walker turned so that his body screened the scene from the other diners—"is *my* boy." From the back, they would appear to be engaged in a friendly conversation. When he dug in with vicious fingers, the man hissed with pain. "Mine, understand?"

The Trinitarian glared. "He's of age." The man had more nerve than he'd given him credit for.

"Meck," said Walker without turning his head. "Whose boy are you?"

A pause and the scrape of a chair, then, "Yours, Wajar." The tremor in her voice filled him with savage delight.

"Do you know who I am?" spluttered the Trinitarian.

"I imagine you're related to someone important." Slowly, Walker released him. "Whereas I am but a one-name. Scandal means nothing to me."

"You wouldn't!"

The swordmaster held his gaze. "Try me."

The Trinitarian's face went the same color as the ashes in a cold brazier.

"As for you . . ." Walker turned to Mehcredi.

What she saw in his face he couldn't be certain, but she rose and took an involuntary step backward, her throat moving as she swallowed. "Don't kill me," she whispered.

"Oh no," said Walker grimly, hustling her off down the street with a merciless grip on her arm. "That would be far too easy."

But because she was Mehcredi, and therefore irrepressible and infuriating, she'd bounced back by the time they reached the chamber in the Three Rivers Inn. "All I wanted was a decent meal," she argued as Walker bolted the door in the dog's hopeful face. "There's nothing wrong with that."

"Really?" Something ugly twisted inside him. "You've got balls, I grant you, but what did you intend to do when he discovered you don't have the cock to go with them?"

She gaped. Even beneath the stain of the blengo juice, he could see the dull red of a flush rise in her cheeks. Her mouth shut with an angry snap. "That's not fair! He was just being nice. He actually lives in the palace, can you believe it? He was telling me all about it. And wait 'til you hear about—"

"I'm sure he was highly entertaining." Walker sat on one of the beds to pull off his boots, his blood buzzing with fright and fury combined. To the seven icy hells with scruples, she'd come within a whisker of discovery and ruination. And all because—he ground his teeth—she wanted someone *decent*. Gods, what would she do next? Who would she choose?

He said, "The man likes boys, *Meck*. He would have taken you there, to the palace."

The angry color receded. "No," she said, her voice thin.

"Yes. To his bed, to *fuck*. Imagine how well that would have gone."

He had to close his eyes for a second. 'Cestors' bones, it didn't bear thinking of. Helpless and raging, unable to reach her, while the Janizars—Oh, gods, gods . . .

Mehcredi tossed her spectacles onto the dresser with a petulant clatter and his eyes snapped open.

"You nearly got yourself killed because you had an itch to scratch," he growled. "That won't happen again." He shrugged out of his robes, his heart hammering. "I told him you were mine and I meant it. Strip."

"What?"

"You heard me." He ripped the shirt off over his head. His pulse pounded hard and heavy between his thighs, his body racing ahead, exulting. "You're about to get exactly what you want. Pleased with yourself?"

Her eyes were huge, the same shade as storm clouds. "But I wasn't going to—" She stopped and started again. "I only said that to make you angry."

"Congratulations," he snarled, reaching out to remove her head cloth with a flip of his wrist. "You succeeded."

"But you don't want me, you said so. Not enough, remember?"

A growl rumbled in his chest. A half step forward and he had her shirt gripped in both fists. A quick wrench, a tearing noise and it ripped straight down the middle. "Fucking breastband." His blade appeared in his hand as if by Magick. "Hold still."

"Walker." She put out a hand. "I changed my mind."

"So have I." Grasping her wrist, he spun her around and slit the laces at the back with a single stroke. The fabric fluttered unheeded to the floor. Dropping the dagger onto one of the narrow beds, he released a long breath of pure relief as he pulled her back into his chest and her breasts filled his palms, warm satiny weight, the blood beating hard just beneath the skin. When his thumbs rasped her nipples, Mehcredi cried out, bucking against him.

Gods, yes! The *ch'qui* surged through his blood with an almost discernable roar, potent as the best brandywine. Exactly as he remembered, but this time . . . this time, he'd be deep inside her when he came. Unable to deny the instinctive desire to thrust, he pressed his cock against her gorgeous ass, eyes sliding shut with the delightful friction.

She rose on tiptoe against him, her head falling back on his shoulder, baring the long lovely line of her throat. Everything male in him roared with triumph. *His!*

Bending his head, Walker buried his nose behind her ear and inhaled deeply. Loosening the laces of her trews, he skimmed a palm over the slight curve of her belly, feeling the nerves flutter in response to his touch, her breathy gasps and sighs.

The trews slipped to her hips, hung for an interminable second and slithered down to pool at her boots. His fingertips brushed a silky tuft of hair, his smallest finger tracing the tender crease where hip met thigh. Gods, he had to see!

In a single smooth movement, he swung her up into his arms, ignoring the yelp of surprise. Mehcredi the assassin was hardly a lightweight, but at this moment, he could have carried her against his heart from one end of the Spice Trail to the other.

Two steps and he had her on one of the beds, tugging off her boots with ruthless dispatch, ridding her of the trews. He thought she might be speaking, but the words were a meaningless jumble on the periphery of his consciousness. He couldn't take his eyes from the juncture of her thighs, the sweet cleft bisecting a plump little mound.

Nearly bare, no more than the thinnest silkiest covering of fine blond hair. 'Cestors save him. He couldn't breathe.

Her eyes wide and smoky, Mehcredi pressed her thighs together. She was blushing, so fiercely that the rosy color began on the pale silky skin of her breasts and extended upward, to disappear under the brown of blengo juice. Suddenly, Walker loathed that stain, and the necessity for it. He wanted his assassin as the gods intended, all long strong limbs and cool blond beauty.

"What?" he rasped. "What did you say?"

"Your hair," she whispered, folding her arms across her breasts. "Untie your hair."

Even a single word required concentration. "Wait." Kicking off his boots, he unlaced his trews and let them drop.

Mehcredi made a noise like a surprised kitten, but Walker gave her no time to stare, descending on her like a storm front, grabbing her wrists and pressing them into the pillow.

Skin against skin, all the way from thigh to shoulder. Mind-numbing, cock-searing sizzle. The breath punched out of her in a gusty rush and she undulated beneath him, all woman. "*Oh,*" she whispered. Her lashes fluttered. "That's—You feel—Oh, gods."

It was difficult, but Walker forced himself to loosen his grip. Then he pulled the tie from his hair and shook his head. When he bent to nuzzle the pit of her throat, a curtain of sable silk spilled onto her shoulder and slithered over her breast. Another of those small shocked noises and she turned her head, her lips brushing his ear in a shy caress. Fingertips skated gingerly across his shoulder blade.

Mine.

He slid a hand under her neck, where the fine hairs were soft and life pulsed warm beneath the skin. So fragile for all her strength. A quick twist, that was all it would take to end her. His guts clenched. No more intrusive questions, no more foolish trust and big eyes, that quicksilver intelligence gone forever, condemning him to the dark.

Never.

Fitting his lips to hers, Walker set himself to seduce her with all the ruthless skill of which he was capable. Her lips, at first cool and smooth beneath his, warmed and grew pliant. When they parted on a sigh, he slipped inside, caressing her tongue with his, not coaxing or asking permission, but demanding. Mehcredi quivered. With a little moan, she dug her fingers into his skin, her hips rising against his. The kiss became deeper, wetter, harder. Nothing existed save the woman beneath him—and the green sapling strength of the *ch'qui* filling his balls and cock, the pressure and scalding heat driving him out of his mind.

He tore himself away to lick a trail down the side of her neck, tasting blengo juice and hot skin. But when he reached her breast, the taste changed—pure Mehcredi, satin smooth and hot cream, flavored with the dark spice of the Mark. A kind of purr-growl vibrating deep in his chest, Walker stroked her distended nipple with his tongue. Sex and Magick exploded in his mouth, sweet and fiery as summerberries soaked in raw spirits.

Mehcredi didn't scream as he'd half expected. Instead, she choked and went rigid, her fingers spearing into his hair and gripping hard. Ignoring the pain in his scalp, Walker redoubled his efforts, licking all around the crinkled velvet of her areola before returning to suckle her deep, compressing nerve-rich flesh between his tongue and hard palate. *Sweet,* something babbled in his head. *Gods, so sweet.*

He nudged her legs apart with his knee and without preamble, skimmed eager fingers over her cleft. *Yes, godsdammit, yes!* She was flowering for him, plump with desire, her delicate folds slick and hot, open as a velvety, full-bloom rose. His cock leaped, ravening.

When he strummed the prominent bump of her clitoris with his thumb, she keened with pleasure, her head thrashing on the pillow. Walker inserted the tip of one finger into the tight sucking entrance of her body and rotated it, very gently. With a last regretful lick, he lifted his head from the temptingly ripe gleam of a wet nipple.

"Tell me you still want this." Was that his voice, so guttural it was barely human?

Mehcredi's laugh came out more like a sob. "What do you think?" Her fingers trembled as she reached up to tuck a lock of hair behind his ear. She swallowed hard. "Don't stop."

"I won't."

Utterly shameless, she squirmed, her thighs falling open beautifully as she bore down, trying to impale herself on his finger. Such beautiful strength, like a slippery velvet vise. *Fuck.* He'd never been so hard in his life, so engorged with desire the tender skin of his cock felt like it might split, his balls tense and ripe, drawn up hard into his body.

His brain had degenerated to a lusty soup where an errant thought whimpered for his attention. *Irrevocable,* it wailed. *Never the same. Never again.*

'Cestors' bones, who the fuck cared? Walker bit the inside of his cheek, using the small pain to anchor himself. "Ready?"

"I don't know." Her eyes turned nearly as dark as his. "*Nngh!* Sister have mercy, do that again."

Instead, he settled into the cradle of her pelvis, the broad head of his cock nosing against wet satin. Eyes rolling back in his head with the effort of restraint, he flexed his hips. Probing.

Her knee rose against his hip and he hooked an arm beneath it, splaying her open, leaning forward, covering her with his body, making her prey.

"Walker?"

Ah, *there*. "Mmm. What?"

"Will it hurt?"

22

Walker froze above her, his face stark, and once again, she was trapped by his compelling hunter's gaze. She hadn't thought it possible to feel so many sensations at once, so much emotion. Every nerve under her skin sang in concert, greedy lip-smacking hallelujahs. She felt feverish, dizzy with it all, a feast for her starved senses. Her mouth watered with the need to bite off huge chunks of the physical gorgeousness of it—of him. Then she'd be able to keep this forever, pull it out of memory to roll around her mouth and savor at leisure.

Sweet Sister, just the press of his weight was amazing. She'd had no idea—how could she?—that a man's body would be so heavy, so incredibly solid, all bone and muscle clad in satiny resilient bronze. Godsdammit, she felt *small*.

Nor had she realized sex was so . . . wet . . . so hot. So splendidly wicked. The head of his cock shifted against her most secret flesh, a smooth dense presence. Every insistent slide, each slippery rub, forced a gasp out of her, sent vicious tingles surging through her body, not just in her loins, but up her spine, into her belly and over her ribs. Compressed by the wall of his chest, her breasts ached, already desperate for his fingers, his mouth.

Panting, her pulse juddering in her ears, she ran her fingers through the cool silk of his hair, over and over, as she'd always longed to do, watching him think. He was searching for words, she could tell. And wasn't that flash of insight a complete surprise?

At last, he said, "Hurt? I don't know, but I imagine so." Every muscle in his body had turned to stone, the breadth of his shoulders setting like a girder, but his head dropped so the curtain of hair concealed his face. "Think quick, Mehcredi." He sounded like he'd gargled with gravel. "My willpower is . . . limited."

Her laugh bounced off the walls. Still smiling, she reared up to press her mouth to his and he hissed as cock flesh slid through her slippery folds. How the touch of him could . . . well, *sear* like that when she was so wet remained a mystery.

"Don't care," she said, fizzing with joy. "Hard and fast, Walker." Grinning, she nipped his lower lip. "Do it."

Walker's hips drew back, buttocks flexing. She'd expected another of those deep sensual growls, but instead, he surged forward with a pained groan, driving what felt like a tree trunk partway into her body.

The breath left her in a strangled shriek.

Walker froze, bracing himself over her on his forearms, shuddering. "Mehcredi? Love?"

"Shit," she said through gritted teeth. "Stings like a bitch. *Move.*" Wrapping her long legs around his hips, she dug in with her heels.

A long release of breath and Walker thrust again, not stopping this time until he was wedged hard and high inside her. There he stopped, chest heaving. "Better?"

They were as close as it was possible for two people to be. Sweet Sister of mercy, a part of his body was *inside* hers. And yes, it did hurt, though the initial sting was fading to a dull ache.

Mehcredi didn't know how she knew, but for some reason she was completely assured he wouldn't move until she signified she was ready. Gods, it was such a luxury to be able to stare into his face, close enough to count each fabulous eyelash, to drown in eyes gone the warm deep brown she loved, to know she could kiss his mouth until she died of the sheer pleasure. Wonderingly, she raised a trembling hand and laid her fingertips against the firm softness of his lips.

"Godsdammit," he growled. "I have to—I can't—" Turning his head, he blew out a breath and nipped her index finger. His hips shimmied the slightest bit as if he were powerless to prevent it.

Oh. It didn't feel so bad, not now. Cautiously, Mehcredi clenched her internal muscles against the intruder. If she concentrated, she could feel their heartbeats pulsing in concert, separated by only the thinnest of membranes. Being crammed with unyielding flesh was . . . interesting. His shaft was imperious, hot and hard and thick, throbbing against the muscular resilient walls of her sheath. When she gave an experimental wriggle, it kicked inside her, the most extraordinary sensation.

Walker made the strangest noise, deep in his throat, almost a whine.

"Fascinating," she murmured, arching into him, running her palms down over the intoxicating sweep of a strong spine, from trim waist to taut buttocks. Beautiful, simply beautiful. She gripped, feeling quivering tension beneath her fingertips, the instinctive desire of the male animal to mate, to power into his female until he spilled.

Walker grunted, every muscle locked, the tendons in his neck taut. He could have been carved of cedderwood except for the pulse ticking wildly in his throat and the tremors that shook him, bone deep. Revelation burst in her brain, so bright that she blinked, awed. Gods, *this* was discipline, this was control. And it was costing him dearly. All because he didn't want to cause her pain. Sister save her, on some level, the swordmaster must really care.

"I'm fine." She smiled through incipient tears. "It can't be harder than the *nea-kata*, can it?" Nuzzling his throat, she inhaled great gulps of clean male sweat and the dark spice that was uniquely Walker, building her courage.

Then she shot him a blazing all-out grin. "Welderyn," she whispered. "Welderyn of the Shar. C'mon, show me what I've been missing."

He didn't speak, just dropped his head into the curve between neck and shoulder and flexed his hips, rocking into her slowly. Mehcredi gasped, startled by a wave of tingling pleasure. With each thrust, he increased the range of movement a little, the skin of his shaft sliding against clasping walls, caressing and finessing, a divinely dirty, slippery duet.

The sting of his first entry paled into insignificance in comparison with the rush of sensation building deep in her pelvis. Like a lover vine gone rampant in the first flush of spring, curling and twining, encasing her in coils of pleasure. Tilting her hips, she opened herself, one fist in the waterfall of his hair, the other in her mouth to stifle the moans.

"No." Walker swiveled his hips, which changed the angle just enough to hit a sweet spot that forced a throaty cry out of her. Reaching up, he grasped her wrist, pinning it to the pillow. "Don't." Another couple of thrusts, deep and slow and luscious. "Let me hear you."

"Oh gods." Her neck went loose, her head rolling from side to side on the pillow. "What do I—*Ah!* What do I do?"

"Nothing." Gradually, he increased the tempo, sweat beading his forehead and glistening on his shoulders. "Just . . . take me."

Mehcredi opened her mouth, then shut it again. Smooth and hot, Walker was moving as if they'd both been oiled, each withdrawal a delicious drag against clinging tissues reluctant to release his girth, each push within filling her all the way to her womb with hot hard cock. Vestiges of the ache lingered, but overwhelmed by pleasure as she was, they no longer mattered.

"Good." She gulped. "It's good."

Walker paused, buried inside her to the hilt, his balls a soft warm presence nudging sensitive folds. "You sure?" His shoulders relaxed. "Fuck, you're tight." A lock of raven hair flopped over his forehead, his bronzed face ruddy with passion and effort, and his teeth flashed in a smile so broad it qualified as a grin.

Mehcredi choked. Gods, this was the boy he'd been all those years ago, before the Trinitarians had robbed him of everything worth having—serious and reserved by nature, but with a well of sweetness and joy for those he loved. She thought she saw a shy mischief there, overlaid by the satisfaction of a randy lad who'd scored.

"Hold on," he murmured, slipping his arms beneath her knees and splaying her open in a way that was positively embarrassing.

"Nngh." She clutched his shoulders as he leaned into her, putting pressure on that sensitive spot at the top of her cleft. "Gods. Whoo. Aargh."

Another glimpse of the grin that wrung her heart. "You make the best noises. Going to scream for me?"

"M-maybe."

With a dark chuckle, he bent his head to lave the Mark, and she squirmed, cursing.

Abruptly, Walker tensed. "*Shit.* Mehcredi—" Gripping her shoulders, he pulled out and surged back in, the pace racking up until he was thundering into her, hard and fast, the bed rocking to the rhythm.

She had no breath to scream, though she wanted to—*needed* to. The new angle added an extra dimension, hitting her high with jolts of silvery sensation, while his cock powered into the core of her, a pumping counterpoint of lusty delight. Shocked, she recognized the dark blossom of energy suffusing her sex, her belly, her heart. Back in the House of Swords, when she'd brought herself to orgasm wearing his shirt, she'd feared she might die, but now she never doubted Walker would keep her safe, like a tall stalwart tree she could cling to in a storm.

Mehcredi dug her fingers into flexing muscle, her head reeling, her body hurtling toward a shattering climax. Was this what Magick was? What a shaman felt? A great vortex of whirling sparkling energy, fascinating and terrifying at once?

For an endless moment, she hovered on the edge of the abyss, whimpering, unable to fall, unable to look away. From very far away, she heard Walker groan. Then his voice, almost unrecognizable, muttering something in what must be Shar. His knuckles brushed her stomach, his fingers furrowing between the lips of her sex to the place where she burned.

When he pressed, she broke, crying out, clinging to his shoulders, while the room and everything in it spun away and she whirled among the heavens, a mote made of starstuff, as he'd said, perfect and beautiful. Her body bucked and writhed. Walker cursed, gritting his teeth.

But Mehcredi didn't hear. Because strangest of all, as she quieted, panting, there was the same vivid sensation of the welcome shade of a great green tree, its branches a shelter that would never fail her. She'd never had a home—well, not in the sense of a place of her own, a refuge specially shaped for her heart and mind and body. But as she relaxed, she couldn't help but wonder . . . Was this what it felt like?

"Ah, fuck!"

Mehcredi blinked. Walker threw his head back, the hair whipping about his shoulders. His rhythm remained powerful, but it had grown choppy.

"I've got you," she said, wrapping her long limbs around him, as if he'd been a tree in truth, and she a lover vine.

The swordmaster groaned as if she'd reached into his chest and torn his heart out still beating. Then he froze, jammed deep, his cock rippling and jerking with the force of his climax.

Slowly, still breathing hard, he bent his elbows, until she could straighten her legs. Dipping his head, he snugged his nose into the curve of her neck, his hair brushing her cheek. Warm lips caressed the tender skin behind her ear. "Ah, *carazada*," he murmured, no more than a thread of sound replete with satisfaction. "That was good." His long body relaxed against her.

Mehcredi gathered up a fall of raven black and rubbed it against her cheek. So cool, so beautiful. "What's that?"

"Mmm?"

"Cara—What you called me?"

"Nothing." After a pause, he sighed and pushed up on one elbow. "Stay there."

Her first impulse was to clutch him to her. Instead, she said, "Don't go. This is nice."

She got a heavy-lidded black stare, all swordmaster, but Walker didn't speak. Gently, but firmly, he peeled himself away and went over to the water bucket.

Mehcredi shivered, the wash of his seed cooling on her thighs. The room reeked, a sharp, sweetish smell that must be sex. She wrinkled her nose, thinking about it, but no, she didn't feel small or dirty, not this time.

The washcloth plopped back into the bucket, accompanied by Walker's exclamation of disgust. "Godsdammit, the water's cold." He fixed her with a commanding eye. "Don't get up."

Even doing something as mundane as giving his genitals a casual swipe with a dirty shirt, he was a poem of long graceful muscle clad in gleaming bronze. Mehcredi drank him in, fixing every detail in her mind while she could. She'd known he had very little body hair, but her fingers itched to stroke the small glossy thatch that surrounded his cock. Would it be wiry, or as silky as the hair on his head? His scrotum was so close to bare she could see the plump curve of his balls nestled inside the tender rosy skin.

She mourned as he stepped into his trews, laced them up. "Where are you going?"

"Won't be long." With a single yank, he pulled the cover off the other bed and flung it over her. Another level stare. "Do not move."

"Mmm." Mehcredi yawned. The muscles in her thighs were complaining, but she was too boneless to be particularly bothered. As the door clicked shut, her eyelids slid down.

She woke to a cool rush of air, the dip of the mattress. Something wet and warm and soft traveled over her belly. Strong hands parted her legs. She forced her eyes open. "Nngh?"

"Only me." He had a bowl of water on the nightstand and a clean soft cloth in his hands. As he stared down at her thighs, a frown gathered and his lips tightened. "Hold still. I won't hurt you."

Very gently, he ran the cloth over her inner thighs and up to her sex. When she hissed, he raised a brow. "Sore?"

Emotion closed her throat, so much so that the words emerged in a cracked whisper. "A little."

The movement of the cloth stopped. "You're crying!"

She sniffed. "No, I'm not."

"How bad is it? I thought—"

Reaching out, she touched his shoulder with her fingertips. "It's just—" She fought to regain her composure. "I've never had anyone . . . do anything like . . . look after me before."

A long silence, but he rinsed the cloth out again, laid it between her legs and held it in place. His head was bent so she couldn't see his face through the shining curtain of his hair.

"Walker? Would you—?"

He didn't turn his head. "What?"

"Take off those stupid trews."

That surprised a bark of laughter out of him. Mehcredi glowed with triumph.

A dark brow winged up. "You want to look?"

"You're looking at me," she pointed out.

"True." Walker rose and shucked the trews with no trace of self-consciousness. He returned to the bed with a small towel in his hands. "You're worth looking at," he said, patting her dry.

He'd called her magnificent once. Deeply pleased, Mehcredi essayed a glance from under her lashes. "All men like to look at naked women."

"Except your Trinitarian friend," he said dryly. "Which, as you'll recall, was the problem."

Godsdammit, she'd wrong-footed herself. And it had all been going so beautifully. She pressed her palms to her hot cheeks. "Can we not talk about that? Please?"

Walker drew the covers up to her waist and turned toward the other bed. "Sleep. We have another long day tomorrow."

Shit, he was disappearing behind his walls of ice and she couldn't bear it! She'd thought fucking would make everything different. Wasn't that how it worked? Rearing up, Mehcredi grabbed his hand and tugged. "No!" She swallowed hard. "Aren't you supposed to stay here with me and . . . ah, cuddle? Or something? Isn't that part of it?"

"Not necessarily." His brows drew together, but his gaze had wandered to her nipples, which were puckering a little in the evening air. "Anyway, it's a bad idea." Though his voice was cool, his fingers curled around hers.

Heartened, she dropped her lower lip and arched her back. "I'm cold," she said, as plaintively as she knew how.

Another brief chuckle, so rusty it sounded disused. "You'll warm up," he said, but he slid his lean length in beside her. " 'Cestors, this bed is narrow."

"Mm," she agreed, closing her eyes in order to appreciate every smooth warm inch. But when she tried to wriggle closer, her elbow hit the wall. "Ow!"

"For the gods' sakes, come here."

A few seconds later, she was lying with her head pillowed on his shoulder, wide-eyed with shock. Sweet Sister of mercy, they fit together like two parts of a puzzle. Cautiously, she snuggled in closer, lifting one leg to rest over his. Her entire body humming with bliss, she drew wobbly circles on the hard planes of his chest with the very tips of her fingers.

After a few minutes, he laid a hand over hers, pressing her palm flat against him. "Tickles."

His heart beat steadily, cupped beneath her hand like something precious, his nipple a fleshy pebble nudging her palm.

"Is fucking always like that?" she asked sleepily.

"No," he said immediately. "Next time will be better." The instant the words left his lips, his breath caught, but Mehcredi's brain was too mazed, too warm and comfortable, to pay attention.

"I'll die," she said with complete conviction.

The only response was a grunt, but when she risked a glance, his mouth had softened. Those absurdly extravagant lashes lay against his skin like a delicate fan. Vaguely, she wondered if they were longer than her own and whether there was a way to measure. She was still considering it when sleep rolled over her.

The Necromancer shot bolt upright in bed, his heart thudding. He'd been dreaming. He scrubbed his hands over his face, a shocking thrill running through him at the feel of a stranger's features, the big nose and heavy chin with its persistent stubble. Would he ever make this meaty, ill-fitting suit truly his own?

The dream had taken him back to his slum childhood, his skinny ass at the mercy of Tolaf, the foul old sodomite. Though now he came to consider the matter, it was probably the drink that aged the man. He couldn't have been much more than forty. There was certainly nothing wrong with his intellect—when he was sober.

"My lord?" The slave curled up on the floor beside the bed raised his head.

"Iced water."

"Yes, Pasha." The boy whisked himself out the door.

But he'd made his peace with that bargain years ago. By Shaitan, it had been worth all the pain and indignity, the crushing loss of a little boy's soul. Tolaf had taught him well and he'd soaked it up, numbers, letters, philosophy and logic—all the knowledge he'd craved. His thick lips curved in a grim smile. The man had taught him to read and shown him something of Magick. And once he'd looked full in the face of the Dark Arts, he'd seen that knowledge was power and power was above petty morality. Besides, Tolaf's protracted demise had been as much an artistic exercise as a scholarly one. The Necromancer flattered himself he'd done well for one so young.

Taking the chilled goblet, he waved the slave away. No, in the dream, he'd been running down a dark alley in the Melting Pot, his bare feet slipping on the wet cobbles and then—somehow he was whirling among the stars.

Thoughtfully, he sipped, clearing his mind, backtracking through the dream mists. The water slid down his throat like an icy finger and he shivered. This wasn't ephemeral in the usual way of dreams. It had substance, *significance*.

He'd approached godhead once before, borne high on the death energy of a seelie, so close he could have reached out and with a contemptuous flick of the fingers—Gods damn Deiter to the seven icy hells and his fucking fire witch with him.

The Necromancer rolled the cup across his hot cheeks, thinking. The dream had been very like that, he'd half expected to see the Great Pattern, the godsbedamned Pentacle etched across the face of the cosmos, and yet . . . He chewed a thumbnail. Rocking in the cradle of the chill winds that whispered across the endless deeps of space, content simply to be.

Content? That wasn't like him at all.

He shoved an embroidered pillow in the small of his back. Because the presence in the dream had been something else, a . . . a creature, ancient beyond human reckoning of time, so alien as to be beyond imagining.

But what?

23

Was it a demon?

No, there was none of Xotclic's vivid self-awareness, its ravening appetite. Eons had drifted past and the . . . thing he'd sensed in the dream remained tranquil, absorbing low-level energy, needing nothing, knowing nothing of desire. He'd never seen anything like it. His pulse quickened.

"Take this." Without looking, he thrust out an arm and the slave relieved him of the goblet.

Clasping his hands loosely over his stomach, the Necromancer settled back, regulating his breathing, letting his consciousness spiral back into the dream-fugue, down, down . . .

Ah. Spawned in the heart of a dying star and cast forth as a thin veil across the vacuum. So close to nothing, it tempted him with the peace of dissolution, of oneness with everything that was and ever could be.

For a while, he drifted, half tranced, half dozing.

A dozen motes of brightness appeared as pinpoints in the void. Slowly, the creature swung its vast attention toward that sector of the dark and observed the strange objects resolve themselves into sleek, shiny ovals that unfurled impossibly delicate gossamer wings. Slingshot sails, glittering against the black like nets of fire and ice.

The Necromancer smiled.

Because in that moment, the creature understood for the first time what it was to hunger. The fragile life forms cocooned within the metal shells blazed hotter to its senses than any sun, unutterably enticing, tempting beyond endurance. It stirred, fascinated. Rippling, it extended its substance, enveloping the silver starships in a leisurely, massive embrace.

Yes! This was what had woken him, pain and longing, a howl of anguish on a cosmic scale. Because the creature discovered it couldn't pull away. The lure of the life forces within the metal hulls held it hypnotized, even as its weight forced the starships off course. As they were caught by the gravity of the Sibling Moons, the heat of their power sources seared the stuff of which the being was made. It screamed without sound, broadcasting pain in tangible waves that puckered its semitransparent surface into a million separate depressions of agony.

The starships entered the atmosphere of Palimpsest in a fiery lurch over the desert, near out of control, and with them went the creature, sundering, splitting, becoming countless motes, forever divided, forever seeking wholeness.

Wounded near to death, it fled, seeking refuge. In the cool depths of an extinct volcano, it brooded, regaining its strength. Millennia passed in the dripping darkness while it thought leviathan thoughts, growing accustomed to its new existence as a hive organism. Until the world grew warmer, uncomfortably warmer.

The Necromancer's eyes blinked open. So long ago. By Shaitan, the Technomages had hushed it up perfectly. Did they know of the creature? His brain raced, his prodigious intellect sorting and sifting—impressions, rumors, visions . . .

The creature endured until the suffering became too great to be borne. Then it rose, a wave of sentient fragments covering the land from horizon to horizon, and ventured out, looking for the cold. But it didn't forget the luscious, liquid brilliance of the human spirit. It could never forget. Along the way, the dwelling places of men enticed it. The soft, warm glow of life energy drew it irresistibly. The harder the death, the greater the nourishment.

Of course! He snapped his fingers. The village headman's shoulders had slumped with relief when he saw the guards. No wonder he'd been delighted to bow before his new lord. Djinns, he'd muttered, out among the wadis and sand cliffs, death swooping from the sky, but the Necromancer had had no patience with such superstitious nonsense.

Gods, he'd been a blind fool. There was no time to waste. This was what the Dark Lord had intended for him to see all along. The so-called djinns and the wounded space creature—they were one and the same.

Rolling over, he slapped the snoozing slave. "Up, up! Get the guard captain!"

"But, my lord . . ." stammered the boy, his head turning to peer out the window at the darkness. "Um, now?"

"No," snarled the Necromancer, "at your fucking convenience. What do you think?"

His backhander sent the slave reeling toward the door, clutching at his face. "Yes, Pasha," he mumbled.

The patter of his footsteps receded down the passageway.

❧

It was still dark when Mehcredi woke. She raised her head from the firm warm pillow beneath her cheek and blinked into the gloom.

A heartbeat later, the mists of sleep cleared with an almost audible snap. Sweet Sister in the sky! She was in bed with the swordmaster, lying half on, half off, his sleeping body, sandwiched between him and the wall. And gods, they'd done it, they'd . . . fucked.

The realization, the very real heat radiating from the muscled form plastered against her, made her head swim. In wonder, scarcely daring to breathe, she drifted a palm over the band of heavy muscle on Walker's chest. Sister save her, it was true! It had been every bit as amazing as she'd hoped. What's more, she'd asked him to stay, and by all the gods, he had. Joy blossomed within her, glowing like a summer rose opening its face to the sun.

Oh, she was so glad she'd woken. Why waste this delicious feeling on sleep? The opportunity would probably never come again. Her stomach flipped. *Next time will be better,* he'd said. Had he enjoyed it? Had he enjoyed *her*? He hadn't said much, but then he never did.

With the utmost care, she lowered her cheek to the warm breathing expanse of his chest. Walker slept on with self-contained grace, the way he did everything, his breath deep and even.

He'd climaxed, found his pleasure, though she imagined that wouldn't be too difficult for most men. Her lips quirked. Except possibly her Trinitarian friend. She resisted the impulse to shake her head at her own stupidity. How could she have missed it? But the man had been downright entertaining. She'd been so interested in the palace gossip, so busy memorizing the wild rumors about a new kind of demon—a djinn he'd called it—that she'd forgotten to watch his face. *Forget it,* she told herself sternly. *Enjoy what you have before it disappears.* If she held her breath, she could hear the beat of his heart against her ear, a steady, reassuring rhythm. Gingerly, she skated her fingertips over the satin of his skin. So beautiful, so male. Gods, she was torn! Part of her yearned to sink deep into the comfort and delight of such close proximity, never mind that he wasn't even conscious. Everything she'd ever longed for and known she could never have. She'd been starving all her life and here was a feast, so sumptuous it made her dizzy with the possibilities.

It should be enough, and yet, her mouth watered for more, every nerve on edge with sexual desire. She shook with the need to explore all the fascinating dips and contours with her hands, her mouth, gods, even her nose. It was insane. Trembling, she buried her face against him and inhaled, filling her lungs, imprinting the smell and texture of his skin upon her senses.

Even worse, it was still too dark to see and curiosity was killing her. What would happen if she reached down and touched him *there*, between his strong thighs? She let out a soundless huff of frustration. He'd wake and throw her off. But she'd never seen anything as extraordinary as his cock, jutting out clear of his body, hard and thick and deliciously threatening. But after he'd finished, it had looked quite different, softer, nestled in the thatch of his pubic hair, his balls an intriguing shadow behind. She wanted to pet it, stroke a little and see if he liked it. He'd stroked her, after all. Her cheeks got hot. Godsdammit, he'd had his fingers *inside* her.

Walker's breath hitched and he shifted slightly, his head rolling on the pillow. Mehcredi froze. But after a moment, he murmured a few words in what she thought might be Shar, turned his face into her hair and slipped more deeply into sleep.

She lay for what seemed like hours, staring into the dark, all her attention focused on the points of contact between them. The strength of his thigh along hers, the bump of a hip bone, the breadth of his chest where the softness of her breast was pressed, the strong cage of his ribs, rising and falling with his respiration. If she lifted her head . . . Holding her breath, she did so. Ah . . . With the tip of her tongue she touched the strong brown column of his neck, tasting salt and musk and hot man. He didn't stir.

Mehcredi allowed herself to sink into sensation, going deeper layer by layer, until she was centered, grounded as if by the *nea-kata*. Gratefully, she surrendered, accepting something about herself she'd never fully articulated. She hadn't known how before—before Walker.

She didn't know what love was, what people meant when they said they loved one another. They were words and therefore easy to come by. *I'd die for him,* she'd said to Abad.

Only words?

Instinctively, Mehcredi clung closer, placing her parted lips against his skin, breathing him in.

Not empty words, but truth. Because she would. Not gladly— that was stupid—but if there was no other way. She belonged to the swordmaster, to this reserved difficult man, more surely, more completely, than if he'd purchased her with coin at a slave market. Her life was entwined with his because that was . . . well, the way it was. Frowning at the vague outline of the nightstand, she swallowed hard.

Walker would complete his vengeance, she didn't doubt it for an instant. Then what? He'd return to Caracole, to his House of Swords, to his garden and the fighting salle. She could probably hire on as a bodyguard for some noblelady, or even try for the Palace Guard. Walker had a friend there, she thought, a man called Rhio. He might help.

If this night was all there was . . .

She'd make the most of it, memorize every sensation, use all her senses. Ask for more. When it was over, it would be over. Once she accepted that, by all the gods, what did she have to lose?

The cool light of dawn was pushing back the shadows. Cautiously, she raised her head, glancing down the length of his body. She'd never be able to think of words adequate to describe him, not if she lived forever. Not an ounce of fat, all those shapely muscles on display, the scars marring the smooth bronze of his skin. He had the most beautiful legs she'd ever seen on a man, long and strong and graceful, roped with muscle.

Mehcredi frowned. The swordmaster ought to take better care of himself—eat more and keep away from demons and bad men bearing sharp-edged weapons.

With the utmost care, she disengaged herself until she could sit up and look her fill. Her gaze skittered away from his genitals, then returned. Fascinated, she stretched out a hand, then snatched it back. No, no, no. Bad idea.

His nipples were as dark as Concordian chocolat, not as broad as hers. Were they as sensitive? Would they feel velvety against her lips?

She wouldn't, she *wouldn't*. Unable to resist, Mehcredi hovered a palm an inch away from a brown disk, wanting desperately to touch, but not bold enough. When Walker didn't stir, she let out a shaky breath. His gorgeous heat burned her flesh. To her astonishment, his nipple crinkled, drawing up as if to nuzzle into her palm. A wave of gooseflesh followed, racing across his chest, pebbling the nipple on the other side.

Shaking all over, she withdrew her hand, flexing her tingling fingers. A coil of tension settled at the base of her spine, a series of flutters making her stomach flip.

Imagination. Must be.

Leaning forward, she ran her hands over his body, keeping a scrupulous inch from contact. Over his ribs, his sternum, the tight cup of his navel, his hip bone. The skin of her palms felt scorched, primeval energy arcing from him to her and back again. It had to be Walker's Magick, because she had none.

Her heart drumming, she focused on his groin. His cock lay curved, quiescent against a hard thigh, the heart-shaped head now shielded by his foreskin. She bent a little. He smelled muskier there, but she didn't mind it, not at all.

She'd never been so curious in her life. How could a body part transform itself so completely, as if it had a mind of its own? Were all men like this?

It stirred. *Twitched.* Mehcredi's mouth dropped open. Shocked, she stared down at her own hand, hovering over Walker's cock, the heat blazing between their flesh. Her eyes growing rounder and rounder, she watched the shaft move like a sleepy animal, swelling and straightening, until the foreskin slipped back to show the head, smooth and ruddy, with a little slit at the top. She peered, leaning closer still. The skin of his member looked as soft as finest chamois, but it was roped by tracery of blue veins, growing more prominent by the second. And, oh yes, his balls had drawn up against his body, tight and hard. Completely enthralled, she began to shift her hand toward them. Who knew what might happen?

Long brown fingers appeared in her field of vision, cradling Walker's cock with casual competence. An iron hand clamped over her wrist.

"Mehcredi."

Her head whipped around to meet a flat obsidian stare. "What the hell are you doing?" asked the swordmaster.

The Necromancer leaned forward over the saddle and surveyed the collection of poor tents clustered round a seep trickling out of a gray rock face. About a dozen contorted figures lay in the stony gravel, some of them still clutching weapons that had clearly proved useless. Corpsebirds circled lazily overhead, riding the hot desert wind. "You're telling me no one survived?"

The guard captain shifted uneasily. "It appears so, Pasha. But I've sent men to check in the hills."

As he spoke, a soldier appeared from behind a clump of boulders, driving a small group of people before him. The guard captain's shoulders slumped with relief.

"Ah." The Necromancer used a fold of his head cloth to blot the sweat on his face. His nose wrinkled with distaste. Nyzarl had liked his food heavily spiced and fatty, and although he'd startled the cook by demanding plain, well-cooked fare, his new body still sweated like a vanbeast. As the spices worked their way out through his skin, he smelled like one too.

"What did you see?" he asked an old man with a toothless face so seamed with lines it looked like a badly cured hide. "Who did this?"

"D-djinns," quavered the old man. "Hundreds of djinns."

"Describe them."

But he couldn't, not to the Necromancer's satisfaction. The djinns had apparently ridden into the camp on the wind, invisible and deadly. None of which was any use.

With an irritated grunt, the Necromancer swung down heavily from his horse. "Come here."

The ceaseless babble dried up when the soldier shoved the old man forward. A skinny middle-aged woman stepped up with him, her arm around his waist for support. The Necromancer flexed his thick fingers. It had been so long. Could he still do it?

"P-Pasha?" said the old man. Tears glittered in his rheumy eyes, made streaks in the dust on his cheeks.

"Think of the djinns." The Necromancer wrapped his whole big hand around the man's face. "Oh, and keep breathing." He closed his eyes, concentrating.

The Sibling Moons had been high. They'd been celebrating something, a marriage perhaps, grouped around the fire, their plaintive music echoing across the stony plain. A young woman played a finger drum, a man blew notes on a simple wooden flute.

Death swept in an acrid cloud down the wadi, the djinns fanning out over the open ground in vortexes of roiling light, barely visible despite the soft brilliance of the Siblings. Rising swiftly from below the threshold of hearing, a whine built to a piercing shriek that penetrated the bones of the skull. Men and women grimaced with pain and slapped their hands over their ears. An elder stumbled to her knees, the eyes rolling back in her head. A vicious, metallic stench rolled over the desert, clawing at throats and making eyes tear.

Like the rest, the young woman fled, the small drum slipping from her grasp to bounce away across the pebbled ground, tassels waving. She was kin to the old man, close, possibly a daughter. A pulsing thickness formed in the air, one of the djinns hovering directly in her path. It swooped. Her shrill cry was cut off by a cracking report, echoing above the unbearable wall of noise.

By the time the old man reached her, every muscle was racked and bowed, her spine arching hard with pain. A swelling the size of a small bird's egg trembled beneath the skin of her shoulder. When he touched it with a fingertip, the dreadful thing *skittered*, burrowing deeper into the woman's flesh.

Her mouth opened in a soundless scream, her eyes stretched wide. "Knife," she gasped, her clotted gurgle an obscene parody of human speech. "Da. Kill. Me."

She made a supreme effort. "Da, as you love me. Argh!" The last word emerged as a bubbling shriek. "*Please!*"

The old man's fingers clenched on the hilt of his blade, but before he could move, his daughter's ribs parted with a sodden crack and her heart exploded outward in a shatter of bone and torn flesh.

Well, that explained the extraordinary pattern of the injuries.

The night sky boiled and stank as the creatures rolled away across the plain, the cruel whine of their passage diminishing as the distance increased.

The old man wiped his daughter's blood from his eyes and stumbled to his feet. His fingers were icy cold and spots gathered before his eyes. Before the wave of darkness could pull him under, the Necromancer let him go. The old man collapsed, the middle-aged woman trying desperately to support him as his body convulsed with grief and horror.

"I've seen enough." Remounting, the Necromancer commandeered the guard captain's shoulder as a crutch, enjoying the man's instinctive flinch.

"My lord?"

"What?"

The guard captain's throat moved. "Was it djinns? Truly?"

"Oh yes." The Necromancer gathered up the reins. "But it's all one."

"Yes, my lord. Ah, my lord?"

"Now what?"

The man indicated the sorry little group. "What about them?"

"Bring them."

The woman fell to her knees, making the sign of the Three, over and over. "Oh, thank you, Pasha. Thank you."

The Necromancer's smile showed all Nyzarl's large white teeth. "Don't thank me yet," he advised, and trotted away.

❧

Mehcredi's eyes were so wide, Walker could see the whites all around.

"Doing? Uh. I was . . ." A violent flush stained those glorious tits with rosy color. "I was only looking. I didn't touch anything, I swear." Her gaze swiveled back to his groin as if drawn by a magnet.

His hips arched instinctively, his cock hardening under her attention, the stupid godsbedamned thing. For a moment, he couldn't speak, a battle going on in his throat. He had the strangest desire to laugh, but it was accompanied by a tenderness so piercing it very nearly choked him.

"Tell me what you're thinking." Mehcredi laid warm fingertips on his thigh, the muscle jumping beneath her touch. "Are you angry?"

"No," he said. "Not with you."

There couldn't be any doubt Mehcredi of Lonefell was the strangest woman on all of Palimpsest, but godsdammit, she was also so brave and so beautiful it was painful to watch her. After a childhood like hers, let alone a career as an assassin, how could she remain so essentially unsullied, so . . . sweet?

"Are you sorry?" he asked, knowing whatever tumbled out of that pretty mouth would be the unvarnished truth. "For what we did?"

Her luminous gaze went wide again. "Are you joking? Of course not." She twinkled at him. "What about you? Any regrets?" But the smile slipped a little on the final word.

There was a stain on the ceiling shaped roughly like a map of the Isles. "I took a gift that wasn't meant for me." He lowered his gaze to her face and kept it there. "If I was a better man, I'd regret it."

He didn't expect the lick of temper that had him pulling her back into his arms, her long body supple and warm against his. She landed on his chest with a muffled yelp of surprise. "But I'm not and I don't."

Walker speared his fingers into her cropped hair and pulled Mehcredi's mouth down to his, plundering. Such a silky, desperate little tongue, twining with his, growing bolder with every passing second, such gorgeous incoherent noises, deep in her throat. 'Cestors' bones, he didn't find her endearing, he positively didn't—only delightfully fuckable.

24

She was trying to keep up, but godsdammit, a woman had to breathe. Walker would let her up for air, then drag her down again until she was drugged with kissing, his clever lips and tongue luring her further and further from safety, to a place where nothing existed but his warmth and heat, one hand holding her head at the angle he required, while the other plucked at an aching nipple.

Then he gripped her ass in both hands and hauled her even more firmly on top of him. There went that amazing sizzle again, from shoulder to thigh, lighting her up like tiny firecrackers just beneath the skin. His cock dug into her stomach, as hot and as hard as a brand. When a heavy hand in the small of her back pressed her down against it, everything in her belly clenched.

Gasping into his mouth, she took a fistful of raven hair and tugged. Lingeringly, Walker withdrew, nibbling her lower lip, licking the corner of her mouth. Finally, he dusted feathery kisses over her cheekbones, her brows, her eyelids. Sister, if he didn't stop it, the slew of emotions bubbling inside her would spill over and she'd be weeping all over him like a half-wit.

"I c-can't—" She gasped.

"Can't what?" The thumb stroking her brow stopped in midcaress. Walker frowned. "I thought—Shit, does it still hurt?"

"What? No, I'm fine. It's just—Oof!"

With no apparent effort, he flipped her over and kneeled up between her legs, scanning her body. Warm callused palms skimmed up the inside of her thighs and urged her legs open.

Mehcredi squirmed.

"Hold still."

Oh, that was his swordmaster's voice. She glanced up from under her lashes. Well, hell. There was no expression on his face, or none that she could detect. His eyes were completely black, fixed on her most private place. Instinctively, she slipped a hand down, intending to cover herself.

"No." Gently but firmly, he moved it aside.

Exposed. Vulnerable. A silvery jolt of sensation hit her behind the pubis, seemingly out of nowhere. Quite distinctly, she felt wetness seep out of her, the lips of her sex grow plump and moist. A tiny noise escaped, panic and arousal mixed. She thought his mouth softened, but she couldn't be sure.

"What are you thinking?" she whispered, desperate.

Walker came down on his elbows. He drifted a forefinger over the crease where hip met thigh. "There's an orchid that only grows where there's water in the desert," he said, deep and almost meditative. The finger skimmed across the outer lips of her sex and she shivered. "It's shy and rare and very lovely."

"What are you talk—?"

"Sshh." He flicked a stern glance at her. "You will tell me at once if there is pain." Then he settled even closer, so close his breath puffed across wet flesh and she couldn't hold back a whimper.

"The petals are ruffled and delicate, a pale pink." Featherlight, he stroked all the way from the top of her cleft to her anus—and back again. He dabbled a thoughtful finger in the juices now spilling out of her, holding her down with the other hand when she bucked. "But they deepen to rose at the throat." Very gently, he spread her inner lips with his thumbs, massaging with light circular movements.

Godsdammit, the fluttery feelings behind her pubic bone were piling up, one on top of the other, coalescing into dark waves of erotic heat, coming at her over and over, robbing her of the ability to think. "I'm—" Her voice cracked. "I'm a flower?"

"Mm." One finger advanced a careful inch, resting just within the entrance to her body. His head dipped. "The nectar is plentiful, honey sweet, and . . . intoxicating."

Without warning, his tongue flicked out and curled around the ultrasensitive bump of flesh at the apex of her cleft.

Mehcredi shrieked, writhing. With a rusty chuckle, Walker pinned her down with both forearms on her thighs. "It's also"—he inhaled deeply—"said to be a potent aphrodisiac."

Then he dragged the flat of his tongue along the same path his finger had taken, again and again, licking and laving, nibbling and stroking. Every fold, every ruffle and crease. A kind of continuous purr-growl rumbled in his throat, buzzing against her.

Oh gods, oh sweet Sister of mercy. *Fuck!*

She'd never imagined anything so exquisite, so excruciating. Hadn't known this was possible, that a man would do this, take pleasure in it. Because even she couldn't doubt that he did. On one level, the muscular warmth and wetness was comforting against her most sensitive tissues, on another, it was torture. Because for some reason, he kept missing the burning knot of flesh where she needed pressure so badly.

She sank desperate fingers into his hair. "Please! Shit, *please!*"

A dark chuckle, a caressing nuzzle. "What do you need, *carazada?*"

"I don't know!" she wailed. With her last remnant of sanity, she glared down at him over the curve of her belly. "But you do."

Walker didn't answer, but he licked his lips, shot her one of those unexpected, earthshaking smiles and bent his head.

"Such a pretty little clit," he crooned, sucking the place that ached right into his mouth, pressing the hood back with the pointed tip of his tongue.

"Nngh!" Mehcredi sucked in air. "Clit? What's a—?" He did some kind of spiraling lick thing and her pelvis lifted clean off the mattress. "Oh, gods!"

The sensations were so intense, it took her a moment to realize he'd slipped a finger deep inside her. "C'mon, little one," he murmured. "For me." He twisted his wrist, his fingertip stroking against an achingly sweet spot she hadn't known she had. It pressed up against— what was it?—her *clit* from the inside, and when he drew the jut of it into the wet heat of his mouth to suckle, her head thrashed on the pillow, her mouth falling open to scream. But because there was no air left in the world, all she could produce were embarrassing noises like an incoherent kitten.

Not that the swordmaster seemed to care. Humming with apparent delight, he kept up the rhythm of mouth and finger. Oh gods, *fingers*, because now he was circling the pucker of her anus with his smallest finger, wet with her juices. She'd never heard of anything so thoroughly wicked, so dirty, in her life.

She was going to fly apart, disintegrate, dissolve. He was killing her. Hadn't she said she'd die if it got any better? It wasn't possible for one body to contain this much sensation, let alone for one human being to do this to another. Her heart beat like a gong, reverberating between her thighs.

"*Walker.*" Thrashing like a sapling in a storm, she stretched out a hand, seeking. "Gods! Ah!"

Warm, strong fingers closed over hers. And suddenly, she was anchored, as securely as the world tree she'd dreamed of, with its great taproots reaching deep into rich soil.

For the space of two heartbeats, Walker continued to push her to the very brink. For a timeless instant, she hovered. Then, without fuss, all the tension released, a luscious swell of honey heat spreading through her loins and sweeping up her spine to make her head spin. Stars twinkled behind her lids and the breath whistled out of her on a long exhalation. Slowly, she sank back into her body, the mattress soft beneath her.

Down the street, she heard the clank of someone opening shutters, and closer, the scrabble of claws on the stairs, a snuffling whine under the door. She cleared her throat. "Was I loud?" she said without opening her eyes.

"You screamed very prettily." Walker's voice sounded tight, each word bitten off.

Mehcredi levered her eyes open.

Shit! Her legs were draped over his shoulders and her fist was buried in his hair. How had that happened? Releasing him, she struggled up on her elbows, a ferocious blush suffusing her whole upper body. Walker cooperated by straightening, allowing her legs to slip to the bed.

"Oh gods, I'm sor . . ." The words trailed off.

He knelt between her spread legs, his high cheekbones ruddy with a sexual flush, thighs rock hard with tension. "Don't move," he grated, taking his cock in a businesslike grip. "My . . . turn."

Mehcredi watched open-mouthed as he jerked his fist up and down, his thumb sweeping over the head, now a deep rosy red and shiny with juices, on every pass. Gods, it looked brutal, but also wonderfully . . . *raw*. Such a private man, yet he was exposing his soul as much as his body. How many other women had seen him like this? The thought was a canker, a worm in paradise. She pushed it aside. *Enjoy the moment, only the moment.*

"Fuck." His hair whipped about his shoulders, the tendons in his neck standing taut. "Ah gods, *fuck*."

He froze, caught at the exquisite apex of his pleasure, unapologetically starkly male, an image she knew she'd carry to the grave. Then his cock rippled, spurting warm globs of cream across her belly, Walker squeezing, milking it to the end. He cursed in Shar, his chest heaving.

At last, his lashes fluttered down on a cross between a groan and sigh. "There," he murmured, coming down over her so their skin was sealed together. "What do you think, Mehcredi of Lonefell?"

"Messy," she said, taking a surreptitious nibble where neck met shoulder.

One of those rusty chuckles. "Sex is. Inevitably, gloriously messy."

She hesitated. "Is that how most people fuck? Like we did?"

She felt him shrug. "Some do, some don't."

Her voice rose. "You mean there are other ways to do it?"

"It's a physical skill like any other." Walker reached out a long arm and snagged the damp cloth. His lips twitched. "Think of it as being like the *nea-kata*. There are many levels to master."

There was *more*? Sister save her!

Sitting up, he swabbed at her skin, while she suppressed the impulse to drag him back down.

"Walker?"

"Yes, Mehcredi?"

"Do you think—Could I learn to be good at it?"

He froze, every muscle rigid, and she could have wept.

After an interminable pause, he passed over the towel and rose to shake out his trews. "I suspect," he said in a voice as dry as the desert, "that you're naturally gifted."

As the last guttural syllables of its name died in the air, Xotclic stepped out of yet another green cloud, this one tinged with streaks of a rusty red. It had fed then, and within the last few days.

The Necromancer pursed his lips. The local village was too useful for the demon to use it as a feeding ground. The headman was eager to please the new Pasha, his people a handy source of labor.

"We need to talk," he said shortly.

The huge dark eyes regarded him with detached curiosity. "Ss?"

"You took a child from the village two days ago. Another one."

Xotclic's nostril holes flared, but that was the only reaction.

The Necromancer took a careful sip of his chilled manda juice. "Don't do it again."

The demon hissed its displeasure, the forked tongue flickering over the lipless gash of a mouth. For a hideous moment, the leering face of Tolaf shimmered behind its scaly visage.

Controlling his instinctive flinch, the Necromancer set the cup aside with a decisive clink. He was pleased to see his hand remained steady. "I do not doubt your intelligence, Xotclic. As I will explain in a moment, the villagers are useful. I have given you your freedom. You can step out of your mist and feed anywhere you please. Is that not so?"

The horny plates on the creature's chest lifted and settled with a tiny clattering sound, like mandibles rubbing together. "Ss."

Nyzarl's heart pounded in his massive chest. By Shaitan, the man had been a coward. No wonder, given his woeful lack of self-discipline. But the Necromancer was purging the dross from this body, eating well and sparingly. Already, he'd had to cinch his belt two holes tighter, he sweated less and his wind was greatly improved.

"Well then, do so. Somewhere far from here."

Xotclic folded one set of arms across its chest and leaned against the wall. Its hideous head tilted to one side. As clearly as if it could speak, its posture said, *Yeah, and so?*

"I called you here to listen to a proposition."

"Ss?"

"We have exchanged Names. That makes us partners, of a sort."

"Ss." The lipless mouth stretched, the chest plates quivered. The Necromancer avoided looking at what writhed beneath them.

He suspected the demon was amused. To the seven icy hells with the bastard, he needed its cooperation, its advice even.

"I have found a pet for us, a weapon I"—he caught himself—"*we* can use to hold the world to ransom. Enough corpses to glut even you."

Xotclic slid down the wall, hunkering comfortably, though its legs folded the wrong way, an ugly parody of a long-legged bird.

The Necromancer released a careful breath. He suspected that if he touched the demon, the power of the True Names combined with his own Dark Arts would allow mind-to-mind communication, but that was a risk he was not yet prepared to take.

Choosing his words, he described his vision as accurately as possible, the alien creature drifting in the deep reaches of space, its pain and dissolution in the atmosphere of Palimpsest. He recounted the trip into the desert, the old man's story and the djinns of death riding on the hot winds.

When he finished, the demon stared at him in silence, a third hand rubbing its chin in a weirdly human gesture, its eyes very bright. At last, it opened its mouth and emitted a string of grating, high-pitched sounds, redolent of doubt and ending with what was obviously a question.

"Yes. It's damaged, I'm almost certain," said the Necromancer, chewing a thumbnail. "Dying. That's what Dotty said, in the two minutes she made any sense at all."

"Ss." When Xotclic nodded, its neck creaked.

"It should be one djinn, not many," the Necromancer mused aloud. "It was a single entity out in space, where it's cold and dark."

Creak, creak. "Ss."

"The damn thing's no use to us dead. If I could get it away from the heat, out of the desert . . ."

"Ss."

"Take it north, to the ice fields." When his gaze met the demon's, he smiled. "Fortunately, I have maps. Even better, I have a guide to take us to its most recent location."

"Ss!" hissed Xotclic, coming off the wall to wave all four arms in the air. Its chest plates clattered with excitement.

Walker couldn't believe how stupid he'd been, how catastrophically he'd missed his step. As he turned to leave their chamber at the inn, Mehcredi grabbed his hand and pressed it briefly to her lips. "Uh, thanks," she said, her voice as husky as a boy's, before walking past him with her head held high.

He stood there like a fool, watching her trim ass as she moved away from him with that swinging mannish stride, and his heart turned a somersault in his chest. He had to wait for a moment for the black spots to clear from his vision before he could follow her down the stairs. For the first time in his adult life, he was grateful to be the only living speaker of Shar. *Carazada*, he'd called her. 'Cestors save him! Let alone the rest of it. Lust fogged a man's brain, not a doubt of it.

He caught up with her in the street, holding the gut flutters at bay with sheer willpower. They weren't panic, or anything like it, for the simple reason that he couldn't afford such stupidity, not now when he had to make everything clear.

"So," he said briskly. "I assume you've got that out of your system?" He showed his teeth. "Scratched the itch?"

Her eyes flickered behind the tinted spectacles. "I suppose so." She turned her head to watch a veiled woman walk by, a tousle-haired child on one hip, a huge pottery jar balanced on the other. "Amazing," she murmured, and he wondered what she was thinking.

She lengthened her stride. "What are we doing today?"

And that was it. His brows rose. Well, not so difficult after all. He should have known—no tears, no female weakness, not Mehcredi the assassin. Godsdammit, she was mighty cool about her first sexual experience. It had been . . . extraordinary. Any other woman would be overwhelmed, the emotional effects still reverberating deep inside. If he could feel it, hardened as he was, why didn't she?

Aloud, he said, "I want to buy a couple of desert ponies, and then stock up on supplies. We need waterskins, among other things. We'll ride out late in the day, when it's cooler. If we travel all night, we'll be at Nyzarl's before dawn."

And that was precisely what they'd done. With the addition of a broad-brimmed floppy hat for Mehcredi. He'd overruled her objections. Blengo juice or no, he refused to take any more chances with that tender skin, not out in the deep desert.

A long bruising ride later, Walker sat cross-legged at the lip of a cave in the hills behind the diabloman's estate, feeding a small smokeless fire. Behind him, he could hear the soft regular sigh of Mehcredi's breath as she slept, the dog curled against her hip. She'd carried the damn animal across the bow of her saddle all the way from Trimegrace. He'd sat bolt upright as to the manner born, tongue lolling happily. He even had a name now—Scrounger, but she called him Scrounge.

For a lone assassin, she was collecting dependents at a remarkable rate. First, a stray cur, and now—

Brooding, he gazed into the heart of the fire and reached for the *ch'qui*. "Cenda, are you there?" he whispered, feeling like a fool. "Cenda!"

Nothing.

When he tried again, a twig rippled, putting out a couple of hopeful green leaves, only to have them blacken and shrivel in the hungry flames. Walker's lips tightened. Godsdammit, for once in his life, nothing would have pleased him more than to speak with Deiter.

Delighted with a fresh audience, the horse trader in Trimegrace had lingered over the cups of bitterbrew, regaling them with gory tales of the desert djinns. Safe in his shabby stable, the man's eyes had shone with a mixture of horror, relief and glee, but fuck it, everything he said fit with the evidence of the caravan they'd found destroyed on the road. Especially the wounds.

More to the point, Walker had found Deiter's nameless evil. *Djinns.* He snorted. What did the old wizard think he and his little band of heroes were going to do? Gallop into Trinitaria on snow-white horses and kill the things? Or was Walker supposed to do that? He ground out a curse, poking another stick into the fire.

The Sibling Moons had sunk below the horizon, the Brother a reluctant red glower retreating behind the shoulders of the arid hills. Dawn wasn't far off. By the First Father, nothing compared with the smell of home, the ancient odor of dust and stone, mixed with the resin tang of the small hardy conifers that scraped a meager existence up here.

Walker blinked out at the shadowed landscape, noting where dawn light illuminated the gray and pink and yellow of cliff faces, the dense shadows where night still lay pooled in the wadis. He half expected Owen and Brennard to appear from out of the rocks, Amae trotting at their heels. They'd ignore her chatter with brotherly disdain, one keeping a watchful eye on her while the other scanned the terrain. Ensuring her safety.

And this was fucking useless. Rising, he scattered the fire and stamped out the embers. He circled up behind the cave, discovering a sandmat in one of the traps he'd set. With a grunt of satisfaction, he skewered it behind the head, rolled it up and stuffed it into a rough net he wove out of feathergrass.

Turning to the west, he stared at the white cluster of buildings and the startling patch of green that was Nyzarl's estate. A blight on the ancestral lands of the Shar. These ancient rounded hills were *his*. He knew every fold of them, every spring and seep, all the plants and animals, from the packs of lean direwolves to the painted dogs with their huge furry ears and high-pitched yips. For every creature, no matter how small or how venomous, there was an ancestral Song, handed from parent to child, generation after untold generation.

And all of them would end with him.

His mouth was full of an acrid taste like bitterbrew. How much of Shar culture had he forgotten already? How much was lost because he'd been too young to be trusted with it? As for the faces of his kin— the harder he tried to hold on to them, the faster they slipped from his mind.

As his tally of diablomen grew, the moments of disorientation increased, running together until there were times he knew he approached dissolution. Not all the gardens in the world, nor the framework of the *nea-kata*, were strong enough to keep his spirit from fading from this life, his Song dying away. Soon it would be no more than another tiny voice among the seven million Songs of the Ancestors, echoing from star to star.

Mehcredi's warm body, sealed the length of his in a narrow bed, that had helped. He'd felt her heart beat next to his, tasted her on his tongue, and felt *real*. Solid.

His lips twisted. Very sweet. A distraction that might very well kill him.

Scrubbing his hands over his face, Walker ducked into the cave to stow the sandmat in a dark corner. As he wove finger bones into his braids with steady fingers, he wondered if he'd be back. Well, if he wasn't, Mehcredi had the horses and the supplies. The ponies were hobbled in the shade, fed and watered. He'd pointed out all the landmarks during the journey. When he'd drawn scratch maps in the dirt, she'd grasped the concept straightaway. He'd taught her so much already. She'd cope.

His death would release her from the Mark. That beautiful breast would return to its unmarred perfection. He wished he could look upon it one last time.

But even standing over her sleeping form, he didn't waver. She was curled up like a child, a hand beneath her cheek, her lips soft and slightly parted. A bright spirit meant for a long and happy life.

Mehcredi had called him by name, not once, but twice. *Welderyn, show me what I've been missing.* She even got the inflection right.

When Scrounge raised a shaggy head, Walker bent to rub him behind the ears, but he didn't trust himself to touch the assassin. Welderyn'd'haraleen't'Lenquisquilirian wasn't going to fail her too. Slowly, he backed away, then turned to negotiate the rocky scree. He passed into the well of shadow at the base of the wadi, no more than a presence on the wind, silent and deadly as a lone direwolf on the hunt.

25

"Gone?" said Walker with deadly calm. "What do you mean, *gone?*" He settled on the fusty bed next to the man's hip, his guts churning. He felt as if he'd run full tilt into a brick wall.

The man fumbled the bedclothes up to his chin and hung on with a white-knuckled grip. What, did he think Walker intended to rape him?

"Left d-day b-before yesterday. T-took almost everyb-body." When he realized what he'd revealed, his face went a nasty shade of gray green.

"Shit! Here, you fool." Walker snatched up the brandywine bottle from the floor and thrust it into the other man's palsied hands. "What's your position here?"

Judging by the way the man tilted it, there were only dregs left, but his face regained a little color after he'd swallowed. "S-steward." His gaze flickered over the finger bones in Walker's hair and he made the sign of the Three. "W-what do you want?"

Walker's lips pulled back from his teeth and the man blanched. "Nerajyb Nyzarl."

"He's Nerajyb Nyzarl Necros now," said the steward with an odd sort of dignity. "It t-took my lord a little while to settle on the third name but I sent the p-papers by courier the same day he left."

"Did you indeed?" murmured Walker, all silky menace. He leaned forward, ignoring the man's sour breath. "Where has he gone?"

The steward made a noise like a whipped dog. "I can't t-tell you that. He—He swore he'd g-give me to the d-demon. I can't fuck up, not again." He reached out to clutch at the swordmaster's sleeve, but Walker swayed back, out of the way.

He gave a thin smile. "That's only a probability. What is certain, however, is that you will die"—a blade glinted in his hand—"here and now, if you don't tell me what I want to know." Placing the point under the man's chin, he leaned forward, the finger bones clattering softly. "Slice by slice, piece by piece."

The steward moaned and his eyes rolled back in his head.

"He's gone to find them," said a husky contralto. "The djinns, I mean."

Mehcredi perched on the windowsill, one long leg thrust into the room. Scrounge wriggled under her arm, whining.

Could this get any better? Walker stalked toward her, knowing there was murder in his eyes and not caring. "What the hell are you doing here?" He'd heard the quiet movements outside, but put it down to the other servants, waking. Godsdammit, she'd made him soft.

"Following you," she said placidly, and released the dog. To the steward, she said, "Did all the guards go with him?"

"N-no." He pulled in a small rattled breath. "Habrik stayed behind, but he's got a b-bad leg. He got kicked by—"

With a growl, Walker ripped the covers out of the man's grip, exposing a long body clad in a grubby nightshirt. The steward clamped his bony knees together.

"Just a minute," said Mehcredi, crossing the room to peer through a doorway on the far side. "That's your office, isn't it?"

The steward swallowed, a prominent Adam's apple bobbing in his skinny throat.

She gazed at him thoughtfully. "You're frightened out of your wits," she said on a note of discovery. "We'll tie you up," she offered. "Knock you out. That would help, wouldn't it?"

Walker bit the inside of his cheek, his usual mental balance decidedly off-kilter. If he laughed now, he'd never stop. "Turn your head away," he growled at the trembling steward. "If you piss yourself, I'll leave you to lie in it, I swear."

His fist caught the man behind the ear and he slumped to the mattress with a choking grunt. Walker picked him up by the front of his nightshirt and punched him three times in rapid succession, face, kidneys, gut.

"Stop!" Strong slender fingers dug into his forearm. The dog gave a single sharp yip. "Walker, are you out of your mind?"

"No." Walker rubbed his bruised knuckles. Even under the blengo juice, she was pale. Stepping closer, he jabbed his fingers none too gently into her neck.

"Ow!" She clapped her hand to the spot, scowling.

"I could have done it that way, but he'll need the bruises to show the others." He glared, feeling distinctly ill-used. Gripping the sheet, he gave it a vicious jerk. The fabric was so threadbare it ripped easily, the raw tearing sound startling in the early-morning hush.

"Godsdammit, Mehcredi, why didn't you stay where I left you?" He tossed the first strip to her and tore off another.

She busied herself wrapping the makeshift tie around the steward's ankles. "You're joking."

Walker secured the man's wrists, then hog-tied them to his feet. "I never joke."

Mehcredi frowned at him as they dragged the limp body off the bed and dumped it on the floor. "I thought you were supposed to understand women."

With a certain wicked satisfaction, Walker scooped up a dirty sock from under the bed and jammed it into the steward's slack mouth. "The man isn't born who does that."

Mehcredi's lips twitched, but she said nothing.

The steward's office was tidier than his sleeping quarters, but only barely. A few minutes searching through the haphazard piles of paper on the rickety desk revealed a sheaf of to-do lists written in a small crabbed hand. Walker rifled through them. "The steward's right. Nyzarl took almost the entire household. Bastard likes to travel in comfort."

Mehcredi lifted a glowing face. "Look." She brandished a roll of parchment. "I found a map."

"Don't need it," said Walker frowning down at the list in his hand. Gods, the diabloman had even taken his fancy cook, plus his strongbox. "That many people will leave a trail a blind man could follow."

Her face fell.

"On the other hand . . ." He sighed. "Give it here."

After a few minutes' study, he pointed to an area circled in pencil. "This looks like the approximate area where the djinns have been worst. You could be right."

"What do you think he wants with them?"

"Nothing good," said Walker grimly. "Let's go." Scrounge trotting happily behind, they negotiated the maze of buildings, emerging from the shadows into the blazing sunlight where the rear of the estate butted up against gray rocky hills. The only person about was an elderly man who shuffled toward an outdoor privy, scratching his privates and muttering to himself.

Mehcredi kept up easily enough, though she was noisy on the scree slopes, pebbles clattering from beneath her feet. Even behind the tinted spectacles, she squinted in the light that bounced off the rocks, baking and relentless.

"Where's your hat?" Walker said irritably.

She rolled her shoulders, blotted her face with her sleeve. "In the cave. It annoys me."

Pausing in the shade of a narrow wadi, she turned to face him, her hands on her hips. "You didn't even say good-bye."

Walker shouldered past her. "Wasn't much point."

After a short tingling silence, she scrambled after him. "Why? Were you going to come back?"

"I don't know." He whirled around so abruptly, she slammed into his chest. "What do you take me for, Mehcredi?"

Pushing the glasses down, she peered over the top of them. "I don't know," she said seriously. "I've told you that."

"You want to know what I was thinking? All right!" Gripping her upper arms, he pulled her up the inch necessary to make up the difference in their heights. He thrust his face into hers. "Every time, the odds are against me and every time they get slimmer. Every diabloman, every demon, every kill. 'Cestors' bones, it's a miracle I've survived this far."

The dog whined, butting his head between them. Walker ignored him.

"All that matters is the vengeance of my people. Do you understand?" He gave a harsh bark of laughter. "I don't fucking care if I live or die as long as I don't fail. And every demon is stronger than me."

Mehcredi opened her mouth and closed it again.

"Very wise," he said. "You think I'm going to take an innocent into that? I've got the blood of the Shar on my hands. I won't add yours."

His chest heaving, he stepped back, releasing her, his temples throbbing. How the fuck did she provoke him into losing control? This wasn't who he was. Closing his eyes, he tried to ground himself, reaching for the *ch'qui*, the strength that never failed, but it was like trying to grasp a fog.

"Stop for a minute," she said. "Here." A water flask was thrust into his hands.

Walker ground his teeth, but he took a swallow of tepid water.

"I've been meaning to ask. How exactly do you kill a demon?" Her grin was shaky, but it was a grin nonetheless. "In case I meet one, you know?"

Suddenly, he felt unutterably weary. "You get the diabloman alone and kill him first," he said, leading the way up the final slope to the cave. "Before he can call his demon, though his death will bring it at once, out of sheer curiosity, if nothing else."

He leaned against the wall, watching her strip off the outer layers of clothing. The cave was a couple of degrees cooler than the world outside, but that didn't mean it wasn't hot. The roots of her hair were showing blond, but he didn't have any more blengos.

"Then what?" she said.

He shrugged. "It's you against a demon. They're all different—mandibles, pincers, mind games, illusions, barbed tails. I find hacking the head off works pretty well." Pushing away from the wall, he said, "We should eat. Get some rest. We'll be traveling at night again."

Retrieving the sandmat, he shook it out of the net and drew his knife.

"Sister, what *is* that?" Mehcredi crouched to peer, the dog at her side. "It looks like a pancake."

Walker flipped the animal over to expose the small circular mouth full of needle teeth. "A desert creature called a sandmat. But this is only a small one. I've seen some as big as a tablecloth. Good eating if you're careful."

She reached out to touch the muscled underside with a fingertip. "Careful?"

"The venom sacs are full of poison." Running the point of the knife around the mouth revealed three pulpy purplish glands. "Sand-mats kill by dropping over their prey and squeezing to hold them still. Once they bite, it's all over." He popped the glands onto a flat stone. Working quickly, he followed up by gutting the creature.

Mehcredi pulled a face. "That's disgusting!"

"City girl," he said without rancor. "You want something good to eat, you put up with a bit of mess. Don't let the dog go."

"Like sex," she said thoughtfully. "That's what you said—good, but messy." She tilted her head to one side. "Funny, I didn't mind that part at all."

Gods, she was right. She hadn't minded. *Wet and hot, earthy and eager. Slick for him.* Taking the stone, Walker stepped out of the cave and wedged it in the fork of the nearest tree, well out of Scrounge's reach. By the time he returned, he had command of himself.

"Yes," he said with perfect calm. "Now you know. I'll finish skinning this. Go see if you can find some wood for a fire, will you? Take the dog with you, and for 'Cestors' sake, put your hat on."

A short time later, the dog lay in a dark corner, crunching bones. The assassin sat cross-legged across the fire, contentedly licking her fingers.

"I'll get the bedrolls," Walker said to the rocky ceiling.

When he laid them out at either end of the cave, she hesitated, then said, "Walker, can we—?"

"Sleep," he said brusquely. "You'll need it."

Stretching out across the entrance to the cave, he turned his back on her stoic face. He didn't know why, but the matter-of-fact resignation—hell, as if rejection was no more than what she expected—hurt him more than the initial flinch she hadn't been able to suppress.

Resolutely, he closed his eyes. What was done was done. It should not have been done and he was a fool, but it was too late now. How fortunate that first loves, by their very nature, tended to burn out quickly.

For the first time, he found himself wondering what Mam would have thought of Mehcredi of Lonefell. Like all the Shar, she'd respected courage, his mother. By the Ancestors, she'd been a warrior, as strong as these ancient hills, and equally enduring. Walker had been twelve when his father left on a hunting trip and never returned, swept away by a flash flood that roared down a wadi. He remembered his mother at the death rites, singing Da's Song, her spine as straight as a quarter-staff, not a tear on her cheek.

And yet . . . He'd been lucky, hadn't he? He'd been well mothered. To say nothing of his noisy, brawling, loving siblings. Mehcredi had had no one, and nothing.

How, in the gods' names, had she turned out sane, her spirit untarnished, as bright and shiny as a newly minted coin?

A bittersweet smile curved his lips. Mam would have hustled Mehcredi into the family tent, woven beads and feathers into her hair and made her a Song of her own. How would it begin?

Mulling over the first line, he sank into a fitful doze.

Mehcredi couldn't work out how he did it, but even leading his pony over the rough spots, the swordmaster blended into the landscape, became a part of the desert at night, as soundless as she imagined the djinns to be. While she toiled along behind him in a graceless scramble, the sweat chilling on her skin in the cold dry air.

Even though they could have been alone in the world, he kept to the moonshadow, following the broad swath of broken bushes and churned-up dirt that marked the passage of Nyzarl's party.

He waited for her to catch up. "We should stop soon, find a place to hole up for the day."

Poor Scrounge flopped at their feet, panting. Mehcredi bent to pat him, taking comfort from the wiry fur beneath her fingers, the swipe of a hot tongue across her wrist.

They'd been traveling for two nights now, and each day had been the same. Eat and rest. Monosyllabic conversation. But other times, he'd talk, almost as if he were thinking aloud, about the painted dogs and the way the pack cared for the old and the sick more tenderly than most humans. Or about tygres, so rare as to be almost a legend, but real enough with their striped hides and yellow eyes and paws like dinnerplates armed with scimitars.

She wondered if it was the only kindness he thought he could show her. Because he took scrupulous care to avoid touching. If she stepped close, which she did at every opportunity, he'd freeze for a second and then move aside. She still ached, great daft lump that she was—who'd have thought it would hurt so much?—but she loved the sound of his voice, deep and slow, every word measured and considered. It did help—a little.

"Do you know where we are?" she asked. Stupid question.

The silvery light of the Sister caressed his high cheekbones, shadowing his eyes. An errant breeze flirted with his hair, falling in a long tail down his back. He gazed down to the place where the valley floor forked, another line of rocky hills joining the first, as stubborn and timeless as the bones of some gargantuan prehistoric creature poking up out of the subsoil.

Cool and remote, he said, "There's water to the east, not far. Would you like to bathe?"

Mehcredi laughed. "You have to ask? Gods, I can smell myself."

But all he said was, "Come then." Without another word, he mounted and turned east, into the hills.

An hour later, they had to dismount and lead the ponies into a rocky defile that grew progressively narrower until their shoulders brushed the walls and the animals whickered with nerves.

"Where are we?" For some reason, she felt she had to whisper.

"Nearly there."

Abruptly, he turned left, reaching back to grasp her wrist. "Careful."

"Walker, what—?"

"We're on a ledge above a long drop."

Mehcredi stared to her right. All she could see was the silhouette of rocky ramparts, sharp-toothed against the starry sky and beneath them a pool of inky darkness, but instinctively, she knew that below lay nothing but empty air. All the hair on the back of her neck stood up. Scrounge pressed right up against her calf, trembling.

"Not much farther. I've got you."

She peered at his dim outline, listening with her whole body. There was a suppressed note in his voice, full of tension and . . . excitement.

"It opens up here. Stand still a minute."

The reins were taken from her hands and the ponies led away. A few moments later, Walker reappeared at her side and drew her about another fifteen feet along the trail.

"Here will do," he said.

With one hand, Mehcredi patted the reassuring bulk of stone at her back. She heard rustling, as if a whole field of feathergrass thrashed in the wind. After a moment, Walker said, "Sit down and lean back. You're safe."

With a sigh of relief, she sank onto a soft mat of feathergrass. "Gods, you're useful."

"I live to serve," he said, very dry, and she chuckled.

"What are we doing here?" she asked as he lowered himself beside her.

"Waiting."

"Oh." Mehcredi wrapped her arms around herself. It was plain wrong that a place so hot during the day should be so bloody cold at night. "What for?"

"Dawn," he said repressively.

"But why—?"

"Mehcredi." He turned his head to look into her face and she wondered if his night vision was keener than hers. She wouldn't be surprised. "Shut up and wait for the surprise, all right?"

26

Walker said, "You're shaking. Are you scared?"

"Just cold." Mehcredi set her jaw. "I lived through the Lonefell winters." She edged a little closer. "Must be out of practice."

A short pause and he drew her under his arm, into all that wonderful heat, spiced with healthy male sweat and something that was uniquely Walker.

Bliss.

Gingerly, she snuggled closer and laid her head on his shoulder.

"Better?"

"Oh, yes." She smiled into the folds of his robe.

Callused fingers nudged her chin around, toward the unseen void before them. "You have to look out there," he said, "or you'll miss it."

"Mmm."

Mehcredi blinked sleepily as the Sister sank gracefully behind the ramparts, followed by the martial red crescent of the Brother. Muscle by muscle, she relaxed into Walker's firm body, conforming her shape to his, soft where he was hard. One star at a time, the night sky faded to a pale gray.

Peace. This was peace.

The place where she fitted, a puzzle piece finally come home. Oh, it was transitory, she knew that. Walker didn't want her, not truly. But now she knew what it was, she could strive for it again. Because life went on, a day at a time. Regardless of misery, you went on living, breathing, eating, sleeping. *Yearning.*

When it was all over, she'd still have this—the shining knowledge of what was possible, if she was incredibly, extraordinarily lucky. Carefully, she took a fold of his robe between her fingers, watching the gray cliffs flush with color—rose and lavender and yellow. Light spooled out, banishing wells and stripes of shadow, slithering down the cliffs.

A mist rose gently out of the valley below, gossamer streamers twisting and spiraling in the light, only to dissipate in the upper atmosphere. Mehcredi caught her breath, staring. Almost shyly, dawn revealed a jeweled cup, an oval basin bisected by a silver stream that poured out of the cliff in an arching frothy stream of sparkling joy, only to disappear beneath a forbidding dome of rock on the farther side. It was bordered so densely by stands of cedderwoods and widow's hair trees that only enticing glimpses of the water could be seen, winking between the leaves. The valley was carpeted with a type of grass she hadn't seen before, about knee-high and topped with silvery purple tassels that danced in an unseen breeze.

Mehcredi licked dry lips. "What is it?"

"The Spring of Shiloh. Sacred to the Shar."

Slowly, she sat up. "It's . . . it's beautiful."

"Yes."

The swordmaster gazed out over the valley, his jaw set. "We are the first to see it since . . . since . . ." He swallowed, blinking hard.

She could have sworn she heard the snap as her heart broke for him. She lifted her fingers to brush his cheekbone. "Don't be sad," she said. "Please, don't."

With a dismissive shrug, he stilled her hand in his, but after a moment, he slipped an arm around her waist to pull her close. "They are worthy of grief."

She managed a shaky smile. "Yes, I know."

Scrounge barked, shattering the silence. He stood at the head of a narrow path, prancing with impatience, tail waving.

Walker stood and pulled Mehcredi to her feet. "Let's go."

Smelling the water, the ponies were eager enough, but the track had their eyes rolling. Barely wide enough for a single person, it switchbacked down the slope, made difficult with rocks and tree roots. At one point, it passed so close to the waterfall, the air was full of moisture and thunder, every surface slippery and treacherous.

Pausing to catch her breath, Mehcredi's attention was caught by a flash of green. She had to go up on her tiptoes and reach up over her head, but she snagged the trailing stem and drew it down for a closer inspection. Bedewed with the river's mist, velvety petals of the palest pink shone almost luminescent in the shadow of the cliff.

Her belly clenched, heat rushed to her cheeks.

When she raised the bloom to her nose and inhaled, she smelled liquid honey, musky and intoxicating. She dabbled a finger into the rosy heart, licked at the nectar like a cat. Delicious. Gods, it did look like—Her flush intensified.

"Mehcredi, are you all right?"

Up ahead, Walker had turned. He stood at the head of his pony, looking back over his shoulder. His dark gaze flicked from her mouth to the flower and back again, stopped and clung. He might as well have reached out and touched her. Laid his lips against hers.

The wave of heat was instantaneous, roaring over her as if she'd been dipped in flames. Only a second or two, but she was left leaning against the damp stone at her back for support, seared to the bones.

Walker's face shuttered. Without another word, he swung around and continued down the trail.

But she'd seen it—heat, passion, *want*.

Turning her face to the spray, she laughed aloud for sheer joy—not only because of what she'd seen, though that was enough to set her blood bubbling, but—oh, sweet Sister of mercy—she'd *recognized* it! She'd read his expression and got it right, she was as certain of it as her next breath.

Lifting the orchid to her face, she breathed, "Thank you," into its sweet-smelling heart, dropped the lightest of kisses on a cool satiny petal and replaced the stem where she'd found it.

"C'mon," she said to Scrounge, who was watching with one ear up and the other down. "I'll carry you the rest of the way."

Her feet lighter than air, she danced down the precipitous path, the pony clip-clopping gingerly behind. A cold nose nudged her cheek and a warm tongue swiped her skin. "Stop that." But instead of pushing the dog away, she hugged him closer.

She was getting better at it, she was!

Striving for calm, she set herself to think rationally, to remember. Start with the steward. She'd caught the flavor of the man's fear at once, trapped between the wrath of two equally terrifying men—Walker in the here and now, his dreadful master in the future. Everything he felt had been blatantly obvious, but still . . .

The horse trader had been a greedy, mean-spirited man, the sort who'd knife a friend in a dark alley for the price of a thin beer. Now how had she known that? The lip-smacking glee with which he'd described the wounds left by the djinns, something about his small dark eyes, the way he'd rubbed his hands together—they'd all been clues she'd processed without realizing what she did.

And gods, these were strangers, while Walker was the person she knew best in the whole world. She'd seen the swordmaster's soul stripped bare, seen him in the grip of almost every human emotion, coldly furious, borne down by grief and guilt, consumed by lust—and yet he could be so tender he made her heart ache. Godsdammit, how many people had seen the swordmaster smile, let alone laugh? But she had, *she*, Mehcredi of Lonefell, failed assassin and passable swordswoman, owner of a scruffy mongrel and . . . companion to the most fascinating man on Palimpsest.

Her heart soaring, she tightened her grip on Scrounge's sturdy ribcage until he whined in protest.

As the path began to widen, she reached for the old sense of separateness, the crystal walls that closed her off from so-called normal people.

Oh, still there.

Crossly, Mehcredi rolled her shoulders. Godsdammit, Abad the waggoner had liked Meck, hadn't he? She'd managed a perfectly ordinary conversation with no problem at all. With the Trinitarian lord in Trimegrace, she'd missed the sexual lures because she'd been so focused on the interesting things he said, not what he did.

Her jaw set in a stubborn line. All right then. Actions, not words.

And paying attention.

The rump of Walker's pony vanished around a corner and automatically, she followed, brow furrowed. She stopped. Spread out before her, basking green in the sun, the impact of the hidden valley was so visceral, it was like running into a wall. After days in the rocky desert, it stole the breath, pouring over the spirit like a soothing balm.

Walker stared. His chest rose and fell with the force of his respiration, color high in his face.

"Gods, it's gorgeous." For some reason, she had to whisper. Stooping, she tipped the dog out of her arms. With a joyous yip, he disappeared into the long grass, his passage marked by wildly waving tassels.

"I'd forgotten," Walker murmured, almost as if he spoke to himself. "How could I have forgotten?" Dropping the reins, he took a few steps forward and sank to his knees in the grass. He sank the fingers of one hand into the dirt, his head bowed. "The *ch'qui* is so strong here."

"The chi what? You've said that before. What is it?"

Slowly, he rose, tilting his palm to let a stream of dark soil trickle down. "It's what makes me a shaman," he said at last.

"You get your Magick out of the dirt?"

His lips twitched. "A gross simplification. The *ch'qui* is the soul of the world, its life force, if you will."

Mehcredi released her pony to wander down to the pool at the base of the falls. Its fellow was already there, nose buried in the foaming water.

She thought about the chi thing for a moment. "That's why you love your garden."

"Yes." Walking up to a magnificent widow's hair tree, he reached up to run his fingers over a dangling twig verdant with green. The tree swayed in the breeze, bending over him. Another twig swayed down to brush his cheek as gently as a lover. His throat moved as he closed his eyes.

"It's why your garden loves you," she said, her pulse thudding with another flash of insight. "It's what you use to grow soft beds out of ordinary feathergrass. Gods what else can you do?"

His black gaze dropped to her breasts. Immediately, the Mark flared to life, not burning, but tingling soft as the brush of orchid petals. She moistened her lips. "Apart from that."

"You sure you want to know?" He moved away, the grass swishing around his knees. From somewhere deeper in the trees, a bird chorus started up, shrill and scolding. Walker smiled. "Ganglebirds. I haven't heard that call in years."

Scrounge barked, hysterical with excitement. With a whoosh, four of the most extraordinary birds Mehcredi had ever seen took to the air. They were solidly crimson, with thin snaky necks and bright yellow beaks. Long, stick-thin legs trailed beneath them as they honked their displeasure, while the dog capered about below, barking furious threats.

"We'll tether the ponies here. They're safe enough. I want to set up camp and get clean." Bending, he retrieved something from the grass. "Here." He handed her a single red feather.

Absurdly pleased, Mehcredi stammered her thanks, but he was already several steps ahead of her, his hair shining blue black in the sun.

Half an hour later, he'd woven another spacious bower out of willing ticklewhisker bushes, but this time, in what she could only suppose was a fit of whimsy, he coaxed a wild lover vine to knot it all together.

"We have to be back up the cliff path before it's dark, but there's time to wash and eat and sleep." He pointed toward the waterfall. "You go that way. I'll be downstream. Yell if you need me."

Mehcredi surveyed the sun-shot water of the pool with the deepest misgivings. It ranged from a golden brown at the edges to a solid dark green in the middle. The swordmaster hadn't asked if she could swim. She couldn't, of course, but gods, how she longed to be clean.

After a little, she shrugged, stripped and waded in where the stream flowed quick and shallow over a big flat rock. Gasping at the first chill, she splashed water over her breasts, while her nipples crimped and the Mark glowed a darker shade of green bronze beneath the white of her skin.

Scrounge appeared out of the bushes, stretched out on a sun-warmed rock and watched her with a wary brown eye. Mehcredi giggled. "Relax." She showed her empty hands. "See? No soap."

Instead, she scooped up handfuls of fine river sand from between the rocks and used that to scrub her skin. Sister, it was good to feel clean! Greatly daring, she dipped her head below the surface and opened her eyes, watching tiny, silver fish dart for cover among the rocks. Where did they come from, out here in the desert?

Climbing out, she joined Scrounge on his rock. In the dappled shade, the sun was no more than pleasantly warm on her shoulders, the coolness coming off the water keeping the temperature comfortable. When a crimson cloud of ganglebirds returned to stalk in the shallows on their improbable legs, Scrounge growled, but she dug her fingers into his ruff and gave him a warning shake. Eventually he subsided, yawned and went to sleep.

Deeply content, Mehcredi watched the ganglebirds fish, while the sun and the breeze dried her skin.

Walker floated on his back, spread-eagle, buoyed up by the water, and found a small measure of peace. Once he'd thought this hidden valley was his heart's home. Now he knew no such place existed, but the beauty of it, the whisper of Ancestral voices in the waving grass—all that eased his soul. Clouds scudded across the sky and the widow's hair trees that fringed the pool tossed their translucent pale green leaves in the light breeze.

It was so quiet he heard Mehcredi and the dog pushing through bushes and grass for some time before they appeared. He should teach her to walk like a Shar. A few words of encouragement, and she'd pick it up quickly enough. She did so much better when he praised her.

Lazily, he let his feet sink so he could tread water, enjoying the silken swish of it over his chest and shoulders, the chill closing like a cold fist around his ankles where the pool was deepest.

The touchme bushes chimed a greeting and Mehcredi stepped forward to perch on a rock. By way of greeting, she held out her hat, full of ripe, red summerberries. "Look what I found. Want some?"

Her lips were shiny with juice, her fingers stained. 'Cestors be thanked she wasn't nude, as he'd half feared, but all she wore was an unlaced shirt.

"No."

Actually, the shirt made it worse, concealing and enticing, exposing a pale mouthwatering length of endless leg. Godsdammit, she even had pretty feet—way too big to be called dainty, but nicely proportioned with high arches. She'd tucked the crimson ganglebird plume behind one ear, where it bobbed jauntily. Ridiculous, especially with her two-tone hair. Walker's gut clenched and his cock filled, a heavy, unwelcome pull in his groin.

Irritation made him snappish. "You've ruined your hat."

"I'll wash it before we go." A grin lit her face. "Won't take more than a minute to dry. You clean yet?" Her eyes twinkled.

A Shar had his pride. Gritting his teeth, he dived deep, sculling down through the shadow of the cliff, where the water was shockingly cold. In a single motion, he burst out of the water, stepped up onto a handy rock and grabbed his shirt from a bush. His back turned, he shrugged into the sleeves, gathering his hair into a heavy rope and squeezing out the moisture.

"Walker?"

"What?" He heard her move, felt her breath against his shoulder blade.

Sticky fingers brushed fabric aside, glanced over the scars on his hip. "How did you get this?"

Smoothly, he made a half turn, shifted away. "I met a demon— with claws—and I was careless." He breathed in through his nose, reaching for his battle self, cold and hard. Shit, wrong word. Not hard, not—

"It must have been huge. Look"—stepping right into his space, Mehcredi tried to match her fingers to the ugly furrows—"my hand doesn't even come close."

Walker stared, half mesmerized by her touch. She must have gobbled up summerberries as eagerly as a child, the evidence was all over her fingers, and now on him. But 'Cestors help him, she was no child.

He wanted to tug at his hair to still the clamor. Justifications, arguments, rationalizations—they flew at him like corpsebirds, jeering and jangling and squawking so loud he couldn't think straight. Yes, Mehcredi was a woman grown, but her heart was as innocent as a babe's. Yes, he was the first man to treat her with any sort of consideration whatsoever. Yes, she was magnificently strong and healthy, driven by natural physical needs. No wonder she'd lighted on him to break her drought. Gods, yes, look at the damage he'd done with proximity and a little misplaced kindness. And then he'd compounded the disaster by making love to her, though she'd called it fucking. So direct.

His breath caught at the memory. *Carazada* . . .

Even worse, he'd let her see further into his soul than . . . well, than anyone. And wasn't that an even more unwelcome realization?

'Cestors save her, he was so dark, so broken, and she thought of him as a hero to be healed as if they were characters in some stupid romance.

But he wasn't. He was beyond salvation, cynical and cold. Empty, save for his vengeance. By the seven million Songs, he'd grown used to the shape of his life. It was like wearing in a pair of ill-fitting boots— there'd be discomfort, pain even, until bones and flesh conformed to leather. In the end, the shoes hardly pinched at all.

But the crippling damage was done.

"Don't—" he growled, but she lifted a summerberry to his lips, leaning right into him to do it, bracing herself with a hand on his hip. She could hardly miss the rigid length poking into her stomach.

Sweetness burst across his tongue, exploding in his bloodstream, making him light-headed. Brutally, he quelled the urge to lick every trace of juice from her fingers. Instead, he gripped her wrist, staring down into wide eyes gone dark as pewter.

Mehcredi smiled, though her lips trembled. "Good, aren't they?" Her lashes fluttered. The hand on his hip fumbled down to his cock. Despite everything he could do, it leaped into her fist. By the time he closed hard fingers over hers it was too late.

An incredible suspicion entered his mind. "Godsdammit, Meh-credi, are you *playing* me?"

"Um, yes?" When nervous tension made her grip tighten, he had to bite back a groan. "Is it working?"

27

Trapped, as neatly as a sandmat in a snare. But unlike the sandmat, Walker was no dumb beast. He understood the consequences of capture, knew he should be making frantic efforts to escape, yet he had not the slightest inclination to do so.

Whatever you do, you'll hurt her, whispered the voice of temptation, clear as a bell through the corpsebirds of confusion. *But you can teach her, love her—fuck her—right here, right now. Why not?*

"Mehcredi," he said hoarsely. "Last chance. *Back off.*"

She had her cheek pressed into his chest, fucking *purring*, her hips undulating against his. When her thumb began to brush absently over the head of his shaft, it was simply beyond him to stop her.

"You've never lied to me, Walker," she said against his thundering heart. "Not once." She raised a flushed face to his.

"You're the person I know best in the whole world—the gods know I've tried to understand you with everything I have." She drew a shuddering breath that vibrated through him, sending hot chills up his spine. "Tell me you don't want me and I'll stop, I promise."

"That's not the point!" The cry was wrenched out of him.

They were both shaking now, dragging in air with great hard heavy gulps.

"No," whispered Mehcredi, "*this* is the point." Quivering like a tree in a storm, she pressed trembling lips to his, simultaneously giving his cock a shy squeeze.

Gods! Sweeter than summerberries, hotter than the desert at noon, with an undertone of wild Magick that raced through his blood like the *ch'qui* gone mad. A roaring in his ears, Walker wrapped a hand around the back of her neck and sank into her mouth like a man dying of thirst.

More, more! The beat echoed in his head, in his heart, his cock, his balls. His soul answered: *Never enough.* Never, ever. Gods, he'd never have his fill of her.

Mehcredi gave as good as she got, writhing against him. When he squeezed the fingers beneath his, guiding her in the rough rhythm he liked, she growled deep in her throat, gripping him gorgeously hard, and hiking a leg up over his hip. His knuckles slid over the slick flesh of her core, shockingly hot and wet. Open for him.

Walker froze, every rational thought lost in a soft red explosion, a drumming refrain of want, want—*want.* The next few moments disappeared, just . . . fell out of the world. When he came back to himself, he had Mehcredi slammed up against the trunk of a widow's hair tree—'Cestors be thanked they were smooth-barked. Her long legs were wrapped tight around his waist, his hands full of the creamy curves of her buttocks and she was raising herself to take him, her fingers digging into his shoulders.

Gods, she was mewling like a godsbedamned tygre cub.

He'd never seen anything so erotic, so earthy and splendid in his life.

Animal instinct had him surging forward. He was wedged halfway before he had time to think, the seed boiling in his balls, at the base of his cock.

When their eyes met, her face bloomed in a wild wicked grin. "More!" she gasped. Then she threw her head back and laughed, the sound ringing around them like pure joy.

The slide home was so sweet, so dirty, Walker rested his forehead against hers, panting. "Won't last." He sucked in a huge breath. "Sorry."

"Nngh." She wriggled and clenched, sighing with pleasure. "We can do it again, right?"

Walker flexed his hips, trying to keep it slow, reaching for the control he was sure he'd left some-fucking-where. "In a . . . little . . . while. Oh gods."

He'd be fine if she'd damn well stay still, let him catch his breath, but gods no, Mehcredi the assassin was too strong, too willful for that. Like the green summer surge of the *ch'qui*, a time when the sap rose and buds and leaves burst forth in wild profusion, she was what she was, a force of nature.

"Let yourself go," she whispered, nipping his earlobe, a sharp stinging sensation. "I won't break."

"Stop . . . pushing."

Her chuckle was deep and rich. "I think you like it." With no more warning than a soft intake of air, she clamped down hard on his girth.

Walker's head swam. He powered through the hot clasp, thrusting again and again, harder and harder, slamming her against the tree. A small part of his brain was conscious of Mehcredi's voice, urging him on with keening cries that grew higher and more desperate with every thrust. Ah gods, how he loved those sounds, so quintessentially female! Her heels drummed in the small of his back. His wet hair fell in his eyes, but he couldn't spare a hand to tuck it back.

Nothing mattered save the godsawful, wonderful pressure in his balls and the woman in his arms, alternately shuddering and calling his name as they worked closer and closer toward a shattering climax. Growling deep in his throat, he hitched her higher, stroking hard and deep as she raced him to the finish.

"Argh, gods! There . . . ah, there!" Her legs tightened around him like a vise and her body arched up in a long beautiful bow. "*Walker!*"

Thank all the gods. Walker released the last vestiges of control. His buttocks hollowed as he tensed, caught by the searing intensity of the boiling rush from balls to cock. But even as exquisite pleasure rippled the length of his shaft, even as he squeezed his eyes shut, groaning his relief into the curve of her neck, he knew.

He'd done precisely as she'd asked—*he'd let go.* Somehow, somewhere along the line, he'd surrendered some part of himself—his heart, his soul—who the hell knew exactly? Still reeling, he turned his head to nuzzle at Mehcredi's neck, getting a breathy mumble in response. Worse, if he wasn't careful, he'd compromise his duty to his people. Because for the first time since the death of the Shar, he had a vulnerable spot.

You had nothing left to lose before, whispered the voice of reason, the voice he was coming to loathe. *Now you do.*

All because of a child-woman, a person with no earthly idea of how relationships worked. Not that he was any pattern card in that respect, he had to admit. A fine pair.

He eased back, supporting her until she could stand. Mehcredi leaned against his shoulder and gave a long low whistle, like a boy. "My knees don't work anymore."

Just like that, she made him smile. Father's balls, this had fucking disaster written all over it. He must have been mad to think of bringing her within a hundred miles of Nyzarl . . .

The gods hold hostage the ones we love. The Ancestors had a proverb for every occasion. Very wise.

From where he stood on a rocky eminence, the Necromancer could see a storm building to the west. But the clouds behaved strangely, roiling about close to the ground, distorting the air so that it shimmered. The breeze picked up, bringing with it an acrid flavor that caught at the back of the throat.

Ah. The old man had done well, guiding them through the endless arid hills. This was the spot.

His robes fluttering, the Necromancer braced himself against the increasing wind, enjoying the sensation of strength. "You are watching, Xotclic?"

That feeling at the base of his skull, like the brush of abrasive fingertips, a whisper on the rising wind. "Ss."

"Pasha." The old man appeared at the Necromancer's side as if he'd sprung out of the stony soil. He wrung his gnarled hands. "Please. Send a man to warn them." He indicated the small settlement below, a collection of mud huts and crude animal pens, crouched next to a muddy seep.

"Too late." The Necromancer glanced at his guard captain. "Keep our people behind the ridge, out of sight."

Hopping from foot to foot in his agitation, the old man broke into a torrent of incoherent words, curses and pleas, even tears.

"Quiet." The Necromancer closed his eyes, extending his other senses. The space creature seethed with the agony of separation, radiating its own strange Magick. Driven by blind all-consuming hunger, it didn't kill for pleasure. It had no intelligence as such, no moral sense. All it knew was that the energy released by death eased the pain. But he'd guessed right enough. Without his intervention, the space djinn would die in the dry desert heat.

His eyes bright with interest, he watched the air boil and thicken, people emerge from their tents and try to run. The men thrust the women and children behind them, jabbing with staffs and swords, but it was useless. Sharp reports echoed across the desert, competing with screams of the wounded. The Necromancer's gaze narrowed as a young woman snatched up a burning brand from the campfire and skewered the djinn descending on a child.

With an ear-aching shriek, it exploded in glittering shards that twisted slowly in the wind and fluttered to the valley floor.

"Highly sensitive to heat." Dotty's voice came from behind him. "Did you hear? It went . . . pop." She giggled. "Pop, pop, pop."

"Should enjoy the glaciers in the north then."

"Oh, yes." A stifled snort of merriment. "If it doesn't kill you before you can offer to show it the way."

The camp was strewn with bodies, a half dozen or so still writhing, agony spilling out of them in high-pitched whimpers and moans. The djinn stones he'd seen in the old man's mind, boring through living flesh until they reached the heart and shattered it. What an extraordinarily creative way to kill.

Gathering his robes around him, the Necromancer smiled at Dotty. "I don't think so." He strode toward the carnage, Nyzarl's strong heart pumping hard in his breast. "Come, Xotclic, there's enough for both of us."

"Ss."

※

Walker's white teeth ripped the last shred of meat from a sandmat bone. Tossing it to the expectant Scrounge, he lay back in the bower and stacked his hands behind his head. Speckled shadows dappled his long limbs.

Mehcredi longed to dapple them too. With her tongue.

"It's nice, isn't it?" she said. "Not wearing clothes, I mean."

He shrugged. "Go to sleep."

She touched a knot on his collarbone. "How did you break it?"

"Jumped out of a second-story window."

"And this one?" A pale ugly ripple on the dark skin of one forearm.

"A diabloman with a throwing star."

"What about—?"

He grabbed her wrist. "What are you doing, Mehcredi?"

"Exploring." She lowered her gaze to his groin, where his shaft lay quietly against a hard thigh. "I've never seen a naked man before, not close-up." She leaned forward. "Oh, look, it moved!"

"Godsdammit!" He came up on one elbow, the hard planes of his face flushed.

She'd never have another chance. Mehcredi laid a palm against the center of his chest. "Let me?" she said. "I'll be gentle, I promise."

For the space of three or four heartbeats, Walker stared at her, his eyes glittering. Then he blinked, a sweep of long sooty lashes. "What the hell." He relaxed, shoving his pack under his head as a pillow. "Be my guest."

Oh, gods. She wasn't going to rush this, not for anything. Her heart stumbling with excitement, she began with his hands, comparing their palms, stroking up over the muscled swell of biceps to the strong neck and broad shoulders, the complex struts of his collarbones and ribcage. Except for the scars, his skin was so smooth.

His eyes were closed, his face calm.

When Mehcredi pressed a kiss to the knot on his collarbone, he huffed out a breath but he didn't stop her. Encouraged, she ran her hands over his ribs. Walker twitched. "Ticklish?" she asked.

One dark eye opened. "No." It fell shut again.

A lie if ever she'd heard one. Grinning to herself, Mehcredi transferred her attentions to the muscled planes of his chest. His heart thudded beneath her fingertips, strong and a little fast. Fascinated, she stroked over ridges and dips, luxuriating in his heat, his sheer solidity. Gooseflesh chased her touch. A warm dark brown, his nipples drew up into small peaks. Her own nipples tingled in response. She'd loved him touching them, suckling them.

Gods, he was a banquet, stretched out before her!

She stared, her brows knitted. His cock had expanded, it looked . . . tighter, the soft skin slipping back to reveal the first hint of a broad rosy head.

Keeping a cautious eye on it, she extended her tongue and licked around one nipple. He tasted good, clean and salty, his flesh like crinkled velvet. Untouched, his shaft stirred, filling.

"Mehcredi." His fingers skated over her shoulder to tangle in her hair.

"Not stopping." Gently, she tugged the other nipple between her teeth, and unable to resist, reached down to cradle his cock in her hand.

With a soft curse, Walker arched his hips, thrusting into her loose fist. Mehcredi lifted her head. Gods, he was swelling in her grip, the most amazing thing she'd ever seen, hot and throbbing and so *alive*. Experimentally, she squeezed, sliding soft delicate skin over an iron-hard core.

Walker swore again.

"Does it feel good?"

"Yes. Gods!" A pause. "Could be better." His jaw was set, the tendons in his neck taut. "Use your mouth."

Sensory memory made the nerves behind her pubic bone contract in a silvery spasm. Lips, tongue, fingers. That night in the Three Rivers Inn, he'd made her throb, sent her flying. Surely she could do the same for him now?

Walker shifted his legs apart so she could kneel between them. Mehcredi had to swallow hard. Sweet Sister, her mouth was watering.

He was ferociously erect now, stiff and quivering, the heart-shaped head of his cock completely exposed, shining with moisture. When she bent her head to swipe her tongue across the curve of it, Walker inhaled sharply. Salty, a little bitter, the texture smooth and dense like a ripe fruit.

Impatiently, she shoved his knee aside with her shoulder, opening him up so she could run her fingers over his balls. The swordmaster jerked once, then froze, his breath going raspy. Almost hairless, weighty and swollen, rosy and hot with life.

A single blow and he'd be in agony. Gods, it wasn't possible for a man to make himself more vulnerable.

Mehcredi met the hot midnight gaze over the muscled length of his body. His eyes glittered when she licked her lips. "Tell me what you like."

"Lick. Suck." He fell back, an arm over his eyes and his throat bobbed as he swallowed. "No teeth."

"All right." Dipping her head, Mehcredi ran the flat of her tongue over the ridge that bisected his scrotum, progressing with a long luxurious sweep up the underside of his straining shaft. She finished with a spiral lick around his cock head, whisking the tip of her tongue into the little slit there.

Walker grunted and his free hand clenched in the robes beneath him, so she did it again. And again.

She didn't know quite what to call the sounds he made—Groans? Growls? Whines? But his hips were rising to meet her and she was drunk on erotic power. Her sex was so wet and puffy, she could pleasure herself simply by pressing her thighs together. Her heart singing, she fisted him at the root, cradled his hot heavy balls in her palm and sucked down as much of the rest as she could, relishing the way his girth stretched her lips, his weight sliding velvet smooth over her tongue. His heart's blood pulsed beneath the thin skin. He tasted musky and strong, with a hint of bitterness like tears, like nothing she'd ever known.

When his fingers speared into her hair, she fumbled, choking. He loosened his grip. "Sorry."

Mehcredi hauled in a breath and rolled her shoulders. She relaxed, allowing him to dictate the rhythm. With an inward grin, she got in a sly lash of the tongue on the sensitive head at every pass.

At this moment, Walker was hers, and hers alone. He wasn't thinking of all he'd lost or of killing diablomen; his whole world was under her control—she, Mehcredi of Lonefell, pleasuring him until he groaned and bucked, begging wordlessly for release.

He tugged sharply.

"Mmm?" she murmured, ramping up the suction, loving the way he shuddered.

"Stop," he grated. "Ride me."

Every nerve and muscle in her pelvis tensed with emptiness and yearning. Moisture trickled down her thigh. Mehcredi bestowed a final nibble around the soft wrinkled collar of his foreskin.

Walker set his hands at her waist and helped her to scramble over him. "Put me inside you."

Panting, Mehcredi fumbled about beneath her. "People do it like this?"

His teeth flashed. "Think of it as the next level in the *nea-kata* of fucking. Take your time."

Inch by inch, she sank down, impaling herself. Her eyes wide, she gazed down at the muscled man beneath her. "Feels different," she managed. "Fuller." She clamped down, wriggled. "Gods!"

Walker cupped her breasts, tugging at her aching nipples with clever fingers. Although his face was stark with desire, she told herself the curve of his lips was tender. "Most women like it this way. Gives them control." He lifted into her. "Fuck me, *cara*—Mehcredi."

So she did, using the strength of her thighs to lift, dropping back carefully at first, then faster and faster, gasping with the effort and the jolt of pleasure each time she took him to the hilt.

"Go on." Walker's eyes were black as sin, his cheekbones ruddy with a sexual flush. "I won't break. 'Cestors' bones, you're gorgeous. Like a Battle Maiden."

He was moving with her now, rising and falling, flying with her. Climax hovered close, a breath away, but she couldn't . . . couldn't. Throwing her head back, Mehcredi keened her frustration.

Slipping his hand over her stomach and into her sparse curls, Walker grinned. "Let me show you . . . *ah, gods!* . . . another advantage." He pressed the pad of his forefinger against her clit, so that on the next downward thrust, every nerve burst into flame. The great coil of tension released, the whiplash so glorious, so vicious, that she stiffened, shrieked, then collapsed onto his chest as if she'd been poleaxed.

Walker's arms tightened around her like steel bands. His hips hammered upward. One stroke, two, three. Then he groaned, burying his face in the crook of her neck, his breath hot and rushed. The wet wash of his seed spurted inside her.

The long grass whispered its secret songs, the stream chuckled at its own joke and Scrounge crunched on a bone.

Beneath her, the swordmaster relaxed, his palms drifted soothingly up and down her spine. She thought she heard him whisper, "Ah, *carazada*," but that was probably imagination.

When they emerged from the hidden valley a few hours later, all they had to do was head for the circling cloud of corpsebirds. The old man lay a little distance away upwind of the carnage, propped up against a rock, a knife and a water flask in his lap. He looked up at them without surprise, his rheumy eyes empty and tranquil.

Walker squatted beside him and took his hand. "What happened here, Eldest?"

"The Pasha would not let me warn them." His head rolled feebly. "I have borne enough. First my village, all my kin, now this."

"The djinns?"

Mehcredi picked up the flask and helped the old man to drink. Water trickled from the corners of his slack mouth. "He stood and watched. *Smiling.*"

28

"You mean Nerajyb Nyzarl?" Walker's voice was completely without inflection. "Where is he now?"

"Gone west." The old man shrugged. "Following the djinns. Gods, he *spoke* with them. I saw him." His eyes slid shut and the breath rattled in his wattled throat.

"Eldest." Walker leaned closer. "What did you hear?"

"Nothing." A feeble shrug. "Gibberish. The ice in the north. He said something about the ice fields, the stars, deep space. Nonsense."

"That's not much. And godsdammit, there are any number of routes they could take." The swordmaster's brows drew together. "One set of tracks comes in here, but two leave. Did he send a group back to his estate?"

The old man nodded.

"Why didn't you go?" asked Mehcredi. "You could have traveled in comfort in a wagon. Found a healer."

Slowly, the old man focused on her face. "You're a stranger," he said. "You don't know. Something is broken inside." He pressed a trembling fist to his chest. "I have chosen. This is my end."

The breeze shifted, bringing with it the sweet fetid reek of blood. Mehcredi drew a fold of her head cloth over her nose, bile rising in her throat. The dog pressed closer to her legs, shivering. "Did no one survive?"

The old man made a weary noise. "Some took longer to die than others. The young and the strong." Slow tears oozed from the corners of his eyes.

Walker rubbed a gentle thumb over the back of the veined hand. "I know it's painful, Eldest, but if you can tell me about their weapons, I can destroy them."

"You think?" What started as a chuckle became a wheezing cough.

"They fling . . . stones." The old man shuddered. "Evil things, like parasites. They worm through the flesh. Ah gods, the children, the screams . . ."

"Wait here." Walker got to his feet. "I won't be long." He strode away and the corpsebirds rose, scolding as he approached.

"You're a strange one." The old man groped for Mehcredi's hand.

She tried to smile as she clasped fingers like a bunch of winter twigs. "I know."

"Pretty for a lad."

She snorted. "I'm not pretty, but I'm not a lad either."

"Ah." The old man considered. "He knows?"

"Oh, yes."

"Just as well, the way he looks at ye."

Mehcredi thought about it. *Magnificent*, he'd said. "Maybe."

They lapsed into silence.

When Walker returned, he was white to the lips. "The same as the caravan," he said. "But these were families. Children—" He broke off, his heavy-lidded gaze so intent on Mehcredi's face, he could have been engraving her features on his soul.

Heat rose in her cheeks. "What?"

"Nothing." But the gray tinge beneath the bronze of his skin made her uneasy.

She touched his knee. "Walker—"

He turned away. "Eldest, can you hold on a little longer?"

The old man murmured his assent.

"Mehcredi, come with me." Taking the ponies, Walker stalked away up the valley, until they were screened by a rocky outcrop. "Here." Shoving both sets of reins into her hands, he crouched to redistribute the contents of their packs.

"What are you doing?" she asked with deep misgiving.

"I want you to go back to Caracole, the fastest way possible. I'm giving you almost all of the money and the steward's map. Ride hard for Belizare and buy passage on a ship there. Sell the pony and take a galley if you have to. If you hustle it shouldn't take more than four or five days. Do you remember Rose?"

She shut her mouth with a snap. "No! I mean, yes, of course I remember her, but this is stupid. I'm not going."

The swordmaster continued as if she hadn't spoken. "Go straight to The Garden and ask for her. She'll haul Deiter out of a bottle long enough to listen to you and the queen will listen to him."

Mehcredi set her hands on her hips, her guts heaving. "Do you have some sort of death wish?" Walker stiffened, shooting her a murderous glare. She winced. *Tactful as ever, half-wit.*

Hastily, she regrouped. "Look, you can't take on Nyzarl and his demon and the Sister knows how many djinns all by yourself."

"I don't intend to. But we can't afford to lose track of them either. They don't seem to move fast and Nyzarl's wagons will slow them down. If I can circle around the first wave, I can warn the people in the settlements ahead." His mouth twisted. "I've waited fifteen years for Nyzarl. I can wait a little longer. But the djinns . . ." He shook his head. "Deiter and his godsbedamned bargains. The old bastard couldn't lie straight in bed, but I have to know who this woman is. You tell him everything you can."

"He won't listen to me. And Prue and the others . . . They hate me."

Walker tightened the last strap with a vicious jerk. "Convince them."

"I'm not going." All that way alone? Gods, he must be mad.

"Yes, you are."

"No." What would she do without him, how would she manage even the most ordinary of conversations, great lump that she was? And besides, besides . . .

"Your Mark!" she exclaimed in triumph. She patted her breast. "I can't leave you, even if I wanted to—which I don't."

Walker gripped her shoulders in strong hands. "I put it on, you think I can't remove it?"

Instinctively, she folded her arms across her chest. "Do you have to?"

He shifted closer, cradling her face in his callused palms. "Don't you understand? Many lives depend on you, Mehcredi, mine included."

"I can't do it," she whispered. "I don't know how. And I'll never see you again."

"You can do whatever you set your mind to," he said, spacing every word for emphasis, his eyes boring into hers. "I believe in you. You underestimate yourself, Mehcredi. It's your greatest fault."

"It is?" She must be goggling.

Walker's lips curved, the smile warming his eyes. Mehcredi caught her breath. "Let's see, hmm? Intelligent"—he ticked them off on his fingers—"quick-thinking, resourceful, more than passable with a blade. And brave, so brave you frighten me." He pressed a fleeting kiss to her temple and stepped back.

The smile died. "If you refuse to leave me, I will leave you." He brushed his fingertips over the skin behind her ears, raising goose bumps. "A quick nerve pinch and I'll have all the time I need. This is Shar land. You'll never find me."

Mehcredi turned away. "You've thought of everything," she said bitterly.

"Yes." A heavy arm curled over her shoulders. "Undo your laces."

Dully, she shook her head. "You do it." Closing her eyes, she laid her head against his shoulder and braced herself. "Will it hurt?"

She thought she heard him sigh. "Yes, but not you."

Before she could demand an explanation, warm fingers slid under her shirt to trace the Mark, all the way from her cleavage to the swirl that embraced her nipple, and she could no longer think at all. Walker's breath changed, became deeper and rougher, his heart thudding beneath her ear. He cradled her breast, his thumb idly rasping her nipple until it stood proud and long.

Softly, he began crooning, a two-note chant so completely subvocal that she sensed, rather than heard it. The Marked flesh flared and tingled, the way it did when he made love to her, but after a few seconds, the sensation faded and bled away. She tensed, groping after it, tears stinging her eyes.

"Sshh." Warm firm lips ghosted over her hair, drifted over her forehead, her eyelids. "It's for the best." Slowly, he withdrew his hand. A whisper so soft she wasn't sure she'd heard it. "Ah, *carazada*."

"There." He put her away from him. "Wear your breastband, Meck, my lad."

Mehcredi shot him a furious look. "And the spectacles and the head cloth and the stupid hat." Her lip curled. "You're not my bloody mother."

He ignored this. "Tell Cenda to light a fire every night. I'll do the same."

Silence fell as they stared at each other. "Mehcredi." Walker cleared his throat. "Go."

Her hands fisted by her sides. Godsdammit, how could he stand there all dark and impassive while she was bleeding inside?

"What are you thinking?" she rasped. "One last time, tell me."

But he shook his head. "I don't—I can't—Ah, fuck!" Yanking her into his arms, he kissed her so hard her lips felt bruised. Abruptly, the pressure gentled and he was holding her face between his palms.

"Your penance is done, assassin," he said softly. "Now make something worthy of it. Get on that fucking pony, ride like hell and *live*." Dropping his hands, he took a step back. "For me."

Spinning on his heel, he walked away, his back ramrod straight, the tail of his hair swaying with every supple stride. But her tears blurred his outline long before he disappeared around the outcrop.

Fuck it all to the seven icy hells. Mehcredi kicked an inoffensive rock so hard she hurt her toes. Then she scooped up the dog and clambered onto the pony. As they trotted away down the valley, Scrounge stretched up to lick the tears from her cheeks.

The old man levered his eyes open when Walker touched his shoulder. "That you, lad?"

"Yes, Eldest." Walker rubbed the heel of his hand over his chest, where the tightness was worst.

"Sent her back to the city, did you?" He coughed, spittle running out of the corner of his mouth. "Clever."

The last time Walker had experienced such gut-wrenching terror he'd been fighting to the death as diablomen and their demons destroyed everything he'd ever known or loved. But now—Gods! As he'd stood among the human detritus the djinns had left behind, realization hit him like a mailed fist in the gut. There was no defense against them. Nothing these people had done had saved even a single life. They were desert folk, tough and brave and desperate. They'd tried everything, he could work that out from the weapons scattered about—staffs, swords, even a crossbow.

His cursed imagination had supplied a vision of Mehcredi's body, her long straight limbs impossibly contorted, her luminous eyes dull as marbles, blood running red over ivory skin—He swallowed hard, his guts heaving. Shit, he could still see it, even now, so vivid, so real, the image had the dark force of premonition.

Not again. Fuck, *not again*! 'Cestors be thanked, a plan had come to him. Get her away, get her far away. And as a bonus, she could tell Deiter all about the fucking djinns. It worked on any number of levels.

Walker shrugged. "Safer there than here. And she can pass for a boy."

"Mmm." The old man's head fell to one side.

Walker felt for a pulse and found a weak thready beat. "Eldest," he said softly. "Can you hear me?"

After a long time, the old man croaked, "You . . . better go."

Cupping the old man's cheek, Walker said, "My hands are steady. Do you wish me to do it, quick and clean? It would be my honor."

When he got a murmur of assent, Walker drew the long dagger from his belt.

"Wait. Forgot." Gnarled fingers found their way to his wrist. "Fire. Fire kills them. I saw . . . You understand?"

His heart leaped. "Yes, Eldest, I understand."

"Good." The hand fell away. "I am ready."

"I will sing the Song of Death for you," Walker promised. "Go in peace to your Ancestors, Eldest."

The Necromancer swiped the last piece of bread around his plate. Light tasty sauces, fresh fruit and vegetables. By Shaitan, bringing Cook had been one of his more inspired ideas. Pushing back his chair, he flexed a bicep, relishing the smooth clench and release of power-ful muscle. Nyzarl's body—*his* body—delighted him more with every passing day. Even better, the store of Dark Magick within him seethed and roiled, ready to his hand at any moment. If truth be told, he felt as giddy as a girl. Or as if he were a little drunk. So many deaths, so much energy and pain . . . Ah, it was truly splendid!

Smiling, he rested his chin on his clasped hands. The room was simply furnished, but comfortable enough. It would be churlish to be fussy. After all, the house had belonged to the mayor. It was no one's fault that the town was small and not particularly prosperous.

What should he do? Sipping his wine, he rolled it around his mouth. There were so many possible strategies, all he need do was pick the one that suited him best. Hold Caracole to ransom? Gods, he'd love to see Queen Sikara's face, the bitch. But why stop there? This entire world could be his, Palimpsest in the palm of his hand. He'd close his fist and squeeze the juice out of it.

He cocked his head to one side, considering. Perhaps he should do that.

Kill one man, and you were an assassin, but killing millions—that made you a conqueror. Hmm, he quite liked the sound of that. He could get a fancy uniform with lots of braid on it. The Necromancer's mouth twisted with derision.

No, no, he had a better idea. What if he destroyed everyone, a whole world, a universe? He laughed aloud. He'd be a god. All-knowing, immortal, the Great Pattern at his mercy to stomp and splinter and wreck and—No wonder he was dizzy.

So why was he surrounded by incompetence? Why was it necessary for him to do everything himself? The smile became a scowl. He had an experienced guard captain and a Scientist with a brilliant—if broken—mind.

It was imperative Dotty keep the djinn alive, but all she could do was bleat and wring her hands and say it needed the ice. So much for constructive suggestions. As for the guard captain—the Necromancer ground his teeth—the idiot was useless. Take today, for example: The djinn had descended on the town with an eldritch howl of pure hunger, only to find it empty. Every living creature had fled.

Not for the first time, the towns and villages in the djinn's path had been warned. The guard captain had nearly pissed himself with terror, but he'd confessed he was helpless. Whoever it was came and went like a ghost.

Sighing, the Necromancer worried at a thumbnail. Xotclic drifted in and out on its noxious green cloud, like a casual spectator at a traveling show, one with a healthy appetite. The demon would have to be dealt with, but that was a problem for another time.

They'd have to move faster, there was nothing else for it. Another twenty miles west and they could swing away from this accursed heat, toward the north.

His lower lip jutting, the Necromancer composed himself to build a vivid image of snowcapped peaks and glacial flows. Drawing on his Dark Arts, he reached out for the fiery, tormented consciousness of the djinn. *Look at it,* he crooned. *Peace and silence and the cold, cold dark. You will be healed. You will be one again. Soon, soon.*

29

A hard hand shook her shoulder. "Quarter cred."

"Wha—?" Mehcredi blinked at the burly figure of the skiffwoman.

"Wake up, lad." The woman gestured at a wide two-story building lit up as if for a carnivale. Music echoed across the water, something sprightly with a lot of strings. "The Garden." She grinned and rubbed Scrounge's ears. "Won't charge ye fer the cheeky one."

"Uh, thanks." Still muddled with sleep, Mehcredi dug the small coin out of her belt pouch. On shaky aching legs, she climbed the water stairs, but when she reached the top, her steps slowed as if she'd walked ankle deep into a mire.

Sweet Sister of mercy, she'd done it! Who knew?

You underestimate yourself, Mehcredi.

Godsdammit, Walker had been right. Again.

For the hundredth, thousandth time, her stomach churned at the thought of him. Did he live? Only the fire witch could tell her. Drawing a deep breath, Mehcredi squared her shoulders. The bruise there still ached, a sullen fire in her flesh. First things first. Find the oh-so-beautiful Rose and Deiter the wizard, make Cenda look into the fire. There'd be time for sleep when she knew he was safe.

Scrounge frisking about at her heels, she walked down the lantern-lit path and through the doors flung wide in welcome. The party noises came from a spacious room on her right, painted in cream and gold and lined with mirrors. A stocky serving man in livery blocked her progress.

He shoved the edge of the tray he carried into her belly. "Invitation only," he said. "An' I'm bettin' you don't have one."

"I need to see Rose."

"You and every other man in Caracole." The man grunted. "Though . . ." He looked her up and down and his brow furrowed. "Ye don't look the type. Off with ye, lad."

"I have to see Rose."

The serving man lost patience. "Well, ye can't." He clamped a meaty hand on her shoulder. "Hop it."

After the rough stable hands she'd encountered at every stop, the surly, barefoot sailors who spat next to her feet after a single glance at her head cloth and robes, and the pair of thugs who'd cornered her behind a dockside tavern in Belizare, this man was laughable. Almost absently, Mehcredi grabbed the tray, rammed it upward into his throat and slammed her fist into his sternum. She was already well into the party room before the crash echoed around the hall. With the utmost concentration, Scrounge quartered the floor behind her, snuffling up escaping canapés.

Heads turned, chatter ceased. A few faltering scrapes and the musicians lowered their bows. For once in her life, she didn't give a good godsdamn if the whole world was looking. She scanned the faces—shocked, amused or alarmed, according to temperament—until—Yes! Rosarina of The Garden stood by the tall windows on the other side of the room, elegant brows arched in mild surprise.

Yes!

Mehcredi surged forward, so focused on Rose that she didn't notice the small woman planted in her path until she almost mowed her down.

"*You!*" Although she had to tilt her head way back to catch Mehcredi's eye, Prue McGuire didn't appear to be intimidated in the least. Her aquamarine gaze blazed with fury. "What the hell do you want, *assassin?*"

Firmly, but gently, Mehcredi set her aside. "Rose."

"Not so fast," said a deep melodious voice. A huge hand curled around her sword arm.

Mehcredi raised her eyes from the top button of a fine linen shirt. *Shit.* "I'm sorry about . . . about . . ." she said to Erik the Golden.

Hell. She gave up. "Godsdammit, I have to talk to Rose. Walker sent me." The urgency of four interminable days had her vibrating with tension, shuddering deep in her bones. She was going to snap and when she did it wouldn't be pretty. She clenched her teeth on the violence simmering beneath the surface. "*Please.*"

"Walker?" Rose stood at Erik's elbow, clad in a cream-colored thing that skimmed over her voluptuous body and turned her eyes almost navy blue. Her dark shining hair was threaded through with pearls. When she nodded at the small orchestra, the music started up again. Slowly, conversations resumed, people turned away. "Where is he? Is he all right?"

"He was when I left him." Beyond patience, Mehcredi bared her teeth at Erik. "Let go of me. Now."

Slowly enough to make a point, Erik released her.

"She's an assassin," snapped Prue. "I don't trust her."

Mehcredi scowled. "And I don't give a fuck." She scanned the crowd. "I need Cenda. And the old wizard." She shifted her attention to Rose. "Walker said you'd get them for me."

"Where in the gods' names have you come from?" Rose said slowly. Her eyes flickered from Mehcredi's hair to her shabby boots. "You look like hell."

Mehcredi snorted. As if it mattered. Aloud, she said, "From the deep desert, south of Trimegrace."

"This way," said Rose decisively, skirts swirling as she turned toward the door.

"Rose—" Prue flung up her hands. "Oh, all right. What about the Spring Green Parlor?"

"That'll do." Though she had inches on them both, the two women flanked Mehcredi as if she were a prisoner. "Erik," said Rose, "would you be a dear and find the Purist? Sling him over your shoulder if you have to."

Erik grumbled something under his breath, but he strode away, head and shoulders taller than every other man in the room.

"Sit." In the Spring Green Parlor, Prue gave Mehcredi an impatient shove toward a squashy sofa. "You too." When she leveled a stern finger at Scrounge, he plopped his furry rump down on the rug and grinned.

Ah gods, the cushions felt good on her aching ass, her poor legs. To reach Belizare, she'd ridden for three days and two nights straight, pausing only to sell one horse and buy another. More than once, she'd dozed off in the saddle, even knowing how risky it was. When she ate, it was because she needed fuel. Mehcredi's head swam.

"When did you last sleep?" said Rose, a pucker between her brows. She gave the bellpull near the door a decisive jerk.

"On the ship." There hadn't been anything else to do during her passage across the Three-Pronged Strait, but despite the bone-deep exhaustion, she'd wake with a start every couple of hours, her heart trying to beat its way out of her chest.

A girl with a face like a merry flower appeared in the doorway. "Mistress?"

"Ah, Tansy." Coming to her feet, Prue patted Rose on the shoulder. "Don't get up," she said, and walked out into the hall to confer with the girl.

They were a team, thought Mehcredi, *friends*. Such ease, how she envied it, knowing it was beyond her. As if he understood, Scrounge pushed his shaggy head under her elbow.

Footsteps sounded in the passage, a querulous voice was raised in protest. Suddenly, the parlor was full of people—big Erik hauling the old wizard over the threshold, a tall slim woman with astonishing swathes of red hair at her temples, a lean dangerous-looking man she hadn't seen before, and—

"Florien!" It was downright astonishing how pleased she was to see the boy's wary grin, the nonchalant hunch of a bony shoulder. With a happy whine, Scrounge bounced over to greet him.

The boy glanced up as he knelt to scratch the dog's ears. "Hey, assassin."

Deiter fixed him with a baleful eye. "Off with you, slum rat."

"No," said Mehcredi.

"He stays," rumbled Erik.

The woman with the fire-bright hair—who had to be Cenda—said, "He'll only listen at the keyhole anyway."

"You've got a way with you, lad, and no mistake," the lean man said to Florien, and his elegant lips quirked. As he closed the door, his attention shifted to Mehcredi. "I'm Gray," he said and slipped an arm around the fire witch's slender waist. "This is Cenda."

At last! Mehcredi leaned toward the other woman. "Light a fire," she demanded. "Do that . . . talking Magick thing. Now."

Prue made a disgusted noise, but Deiter curled a lip, exposing wine-stained teeth. "You're not among friends here, assassin. Ask nicely."

Mehcredi surged to her feet. "I don't *want* your godsbedamned friendship, wizard. All I want to know is if Walker . . ." She stumbled. "If . . . he lives."

"Got you there, Purist," said Cenda mildly. "I could have scried for him days ago, but you had to go on a bender—"

"Bah!" Deiter sank into a chair, his hands trembling. "Get on with it, girl, and remember what I taught you."

Mehcredi wasn't sure what she expected, but Cenda reached into her hair and withdrew a gold ornament shaped like a lizard. Except . . . when the fire witch cupped it in her hand, it sat up on its haunches and *grew*, its eyes gleaming a fiery sapphire. Smiling, Cenda kissed it on the nose and shooed it into the fireplace. Out of the corner of her eye, Mehcredi caught Gray's flinch.

Flames sprang up with a whoosh, the creature dancing an ecstatic sarabande at the heart of the blaze. "It's a salamander," murmured a soft voice and Mehcredi jumped. Completely at ease, Rose sat to her left in a spindly chair, those strange beautiful eyes missing nothing.

Mehcredi fell to her knees beside Cenda on the hearth rug. "Is he there?" she rasped. "Can you feel him?"

The fire witch's amber eyes widened, then narrowed. When she reached out to brush a tear from Mehcredi's cheek, it sizzled on her fingertip. "I'll do my best," she said gravely. "But scrying like this is still very new to me."

Mehcredi clamped a hand over the fire witch's knee. "Please."

Cenda dropped her gaze and the gold bracelet around her wrist uncoiled, reared up and hissed a challenge. Sweet Sister! Mehcredi snatched her hand back.

With a small satisfied smile, Cenda leaned toward the fire and thrust both hands into the heart of the fire. Mehcredi's jaw sagged.

Godsdammit, how could she do that?

Cenda trickled streamers of flame through her fingers like ribbons, stroking and weaving. She closed her eyes. "Walker? Walker, can you hear me?"

Nothing but the crackle and hiss of the flames and the expectant breath of the people in the room. The orchestra in the party room launched into a plaintive melody.

Cenda's head dropped. "I can't . . . It's like a wall. There's nothing there."

Mehcredi clutched her arm, heedless of salamanders. "Do it again! He said he'd make a fire every night. He promised!"

In a single smooth movement, Gray came to crouch at the witch's other side, his shadow flickering oddly on the wall. "Come on, sweetheart," he murmured.

That was all, but Cenda pushed a lock of blazing red hair out of her eyes and reached into the flames once more.

"Wait." Deiter struggled to his feet. "Help me, boy." His fingers sank into Florien's bony shoulder. The boy growled a curse, but he supported the old wizard across the room.

Deiter transferred his grip to the back of Cenda's neck.

She winced. "Purist, is this wise?"

"Shut up, girl, and do it. Take power from me as you need it. Erik, you keep the flames high. Prue, stay over there, hear?"

Prue returned the old man's scowl with a sneer. Erik the Golden nodded, flexing his fingers and humming under his breath.

"Assassin, move those pretty tits if you don't want 'em singed." Deiter leered.

She must be gaping like a half-wit. Honestly, these people were the most extraordinary—

With a coughing whoosh, the fire exploded into a mass of flame that writhed up the chimney like a blazing tree. Rose's fingers gripped the back of Mehcredi's shirt and yanked, just in time.

"Walker?" whispered Cenda. "Five-it, *Walker?*"

Deiter began to shudder and Florien slipped under his arm to prop him up. "More," the wizard said through gritted teeth.

Silence. Oh gods, oh gods, he was injured, dead. Gone, gone forev—

"Sscenda." So faint, it could have been the sound of the salamander dancing.

"There!" Mehcredi lunged forward, so close she thought her eyebrows crisped. "Walker, Walker, are you all right?"

"He can't hear you," Rose said quietly. "Only Cenda."

Erik kept crooning, Cenda's busy fingers plaited fire ribbons. "Go on, Walker," she said. "I'm listening."

As the tongues of fire writhed, Mehcredi thought she caught a glimpse of high cheekbones, a blade of a nose.

"Sscenda." An agonizing pause. "Iss Mehcredi there?"

"I'm here," Mehcredi cried, tears slipping down her cheeks. "Walker, I'm here. Cenda, for the gods' sakes, tell him."

Cenda said, "Safe and sound. She's right next to me. Walker, are you all right? Where are you?"

Another lengthy silence, then, "Yess. Jusst north . . . border . . . Cressy Plains."

"Ask him where he thinks the djinns are headed now," demanded Deiter, sweat rolling down his cheeks to dampen his beard.

But before Cenda could speak, Walker's profile firmed in the heart of the blaze. Sweet Sister, he'd plaited finger bones into his hair again. "Lissten. No time. Guardss talk . . . ice fieldss."

"What are they, the djinns? How do we stop them?"

"Woman'ss name." Pause. "Now."

Deiter snarled, "You're a stubborn bastard, shaman. She's called Dancer, that's all I know."

Cenda repeated the words. This time, the silence lasted an eon, but when the crackling whisper came again, it was so distorted Walker's reaction was impossible to gauge. "Fire kills . . . Afraid . . . fire. For resst . . . ask Mehcredi . . . wass there."

"If they're heading for the ice fields via the Cressy Plains, they'll have to go through Guardpass," Rose said suddenly. "Cenda, tell Walker we'll meet him there." When every head turned toward her, she spread her hands in a graceful gesture. "Anyone have a better idea?" She arched a cool brow. "Purist?"

"Why not?" Deiter flapped a hand at her. "I'm only the most powerful wizard in the known universe. A courtesan knows best."

"We'll meet you at Guardpass," said Cenda to the blaze. She was very pale, Mehcredi noticed, leaning hard into Gray's shoulder. "*Walker?*"

"Yess." Or was that the crackle of the dying fire? Walker was gone.

Cenda sagged back into Gray's arms and Rose helped Florien guide the old man into a chair. Then she tugged the bellpull again.

One by one, every person in the room turned to look at Mehcredi. Thank the Sister she was sitting on the floor. Her whole body was awash with knee-trembling, muscle-loosening relief. He was alive, and apparently unhurt. And the first words out of his mouth had been about her!

She blinked at her audience, trying to smile. "Thank you," she said to the fire witch.

There was a tap at the door and Erik opened it to take a laden tray from the pretty girl Mehcredi had seen before. Without a word, he handed Deiter a squat bottle of spirits and a cup.

Prue crossed her arms. "So, assassin, tell us all about the djinns. From the beginning."

"I . . . I . . . ." Mehcredi rubbed her forehead. "I'm no good at telling stories," she said, feeling like a fool.

Prue gave a huff of disgust, but Rose said, "Then we'll ask questions and you answer them."

If it hadn't been for the food on the tray and the piping-hot tisane, Mehcredi would have gone to sleep midsentence. As it was, she could barely focus as everyone in the room, with the exception of the boy and the dog, attempted to turn her skull inside out so they could examine the inner workings of her brain.

Every action and reaction, every conversation and memory. She had to recall them all, word perfect, search her tired mind for every nuance, every useful scrap of information. At least she wasn't stupid enough to tell them what Walker had come to mean to her, what they'd done together in the Three Rivers Inn, let alone at the Spring of Shiloh. Instinctively, she knew the hidden valley was private, a precious jewel the swordmaster had chosen to reveal only to her. She hugged it to her heart, a fragment of joy she could use to shore up her spirit as she described the carnage the djinns left in their wake.

She wasn't sure how long the interrogation lasted—hours it seemed.

She was literally swaying with fatigue when Rose said, "Once you got out of Trinitaria, you were home free, assassin. You said Walker released you from your penance. Why did you come to us?"

Frowning, Mehcredi stared at the perfect, calm face. Wasn't it self-evident? "Because he asked me to."

Prue snorted. "Really?"

Rose studied her face. "You've saved thousands of lives, possibly more once we get the queen to listen."

Mehcredi shrugged. "As long as I've saved his."

"Mm." The courtesan exchanged a long glance with Prue. "It's late. Purist, you're exhausted. Cenda too."

Deiter waved his bottle in a lordly fashion. "I'm much improved, my dear."

Rose ignored him. "I suggest we sleep now and plan first thing in the morning." Her voice softened. "Take the sofa, Mehcredi."

Mehcredi was still shaking her head as soft upholstery received her aching body. Vaguely, she was aware of further conversation, the rustle of clothing, receding footsteps. Someone shoved a cushion under her head and sleep crashed over her in a drugging wave.

A few hours later, she woke in the dark, gasping. She shot bolt upright and something soft slipped to the floor. Oh, a blanket. A cold nose was thrust into her hand.

"Scrounge. Oh, thank the Sister." Shaking, she bent to hug him. She wrinkled her nose. "We need a bath, both of us." She could see her attic room in the House of Swords, the steaming tubs in the bathhouse. A wave of longing swept over her.

She tiptoed to the door, listening. The building was wrapped in that breathing silence peculiar to a sleeping house. Mehcredi felt in her belt pouch. Enough for a skiff, but if there were none to be found at this hour she'd damn well walk.

"C'mon," she said to the dog. "Let's go home."

30

"Did ye hafta kill anyone?"

Mehcredi shot a sideways glance at Florien slouched like a sack of taters on a sturdy pony. As the worst rider, the boy had gravitated to the rear of their little cavalcade. Deiter wasn't much better. The old man certainly complained enough. What the hell use he might be, she couldn't discern. Mehcredi gazed thoughtfully at the rest of the party, which included a company of guards supplied by the queen. The soldiers flanked the group, looking tough and competent. In the Sister's name, what sort of connection did these people have with Queen Sikara?

"Not quite," she said repressively. Gods, she'd been lucky. Yes, but she'd also been well taught.

"Not quite?" The boy's eyes shone. "What does that mean?"

"Two men tried to rob me." Or worse.

Florien bounced in the saddle. "Yah?"

"I had my blades, they had short staffs. It was dark. I . . ." Automatically, Mehcredi rubbed her shoulder. The bruise had flowered nicely, purple and green. "They were noisy. Thought I'd be easy, I guess."

"But ye weren't, were ye?"

A wry smile twisted her lips. "No. I took the staff away from the short one and broke his wrist with it. I . . . knifed the other." She shivered. The blade had slid through fabric and flesh as if they were butter. She hadn't thought it could be so easy to end a life. But then metal grated on bone and the man had howled and fallen back.

"Ooh, where?" Florien's dark eyes sparkled with relish. "In the guts? Did he yell?"

"Shoulder," said Mehcredi.

"Dai's been teachin' me, same as Walker taught you." Florien's skinny chest puffed out. "He says I got promise."

At the House of Swords, she'd had so little time with Dai. At first, the silence had been awkward, but then the swordsman gave one of his hoarse chuckles and pulled her into a brief hard hug. It seemed that despite everything she'd done, she had a friend of sorts. Mehcredi sighed. He still sounded . . . terrible, all raspy and ruined, though he swore the pain had left him completely.

"They should have left you with him," she said, frowning.

"I do what I fookin' want." Florien shrugged, then spoiled it by snickering. "Swore I'd follow. Prue an' the old man got mad, but Cenda an' Gray believed me. Hah! So they should," he added darkly.

Yet they'd insisted she come, though she couldn't quite work out why. Not that their wishes were of the slightest consequence. If Walker was waiting at this Guardpass place, she had nowhere else to be. She'd grown to love the House of Swords, but even the exquisite garden was nothing in comparison with the man at its center, the quiet sun around which everything revolved.

Mehcredi listened with half an ear to the conversations around her, fretting. Yesterday, she'd walked out into the swordmaster's garden, basking in the autumn sun, and gazed at it with new eyes, marveling. How was it she hadn't understood before? His personality, his heart and soul, were imprinted on every flower, every branch and leaf. The impact of that realization, the recognition of how far she'd come and what she'd accomplished against all the odds—it caught up with her on the lawn beside the contemplation pool. She *ached* for him—as if the gods had scooped out some essential part of her and callously tossed it aside. Looking back now, she thought she must have lost a few seconds there, because when she regained her senses, she was on her knees with her arms wrapped around the smooth trunk of a widow's hair tree, sobbing. She'd wept for ten minutes straight, her cheek pressed to the silvery bark.

It had helped. By the time a tight-lipped Erik arrived to collect her late in the afternoon, she felt as limp and pale as an overcooked noodle, but calm enough.

"You'll spend the night at The Garden," he said. "We leave at first light."

The brusque delivery couldn't make his deep voice less than beautiful, nothing could, not even reading a laundry list. She smiled at the memory, because he'd done just that. Prue had sent a neatly written list of everything she was to bring. Mehcredi had shrugged, admitted she couldn't read, and handed it back. Three shirts, a warm jacket, gloves if she had them, good boots . . . Erik read on and on, giving her goose bumps. Holy Sister, he was a handsome man, all big and blond, with eyes like a noonday sky.

From beneath her lashes, Mehcredi watched him riding knee to knee with Prue, chuckling when an errant breeze blew a curl into her eye and she batted it away with a laughing glare, the color rising in her vivid, heart-shaped face. Overall, they were a well-favored group. Rose was simply spectacular, while Prue and Cenda each had their own charms, she supposed. As for Gray . . . He was decorative enough, if you preferred dark-haired men—which the gods knew she did—but there was something about him that made all the hair stand up on the back of her neck, something that flickered in the corner of her eye. She worried at her bottom lip, trying to work it out.

Shivering, she turned up the collar of her padded jacket. Her blood had grown thin and warm away from Lonefell. The company was four days out of Caracole now and a chilly wind blustered out of the north to slip sly icy fingers between buttons and fastenings. The coat was Walker's—she'd had no compunction about entering his room and taking it from the cupboard. In fact, it had given her a bittersweet feeling to look at his neatly made bed, to touch the plain wooden brush on his dresser. The garment swam on her a bit and she'd had to roll the sleeves up, but every time she closed her eyes, she felt him near, the smell of his skin and hair.

When Scrounge pressed closer, she opened the jacket and folded him inside, taking comfort from his animal warmth. Every night for three nights, Cenda had crouched over the fire, calling Walker's name, again and again. Nothing. What had begun as a faint unease had rapidly gained momentum, filling Mehcredi's belly with a cold spiky ball of dread. A hideous litany sang in her ears, with every beat of her heart. *He's dead, oh gods, he's dead.* That hard bronze body smashed and broken, the lively black eyes filmed and dull.

And she was stupid. A great daft lump. Mehcredi straightened her spine, forcing herself to take stock of the gentle roll of the plains, the wide fields of stubbled grain, the occasional farmhouse of weathered wood, its roof high-pitched to cater for the winter snow. Who better at survival than Walker, last of the Shar? Not only a warrior without peer, but a shaman with mind-boggling powers. She forced herself to take deep, even breaths.

Up ahead, the guard captain, a broad-faced woman called Yachi, barked a command and the company jingled to a halt. She gestured at the blue bulk of a mountain range in the distance. "Stormsoul Range. We'll be in Guardpass tomorrow night."

Deiter rummaged around under his heavy robe and produced a rolled-up map. Muttering under his breath, he ran a horny forefinger over the parchment. "You're right," he announced.

The captain rolled her eyes but said no more, merely kicking her rangy bay into motion. The guards fell into formation and they were off again.

Farther to the west, beyond that double notch in the mountains, lay Lonefell. Would she ever see the keep again? A wry smile twisted Mehcredi's lips. Who cared? Gods, she'd seen more of the world, had more adventures, than a brute like Taso could conceive of. Well, if adventure meant near wetting yourself with terror but having to squat behind a bush to do it. On the other hand . . . Her mind filled with the vision of Walker stretched out beneath her as she rode him. Her sex clenched involuntarily. He'd been so high and hard, wedged all the way to her womb, filling her so brutally, so exquisitely. And Holy Sister, his face!

Just like that, she was back where she'd begun, caught on the wheel of her fear. *Dead, not dead. Dead, not dead.*

Guardpass couldn't come soon enough.

The tavern turned out to be the largest building in Guardpass, and it felt like every citizen for miles around was crowded into the fusty space. The walls smelled of resinous wood, the floor of ingrained beer. Every so often, a cart clattered up, or a horse, and the double doors swung open to admit a blast of chilly air and another hard-eyed, weather-beaten farmer.

Mehcredi stood with the others at the back of the room, trying to avoid contact with the greasy wall, Scrounge pressed against her calf. Florien perched halfway up the stairs to the upper rooms, hanging over the banister. Purist Deiter and the Guardpass headwoman stood in uneasy proximity on top of a table. Tugging at the three plaits of his beard, the old wizard glared at the crowd, which seethed like a rough stew about to boil over. In the confined space, the uproar battered at Mehcredi's senses, making her head ache.

Springing from a chair to the top of the bar, Yachi produced a surprisingly effective parade-ground bellow. "Settle down!"

Mehcredi blinked, impressed.

"You've heard the Purist. You want to speak, go right ahead, but don't waste my time." The guard captain pointed to a man with a barrel chest and a straggly beard. "You! Spit it out!"

The man flushed and shuffled a bit, but his companions egged him on. "First storms o' winter," he said. "Jest rumors." He shrugged. "Folks get skeered when weather's bad."

Yachi set her hands on her broad hips. "What am I? Chopped liver?" She leaned forward. "The *queen* sent us. Get it?" The words, *you fucking idiot*, echoed unspoken.

Voices overlapped, complaints, jeers, catcalls. A sense of ill usage hung over the assembly.

"Waste o' bloody time!"

A rangy woman shook her head. "Fer the Sister's sake, I have beasts in calf, hay to get. I'm off." She pushed her way to the door.

"I ain't never seen no Magick." A snort of derision. "Not gunna now."

Outside, hoofs rang on the packed earth of the single street. The rider was pushing hard, the animal faltering.

"Sister save us, he's going to explode," Mehcredi murmured, watching Deiter's face slowly turn purple.

A small strong hand gripped her forearm. "Brace yourself," Prue said, for once too preoccupied to bother with the glare she reserved especially for Mehcredi.

Cold air slithered down her spine as the doors opened to admit a latecomer. Deiter's furious gaze lifted, then grew fixed. "Ah," he said.

Heads turned, one by one. The silence spread and pooled like beer leaking from a sprung barrel.

"Walker!" Black spots obscured Mehcredi's vision.

The swordmaster stood framed in the doorway, gaunt as a winter-starved direwolf, a limp body slung over one shoulder. But although the limbs dangled, they jerked so violently Walker had to clamp a hand over the young man's calves to stop the spasmodic kicking.

"No!" Prue blocked Mehcredi's instinctive lunge forward. "Wait."

Walker's head turned as he quartered the room. When his eyes met Mehcredi's, the world settled, fell into place with a click so loud, she couldn't fathom why Prue, standing right next to her, showed no signs of hearing it. His shoulders dropped as if he'd blown out a long breath, then he blinked and looked away, fixing his gaze on Deiter. His cheekbones looked sharp enough to cut, the shadows beneath his eyes like bruises.

The crowd parted as the swordmaster stalked to the bar. Willing hands helped him lay the young man on top of it. In the shocked silence, his moans could be clearly heard, the hollow thud of his heels drumming against polished wood.

"A healer." Walker's voice was scraped so raw, she almost didn't recognize it. The front of his shabby jacket was stiff with blood. "Do you have a healer?"

In the circle of lamplight, something shifted beneath the wounded man's clothing. Walker drew his dagger and sliced the leg of his trews to reveal a round protuberance distorting the flesh of the man's thigh, surging purposefully toward his torso.

The stout innkeeper craned over the bar, his eyes wide. The head-woman made a sound of utter revulsion. "Sister of mercy, what the hell is *that*?"

"It's how the djinns kill. He's young, strong. He had the best chance. I had to—'Cestors' bones, *the healer*?"

"Here." A plump woman pushed to the front, her face as pale as milk. She made the sign of the Sibling Moons. "Can we get him to my house? It's only a step."

At Yachi's gesture, a couple of guards stepped forward. Gently, they lifted the man and carried him out into the night.

"How much time do we have?" Deiter asked Walker.

The shaman shrugged. "They're about a day behind me, spread out over a ten-mile front." He glanced after the wounded man. "He was plain unlucky. There were three of them. Maybe they blew into his farm on an evil wind, or they were advance scouts. By the time I got there, only he and his wife were still alive, and she . . . had no chance."

The silence was absolute. As he rubbed his face, the finger bones swung to and fro, pale against the blue black of his hair. "They grow stronger as the temperature drops. Nyzarl's men talk around the campfires. The djinns are heading for the ice."

"The only other gap in the mountains is miles to the west of here." The headwoman's voice shook. "They'll come through Guardpass. It's the most direct."

"Which gives us an advantage," said a cool voice.

Cenda's hand in his, Gray made his way to Walker's side. With his slanted brows and his shadow flickering ominously behind him, his grin was positively demonic. "Because we have weapons the djinns cannot imagine."

His steely gaze zeroed in on a gnarled individual who looked like a trapper. "You say you don't believe in Magick? Watch, my friend, and learn."

With the impeccable timing of a born showman, he stepped aside to reveal Cenda, her face suffused with embarrassment. But at his nod, she raised her chin and held out her hand, rills of fire bursting from her fingertips. People shuffled backward, the space before her clearing with remarkable rapidity. With a hungry whoosh, the flame expanded, wreathing her arm all the way to the shoulder.

"Five-it!" As the fire winked out, the sleeve of Cenda's shirt fell away in a charred ruin. "I keep forgetting."

In the frozen silence, Gray laughed and kissed her cheek. "Never mind the wardrobe." He gathered the crowd with his gaze. "The djinns are terrified of fire," he said. "But that's not all." With an open-handed flourish, he bowed in the big man's direction. "Erik, my friend?"

Mehcredi shut her sagging jaw. Sister save her, this was better than a play in the theater—not that she'd seen any. What would he do, Erik the Golden? Perhaps he'd sing, the way he had in the Sailor's Lay, the awful night she'd poisoned Dai. He'd been wonderful, mesmerizing.

Crooning under his breath, Erik scooped his open palms through the air. For a moment, nothing happened. Then, slowly, noiselessly, his feet left the floor until he was hovering among the rafters, perfectly composed. "Hmm," he said. "The spiders up here are as big as rats. Innkeeper, you have to see."

The man shook his head. "Yer mad—Aargh! Fuck!" Flailing with terror, he rose majestically toward the ceiling.

"See? Big as ponies."

The innkeeper's gasping curses sounded loud in the silence. After a moment, Erik floated him across to the bar and lowered him gently.

Then he made another, more expansive, gesture. A little breeze ran around the room, ruffling collars and tugging at hats. Gradually, it increased, until the bottles and glasses behind the bar rattled and it became difficult to keep their feet.

"We know heat kills the djinns," said Erik, gazing down at his startled, windblown audience. "And we command two of the primal elements—fire and air."

When he bared his teeth, he didn't look genial at all. "Think about that, my friends." Abruptly, the wind dropped and he landed lightly on his feet, his blue eyes very bright.

Something knotted in Mehcredi's chest. Gods, to think she'd nearly killed him!

"Three," said Deiter. Deliberately, he turned his head to stare at Walker. "Three of the elements." A shaggy brow arched. "Well, shaman?"

Walker leaned stiffly against the bar, expressionless. "I'm no trick pony," he said flatly. "But I'll see what I can do."

The room reverberated with conversation and conjecture, shouted questions and exclamations.

Mehcredi's fists clenched. The devious old bastard! Hadn't Walker done enough? She shouldered her way to Walker's side. "You're covered in blood. Are you hurt?" she demanded, touching the swordmaster's hand. Cold, so cold. From the corner of her eye, she caught Prue's fascinated expression and Gray's amusement.

"The blood's not mine," said Walker, so softly only those in the immediate vicinity could hear.

"Look at you!" Lifting his arm, Mehcredi slid beneath it, propping him up despite his grunt of protest. "You can barely move. When did you last eat? Sleep?"

He blinked down at her. "I . . . don't know."

"Why are you looking at me like that?" she asked, nettled. "Why shouldn't I ask? They're perfectly reasonable questions."

"I don't know that eith—" He broke off when Gray smothered a chuckle. "Never mind."

Rose touched Mehcredi's elbow. "I hired the whole of the top floor." Her lush mouth curved. "It's not as if the host gets a lot of custom. You're last on the right." She gave Mehcredi a little push. "Go. I'll have food and hot water sent up."

"No." Walker's jaw set.

"Good man." Deiter allowed the headwoman to help him down off the table. He rubbed his hands together. "Got any decent wine?" he inquired. "Planning's thirsty work."

Something snapped in Mehcredi's head. She could have sworn she heard it go. In a single smooth movement, she dropped into the chair next to Deiter's and shoved her face into his. "Five minutes to find out what you need to know. Then I'm taking him upstairs."

"Aw, how sweet." Deiter gave her his leering grin. "Behind those toothsome tits beats the heart of a mama wolf."

A big hand wrapped around her upper arm. "Don't," advised Erik. "It's not worth it, I guarantee."

A growl still rumbling in her throat, Mehcredi shoved her blade back into the scabbard. Muscle by muscle, she relaxed. "Five minutes, old man," she said.

Walker had gone past exhaustion and come out the other side, but the images of blood and bone-cracking agony were still painted on the inside of his eyelids. In a parade of horror upon horror, the destruction of the Shar had become confused with the attack of the djinns, so that the two were inextricably linked in his mind until he thought he might choke—or spring up, howling with rage and pain, to tear and rend everything within reach.

He'd had to make choices only the gods should face—who to carry to the healers, who to abandon to a protracted agonized death. The children—Oh, gods.

Vaguely, he was aware he had Mehcredi's hand in a death grip under the table, and that Deiter was firing questions at him—gods, the old man had a nerve! What *exactly* was the extent of his shaman's power? Did it extend beyond plants? Because now they needed more than a gardener, much more.

The wizard leaned forward, his faded eyes intent, blazing with intelligence and purpose. "Can you make the earth shift in its bed, shaman? Can you force boulders to dance to the tune of your Magick?"

"Maybe." Walker sat very straight. If he held himself still he could more or less ignore the gash on his arm, the flash burn across his back. "What are you after, Deiter, an earthquake?"

Deiter raised his wine cup in mock salute. "That'd do it." He turned to the headwoman. "You must have a detailed map of the immediate area. Get it, will you?"

The woman's face darkened with offense, but she pushed back her chair. "Back in a minute."

"Good." The old man raised his voice, speaking to the room at large. "The rest of you can bugger off now. We're going to need every fighting staff you can find, right down to broomsticks and hoe handles. Find 'em and be back here at first light."

"Not so fast, wizard." Yachi sat with a decisive thump. "What are you planning?"

31

Deiter stroked his tripartite beard. "A blow against evil, our first as a group." Walker followed his gaze as it flickered around the odd assortment of people at the table—Cenda and Gray, Erik and Prue, the assassin, Rose, the queen's guards, even Florien. "We may only have three Sides of the Pentacle, but this is what the gods, the Lord and the Lady, intend. Which means we can't fuck it up."

A crease appeared between the captain's thick brows. "Pentacle? What the hell are you talking about?"

The wizard drank deeply. He emerged, smacking his lips. "A trap. A stroke of genius, if I do say so myself."

"That's it." Mehcredi's chair scraped as she rose. "You've had your five minutes."

Thoughts fumbled a slow way through Walker's brain, like roots growing blind in the rich dark under the ground. Waves of sleep tugged at him, though sleep was a pale word for the black depths his body craved.

He thought he heard Deiter mutter, "Pussy-whipped," but it meant no more than the buzzing of a biteme.

Instead, he said harshly, "My kinswoman, Deiter. Where is she?"

A long pause while the old man fiddled with his beard. Walker leaned closer, longing to close his fingers around that wattled throat and squeeze.

Something must have shown in his face, because Deiter drained the last of his wine in a single gulp. "Holdercroft, last I heard."

A village on the Cressy Plains. By the First Father, the djinns had come within thirty miles of it.

"What's she doing there?"

The old man shrugged. "Hell if I know. All I have is a name and a place." He reached for the wine jug. "And more important things to worry about."

"Later," Walker growled. Every muscle in his body protesting, he pushed away from the table.

Rose glanced at Mehcredi's hand linked with his, her lips curving in a faint, knowing smile. Prue looked disapproving. Fuck if he cared.

The stain on Mehcredi's skin had faded to a jaundiced yellow, her bicolored hair poked up in tufts as if she'd been tugging it, and she was worn to the bone. But when he'd stepped in out of the cold, his hideous burden over one shoulder, she was all he'd looked for, all that filled his vision. He'd never seen anything as beautiful in his life. The relief had been exquisite. By the bones of Those Before, he was even glad to see that foolish dog.

As she tugged him into a small chamber, a wry smile quirked his lips. In a world gone mad, Mehcredi the assassin made him sane. She reminded him of what *normal* was, grounded him like the *nea-kata*. How ironic was that?

She was trying to get his jacket off, mumbling under her breath, swearing.

"Mehcredi." He gripped both of her hands in his. "Don't fuss. I can take care of myself."

She raised a brow, her eyes molten with what looked like fury. "The way you have so far?" Jerking herself out of his grasp, she returned to the fastenings of the coat. "Where does it hurt?"

His face felt hot. "I said, *I'll be fine.*" Reaching behind him, he braced himself unobtrusively against the door. The bed wasn't far. If he were careful . . .

Mehcredi went up on tiptoes, which put them nose to nose. "I thought you were dead! Get it? *Dead!* I need—" She stopped, breathing heavily. "Let me . . . Ah, godsdammit, never mind."

Spinning on her heel, she took a couple of quick steps to the small potbellied stove and began shoving kindling into it at a furious rate. Walker stared at the hunch of her shoulders. Shit.

"A mama wolf," he said slowly, sinking onto the lumpy bed. "I don't need . . . mothering, but thank you. Sorry." He rubbed his temples. "Sorry. I was just . . . surprised."

Flummoxed would be more like it. She'd sprung to his defense, for the gods' sakes. She'd faced down Purist Deiter of Concordia, one of the most powerful wizards in the known worlds and a capricious old bastard to boot. Lucky he'd chosen to be amused. Father's balls, did she understand the chance she'd taken? No one took risks like that for him. Why should they? Walker fought his own battles.

"Forget it." Mehcredi clanged the door shut on the leaping flames.

Someone tapped on the door, a harassed-looking serving girl balancing a tray of food in one hand and carrying a steaming bucket with the other.

"Here." Mehcredi handed him the tray and heaved the bucket onto the stove with easy strength.

Gods, yes! Walker had inhaled a huge wedge of meat and bread and cheese before she spoke again. "Want help with your boots?" she asked, as politely as if he were a stranger.

Even lifting the tankard of ale pulled at the burn across his back, the pain like a whiplash made of fire. "If you wouldn't mind," he said with equal courtesy.

Walker gazed down at her bent head as she knelt at his feet, at the white stripe of her parting, and his chest went tight. He'd sent her away for her own safety and 'Cestors knew it had been the right decision. If she'd seen what he'd seen, done what he'd had to do as he tracked the djinns . . . His guts turned over. No, no, not his assassin.

Nonetheless, it had been a choice among evils, an insane risk. He'd had to trust to her brains and courage and pray that the training he'd provided would be sufficient. She didn't need to know he'd created a Song for her and chanted it to the Ancestors every night along the trail. Wearily, he wondered if it had made any difference.

When he reached out to touch her hair, his hands shook. Must be delayed shock. "You made it," he said. When her head lifted, he smoothed a wayward lock behind her ear. "Well done."

"Did you worry?" She swallowed. Her eyes had the luminous look that presaged tears.

Unsmiling, he cradled her warm cheek. "Every minute of every day."

"*Walker.*" Mehcredi surged into his arms. The tankard tumbled from his fingers to the floor and her lips were on his, vital and desperate. Their teeth clinked, until she tilted her head, settled into the fit.

Nothing had ever felt so right, so perfect, as the sweetness of her eager mouth, the press of her strong supple body against his own. Reeling with the pleasure, the sheer relief of it, Walker gripped the back of her head and plundered. Alive and real. Here, in his arms. After the first few frantic seconds, something within him relaxed.

Gods, yes, it said. And *mine.*

Deeper. Slower. *More.*

His shoulders hit the mattress and he hissed with pain.

"What's wrong?" Mehcredi pulled back, frowning.

"Went through a window when the place caught on fire." Wincing, Walker came up on one elbow. "Too slow."

Her eyes flashed. "Don't move, godsdammit." She disappeared out the door at a trot.

By the time she returned, he'd managed to peel off both coat and shirt, cursing under his breath as scabs ripped free. The slice across his biceps oozed blood and he preferred not to think about the burn.

Mehcredi dumped two glass vials and some soft rags on the bed. "That cut needs stitches." She rinsed a cloth in warm water and wrung it out.

"I'd say the healer's busy," said Walker grimly. "Give me that." He held out a hand for the rag.

Mehcredi ignored him, swabbing something dreadful from his knuckles, working her way up his arm. "Where have you been? Talk to me, Walker." The warm water felt wonderful, the care in her gentle hands even better.

So he did, slowly at first, searching for words, sparing her the worst. Her touch firm and deft, she rid him of filth and blood and sweat and dried him carefully with a threadbare towel. Moving behind him on the bed, she slathered scaldcream on the burn and healall on the gash.

"What's a pentacle got to do with anything?" She ripped a dry rag into long strips.

While she bound his wounds, he explained as best he could—fire, air, earth and water.

"Even I know a pentacle's got five sides," she said. "Can't Deiter count?"

"Yes." Walker gave a rusty chuckle. "Drives him mad, not knowing what it means." Gingerly, he stretched out on his good side. The room was warm now, almost cozy. He truly hadn't thought to know such peace again. Sleep beckoned, a long sweet fall into a dark abyss.

He forced his eyes open. "Lie down with me, Mehcredi."

After a small hesitation, she kicked her boots off and came down next to him with a long sigh. "No," he mumbled, plucking at her shirt. "Get it off. Everything."

Another pause. When she stripped, she did it quickly and without coquetry, before putting out the lamp. In the sullen rosy glow of the stove, the womanly swell of her hips, her endless legs, took on a golden glow. With a long contented breath, Walker slid an appreciative palm the length of her spine, unable to resist cupping the taut curve of her superlative ass. He turned his face into the curve of her neck. 'Cestors' bones, that was good!

He let himself fall.

Sometime in the early hours, he woke with a choked cry. He'd been back at the farmhouse, beating the djinns off with a blazing torch, while the farmer's wife writhed in her death agony at his feet. The creatures had screamed as they died, high-pitched shrieks that hurt the ears.

But despite the fact that he'd been struck in the leg, the man clung to his dying wife. Gods, she had no hope, none at all, but the farmer did. Walker knocked him out cold, slung him over the saddle and spurred to a gallop. Out in the yard, two little girls lay dead in a welter of blood. In the dream, the bigger one sat up, her chest a bloody ruin of bone and flesh. "Da!" she screamed. "Don't take our Da!"

Callused palms cupped his face, slim fingers stroked. "Walker, it's me." Mehcredi dotted his face with frantic kisses. "Sshh. It's all right."

A little while later, after his heart had stopped hammering, she freed him from his trews, crooning wordlessly as she feathered her fingers over his cock, coaxing him to an astonishing hardness, though he shouldn't have been surprised. His body knew what it needed—to affirm life, to establish reality in the most primitive way possible. Hitching one leg over his hip, she guided him to her beautiful slippery heat.

Silently, they rocked together in languid bliss. Walker's climax grew like a twining vine from his balls to his cock, all the sweet way to the very tip. When the end came, his seed flowed out of him, not in spurts or ripples, but in a steady stream, until every muscle in his body relaxed, limp and sated. Judging by the pretty gasping cries in his ear, Mehcredi had reached her own pinnacle of pleasure.

His thoughts all muffled and ponderous, all he could do was nuzzle her cheek, and sink toward sleep.

So very, very good. A strange, but lovely, homecoming.

"Here," she whispered, rolling onto her back. A firm grip in his hair, she tugged his head down to rest between her breasts.

Instinctively, Walker stiffened.

"You did this for me, that first time." Her breath stirred his hair. "Please, let me do it for you."

He raised his head half an inch. "It?"

"The post-fuck cuddle." She pressed him back down.

Walker found himself smiling into warm creamy skin. Beneath his ear, her heart thumped in a steady rhythm. His fingers drifted over the pure pale beauty of her left breast, automatically tracing the path his Mark had taken.

"Tingles." She undulated beneath him, purring. "Maybe your Magick's still there."

"Doubtful." Her nipple felt like ruched velvet under his fingertip.

"Walker . . ." She hesitated.

"Mmm?" From ribs to waist to hip, her flanks were a long feminine curve, flowing as beautifully as any plant that grew.

"What am I doing here? I mean . . ." Her lips brushed his forehead in a shy caress. "I know I'm here because you are. You're important— you, and Cenda and Erik, but *me?*"

"The Shar have a saying: *The gods rattle our little lives like dice in a game with no point.*" He frowned. "I have no idea, but you fit somehow."

"Truly?" She sounded so pleased. Then she sighed. "Prue hates me. Erik too. Though Cenda and Gray aren't so bad and Rose is nice."

"You can hardly blame them," he pointed out. "As for Gray and Prue, they have their gifts."

"Like what?" She sounded so skeptical.

"You didn't know?" Walker sat up so he could see her face. The gray light of dawn bleached her features, painted shadows beneath her fine eyes. "Gray is a sorcerer of shadows. Prue is a null witch."

Mehcredi frowned. "Shadows? What shadows? And Prue's nothing like a witch."

"Gray's shadow has a life of its own—a mind, if you will. If you watch, you'll see it move without him. He calls it Shad. They have . . . an interesting relationship." A rusty chuckle bubbled in his throat. "You should see your face."

"And Prue?" croaked Mehcredi, her eyes round.

"Haven't you noticed? You never see Cenda or Deiter anywhere too close to Prue. Magick doesn't work within about ten feet of her." He rolled his shoulders, wincing. "It feels . . . weird, as if part of you is numb."

"So that's how—Florien told me she beat the Necromancer's head in with a shovel, but I couldn't quite believe it." Her brow creased. "What about Erik? He's a wizard and he's all over her."

"Doesn't bother him for some reason. Deiter says, deep down, she actually believes in his Magick. Suspension of disbelief or something like that."

Footsteps went by in the passage outside. A door banged. Someone rattled pots and pans.

Completely unself-conscious, Mehcredi lay naked, lost in thought. Did she have any idea of how appealing she was? Like some strong sleek animal in repose, all supple muscle clothed in voluptuous contours. His Ancestors had been warriors. He was their son, blood and bone. The assassin drew him in a way that was blatantly, shamelessly direct. Like to like. Strength to strength. Even among the Shar, a woman so fierce, yet so uncompromisingly feminine, would be remarked and respected.

Such an innocent, in every way that mattered. But she'd survived the trip back to Caracole without him. 'Cestors' bones, she'd done more than survive—she'd triumphed, *grown*. Gods, what would she become when she spread her wings and truly soared? He'd set her free, whatever the cost. Once all this was done.

He felt empty. Food would help, lots of it.

Turning his back, he reached for his battered pack. "Get dressed," he said. "The others will be waiting."

Mehcredi stood at the lip of the cliff, staring down into the ravine that gave Guardpass its name. The air was full of shouts and oaths, the clink of wooden staves being unloaded and distributed, the jangle of metal and the stamp of hoofs. Deiter and Yachi leaned over a map spread on a camp table, talking to the Guardpass headwoman. Over it all, keened the low moan of the chill wind that blew from the north. It was late afternoon, dull with the clouds low in the sky. A sharp silver sickle, the Sister rose above the shoulder of the range.

She shivered, wishing she'd been able to eat. Not long now.

All the preparations were in place. Florien and Scrounge had been left behind at the tavern, under the stern eye of the host. The boy had been so insulted, he'd very nearly wept with fury, but at the last minute, he'd relented and let Cenda fold him in her arms. In fact, every member of the company save Deiter had farewelled him in one way or another. Standing at the door watching them depart, he'd been the picture of sullen defiance, but Mehcredi suspected he was both surprised and touched. After all, in his place, she would have felt the same.

Teams of men had spent the day sweating with levers and rollers, moving boulders to the cliff edge at the southern end of the pass. Cenda and Erik had disappeared, presumably to practice whatever it was they intended to do together. Deiter did a lot of arm waving and shouting.

As the only one who had experience with the djinns, Walker worked with Yachi, drilling the guards, over and over. Early in the afternoon, the guards split off, each taking charge of a group of grim-faced farmers.

Deiter cupped his hands to his mouth. "*To me!*" he bellowed, his voice echoing off the stone ramparts, obviously amplified by Magick.

Mehcredi narrowed her eyes, estimating. Staffs made of snow birch gleamed pink in the afternoon light, rustling and murmuring like a winter wood in the wind. But there were so few of them, perhaps fifty.

Once the djinns descended in a boiling cloud they'd be overwhelmed. Oh gods . . .

A hard hand settled on her shoulder and she turned.

Walker, the long tail of his hair swinging, finger bones and feathers tightly woven into his braids. Releasing a long breath, Mehcredi stepped into the warmth of his body, slipping an arm around his trim waist. Stiffening, he shot her an unreadable glance but said nothing.

"You lot are just backup," Deiter was telling the citizens of Guardpass. "Make sure none of the filthy things get past you and into the village. Apart from that, keep out of the bloody way." He cocked his head like a wily old bird, listening. "Not long now."

Even the ever-present wind fell silent, waiting.

"Go with Rose and Prue." Walker stepped sideways and Mehcredi's arm fell away.

She watched the two women hurry toward a narrow, winding path that led down the side of the ravine. After about thirty feet, it opened up into a wide ledge and behind that was the large cave Deiter had designated for the care of the wounded. The village healer was already there, grim-faced as she sharpened her instruments and counted her pots of medicaments.

"No," Mehcredi said. "I'm staying to fight with you."

Walker's lips went thin. "You know nothing about killing djinns. You'd be a liability."

"But I can fight!" Hurt, she stared at him. "Or did you lie when you told me I'm good?"

The wind picked up, rising to an ear-aching whistle. Walker hissed. "'Cestors' bones, there's no time for this. Listen to me—" He gripped her upper arms, gave her a little shake. "Only three of us really matter—Erik, Cenda and me. The rest of you are cleanup crew."

The wind whipped Walker's hair. Finger bones clinked softly. At the southern end of the gorge, the air became suddenly agitated, as though a mighty hand stirred it with a giant whisk.

"*Go,*" said the swordmaster coldly. "I cannot do my job until you do."

His black stare bored into her as she backed away down the path. He was still watching when she whirled about, her vision blurred with tears. A small fist grabbed the back of her coat and tugged. "Get in here," snapped Prue McGuire, her mouth tight with tension. "There'll be wounded. You can make yourself useful, assassin."

But Mehcredi set her feet. The ledge in front of the cave was a fine vantage point. In a majestic wave, vortexes of boiling air rolled out of the dusk and into the ravine, billowing toward the four figures standing motionless in their path. An acrid reek filled the narrow space.

Atavistic terror cramped Mehcredi's guts. The stench permeated her clothing, sank into her pores. Sister save her, Walker was going to die! She sank to her knees, gravel biting into her skin.

32

Yachi's voice screamed an order and from the cliff tops arched a shower of arrows. When Cenda raised both hands, every arrow burst into flame.

Ah, so Walker had been right. The djinns *did* die. Mehcredi bared her teeth in a grin of savage delight. The high, wavering shrieks hurt her ears, but it was infinitely satisfying to watch the creatures explode in glittering shards that twisted slowly in the wind and fluttered to the valley floor.

The volleys of arrows forced the djinns out of the air, down between the walls of stone. As they swooped and flew, Cenda threw her head back, opened her mouth and screamed. Fire burst out of her throat, then from her whole body. She looked horribly like a figure on a pyre, yet her flesh was not consumed. A huge fireball blossomed above her head, floating in the cradle of the wind.

Gray stood so close he must be singed, but he only stared at the fire witch, his handsome face contorted with anxiety. Beside him, his shadow danced, never still. Gods, so it was true about the shadow!

But there was no time to think of that. Erik's mouth moved, his hands weaving shapes in the air. The fireball flattened out, expanding across the width of the ravine. With a roar like a thousand angry tygres, it dropped and sped forward, a moving wall of flame. Mehcredi shot to her feet.

The djinns writhed and died, screaming and stinking. At Mehcredi's elbow, Prue hopped from one foot to the other, waving her fists. Rose stood quietly, her hands gripped together at her waist, her eyes dark pits in the pale oval of her face.

Abruptly, Walker dropped to his knees as if he'd been shot by a djinn stone. His head dropped, his hair falling forward to obscure his face. Mehcredi started forward, then stopped when he reached out to place the palms of both hands flat on the ground.

The rock beneath her feet trembled, very slightly.

Walker looked up, his gaze focused on the southern end of the gorge. Mehcredi saw his lips move. A huge boulder on the cliff edge began to rock on its base. With a kind of ponderous grace, it teetered toward open space, then turned end over end, spinning out into the open air. It landed with an echoing crash that shivered in the bones.

Djinns sprayed in all directions and were forced down by another volley of burning arrows.

The first boulder was followed by another, and another, until the valley reverberated with thunderous impacts and the hungry roar of flame. The air swirled with fire and fragmenting djinns and vicious eddies of wind and dust and chips of rock. Mehcredi bent double, coughing. The Brother had risen, bloodred and sullen, casting a hellish glow over the scene. Holy Sister, it was the end of the world.

But she was wrong. With a long grating rumble, the cliff at the southern entrance to the pass split from bottom to top, a dark fissure opening like a crooked wound. So slowly they could have been mired in treacle, tons of rock peeled away, falling hundreds of feet in sandy arabesques. When the dust settled, the opening had disappeared beneath a wall of rubble. The pass was blocked, the djinns trapped inside, the air above them filled with flaming arrows.

Deiter's trap!

But there was no end to the godsbedamned creatures. Even trapped in the narrow defile, at the mercy of Cenda's fire and Erik's wind, the remnants of them continued to press mindlessly north toward Guardpass, the only barrier a group of untried defenders. On a guard's barked order, the ranks of burning staffs moved, the outer ranks thrusting outward, the inner upward. Seen from the vantage point of the cave, the patterns they made were eerily beautiful, like a shoal of phosphorescent fish moving through a dusky sea.

It was extraordinarily effective—until the first formation shuddered and broke. Immediately, it was overwhelmed, submerged under a blanket of boiling air and another kind of screaming began—high-pitched, agonized and all too human.

After that, there was little time to watch, less time to think.

By unspoken agreement, the village healer laid hands on the wounded as they were carried in, using her experience to assess their chances. Cold-blooded, but necessary.

Mehcredi lost count of the number of mouths she pried open to pour in a concentrated sleeping potion. Without a moment's hesitation, she used her knee to keep them still or shoved a smooth stick between snapping teeth. Her fingers slippery with blood, she tied endless tourniquets, knowing it was hopeless, but driven to try.

To save her sanity, she closed her ears to the sounds from the back of the cave where the healer amputated at top-speed with the desperate, brutal efficiency of a battlefield surgeon, assisted by the two biggest and strongest of the queen's guards.

The sweet, fetid smell of blood combined with the djinns' stench to produce a charnel house stink that filled her nose, invaded her head. As the healer labored, bloody to the elbows, she cursed in a constant, vicious undertone audible even over the curses and screams that rose and swirled around the rocky ceiling. The same chilling sounds drifted up from the gorge, muted slightly by the thickness of rock.

There would be the butcher's work of mercy to do soon. Mehcredi shuddered.

Time passed in a delirium of horror.

"*Null witch!*"

Deiter's yell echoed around the stone walls like a thunderclap, thrumming with Magick.

Oh Sister, *Erik!* Prue leaped to her feet, abandoning an elderly man who clutched at his forearm, whining between his teeth. Without a backward look, she ran headlong out of the cave.

In the sudden silence, Mehcredi blinked, rubbing her palms down her trews.

Oh gods, Walker!

The roll of bandages slipped from her fingers and rolled merrily across the ground, but Mehcredi had darted after Prue. No more than five steps from the cave, she stopped as if she'd run into a wall.

On the opposite side of the gorge, stood a man with meaty shoulders and a darkly shadowed jaw. Djinns whirled about his head, detectable as individual whirlwinds thickening the air. Something about them stretched Mehcredi's brain until it hurt, as if they were too alien, too *other*, to be real.

Slowly, trembling, she came forward. Walker was there, still safe, and that was all that mattered.

As Prue hurled herself into Erik's arms, the stranger's eyes narrowed. "Well, well. If it isn't Prue McGuire," he said conversationally. The wind had dropped and his voice carried perfectly in the night air, with the same Magickal reverberation as Deiter's. "I should have known." His teeth gleamed, large and white.

Deiter glared across the narrow space. "Prue?"

She shrugged. "Never seen him before."

"I have." Walker lurched to his feet. His face was gray with exhaustion, his lips bloodless, but when Mehcredi grabbed his arm, he set her aside. "Nerajyb Nyzarl." His tone was chillingly devoid of expression.

The man's smile widened. He bowed. "Nerajyb Nyzarl Necros now."

Walker's lips pulled back from his teeth. "I am Welderyn'd'haraleen't'Lenquisquilirian," he said, and waited.

This close, Mehcredi could see his fists clench, the savage bone-deep shudders. He'd done as Deiter had asked, made boulders dance to the tune of his Magick, but Sister in the sky, what had it cost him?

Nyzarl only shrugged and addressed himself to Deiter. "A bargain," he said. "One wizard to another."

Before Deiter could answer, Walker snarled, "Where's your demon, diabloman? Or do you have new pets now?"

"Ah," said Nyzarl, on a note of discovery. "You have a history with demons. By all means"—he waved a negligent hand—"meet mine." A string of guttural syllables left his mouth, spoken very fast and under his breath. At his side, the air *congealed*. Swiftly, it turned green. Clawed hands appeared, grasping the sides of the cloud and ripping it apart like rotted silk.

Peripherally, Mehcredi was aware of sounds—Cenda's gasp, Gray's curse, Erik's rumble as he drew Prue closer, the growl in the back of Walker's throat—but all her attention was focused on the nightmare that stepped out of the green fog.

This was a demon? This . . . twisted, grinning offense against nature? And Walker had killed *fourteen* of them? Merciful Sister!

Nyzarl trained a calm dark gaze on Deiter's face. "Give me the fire witch and I will take my djinn and my demon and retire to the ice. I swear it."

Cenda recoiled into Gray's embrace. "Purist!" As one, Gray and Shad turned their heads to glare at the old man. Gray's hand dropped to the hilt of his blade.

Ignoring them, Deiter gave an inelegant snort. "Then we are at an impasse. How many djinns are left? Half? Maybe less? Grievous losses."

The demon hissed, the holes that served it for nostrils flaring. A thin forked tongue flickered.

"Xotclic scents your wounded, Deiter. How many of *you* are left? Half? Or less? You can cut your losses, starting now. One small sacrifice. Give me the fire witch."

"Filth." Prue straightened her spine with an almost audible snap. "Take me instead." She scowled at Nyzarl, her aquamarine eyes gem-hard with fury. "Erik, pick me up and float me closer."

Erik looked frankly appalled. "No," he said. "Are you insane?"

Prue stamped a foot. "Look at him. *Look!*"

Nyzarl had backed up a step, glaring at Prue with unconcealed hatred. Despite the cold night air, sweat popped on his brow, rolled down his cheek.

The wind rose. Erik swung Prue up into his arms and drifted a few cautious feet into the gorge.

Nyzarl took another pace backward. The demon's chest plates clattered and its tail lashed, the spikes gouging deep furrows in the rocky ground. The djinns dipped and whirled.

"I don't believe in Magick," snapped Prue. "And Magick doesn't believe in me." She patted Erik's forearm. "Closer, love. I don't see how he did it, but . . ."

Slowly, a smile broke over her vivid little face, a smile so full of implacable purpose that a shiver like a drop of freezing water ran down Mehcredi's spine.

"How are the headaches?" Prue asked politely. "Bad, I hope."

"*Abomination.* Mongrel bitch." Nyzarl's face was very nearly the same color as the demon's cloud. He waved the creature forward. "Xotclic!"

Casually, the demon shambled out into midair, three djinns circling above its head like some outré guard of honor.

"No." Mehcredi gaped in horror.

Long tongues of flame snaked out from Cenda's outthrust fingertips. The djinns exploded with shrieks that pierced the bones of the skull. The demon's horny lipless mouth opened in a snarl, its taloned fingers reaching out to snatch Prue from Erik's arms.

Erik breathed so deeply, his chest expanded to an alarming degree. When he exhaled, the demon tumbled backward in the air, its chest plates clattering. The armored spikes of the tail whipped by so close to Prue's face, she barely had time to jerk her head aside.

Walker swore in Shar. The ground under Nyzarl's feet rippled and a vine sprang out of bare rock to curl around his ankle. Fighting to maintain his balance, the diabloman stretched out his arm, crooking the fingers of one hand, as if he squeezed something in his fist. It looked theatrical, Mehcredi thought, like a bad parody of a wicked wizard.

Nothing happened for a moment, then Deiter groaned, clutching his chest. He staggered back, his breath coming in pained gasps. But as Mehcredi and Rose rushed to support him, he forced a wine-stained grin, his skin tight against the bones of his skull.

"Fuck you," he whispered, the rest lost in muttered incantations. His gaze locked onto Nyzarl's and refused to release him. Slowly, two hectic spots of color returned to the old man's face.

Open-mouthed, Mehcredi watched Nyzarl dancing about, trying to keep his feet as the ground pitched and vines writhed about his legs like snakes. Cenda picked djinns out of the sky and Erik played a grim game of aerial cat and mouse with the demon.

"You lose again, *Necromancer*," called Deiter with relish, though he was breathing hard. "Impasse."

"No, no, we can finish it," cried Prue. She reached out with grasping fingers. "Let me have him."

"Aargh!" A rock rolled right under Nyzarl's foot and he stumbled. "Xotclic!"

"Ss."

The demon shot out a chitinous arm and scooped up the diabloman's substantial form as easily as a child. Nyzarl spat, his spittle a glowing green glob that sizzled. "Shaitan curse you! All of you!"

"Hah!" Prue McGuire glared.

Nyzarl, the demon and the green mist winked out of sight. The remaining djinns rose in a tight cloud until they were no more than moving disturbances in the sky.

Mehcredi didn't hesitate. Stepping up to Walker, she wrapped her arms around him, buried her face in the curve of his neck and hugged as if she could meld their bodies together. The swordmaster froze, then he clamped her to him, his breath gusting rough and warm against her hair.

"Holy Sister, I see it," said Prue's voice, still hoarse with tension, "but I don't believe it."

Mehcredi looked over Walker's shoulder to see her staring.

"Give them time," Rose said equably.

But the damage was done. His color high, Walker released her. Without missing a beat, he turned to Deiter. "They're heading west."

"Lord's balls, I need a drink." One hand massaging his chest, Deiter tottered over to the camp table. "Where's that bloody map?"

With a shaking finger, he traced the route. Mehcredi frowned. If that dot represented Guardpass, and those flowing lines the mountain barrier, then the gap in the range where Deiter was tapping must lead to . . .

Her mouth went dry.

She pushed in next to the old wizard. "Is that—" Ignoring his outraged bellow, she snatched the cup from his fingers and took a healthy gulp. "Is that L-Lonefell?"

∞

Lonefell Keep crouched like a great gray beast, its small slitted windows staring down the rutted winding road that led up from Blay Pass. Behind it, reared a series of snow-topped crags, marching away toward the distant ice. The pale sun glittered off a dark mirror cupped in the fold of a meadow, a small tarn to supply the keep with water, not yet frozen. Winter had yet to tighten its grip on this harsh land. Gods, what a birthplace.

Walker shot a sidelong glance at Mehcredi, who'd gravitated to ride on his left as she always did. One corner of his mouth tucked up in a wry smile. He was almost certain she did it instinctively, knowing she wouldn't impede his sword arm there.

He released a long breath. Small groups of figures marched purposefully back and forth across the bailey, but there were no signs of panic. 'Cestors be thanked, they were in time. The route from Guardpass shaved a day off the trip on the southern side of the range, but nonetheless, it had been two punishing days and most of a night in the saddle. The blisters across his shoulders itched as they healed, every muscle and joint in his body ached, except for his ass, which was numb. But physical discomfort faded in comparison with the jangle of thoughts seething inside his skull. And most of them began and ended with Mehcredi of Lonefell.

She was hunched inside a jacket that he thought might once have been his. It seemed vaguely familiar. From somewhere, she'd procured a blue scarf and wrapped it several times around her neck and over the lower part of her face. Combined with a fur cap pulled low over her eyes, all that was visible was the tip of a pink nose and her strange light eyes. It would be a kindness to tell her she drew attention by being obvious, but he couldn't bring himself to do it. She was so pathetically determined not to show her fear.

Before he knew he was going to do it, he'd reached out to touch her arm. "I'm here," he said, like a fool.

The blazing look of gratitude he got by way of reply just about liquefied his spine. Tired as he was, his balls rippled as if she'd feathered her fingertips over the sensitive skin.

Shifting irritably in the saddle, he glared at the unresponsive mountains. Fuck, he was precisely where he'd sworn not to be, surrounded by—he suppressed a growl—a ragtag band of heroes who held him back and got in his way. Somehow, he'd become *responsible* for them, not an area where he excelled. What's more, he had a woman glued to his side, a woman who needed as much attention as the stray she had cuddled under her coat—*his* coat.

He ground his teeth, tasting the bitter lees of failure and fury. Gods, he'd been so close! The last diabloman had escaped, gods damn it all to the seven icy hells. Prue swore that the black soul of the Necromancer had looked out from behind Nyzarl's eyes and Deiter confirmed it.

The only way Walker knew to make reparation to those he'd loved, to satisfy the savage craving in his soul—and it had been wrenched from his grasp, its absence a sore spot he had to prod at again and again, like a missing tooth.

Bouncing like a bag of bones, the wizard nudged his mount alongside. "Thinking about Nyzarl, shaman?" he said, reaching over to clap Walker on the shoulder. He struck the man's hand away. Mehcredi insisted on touching him whenever and wherever she pleased and he couldn't work why he wasn't able to stop her. It was baffling, but it didn't mean he was fair game for all and sundry.

As if he hadn't noticed, Deiter gave a greasy chuckle. "I'd lay odds his own demon ate him. Horrible way to go."

Walker growled something under his breath, wishing he could scrub his brain clean of the memories of Guardpass. After the slaughter of his kin, he'd thought he was inured to horror, his soul armored with the calluses of suffering. Nothing could be worse than that.

He'd been wrong.

The excruciating effort of forcing the *ch'qui* through the dumb resistance of rock and soil had scraped him right back to the bare nerve. After the battle was over, it took every ounce of warrior discipline he possessed simply to force himself to his feet. When he wrapped his hand around his sword hilt, he half expected to feel bone grate on the metal.

Then the healer had appeared, her face a thing of bone and hollows, and it hadn't been over at all.

"I can't do it alone," she'd said dully. "There are too many and all the sleepbalm's gone. I gave it . . . gave it to the children." She staggered and Gray caught her arm. "Please." Her voice had sunk to a harsh whisper. "Help me. My hands shake. I can't—"

As the company passed through a tall gateway, watched by narrow-eyed guards, Walker drew a rattling breath. He wouldn't think of it, of the butcher's work of mercy. He and Gray and Deiter had done it. Gray had been a mercenary once, he knew what he was about. As for the old wizard, he'd turned out to be surprisingly handy with a blade, but the tears that dampened his grizzled beard, those Walker had not expected. After it was finished, the last screams stilled, he'd reeled out of the cave, past Gray, who was quietly heaving his guts up behind a bush.

"Here." Mehcredi had obtained a bowl of clean water, 'Cestors knew where, but by that stage Walker had no longer cared. He'd plunged his arms in elbow deep. They'd spent the night in the narrow bed in the tavern, locked in a fierce embrace, like children shielding each other from nightmares. Long after she'd drifted off, Walker had stared over the assassin's shoulder into the darkness, running over the *nea-kata* in his head, endlessly, desperately, until sleep crashed over him not long before dawn.

A stocky, barrel-chested man stepped up to greet them as they dismounted. "The baron bids ye welcome to Lonefell Keep." His hand fell to the well-worn hilt of his sword. "We're glad to see ye, Captain," he said to Yachi. "The lads will take the horses. This way."

As the party clattered into a cavernous great hall, Mehcredi fell back until she was slouching among the guards at the rear.

The baron stood before a fireplace big enough to roast a vanbeast whole, his hands clasped behind his back. He was a slim compact man, his dark hair silvered with gray at the temples, the slightest thickening behind his belt buckle. Walker decided his eyes were too close together. "Your timing is impeccable, Captain," the baron said.

He fixed a shrewd gaze on Yachi. "My sentries tell me the foe gathers in the valley beyond the pass." Graciously, he inclined his head. "My grateful thanks to Her Majesty. We need all the help we can get."

"Ah, yes," said Deiter, stepping forward. "About the djinns . . ." He took the other man by the elbow.

The baron's mouth thinned. Disengaging himself with icy courtesy, he beckoned to a serving man. "Is that what they are?" He gestured at a heavy wooden table. "Please, take refreshment and we will discuss how best to use you."

"Not so fast," said the wizard, not at all discomposed. "First, you need to know what we know." He brightened as a serving maid placed a jug and a steaming platter on the table. "Wine! How delightful!"

With a single longing glance at the food, Mehcredi faded into the shadows.

It took Deiter a solid hour to describe the nature of the djinns and to convince the Baron of Lonefell to shut the keep up tight, so the djinns could pass over it on their way north.

In the end, it was Yachi who tipped the balance. "It was bad enough at Guardpass," she said in her blunt way. "And it's narrow there, easier to defend. March out to meet the djinns and it'll be a bloodbath, Baron. I guarantee." Her shudder wasn't faked. "Listen to the Purist here. He understands the godsbedamned things. This way there's a chance—a real chance, mind you—no one will die. It was a hard lesson to learn."

Deiter gave a genteel burp. "It's technically a single creature, a kind of hive mind. No more evil than you or I, but alien and ancient and terminally confused. I got no sense of real aggression, but it's irresistibly drawn to the *ch'qui* released by death."

The more the baron heard, the grimmer his face became. "I can't risk it," he said. "Purist, we could finish up fighting them—it—on every room and stair. Brother preserve us." He made the sign of the Sibling Moons.

"If you don't," Yachi said implacably. "Your losses will be much greater."

"Put all your people in one tower," said Walker. The baron summed him up in a single comprehensive glance and his eyes narrowed.

"Go on," he said, folding his arms.

Walker shrugged. "They'll be packed like fish in a barrel, but in a keep like this, you should be able to defend a single tower easily enough."

Deiter grinned like a moth-eaten direwolf. "And you can leave the Necromancer to me and the Sides. We'll keep the bastard busy with Magick."

The baron's mouth twisted as if he'd bitten into something sour, but he conferred with his sergeant. "All right then, we'll try it your way." His assessing eye skimmed over the company, paused and returned.

His arm shot out. "You!" A stern finger pointed at the shrinking figure of Mehcredi. "Thief! Sergeant, arrest that woman!"

33

The cold stone of the wall at her back bled through her clothing to chill her heart. Mehcredi tore off her cap with one hand, drew her sword with the other and glared at the Baron of Lonefell.

"I took what I was owed!" she shouted. At her feet, Scrounge's lips peeled back from his teeth, the rough fur raised in a ridge all down his spine. From somewhere behind her, came a continuous stream of hair-raising curses. Florien.

A quick quiet step and Walker stood on her left, a naked blade glittering in his hand and a snarl on his handsome face.

Chairs scraped, men swore, a serving maid screamed and dropped a tray. Before Mehcredi could blink, Erik, Gray and the queen's guards were ranged in a semicircle around her, staring at the baron and his men.

"*Quiet!*" bellowed Erik, his trained baritone bouncing off the stone walls.

"What the hell *is* this?" said Deiter into the sudden silence.

An ugly flush colored the baron's cheeks. "This woman," he said, biting off every word, "this *slut*, this misbegotten *bastard*, broke into my strongbox and then fled, like the common thief she is."

"Mehcredi?" asked Deiter, not taking his eyes from the baron.

Spots danced on the periphery of her vision. Gods, it was all over, the adventure, the learning—Walker—everything. *Slut. Half-wit. Ye great daft lump.* How could she have been stupid enough to think she'd escaped? Wherever she went, whatever she did, she carried Lonefell within her, buried deep in her flesh like a malignant seed. She tried to keep her chin up, but words were beyond her.

"See?" The baron's lip curled. "She doesn't deny it."

"You abandoned her to die," said Walker into the thrumming silence. His voice was cold, quiet and very precise.

Mehcredi's heart leaped up into her throat, where it lodged like a boulder, stopping her breath. Cautiously, scarcely daring to hope, she laid trembling fingertips against Walker's side, feeling his warmth.

"She meant less than a dog to you, or anyone else in this godsforsaken place." His flat black gaze bored into the baron. "But Mehcredi of Lonefell is a miracle, a stronger, sweeter spirit than a man like you can imagine."

When a thin smile touched the swordmaster's lips, the baron hissed out a curse, falling back a step. "I have never met a braver soul," said Walker. "I swear by my Ancestors, you touch her at your peril."

The baron's jaw clenched. "This is my keep," he said. "Here, justice is mine."

Prue McGuire set her hands on her hips. "Is this true, assassin? He left you to die?"

Mehcredi wet her lips. "From the moment of my birth." Her heart beat with slow painful thuds. Gods, it hurt.

Prue glanced around the company, gathering murmurs of assent, brisk nods. "Walker's right," she said. "Mehcredi's one of us."

"Yah," said Florien, then blushed.

Mehcredi's jaw dropped.

"Now, Prue," said the wizard, "let's not be hasty."

Prue raised her chin and walked slowly toward him, her hips swaying.

"All right!" Deiter scuttled backward, behind Yachi. "All right, have it your way."

"Baron." With an extravagant bow, Gray said, "Allow me to introduce myself. The Duke of Ombra, at your service. I think what Mistress McGuire is trying to say is that Mehcredi's safety is our price." Lounging against the wall, his shadow nodded its dark head in agreement.

A heated sensation bubbled up behind Mehcredi's breastbone and spread hot happy fingers through her whole body.

"P-price?" spluttered the baron. He turned to Yachi. "Captain, you cannot allow this rabble to dictate—"

"She's earned her place." Yachi fingered the hilt of her sword in a thoughtful kind of way. "Got guts and skills. We need people like that. So do you, noblelord."

The baron looked frankly appalled.

Mehcredi burst into laughter, the bubble of joy rushing out of her in great gasping peals. She barely noticed when Walker pushed her out of the hall and into a dark passageway. Snorting, she laughed on and on, clinging to the swordmaster's shoulders, tears streaming down her cheeks.

"Mehcredi?" He patted her face. "Are you all right?"

"Oh, yes." She threw her arms around him. "Gods, I love you."

Every muscle in his body went rigid.

Ah, what the hell did it matter? It was too late now, way too late. She stared into eyes the color of richest Concordian chocolat, too giddy with life and love and sheer relief to care what he read in her face. "No one's ever—" She swallowed. "Thank you."

The corners of Walker's mouth quirked up in the sweet serious smile she'd grown to crave. "The man's a pompous fool. I enjoyed it."

Her heart caroled. *One of us,* it sang. *Mehcredi's one of us.* She fit. Oh gods, she *belonged.*

When she raised her chin, he bent his dark head and their lips met. Sweet Sister, how she loved the way Walker kissed, as if he had all the time in the world. Strong fingers held her head at the perfect angle. No rush, no slobber, just a mind-numbing combination of tenderness and strength that sent a long sweet pull directly to her sex. Dizzily, she thought he'd been right all along—it *was* like the *nea-kata*, a kind of a dance. But, oh gods, there was no way for her to ruin it, no possibility of a misstep. Whatever she did was right and good and gave him pleasure, she knew it right down to her bones. The power of it, the delight, was heady.

I belong, she thought dazedly. *I have a place in this world. With you.*

Pressing her hips against his, she opened to him, soaring on sensation. Walker slid a hand over her breast, flicking the nipple with his thumb. The kiss segued from carnal to intoxicating. Moaning, Mehcredi tilted her pelvis and rubbed against the rigid column of his cock.

She *belonged*. With the swordmaster, she could be as wild and wanton as she wished. He wouldn't let her fall.

"Please," she gasped into his mouth, not even sure what she begged for, but trusting him to give it to her. "*Please*."

With a muttered curse in Shar, Walker ripped his mouth away. "Where—?" he growled, biting the side of her neck.

Mehcredi fumbled one hand across the wall. There should be a small robing chamber . . . A lifetime ago, it had been the most comfortable of her hidey-holes.

There! She fell back into the sweet-scented dark, Walker's hard body crowding her in a space not much bigger than a wardrobe. Light filtered in through a pair of high narrow windows, the standing mirror reflecting the swaying rack of rich garments and the spindly chair. Her heart sank. There wasn't room to lie down.

Walker jammed the chair under the door latch and turned to face her, his eyes glittering in the dim light. "No screaming," he whispered. "Not a sound." The rumble of voices from the great hall carried clearly through the wall.

He swooped, drowning her so thoroughly in another dark velvet kiss, that she wasn't aware of her trews and underthings pooling around her ankles until cooler air hit her bare bottom. Walker picked her up as though she weighed nothing and spun her around. His deep voice vibrated in her ear. "Bend over the chair and hold on."

How extraordinary. Mehcredi lifted her head to ask what the hell he thought he was doing when a questing forefinger trailed from her clitoris all the way to the pucker of her anus and back. She gurgled, quivering.

"You're dripping," murmured that barely-there voice. The finger slipped inside her. Very gently, Walker twisted it, rubbing, massaging. "So ready for me."

The delicate flesh was engorged with blood, the demanding throb driving her insane. Gods, he could see everything, the most private part of her body offered up to him like a gift. Mehcredi made a guttural noise of sheer desperation. A glance over her shoulder revealed Walker poised to surge forward, every tendon in his neck taut, his eyes glittering with passion. Slick, hot and hard, he sank into her body, stretching succulent flesh to its limits.

"Tight," he gritted, working his way forward inch by inch, until the smooth heat of his balls was jammed up right against her, the fabric of his trews brushing the backs of her thighs.

In the hidden valley, she'd loved how different, how delightful, it was to sit astride and fuck him, but this! The angle was shallow, his bulk and length pressing on something inside so excruciatingly nerve-rich that her clitoris swelled hard in immediate response. In this position, she was virtually helpless, impaled and trapped. At his mercy. *Gods!*

Reaching out, she grabbed a sleeve at random and stuffed it into her mouth.

Walker pulled out, a delicious drag that made her head swim. "Yes," he whispered, setting up a smooth deliberate stroke, nudging her clit from behind every time he hilted.

A warm hand skated up under her shirt, tracing the knobs of her spine, sliding around over her ribs to cradle a throbbing breast. As he increased the pace, he came down over her, his breath a hot rasp in her ear. "Come for me, sweetheart."

Diabolical fingers skimmed over her fluttering belly and parted her sparse curls. Walker thrust ferociously, the chair creaking with the power of his passion. Every stroke shoved her aching clitoris against the heel of his hand.

Whimpering into her makeshift gag, she tried to prolong the sensation, wanting to ride the silvery edge of pleasure forever. Walker shifted his hips, changing the angle. With a muffled howl into the baron's judgment-day jacket, Mehcredi shattered. Everything stopped, breath, sense, the world itself, while she shook with the erotic snap and release of tension. Every muscle in her pelvis bore down hard in a cramping, ecstatic grip.

Dimly, she heard a muffled groan, Walker's breath gusting hot against the nape of her neck. The skin there stung, a small delicious ache. Gods, had he *bitten* her?

She spat out the sleeve, sucking in great gulping breaths. If it hadn't been for Walker's iron grip on her hips, she might have floated away. When she wriggled, he hissed, still hard and huge inside her, his pulse throbbing insistently against the close walls of her sheath. Gods! She turned her head and their eyes locked.

Plates clinked and footsteps pattered past the door. The servants, clearing the table in the great hall. On the other side of the wall, voices rose in argument, the baron cutting them off with a snarled phrase.

The sobbing rasp of Walker's breath filled the close space. He cupped her cheek, pushing her head to the side, toward the mirror. "Watch," he said, no louder than leaves whispering in the wind.

Mehcredi choked. She'd never seen anything so lewd in her life. Walker hadn't removed his trews, only unlacing them enough to free himself, while the curves of her ass glimmered like cream satin in the half-light. As he withdrew, his shaft glistened, wet with her juices. He paused a moment at the top of the stroke, then shoved forward and she could see how he spread the small sucking entrance to her body, her flesh struggling to accommodate his girth.

Sister save her, she felt . . . complete. Filled and fucked and *real*. She watched Walker's buttocks hollow with power as he increased the depth and speed of his thrusts. A hand reached past her and snagged the maroon sleeve.

Mehcredi shook her head. Not necessary. She was still drifting on the warm wash of her climax, unstrung with pleasure.

Walker pressed his chest against her spine, enveloping her completely. Lowering his head, he set his teeth where her neck met her shoulder. "Take it," he groaned into her flesh. "Take *me*."

His hips drew back and he thundered into her, plunging so deep it hurt—and it didn't—or not in a bad way. She bit her lip, her eyes wide. Godsdammit, it wasn't possible, but the aching tension was ramping up again, not as fast as before, but deeper, sweeter. Shuddering, Mehcredi sank her teeth into maroon fabric, fighting the scream building in her throat.

The swordmaster's strokes became choppy. Without warning, he slid an arm around her hips, bracketing her throbbing clit with two fingers. As he let out a strangled groan, jamming himself deep inside, he squeezed—just enough.

Why had she bothered with the gag? Mehcredi thought in a far-away corner of her mind, because when she hit the peak, she couldn't produce a sound louder than a newborn kitten. Unlike the first time, this felt more like unraveling than climax as if the physical act had stripped away emotional layers to expose something essential, vulnerable and trusting. Every muscle in her body went limp.

You claimed me. I'm yours.

Gently, Walker pulled out. Without a word, he turned her around, gathered her into his arms and buried his face in her hair, breathing hard. Humming with pleasure, Mehcredi put out her tongue to lick at the beads of sweat trickling down the smooth brown column of his neck.

"Here," he murmured, pressing a fine white handkerchief between her legs. It had a lace trim and the baron's monogram.

When Mehcredi clapped a hand over her mouth to hold back the giggle, Walker's lips quirked in one of those gorgeous not-quite smiles. Her insides liquefied. She lifted a shaking hand to his hair.

Immediately, the shutters came down, his face smoothing into the familiar mask, but she refused to let it bother her. She trusted him, didn't she? With everything she was.

Frowning, Walker tucked himself away. "Give me five minutes," he murmured. "Then you can go."

Mehcredi lifted her chin to whisper in his ear. "You meant it, didn't you?" she breathed. "What you said to the baron?"

Walker stared into her face, grimmer than ever. "Yes." The pad of his thumb skated across her lower lip. He opened his mouth, closed it again, and turned away to ease the door open. A final, unfathomable glance over his shoulder and he disappeared.

Mehcredi contemplated the soggy mess of the handkerchief in her hand. It wouldn't do to be caught thieving, would it? With a grin of pure mischief, she tucked it into the right-hand pocket of the baron's fine coat.

Cautiously, Mehcredi cracked the door open and peered up at the night sky. Nothing but the wind-tossed dark and a sense of something suspended like a smoke stain in the water, pervasive, palpable.

She shivered.

Deiter had weathered the worst of the baron's fury with amazing patience. After that, it took the rest of the day to check every point of access—to the tower, the great hall and then the whole keep, every door, every window, every cranny, every chink. Accompanied by the baron's men, Erik and Prue had done it, then Cenda and Gray and Walker. Together, Mehcredi and Rose had walked every passage and chamber, cross-checking. But still she fretted.

Two squads of soldiers were stationed in the tower and the great hall with buckets of hot pitch and their quarterstaves. Just in case. Deiter, Cenda and Erik climbed to the top of the tower, ready to deal with the Necromancer. With his usual calm, Walker pointed out that his brand of Magick wasn't likely to be of much use up there. Currently, he was balanced on his heels, his back to the wall on the far side of the huge circular chamber, eyes closed. The Sister knew what he was doing.

Shutting the door, Mehcredi glanced over her shoulder at the crowd packed almost shoulder to shoulder, family groups camped on blankets on the floor, children tearing around squealing with excitement. The atmosphere was already fetid, hot and close, the sense of confusion exacerbated by the babble of a hundred different conversations.

She meant nothing to these people—less than nothing—yet their faces were so familiar. The chief laundress with her poor red hands, the stable lads playing a desultory game of dice, Nedward's kitchen maid sporting a swollen belly, even Taso, skulking in a corner. When their eyes met, he leered and waggled his tongue, but the moment she began to shoulder her way through the press toward him, he scowled and disappeared behind a group of chattering serving women. Coward.

She couldn't let them die.

When it finally came, the song of the djinns was barely audible. The children heard it first. A toddler screamed once, shrill and sharp, and then fell silent, clutching its mother's skirts. The chatter trailed off gradually until the quiet was so profound, the only noise was an ear-aching whine entwined with the icy voice of the wind.

One of the baron's hunting dogs lifted its great shaggy head and bayed a challenge, fur bristling all down its spine. From somewhere unseen, Scrounge barked his defiance, insolence in every syllable. Mehcredi couldn't help but grin. Where was he? Begging scraps from the children probably.

The keening of the wind had grown to a howl. An enormous force buffeted the stone walls of the keep. Every shutter rattled. Around the perimeter of the hall, the guards stood shoulder to shoulder, white-faced. More than one strong hand trembled on the staff it held.

"Hold your water!" Yachi bellowed. "Sit tight. It's just passing through."

The barking became a fusillade, high and frantic. Mehcredi's head whipped around and her guts cramped with horror.

Outside!

Gods, no! The only one in all the world of whose love she could be certain.

With a gasp, she jerked her hand back from the bar across the door.

"*Mehcredi!*" Walker's full-throated bellow reverberated off the stone walls. He skewered her with the intensity of his black stare, every ounce of his formidable will focused on pinning her to the wall. "*Don't.*" She saw his lips shape the word as he began to work his way toward her through the crowd.

But she couldn't listen to Scrounge die, *she couldn't.*

Holy Sister, Sister of mercy, please. Oh, please. Frantically, she glanced around, avoiding Walker's furious gaze. Window, the nearest window. I know he's only a—

Out of the corner of her eye, she saw a skinny leg disappear behind a tapestry and her blood turned to iced water. There was an alcove there, if she recalled correctly, and a— Sweet Sister!

Before she knew she was going to do it, she'd shouldered past an elderly couple and shoved the hanging aside, just as Florien's shabby boots jiggled in a narrow window aperture and vanished into the thrashing darkness. Without hesitation, Mehcredi hurled herself after him, slamming the window shut the moment she gained her feet on the flagged path outside.

34

Crouching, a naked blade in either hand, she peered into the shadows. Nothing. The night was clear, the Sibling Moons blurring every chunk of stone, every blade of grass, with their strange double radiance. "Florien?" she called softly. "You little bastard, wait 'til I get hold of you."

No answer, but the yapping started up again, the other side of a projecting buttress.

The wind shoved her about like a bully. Mehcredi's lips peeled back from her teeth. What the fuck. She'd been bullied by the best. Pushing the whipping hair out of her eyes with the back of her hand, she crept forward.

The boy stood with his back pressed to the tower wall, staring toward the keep gates, his face stark with terror. Scrounge was clasped in his arms, still shouting canine threats at the stream of brown black fur pouring out of the stables. Rats. They scuttled across the bailey to dive into a grate over the kitchen.

Mehcredi barely flinched. Her heart thudding with foreboding, she turned to track Florien's gaze.

A heaving turbulence boiled through Blay Pass, a thousand whirlwinds jostling, jockeying for position. The choir of the djinns swelled to a hellish chorus as they swept through the gates of Lonefell.

Using her whole body, Mehcredi shoved boy and dog into the corner provided by the buttress. Her legs weak with terror, she placed herself in front of them. The air roiled. Lifting her chin, she snarled her defiance.

The bolt of fear was so intense, Walker stood frozen for vital seconds. The great doors boomed as though a huge ghostly fist hammered, demanding admittance.

Snapping out of his paralysis, he grabbed the nearest lantern, his brain spinning, calculating the odds. It would take him too long to work through the press of bodies to Mehcredi's window. Whirling about, he pulled a shutter from the window behind him. As he thrust a leg over the sill, a voice growled, "What the fuck—?"

The baron's sergeant lunged forward to pull him back. Walker clipped the man neatly on the jaw, yanked the quarterstaff out of his hand and tumbled backward into the moonslit bailey. The keening of the djinns had become a concerted howl. They darted and swooped, thickening the air in dizzying patterns that twisted the mind.

Walker opened the lantern, shoving the pitch-covered end of his staff into the flame until it caught. Torch blazing, he ran flat out, stretching into his stride like a direwolf, circling the tower. A thunderclap split the air, accompanied by the vicious roar of a hungry flame. Walker risked a glance upward. On the top of the tower, three small figures were silhouetted against the moons-wracked clouds. The light surrounding them glowed a strange acrid green. Deiter's robes billowed as he staggered back into Erik's arms. The green intensified and the flames resumed.

Cursing, the swordmaster jinked and wove while the wind flailed at the dark air around him. Heart hammering, he sped around the final curve—and there she was, standing foursquare, her legs braced, shielding the boy and the dog with her body. Her face was upturned, gleaming pale as bone in the night and her eyes were wide, fixed on three vortexes of whistling air hovering just above her head.

Walker's guts cramped with horror, the blood congealing in his veins.

The djinns rose a foot, swirling about as if confused by the multiplicity of targets.

Gray stepped out of the well of deep shadow thrown by the tower. "*Boy!*" At his side stood a man-shaped slice of midnight. The hair rose on the back of Walker's neck. *Shad*. Reaching out, it wrapped an impossibly long arm around Florien's waist and drew him back into the shadows, the dog still squirming in his arms.

Gray, Shad and the boy vanished, but Gray's disembodied voice carried clearly enough. "I've got him. Godsdammit, *run!*" A sorcerer of shadows indeed. Gods!

Her back to the wall, Mehcredi panted open-mouthed like an animal.

The djinns collected themselves and swooped like corpsebirds, ignoring Walker completely. Sharp reports split the air, small objects ricocheted off tower walls at all angles. Something scored a furrow in Walker's cheek, but he barely registered it.

He hurled the lighted lantern straight into the thick of them. Glass tinkled and an ear-piercing shriek lingered and died on the freezing air. One down, two to go. Mehcredi was dodging and weaving, cramped as well as protected by the stone at her back.

Walker waded into the fray, swinging his burning staff in a wide circle.

"Mehcredi!" yelled Gray, still cloaked in shadow. "Ten feet to your left. *Quick!*" A darker rectangular space appeared in the tower wall. A doorway.

The second djinn writhed on the point of Walker's quarterstaff, dying in a shower of stinking sparks. Mehcredi edged sideways.

With blinding speed, the remaining djinn lunged, the air exploding around it. Mehcredi reeled back, making the strangest noise, midway between a grunt and a shriek. Folding into herself, she slumped against the wall.

No, no! Not when he'd only just found her.

His brain was frozen in a stasis produced by sheer horror, but his limbs moved with the perfect precision that was the result of decades of training. Walker surged forward, close enough for the translucent creature to brush his arm, a weird touch like congealed water. In a single flowing movement, he speared the djinn with his quarterstaff, bent and scooped Mehcredi up in his arms. She moaned piteously.

He threw himself through the door, sinking to a dusty floor, cradling Mehcredi's quivering body with his own.

Behind him, the door slammed and a bar dropped into place.

"Get a light, lad," gasped Gray's voice. "*Run!*"

Outside, the whistling rose to a crescendo and the door rattled. Florien's footsteps pattered away.

"Where?" Gray said. "Where did it get her?"

An icy ball of dread had taken up residence in Walker's gut. "Not sure." When he passed frantic hands over Mehcredi's torso, she screamed.

"Shit!" He recoiled.

A circle of light appeared, Florien entering through a bricked archway. They were in some kind of cellar, obviously used as a storeroom, judging by the sacks of flour and dried fruit, the huge yellow wheels of cheese.

Mehcredi was still conscious, how he had no idea. Her eyes were squeezed shut and she'd bitten her lip until it bled. The warm ivory of her skin had gone a horrible shade of gray green. Frantic, he sank his fists into her shirt and ripped it down the middle, baring her to the waist.

"Argh!" Her body contorted.

The blood sheeting her side shone black in the wavering light, the boy's hand shaking as he held the lantern aloft. The dog crouched, the moaning sound he made eerily human.

"Candles," said Gray. He gripped the assassin's shoulders and pressed her down. "Florien, *hurry*." Shad leaned forward, joining Gray, his smoky fingers long and thin.

Mehcredi's face distorted in a rictus of excruciating pain. An obscene lump, like a huge, hard carbuncle, slid slowly under the skin of her ribs.

Walker's world tilted on its axis. His vision hazed.

Outside, the noise of the djinns subsided to a fretful buzzing. A last rattle, a whoosh as if a huge volume of air had been sucked out of the world and then all that remained was the moaning of the wind. A pause and a hundred people began to babble, deeper voices shouting orders.

"Healer," Walker croaked. "I'll get—"

A small bony hand grabbed his arm. "Nah," Florien said. "He's busy wit' Cenda an' the old man."

"Cenda?" Gray jumped to his feet. "Shit! Walker, I—"

"Go," Walker said dully. "There's nothing you can do here anyway."

Gray opened his mouth, then shook his head and closed it again. Shad stroked a dark hand over Mehcredi's hair and rose to join him. In perfect step, they charged through the archway at a dead run.

Mehcredi groaned and her eyes snapped open, so dark with pain they were black. "W-Walker?"

"I'm here," he said.

"H-hurts." She grasped the wrist of his knife hand, the manic strength of her grip hard enough to leave bruises. "Cut it out."

But when he touched the tip of his blade to her skin, the djinn stone skittered about as if aware of his intentions. Mehcredi's thin scream echoed off the ceiling.

Walker clenched his teeth on a whimper like a wounded animal. He pulled away, sweat pouring off him. "I'm making it worse."

"Fook," whispered Florien. "It's runnin' away. Fookin' thing's alive."

They waited until the trembling stopped. Mehcredi went still, save for the jerky rise and fall of her breasts.

"L-love you." She stopped to grit her teeth. A runnel of blood trickled down her chin. "Do it." Her hand moved toward the knife, the movement uncoordinated but purposeful. "C-clean and quick."

"Can't."

"*Aaargh!*" Beneath his hands, Mehcredi bucked, clenching her teeth on a long groan. Her spine arched off the floor, the bones cracking.

Florien knelt beside him, shaking. "Fookin' hell. Do something!" His voice was clogged with tears and horror.

A terrible rage moved in Walker like a caged beast. "I won't let you die, Mehcredi. Do you hear me?"

"N-no choice." Incredibly, she tried to smile, though it came out like a grimace. "Worth it though. *Ah gods!*" She writhed for a moment, then went limp. "Every m-minute."

Magick rose within him—the rising sap of spring, the slow inexorable strength of tectonic plates deep below the surface of the earth. His skin grew hot and tight as the power expanded, filling him to the point of pain.

Grimly, Walker brought all his shamanic skills to bear, breathing in the stench of sweat and blood and burning as though it were an exotic perfume. Sinking down beside her, he laid his palm over the breast he'd once Marked, closing his eyes. With a moan, he brushed his lips across her slack mouth, tasting the sweet copper of her blood, feeling the faint warm rush of her breath.

Resolve firmed within him, deep and granite hard, enduring as the earth. What did he have to live for, after all? 'Cestors' bones, if his Magick wasn't good enough, he'd find something else to give—his life if that was what it took.

Very softly, he began to chant the Song he'd made for her and the Mark rose beneath his palm, the lines swimming up from the heart of her, Marking her flawless skin once again. When Walker switched to his own Song, the Mark reached out to twine up his forearm like a vine, toward his own heart.

Ruthlessly, he tore apart the shields between them, exploiting her love for him, staring his own feelings in the face and using them. Not flinching, but accepting with all the grace he could muster. Even when it was hopeless, love had an amazing resilience, stronger even than death. He couldn't gainsay that.

Walker sank into the essence of his assassin. At first, the sensation was disorientating, a long, lateral swoop. Down and down he spiraled through the interstices of a glittering maze, impossibly complex, many layers deep, eerily beautiful, a shifting architecture of energy and soul, shot through with prisms of rainbow color. Starstuff. Awed, he allowed himself to fuse, one more drifting mote in a world of warmth and moving light.

In some kernel of self that dimly recalled logic, he knew the swirling shapes and patterns were only a schema, given to him by the mercy of the Ancestors—a gift of earth Magick to keep him sane.

To feel his spirit mesh with hers was a terrifying lunacy, intoxicating, thrilling. Entranced, he drifted deeper, knowing two lives depended on his shaman's skill. If Mehcredi should die at this moment . . .

The symbolism changed. As he hung, floating and twisting, vivid images flickered by faster than he could absorb them, like a deck of brightly colored fortune cards fanned by an expert hand.

A life, he saw a woman's life. He was privy to the soul of another.

Deeply humbled, he watched myriad scenes flash past in a blurring instant, saw all the dreams and realities that had created the unique being that was Mehcredi of Lonefell. There she was with a cavalcade of strangers—a fat old man with a stained apron tied around his middle; a group of children laughing and pointing; a giant of a man with a Northerner's white blond braids; a woman in a maid's gown, her mouth pinched and angry.

Out o' the way, she snapped. *Ye great daft lump.*

Guards, skiffmen, stable lads, tavern wenches, even the Master of the Assassins' Guild, they accelerated past, so numerous he grew dizzy.

The impact was overwhelming, shocking him to the bones. He'd thought he'd known about her childhood, told himself he understood how Mehcredi the assassin had come to be. What arrogance, what godsbedamned folly. Unforgivable. Seeing it this way was like a length of cold steel in the vitals, a razor edge to slice him into bleeding gobbets of horror and pity and fury.

Mehcredi's existence hadn't been a life—except in the sense that her lungs continued to pump, her heart to beat. A bleak string of hours and days amounting to years of . . . of *nothing*. He could scarcely comprehend it, such a wasteland, people—ordinary, presumably normal human beings—looking right through her or cuffing her out of the way, telling her with every absentminded buffet that she meant less than the kitchen cat.

Fuck, how was it she was even sane?

A dark warrior strode out of Mehcredi's memories. Walker's blood chilled to ice. Reeling, appalled beyond measure, he stared. Leanly muscled, cold-eyed and dangerous, this man stood head and shoulders above the rest like some heroic colossus, impossibly capable, impossibly strong. Finger bones gleamed like ivory in the wealth of his black braids.

Was that how she saw him? A dark hero out of legend? A wounded soul waiting for the love of a good woman? Despite himself, his lip curled. Gods, she was such a baby. Could she have chosen someone less worthy? A man closed to all emotion save savage driving hatred, a cold-blooded executioner. No, of course not. She didn't have the experience, the perception, to see it how pathetic he truly was—trying so desperately to atone for his failure to die with those he'd loved.

Brusquely, he turned aside, looking elsewhere. Ah, there lurked the dark side of Mehcredi, ugly smears of pride, of fear and anger. So she was human. What of it? With a wry smile, Walker withdrew his attention. He'd never thought his assassin a paragon, and he'd trespassed enough.

Brightest of all, shone the strong, glowing beacon of her soul, shot through with courage and humor and an extraordinary innocence.

His guts turned over. On some level, he thought dully, he'd always known. He loved her, this strange tactless girl with her shining honesty and generosity of spirit, so clean and bright in contrast with the dark stains on his own weary soul.

By the First Father, she deserved everything life had to give!

He threw his head back, his fists clenching. *Hear me, You Who Came Before. I am Welderyn'd'haraleen't'Lenquisquilirian, earth shaman, last of the Shar. Give me this woman's life and I swear by my Song, by Your Honored Bones, I will give it back to her.*

He was almost certain he'd squeezed his eyes shut, but nonetheless, he stared deep into the heart of the stars, into primeval chaos and fire, the source of all life.

I will set her free to live. My oath on it, willingly given.

Starstuff sizzled over his skin, crisped his bones, moving through and over him like the *ch'qui*.

Walker gasped as it released him, sloughing off his skin. The final impression lingered, a light caress between his brows, sweet as a mother's farewell. Gods, the thing was done.

He opened his eyes, looking straight at a rangy, straight-backed old woman with a coronet of white hair. She smiled into his eyes, her own a familiar, mesmerizing silver. Irresistibly drawn, Walker drifted closer, noticing as he did so that the image throbbed with an irregular rhythm. It took him a moment to realize the pulse of it was faltering, ebbing further with every beat.

Mehcredi and her future were dying before his eyes.

Fuck! Gasping, he flung his will after the djinn stone, tracking its hideous spoor by the ripped filaments that waved, broken and pathetic in its wake, by the echo of an agonized cry.

In all that energy and light, there was only one void, one space full of . . . *nothing*. Walker swooped, flying toward it, leaving no trace of his passing. The stone felt so utterly alien, so *wrong*, he recoiled instinctively, but to his surprise, he could sense no evil.

Gathering himself, he flung the totality of his will around the thing, squeezing, pulverizing, desperate to obliterate it. The old woman nodded and smiled. But the stone's very otherness made it cold and slick. It slipped through his grasp as if greased and slid away.

The old woman flickered and faded.

Noooo! Walker gave himself to the bargain he'd made, to the wisdom of his Ancestors.

Without hesitation, he hurled himself at the djinn stone and enveloped it, hanging on grimly, ignoring the bone-deep chill, the utter emptiness sucking at his soul.

After an endless time, the thing quivered and grew still. The old woman reappeared and quirked a brow, her expression one of gentle inquiry.

Walker breathed again, but each time he tried to withdraw, the djinn stone would reanimate and strain to be off like a hound on the leash. He was snared, caught forever, as if he held a hungry tygre by the tail.

If he let go, Mehcredi would die—one ugly, screaming inch at a time. But if he didn't, what would be his fate? Would he die with her? He shivered. Perhaps not. A living death as a mindless husk, someone to wipe his ass and shove pap down his throat . . .

Think. *Think.*

Ah well. He'd calculated the cost almost as soon as he'd seen the wound. With slow deliberation, Walker delved deep in his soul for the *ch'qui*, force-feeding his Magick with the stuff until he had silky skeins of it, the same sweet healthy pink as her pretty nipples, glistening with life like the slick ruffles of her eager sex. Petal after petal he formed out of the Magick at his core—his heart, his soul, his life—placing each one with the delicate precision of a surgeon. As he did so, he chanted—snatches of the Song he'd made for her during those endless cold nights on the trail crouched over a tiny campfire, snatches of his own Song—twining them together in a tight spiral of sound and ancient Magick.

When it was done, the last notes fading away, he laid the ugly pellet in the heart of a perfect, dew-kissed desert orchid. One by one, the petals curled over, each overlapping the next, until the djinn stone was encased, its darkness eclipsed by a shell of glimmering pearlescent pink. Walker permitted himself a tired smile. No longer dull and mindlessly cruel, the djinn stone shone with the soft ineffable beauty of starstuff.

Infinitely slowly, he released his grip, a fraction at a time. The thing lay quiescent, Mehcredi shielded from its effects by his Magick—by his *love*.

All around him, like a benediction, broken filaments of light wove together in healing tangles. 'Cestors be thanked. Relief turned his bones to water. All he could manage by way of triumph was a warm glow. He was so drained, he wondered if he'd ever be able to summon the *ch'qui* again.

Vaguely, he considered the implications of giving a part of his soul into another's keeping. He gave a harsh soundless laugh. Now there was the ultimate intimacy for you. So much for keeping the world at arm's length. Would he wither and die when he sent her away? Perhaps he'd have to follow her at a discreet distance for the rest of his life. Exhaustion made it hard to care.

The old woman held out her arms, tears streaking her cheeks. When Walker stroked her white hair, she laid her head thankfully on his shoulder. The beat of her heart grew stronger and stronger, a mighty gong that shook the world, until Walker's own pulse could no longer exist independent of it and they were one.

Closing his eyes, he let the reverberations pull him under.

35

A huge rock was crushing her chest. No, not a rock, a bloody mountain. Mehcredi breathed carefully through her nose. Mustn't annoy the mountain.

"Mehcredi? C'mon, I brought Scrounge. If Prue catches me . . ."

Odd that a mountain should have a boy's voice. Something like a warm wet flannel swiped over her cheek. A doggy tongue. Blech. She levered an eye open.

They looked healthy enough, both of them. Good.

Gods, she was tired. She let the eye flutter shut.

Too late. The darkness wasn't comfortable anymore. Mehcredi groped for sense, for memory, but all that came to her was Walker's face, set with concentration, his body moving in a lithe, savage dance and djinns exploding in showers of evil-smelling sparks all around him.

Djinns!

She gripped Florien's skinny wrist, not noticing him flinch. "He's all right?" She dragged in a rasping breath. "Not—?"

"Walker?" Huffing with displeasure, the boy peeled her fingers away, one by one. "Nah, too fookin' tough."

She could barely croak. "Where—?"

"Talkin' t' Deiter. An' guess what?" He leaned forward, his eyes sparkling. "There's Technomages comin'. A flitter came wit' a message for t' baron."

"Huh." Mehcredi fell back toward sleep, not caring. The dog

jumped onto the bed, turned three circles and settled down with his head draped across her shins. People spoke nearby, a door slammed. She smelled the familiar odors of old stone and tapestries and ashes. She was still at Lonefell then.

And Walker? As she relaxed, a slow certainty swam into her soul. She didn't know how she knew or why, only that she did.

"You're wrong." She spoke without opening her eyes. "Not talking, he's sleeping. So . . . tired . . ." Then she settled back into the darkness as though it were a fine feather bed and slept without dreams.

When she woke again, there was no sign of the dog. Prue McGuire sat in a window seat frowning down at a portable writing desk. One forefinger was stained with ink, a smear of it on her determined little chin.

Mehcredi cleared her throat. Prue set the writing desk aside with a muffled exclamation and bounced to her feet. Merciful Sister, was that a *smile*?

"Here." The other woman offered a cup with a straw. The water slid down Mehcredi's throat, cool and welcome.

Surely she should be dead? Mehcredi struggled to sit up, Prue's arm sliding behind her, helping. So should Walker. Her brow furrowed. In fact, she could swear she could feel his body warmth, sense his masculine vitality. Which was comforting and profoundly unsettling, all at once.

"What . . . happened?"

"In brief?" Prue raised a brow. "Let's see. The idiot dog got trapped outside. The idiot boy went after the dog. You went after the boy and Walker went after you. Which makes you all idiots."

"Know . . . that. Then?"

"Gray and Shad hid the boy and the dog in the shadows, while Walker fought off the djinns." Prue frowned. "But you were hit." She laid a cool hand against Mehcredi's forehead, took her pulse in a businesslike kind of way. "How do you feel?"

"Tired." Mehcredi took stock. "Bruised. Hungry. *Alive*." She stared at Prue, shocked. "I don't understand."

The other woman shrugged. "No one does. Walker did some kind of Magick to save you, but he won't talk about it." She hesitated. "He's spent hours sitting with you. Did you know?"

"No." Mehcredi closed her eyes. Grief tugged at her senses, raw aching regret. "Who's dead?" she asked. "Deiter?"

"What? No, not Deiter." Prue's vivid little face lost some of its color. "Turns out one of the scullery maids thought she'd sneak out in the confusion and hide some silverware in her room, which meant she opened the kitchen door. None of the staff survived, nor did the half dozen guards who went to help." She rubbed her temple. "Not good, but we got off lightly this time. A total of fifteen wounded, three of them children."

Unable to speak, Mehcredi ventured to pat the other woman's hand. Prue sniffed and gave a wobbly smile. "As for Deiter, he's far too tough to kill, the old corpsebird. The Necromancer managed to stop his heart for a couple of minutes up there on the tower, but Cenda and Erik pried the bastard loose. The demon nearly got them half a dozen times."

Her throat moved. "It seemed like forever, the horrible green lights and the flames and the flows of air. I thought Erik was going to d-die. They were very b-brave."

"So were you," Mehcredi said gently. "You had to watch."

Prue's lips trembled, tears streaming down her face.

At a complete loss, Mehcredi patted the small hand again. "Ah, shit," sobbed Prue, folding in on herself. "Sorry— I—"

Mehcredi blinked. What was she supposed to do now? She gave a mental shrug. Ah well, patting seemed to work. Gingerly, she stroked Prue's back, murmuring nonsense, and after a wet five minutes, the other woman seemed to calm. She sat up, fumbling for a handkerchief.

Walker was close by, Mehcredi was sure of it. Merciful Sister, how she longed to see him. Aloud, she said, "So we won then?"

"Not even close."

"But they're gone, the djinns?"

"Oh yes, they passed over Lonefell and kept right on going, but the Necromancer and his demon got away." Prue growled under her breath. "By the Sister, I did better with nothing but a shovel. And for all we know, the djinns are having a nice chilly rest cure in the ice. Wait 'til the little ones put themselves back together into one great big nasty djinn. That'll be something to look forward to."

"Oh."

"Yes, *oh*. All we've got are the Necromancer's lackeys—his guards and servants and a crazy old woman who says she's a Technomage. And there's a cook, but I think the baron wants him now."

Gingerly, Mehcredi pushed back the covers and swung her legs to the floor. "Whoops." The room swam.

"Steady." Prue grabbed her arm.

"I need to pee," Mehcredi said plaintively. Her stomach growled. "And then . . . Is there lunch?"

She waited all the following day, but Walker didn't come.

Prue stood with folded arms while the keep healer examined Mehcredi with brisk distaste. Drawing back, he shook his head. "I don't understand," he said, sounding personally offended. "It's as if the . . . thing never touched her."

Mehcredi scowled. "I'm right here, you know." She pulled her shirt up to show a pink pucker on the smooth creamy skin of her side. "And you're wrong. I have a scar."

"Yes, well." The man made for the door. "You're perfectly healthy. I'll tell the baron you wasted time I could have devoted to others."

Mehcredi showed her teeth. "He'll be thrilled."

In the afternoon, she tracked Walker to the meadow beside the tarn. He was sitting on a rock, skimming stones across the dark surface of the water, remote and beautiful as ever. The wind teased the ends of his hair.

Mehcredi sighed. Ah, hell. "What are you think—?"

She broke off, staring, as Walker lifted haunted eyes to hers. Emotions poured off him, a turbulent flood of them, all tangled together in a dark boiling mass—anguish, guilt, grief, regret, a relief so profound it reached to the depths of the soul. She swayed, her senses reeling with the impact.

A strong hand gripped her arm. "What are you doing out of bed?"

Mehcredi blinked at him. "I'm fine," she said absently. "Good as new. The healer said so. But what's wrong with you?" Why on earth had she thought him difficult to read? Everything he felt was right there, except it was all a dreadful blur, the emotions so dark with pain they were indistinguishable from each other.

Walker's hand lifted to brush her cheek. "How did you survive it?"

She smiled. "You were there. You did . . . whatever you did." She slid her hand into the cool silk of his hair, stepped closer. "Thank you for my life."

"Not that." His arms banded around her, though she didn't think he was aware of what he did. "I meant your childhood. I saw—Gods, I thought I knew, but I had no idea."

In an instinctive desire to soothe, she smoothed a thumb over his eyebrow. "Don't worry about it. I never knew any different." Raising her chin, she brushed her lips over his, teased the corner of his mouth with the tip of her tongue. "Until I met you." She breathed the words into his mouth.

"That's the point." He grabbed her wrists. "You didn't know anything at all," he snarled, the words so raw they sounded as if they'd been ripped bleeding from his heart.

Thrusting her away from him, he turned his head away to stare across the tarn. "We need to talk," he said to the mountain peaks in the distance. His breath puffed in the chilly air.

Mehcredi's belly fluttered with apprehension. "Sounds serious." She tried to chuckle, but it came out all wrong. "Will you teach me to skim stones? I've never been any good at it."

"No," he said flatly. "I won't teach you anything, ever again. Showing you the *nea-kata* was wrong, taking you to Trinitaria was wrong. As for the rest of it—'Cestors forgive me."

Picking up a rounded pebble, he threw it with a vicious flick of the wrist. Numb with shock, Mehcredi watched it skip ten, twelve times before it sank. The cold dark water closed over it without a trace—as if it had never been.

"You—" She wet her lips. "You regret . . . what we did?"

His face was implacable, but the emotions seething beneath the surface sliced into her like razors. If only she could untangle them, work out what was wrong, but the sensations were too overwhelming. She floundered.

"I failed you, Mehcredi, abused your trust."

"What?" She set her hands on her hips. "How?"

Walker's lip curled. "Because your need, your godsbedamned innocence, tempted me beyond endurance." He shrugged. "I'm just a man, more arrogant and stupid than most."

Her hands curled into fists. "Then I'm the one who's stupid because I still don't understand."

"You said you loved me. I thought I knew why—a degree of infatuation was inevitable." His face darkened with self-derision. "Such wide-eyed admiration. I suppose I was flattered. But at least I was honest with you. I knew it would wear off after a time. I've been waiting for it." His throat moved as he swallowed. "And then I saw your life."

He turned to face her, deep creases bracketing his mouth. "Mehcredi, you haven't *had* a life. No kindness, no touching, no love. Nothing human, nothing *real*."

When she would have spoken, he held up a hand. "No, I saw it. I *know*. You're like a brand-new garden, the soil prepared, full of untapped riches. Ready to grow, to become something wonderful and good. And of all the men in the godsbedamned world, I'm the first to treat you with any kind of consideration, the first to touch you as a woman should be touched." His voice dropped. "Look at yourself, Mehcredi. I *made* you."

"Nonsense," she managed. "Walker, I am what I am. I always have been."

"You are *not!*" His shout echoed across the still water. "You think you haven't changed? That being with me hasn't made you different?"

The weight of his anguish made her stagger a little, her boots crunching on the pebbled beach. Gripping her hands together, she said, "Well, yes. You've given me so much, I can never thank—"

He loomed over her. "What I have done," he said, biting off each syllable, "is fuck you over." His lips twisted. "In every possible sense of the word." His voice dropped to a harsh whisper. "It gets better too. Do you have any idea what I had to do to save you?"

She struggled to keep up. "No, but I want to know."

Walker gripped her chin with merciless fingers, his eyes boring into hers, blacker than midnight. "I left you a part of my soul, my Magick, wrapped around the djinn stone. It was the only way I could stop it moving, heal the damage."

His lips pulled back from his teeth. "An unexpected gift, hmm? Like the Mark. And you thought that was bad enough. We're bound, Mehcredi. Soul-linked at a basic level."

"W-what?"

"You heard. You wanted me? Well, you got me. And vice versa." He glared. "You'll never need to ask what I'm thinking again. Fucking ironic, isn't it?"

"I—I—" Dark spots danced in her vision, cold sweat springing up on her forehead.

A muffled curse, and hard hands forced her down on a rock, pressing her head between her knees. The light-headedness receded and terror rushed in to replace it. She sat up.

"*You can read my mind?*" She must be goggling.

"No," he said at once. "No more than you can read mine. But I can sense what you feel." His lips curved in a mirthless smile. "I've done a few experiments, distance lessens the effect. Out of sight, out of mind, so to speak."

Shock had made her brain foggy and slow. Mehcredi fumbled her way back over the whole unbelievable conversation, seizing on the thing that mattered most.

"You don't w-want me?" she said, not caring that she sounded like a child. "I thought you—"

"You thought wrong." Walker ran a hand through his hair. More softly, he said, "Look, Mehcredi, I told you once I believe in you. I still do. You're strong, you're beautiful." For the first time, weary humor lightened his expression. "Some would say you have your own unique charm."

"Then why—?"

"Think about it." The pain and anger had returned, stronger than ever, washing over her in a dark wave. Beneath, she had the sense of an iron resolve. "Can't you work it out for yourself? Why would a man like me want a woman—no a *girl*—like you? You're a blank canvas, an unwritten page. You know so little you fell for the first man to offer you more than his fists and his cock. And now, you're linked to me by Magick, regardless of what you actually want. I took that choice from you."

He turned his back. "Well, I won't have it. My life is complicated enough, assassin. I don't need an encumbrance. You're free. Consider your penance over, well and truly."

"But—" Mehcredi locked her knees. If there was one thing Lonefell had taught her, it was that life plodded on, the heart beat regardless of misery and pain. It was remarkable what the human spirit could endure. "You told the baron I belonged." Her voice was remarkably steady, all things considered. "With you."

Pebbles scattered as he spun around. "No, I didn't. I said you were brave and good. I said I would defend you to my last breath." His laugh lingered in the air, brief and bitter. "Which I did, 'Cestors save me."

The world had gone dark, anguish buffeting her with a demon's wings. *Half-wit,* sneered a cold voice. *Look what ye've done now.*

She couldn't think straight, couldn't think at all, but for some reason, it was imperative he didn't see her crumble. And she wasn't a half-wit. She'd learned so much, about life and death, about the difference between fucking and making love—about herself. Mehcredi of Lonefell *mattered.*

"Yes, you do," he said and she started, realizing she must have spoken aloud. "Which is why I am not for you."

She raised her chin. "Don't you dare say it's for my own good."

He gave a wry smile. "Give me some credit."

"Right then." Her fingernails cut into her palms. What was she supposed to do now? How did one accept such a comprehensive dismissal with any degree of grace? Well, fuck it, she'd do it her way, the only way she knew.

Boldly, she gazed into those hooded eyes. "Thank you for everything you've done for me."

Before she could lose her nerve, she took a single step forward and pressed her lips to his. "Thank you for my life," she said against his mouth.

For a second, Walker's body went completely rigid. Then his hands closed over her upper arms like manacles and he ground his mouth over hers, so hard their teeth clinked and she tasted blood, with no idea of whether it was hers or his.

Just as abruptly, he released her. His long braid flying, he whirled about, stretching out a hand to lean against a tall boulder. "Go now," he said softly. "It's over."

A short pause and Mehcredi's steps receded, crunching over the stony little beach. Walker kept his eyes fixed on the waters of the tarn.

He wouldn't last more than a few moments in the freezing depths. The godsbedamned thing looked like it went down all the way to the roots of the mountains. He'd wager Lonefell tarn refused to give up the bodies it stole.

He'd been wounded many times, he knew the sensations well—the surprise and disbelief, followed by the bright bite of pain, nausea and light-headedness when it was very bad. If it wasn't ridiculous, he'd swear he was in shock now.

He rubbed the heel of his hand over his chest. Distance did lessen the effect, that was true. Even now, as she neared the keep, her pain had faded to a nasty spike behind his breastbone. Infinitely better. Close-up, the full impact of her desolation had combined with his own agony of mind, threatening to unman him completely. He couldn't remember the last time he'd shed a tear. Bleakly, he wondered if he could manage it now. It might be a comfort of sorts.

He hadn't lied, but he hadn't told her the whole of it either. Because the soul-link was a little different for him. A shiver of primitive fear raised all the small hairs on his body. He'd given a part of his soul, his Song, into another's keeping. What would he be without it? *Without her?*

Whatever she thought she felt for him, it couldn't be real, though she certainly believed in it. He couldn't trust it and he wouldn't let her either. The pain was real enough though, first love always hurt. Fuck, he should know—he was experiencing it. Walker ground his teeth together, the irony nearly choking him. Under his feet, the earth gave a long shiver, like an animal emerging from winter sleep. The water in the tarn heaved and slopped over the beach, wetting the toe of his boot.

He caught his breath, startled. By the seven million Songs, he hadn't lost control like that since he was a boy intoxicated by Magick for the first time. He needed to get a grip, focus on the woman who might—just might—be his kin. With an effort of will, he forced himself to start the calculations in his head—supplies for say, two nights on the road, maybe three, feed for his horse. Actually, it would be better if he could buy a second mount from the baron. He'd switch horses, snatch a few hours' sleep here and there, and get to Holdercroft all the faster. He sighed.

Damn Deiter to the icy hells. What were the chances she was Shar? Infinitesimal. But one day he'd face his Ancestors. He couldn't die not knowing. After he'd seen her, he'd be able to stamp out the godsbe-damned persistent flicker of hope. Then, ah, then . . . He'd go home to his House of Swords, to the peace of his garden and the rest of his empty life.

At first he thought the strange vibration in the air was the tarn shifting, still settling back into its stony bed. Then he looked up. A winged shape skimmed over Blay Pass, lights flashing on its underside. The Technomages, right on cue.

36

Walker arrived in the bailey in time to watch the flitter descend, its buzz becoming a deep whine. It hovered for a few moments as if making a decision, then landed with pinpoint precision. His brows rose. It was a big one, a twenty seater, its wings barely clearing the stone walls of the keep.

Mehcredi was completely enthralled. He didn't need to look at her to know she was bouncing on the balls of her feet, silver eyes wide with wonder.

With a polite series of clicks, a rectangular aperture opened in the smooth gray surface and a ramp extended until it reached the grass. A bulky figure broke away from the group of white-clad Technomages framed in the opening. He—it was obviously male with those massive shoulders—strode down the ramp, transplas boots thumping decisively. After a swift glance around the assembled crowd, he demanded, "Who is the first here?"

"I am." The baron stepped forward. "And you are?"

"The Quintus." Cold hazel eyes surveyed the other man from top to toe, traveled over the Pentacle group, inspected Yachi's guards and the baron's men. Then it flicked back to Deiter, who was leaning on Rose's arm. "You are Purist Deiter of Concordia?"

The wizard harrumphed. "Yes. And you're late."

"Come," said the Quintus, obviously a man of few words. He turned back to the flitter. "We can talk on the flight. I have room for a dozen, no more."

"The flight?" asked the baron, recovering. "You only just got here. Where are you going?"

"Back to the Tower."

The baron inhaled sharply. "But that's in Caracole."

Walker's heart lifted. A flitter could do in a couple of hours what would take him days on horseback.

"It is." The Quintus sounded bored.

"We need time to pack," Rose said suddenly.

"Twenty minutes," said the Quintus, favoring her with a long thoughtful glance.

The solidity of him was deceptive, thought Walker, summing up the Technomage with a swordmaster's experienced eye. Yes, he appeared to be foursquare and stocky, his shoulders and arms thick and well muscled, but he moved well, neat and quick. More brawler than swordsman though. His sandy hair was cropped brutally short. Walker fingered the end of his own thick braid. To each his own, he supposed.

When the Quintus turned to address the baron, the numeral five on his collar showed crisp and dark against the pristine white. "Where is the woman who claims to be a colleague?"

Walker frowned. By the bones of Those Before, this man was fifth in the Technomage hierarchy. The attention of a Scientist of such high rank was both reassuring and a little disquieting. In fact, odd though the Technomages might be, there was no mistaking the Quintus for anything save a warrior. The intensity of the man's focus was formidable.

"Bring her closer," the Quintus snapped to the baron's men emerging from the keep with a shambling figure in dusty black robes. Whoever it was appeared to be so weak they were obliged to half carry her. Looming over the woman, the Technomage gripped her chin and tilted her face to the light.

She whimpered, screwing up her eyes. The Quintus stared in silence for a long moment. Then he dropped his hand and took a step back. "This is the Technomage Primus of Sybaris," he said.

"*What?*" Prue rushed forward. She reached out, gripping the front of the woman's robes in clawed fingers. "I have a score to settle with you, *bitch*."

"Let me help," purred Erik, looming over them both. His smile gave Walker the chills.

Cenda elbowed Prue aside, only to recoil into Gray's arms. "Great Lady, it is!" When she straightened, rills of flame burst from her fingertips.

The Primus shrank back. "I'm Dotty," she said. "Just Dotty. I lost my brother." Tears trickled from faded blue eyes. "Or he lost me."

"Stop the bloody playacting," said Gray sharply. "Or I'll let her singe you."

"There will be no singeing." The Quintus had gone very still, his eyes on Cenda's hands. "Put down your weapon." His fingers rested on the worn hilt of the lasegun on his hip. "That means you too," he said to Prue and Erik. "Stand back."

Cenda gave a sharp bitter laugh, and the flames winked out, though Walker noted the tiny salamander in her hair still hissed and spat. With a huff of disgust, Prue shoved the Technomage back into the Quintus's arms.

"The Primus was convicted of crimes against Science," the Quintus said. "By her own Conclave no less. She was sentenced to Repair." He waved a couple of his Technomages forward.

"What does that mean?" asked Rose. "Exactly."

A sandy brow lifted. "Precisely what you think it means. Fifteen minutes."

"Cenda and Gray would be more merciful."

"I don't doubt it. Fourteen minutes."

The Primus reached out to finger the Quintus's collar. "Oh," she said. "Oh, I see." Her spine straightened with a snap. "Well, come on." She snarled at her escort. "I haven't got all day. Science doesn't do itself, you know."

"Uh, yes, Primus," said one of the Technomages, a stout woman with three digits on her collar. Immediately, she went scarlet. "This way," she snapped.

Her head high, the former Primus allowed herself to be assisted up the ramp and into the flitter.

"Now just a minute," barked the baron.

He set his hands on his hips, and for the first time, Walker noticed that he wore a fine coat, fashioned of maroon brocade. Involuntarily, he shot Mehcredi a sideways glance and caught her staring. She appeared to be fascinated, her expression suitably grave, but inside, she was alight with laughter, he knew it in his gut. He'd bet his life she was thinking of that fine handkerchief. What if the baron decided to mop his brow? Walker had to breathe hard through the strange, poignant mix of his feelings, the sweetness mingled with the pain. 'Cestors' bones, this . . . this . . . *connection* was going to kill him.

"What about the safety of my people?" said the baron. "What about the djinns?"

"Oh, you're safe enough—for the moment at any rate." The Quintus regarded him without much interest. "Preliminary analysis shows the thing is definitely dormant. We detoured north to the ice to gather data. We'll return for further observations in the summer."

"Summer?"

The ripple of amusement that passed over the Technomage's face was so fleeting, Walker almost missed it. "When it's warm enough for the creature to rise. I'd suggest you make plans for an evacuation." He raised his voice to be heard over the baron's protests. "Ten minutes, Rosarina."

She paused in midstep to look over her shoulder. "You know who I am?"

"I have dossiers on all of you."

Walker stepped forward. "Then you know I am Walker from the House of Swords."

The deep-set gaze shifted to focus on his face. "The swordmaster. Yes."

"I have business in Holdercroft. Can you let me off there?"

"Yes, but I have work to do at the Tower. I will not wait for you."

"That's fine, I—"

"Me too," said Mehcredi, appearing at Walker's elbow. Curiosity radiated from her. She was almost quivering with it.

The Technomage's brows drew together. "Who are you?" he said. "I have no data on you."

"Mehcredi," she said impatiently. "And Scrounge comes too. He won't pee or anything. I promise."

"Scrounge?"

Mehcredi pointed to the dog, who grinned toothily at the Technomage, ragged tail waving gently.

"No," said the Quintus with decision.

"I can't go without him." Panic flashed across Mehcredi's face. "But I can't stay here, I *can't!*"

Rose walked back over the grass to lay a hand on Mehcredi's shoulder. "We won't leave you behind," she said quietly.

"Speak for yourself," snapped Deiter. Suddenly, he sagged. "I'm an old, old man," he said plaintively, clutching his heart. "I've been wounded. Can we board so I can sit down?"

Cenda patted his arm. "She risked her life for the boy, Purist."

"Yah," said Florien, curling his lip in the wizard's direction.

"All of us or none," rumbled Erik and, beside him, Prue nodded. "Take your pick, Quintus." Though the air wizard didn't as much as glance at Deiter, a freezing wind tugged at the old man's robes. He drew his collar closer about his scrawny neck, glaring.

"Very well." The Quintus sent Mehcredi a cold level glance. "The animal is your responsibility. If it misbehaves, I'll put it out the hatch myself." He ignored Mehcredi's muttered curse. "Five minutes."

Turning on his heel, he vanished into the flitter. A few seconds later, it began to whine, straining against the ropes that held it hobbled to the earth.

"Sister in the sky, my things!" Rose lifted her skirts and sprinted for the keep.

"Five-it!" gasped Cenda, catching up in a couple of strides and speeding past. "Gray," she called over her shoulder. "Don't just stand there!"

Shrugging, Gray followed at a more leisurely pace. One by one, the members of the Pentacle group disappeared, while the baron and his men watched open-mouthed. Walker took his time. No need to rush, he traveled light. Pausing at the entrance of the great hall, he looked back.

Clearly giving orders, Yachi concluded an intense low-voiced discussion with her corporal. The man nodded, snapping off a salute. Squaring her shoulders, the guard captain marched toward the Technomage craft. With a sigh that came from his pointy-toed boots, Deiter hobbled in her wake, the very picture of a harmless old coot.

Walker wished the Quintus the best of luck with him.

Mehcredi wrapped her arms around Scrounge and hung on tight as the flitter vibrated like a smoothly struck gong. The dog's eyes rolled until she could see the whites all around and his poor little heart pattered against his ribs. She wasn't in much better condition. Her ears hurt and she suspected she'd left her stomach behind on the last cloud they'd passed.

As soon as they leveled out, the Quintus gave the controls to a subordinate and shifted to sit next to Deiter. They conversed in low tones, the Scientist writing copious notes with a stylus on a sheet of smooth gray stuff she thought must be transplas. She'd heard of it but never seen it. She sighed. Godsdammit, she'd had an endless stream of questions all ready to ask, but it seemed flying disagreed with her digestion.

No one else had the same problem, it seemed, not even the strange Technomage woman called the Primus. Florien bounced in his seat, his eyes sparkling, while the rest sat at their ease in the big padded chairs, chatting. Of course, Walker didn't chat. She doubted he knew how. Instead, he sat as far from her as possible within the confines of the craft, gazing steadfastly out the small round window at his side, and ignoring her completely.

Mehcredi made a point of ignoring him right back. She might be lost in a black sea of depression and hurt, but she'd rather die than have him know. She set her teeth and endured. With a kind of mean pleasure, she concentrated on her physical discomfort. Let him soul-link to her queasy stomach!

The Quintus had resumed control of the craft. Looking toward the nose of the craft, she could see his broad white-clad back, big hands moving deftly over switches and dials as he orchestrated the landing. Some glowed red, others green and yellow and blue.

The flitter side slipped. So did Mehcredi's insides. Then, Sister be thanked, it settled with a small jarring bump. The whining diminished and ceased, the door clicked open and fresh air rushed in, scented with the threat of snow and resinous timber and horses and . . . beer?

Walker leaped to his feet and was down the ramp in a flash. More slowly, the others rose and followed. The Quintus had set them down neatly, in the center of the market square of Holdercroft. Various townsfolk stood around with their mouths open. A thin woman sat in a graceless puddle of skirts on the edge of the wooden boardwalk that lined the single rutted street, gloved hands pressed to her mouth, her eyes enormous.

Walker spun around. "Well?" he said to Deiter. "Where would she be?"

The old man shrugged. "Damned if I know. It was only a rumor." His face brightened. "Ah, a tavern. Lord's balls, I could do with a drink."

Walker's hand landed in the middle of his chest, rudely halting his forward progress. "Just a godsbedamned minute."

The swordmaster's angry gaze narrowed on the group clustered at the foot of the ramp. "What the hell," he said, biting off each word, "do you people think you're doing? You're going home, remember? To Caracole."

Mehcredi trembled. Sister save her. Fury was the smallest part of what he was feeling. Her head swam with the intensity of it—a stubborn hope he couldn't quite manage to quell, terrible fear, an awful feeling of exposure, all of it underlaced with the near-certainty of disappointment. So savagely she could taste his urgency, Walker longed to get the whole godsbedamned thing over with and get the hell out.

What thing?

Prue sent the swordmaster a seraphic smile. "Meg lives here, Walker. Did you forget? Rose and I want to see the baby."

"Meg?" Mehcredi whispered to Erik.

"Used to be housekeeper at The Garden," Erik rumbled back. "Old friend."

A man came out of the tavern, wiping his hands on the cloth tucked into his belt. "What's all the excite—" His slate-gray eyes widened. "By the Brother!" A huge grin lit up his face. "Yachi!"

Yachi rushed past Mehcredi to pound the man on the back. "Rhio, you old dog!"

Chuckling, Rhio swept her up in a hug, ignoring the elbow she shoved in his gut. "Manhandling a superior officer, Sergeant." Then he ruffled her hair and set her aside.

"Mistress Rose." He bowed politely, but a crease knitted his brows. "And Mistress Prue."

The frown deepened. "Walker." The men exchanged handclasps. "Do you still have the Janizar's sword I gave you?"

"Rhio?" Mehcredi whispered to Erik. "Isn't he—?"

The big man shrugged. "Former Captain of the queen's guard, that's all I know. I've only met him once."

Of course. The man's military carriage was immediately apparent. She wouldn't care to cross him, thought Mehcredi, despite the sprinkle of gray in his dark hair. This Rhio could handle himself.

Rhio's gaze traveled to the Technomage craft, squatting like an improbable bird in the market square. "You came in a flitter," he said slowly. "All of you. A *flitter*? What the hell is going on?"

"Long story," said Walker brusquely. "I'm looking for a woman called—"

"Takeoff in two minutes," said the Quintus cooly from the top of the ramp. "Stand clear."

Slowly, Rose turned to face him. "My thanks," she said in her beautiful voice. "I am indebted to you." Delicate color painted in her cheeks. "We all are."

The Quintus showed his teeth. "I concur." He looked directly into her eyes. "Good-bye, Rosarina." The door slid shut with a decisive hiss. Dust rose in a blinding cloud as the flitter rose smoothly to roof level and beyond. It circled over the village, gaining altitude. Then it did a casual loop-de-loop and, with a sound like a thunderclap, shot off toward the south.

"Show-off," muttered Rose under her breath.

"Come on in," said Rhio, ushering them into a well-kept taproom. "Draught ale good enough?"

Deiter breasted the bar. "Wine? What about wine?"

Who was this woman Walker sought? What was she to him? Mehcredi's heart twisted, seeing the tension in that lean muscular body. He held himself so tightly he was ready to snap. Her fingers trembling, she rubbed Scrounge's ears.

When they settled, Rhio brought a couple of foaming tankards to the table. He grinned when Rose asked, "How's Meg? And the baby?"

"The babe's the cutest thing." Rhio chuckled. "She's got John wound right 'round her chubby little fingers. Have a bite to eat and I'll find you transport out to the farm. Won't take long at—"

Walker stood very still in the center of the room. "Where is the woman called Dancer?"

Rhio stiffened, but he finished serving the ale, clicking the tankards down with quiet precision. When he looked up, his gray gaze had turned to steel. "What do you want with her?"

The air thrummed.

Without fuss, Yachi ranged herself on Rhio's left, her homely face calm and watchful.

"You know her?" Rhio said. His eyes locked with Walker's. "Answer me." A blade had appeared in Rhio's fist.

Mehcredi's breath caught. Gods, the man was good! She hadn't even seen him move. Silently, she pushed her chair back and stood.

A door banged open on the far side of the room. "Rhio, did you see who was on the—Oh!"

A woman paused two steps into the room. She was tall and slim with a wealth of shining black hair, tamed with a couple of silver clips. "I am sorry, I did not realize we had guests. Forgive me, yes?"

Walker fell back a step, his breath hissing from between his teeth. Never in all the time Mehcredi had known him, had he looked so awful, not even after the battle of Guardpass. Instinctively, she moved closer, ready to prop him up. Or to break his fall.

Rhio slipped an arm around the woman's waist. "This is Dancer," he said flatly, threat and promise both clear in his tone.

Walker said nothing, but his throat bobbed as he swallowed.

Dancer's dark eyes flicked from one face to the next, finally returning to Walker. A crease appeared between her straight brows as she studied him. Slowly, horror dawned on her face. Her eyes widened.

She made the strangest sound, a sort of guttural sob, and her beautiful olive-toned skin went the color of putty. "No," she whispered, holding out a hand as if to ward off a nightmare. "It c-can't be." Her eyes rolled up. As she staggered, Rhio caught her.

"Sweetheart. What the fuck—?" He cast Walker a murderous glare. "Talk."

Walker said something in what Mehcredi recognized as Shar, flowing syllables with a rising inflection at the end. A question, he'd asked a question. His knuckles whitened on the back of a chair as he waited, his whole frame shuddering. Mehcredi began to shudder too, the turmoil rolling off him so intense she could scarcely process it and remain upright.

Dancer's eyes fluttered open. "*W-Welderyn?*" She gained her feet, pushing Rhio aside. "But you're dead. They're all—" Her breath caught on a sob.

Walker shook his head. "No," he said in a painful rasp. "Not all." He took a jerky step forward. "Oh, Amae."

37

An instant's silence and Dancer flew to meet him, colliding with Walker's chest so solidly that he grunted. His arms banded around her and he bent his head, their hair mingling in a great fall of black on black.

Gods. "It's her," whispered Mehcredi. Her eyes prickled. "Your sister."

Walker raised his head to stare hungrily into the woman's face. Tears leaked from the corners of his eyes. He framed her cheeks in his hands. "I looked for you," he said. "Everywhere, in every face. Always."

"Fook," hissed a small disgusted voice. "He's cryin' like a girl. *Walker.*"

Prue poked Florien in the ribs. "He's allowed." She sniffed hard. "Come on. Let's leave them to it."

"But it's jest gettin' innerestin'—*Hey!*"

Erik picked the boy up and stuffed him under one arm. "Privacy," he growled. "You may have heard of it."

Still clinging fast to his wine jug, Deiter had to be removed from the bar by main force. "Right again." He smirked, once they were all out on the boardwalk. "Gods, am I good or what?"

Mehcredi leaned against the building, her knees weak. Slowly, she let herself slide down until she could sit, her long legs stretched out in front of her. She hadn't known that joy and grief were so closely intertwined, like a lover vine wrapped around a thorn tree, its gorgeous perfume rising from among the wicked spines. How could she? She hadn't known anything.

"Want to come?"

Mehcredi looked up at Prue. "Uh, where?"

Prue smiled. "To Meg and John's. To see the baby."

Mehcredi struggled to her feet. "I don't know anything about babies." Gods, her head hurt. Unobtrusively, she put a hand behind her and braced herself against the wall.

"Then it's time you learned," Prue said briskly.

What had he said? Distance lessened the effect? "All right," she said.

It worked, to the extent that she dozed off to the rocking of the cart long before they reached the Lammas farm. Meg was tall and fair . . . nice, she thought. And John was a giant, so big she felt waifish beside him. Which was also kind of nice. He was a good-looking man too, his handsome face marred by a dark tattoo that sprawled across one cheekbone. Three times she opened her mouth to ask what it was and three times the conversation moved on before she was able to get a word in.

"Here," said Rose, thrusting a warm wriggling bundle into Mehcredi's arms. "Your turn." As she bent forward over little Annarose, she whispered, "Trinitarian slave tattoo. Tell you after we leave."

Mehcredi looked down into the baby's huge blue eyes and a rosebud mouth. The child hiccupped and a stream of milky drool dribbled down her chin. Mehcredi shot to her feet, panicked. She held a squirming Annarose out at arm's length. "Oh gods, she's sick. What do I—"

Immediately, the baby's face crumpled and she let out an earpiercing wail, tiny fists flailing.

Cenda swooped. "Five-it! Here, give her to me."

In no more than a minute, the fire witch had the little one cooing, reaching out to grab at the swaths of red hair over her temples. Mehcredi blew out a relieved breath. But why was there grief in Cenda's tender expression? Her fingers trembled as she stroked Annarose's cheek. Gray sat close, his arm around her shoulder, his shadow at his side.

A little startled, Mehcredi reached out for another of Meg's curdle pies. What had happened to her crystal bubble, the invisible walls that divided her from normal people? The comfortable chatter of old friends washed over her as she thought it through. Walker was right—she'd *grown* somehow. Given the amazing adventures of the past month, it was hardly surprising. But still . . .

From under her lashes, she studied the other people in Meg's comfortable sitting room. Sitting tucked into Erik's arm, Prue's whole body radiated contentment, her face animated. Yes, she was delighted to be among friends. Rose too. She'd blushed with pleasure on hearing Meg and John had named the baby after her. The depth and ease of the long-standing friendship between them was beautiful to see.

Gods, Rosarina of The Garden was a lovely creature. The Dark Rose, Walker had called her. Mehcredi didn't doubt that every man in Caracole wanted her, but what thoughts moved behind those strange beautiful eyes? Did it anger Rose that most people saw only the sensual façade and not the piercing intelligence beneath?

Mehcredi's heart quickened with excitement. Merciful Sister, she could do this! Who'd have thought? It wasn't easy, because she wasn't in the habit of this kind of analysis, but when she made the effort, paid attention—

All right, all right, what next? Rose had stopped her asking about John's tattoo and what the courtesan didn't know about manners wasn't worth knowing. So if she trusted the woman's judgment— and she did—the question would have been rude, even distressing. Mehcredi bit her lip. Godsdammit, she didn't want to upset their hosts.

She stole another glance at Cenda and Gray, playing peekaboo with the baby. Fine. She'd show some of the discipline Walker loved so much. She'd wait to get Rose on her own and then she'd find out everything she needed to know about her new—her new—

Her thoughts stuttered to a halt.

Friends, she'd been about to call them *friends*. But Mehcredi of Lonefell didn't have friends, she didn't have anyone. Only a swordmaster who didn't love her and a little dog who did.

Her heart turned a complete somersault in her chest. She couldn't breathe. Sister in the sky, how had it happened? Her hitherto empty life was full of *people*, a maze of relationships, connections and obligations. She rubbed her forehead. So complicated, so difficult to negotiate. *One of us*, Prue had said to the baron. What did that mean—exactly?

Rose patted her hand. "Are you all right?" she whispered. "You look very pale." She chuckled. "Well, paler than usual, which is saying something."

Mehcredi's eyes filled with tears.

"Mehcredi?" Rose's finely shaped brows drew together in a frown. "What's wrong? Tell me."

Mehcredi swallowed hard. "Nothing," she managed. "Nothing at all." She stumbled to her feet. "I'm going to . . . to . . . check on the dog."

She reached the stables before the storm hit her. Reeling into the first empty stall, she collapsed on a straw bale and let the tears come, the sobs gathering in her chest like hard heavy stones, hurting as they wrenched out of her. Scrounge thrust himself into her arms, licking her face and whining. She clung to his small warm body, the only solid thing in a topsy-turvy world.

But such intensity couldn't last long. When the storm passed, she lay panting, scoured out. Around her, big hoofs scuffled and a horse gave a soft puzzled whicker. Slowly, Mehcredi sat up. She felt bruised and battered, her ribs aching and her throat scratchy, but oh gods, she was . . . *whole*, complete in a way she'd never known before, a full participant in a busy, messy, difficult world. No more standing in the cold, staring through the glass. She was truly on the inside now, a fully paid up member of the human race.

With a final sniff, she stretched her arms over her head, working the kinks out of her back. She still had what she'd been born with—a bloody-minded determination to survive—but now that she came to tally up the rest . . . Her breath caught. Sweet Sister, such riches!

At the most basic level, she had a skill, a means of making her way in the world. Walker had said her sword work was competent enough. She could probably hire on with a caravan. Extending a foot, she rubbed Scrounge's belly, smiling as he squirmed, huffing with delight. In the *nea-kata*, she had both a professional tool and a path toward inner peace—if she was strong enough to work with it.

Walker had given her the gift of his trust, he'd proven it many times over. But gods, so had Rose and Prue. The thought filled her with awe and panic combined. Her fists clenched. She knew nothing about friendship or how it worked, but that didn't mean a godsbedamned thing. She'd rather die than mess this up.

A door banged, cheerful voices were raised. Scrounge leaped up and trotted out of the barn, tail waving.

Mehcredi frowned, chasing the train of thought. She'd been part of a . . . a *team*, had made her own contribution toward their common purpose. Godsdammit, she'd paid her dues. Reflexively, she pressed the heel of her hand against the scar on her side. It didn't hurt anymore but it itched, so viciously there were times she yearned to scratch herself bloody. A piece of his soul, wrapped around the djinn stone in her flesh, the strangest—the most precious—of all the gifts Walker had given her.

Experimentally, she reached for him, but he was only a faint warm glow, hovering on the periphery of her consciousness. She'd feel it like a blade to the guts if that steady beacon winked out, if he . . . died. She knew that, all the way to the marrow of her bones.

A skinny shape darkened the doorway. "Ye comin'?" said Florien, Scrounge frisking about his heels.

"Mm." Deep in thought, Mehcredi walked out into the afternoon shadows and climbed into the backseat of the wagon.

She had resources now, more than she'd ever expected. She wasn't a daft lump or a half-wit slut, she was a sword for hire, a friend—and a woman a man might desire, in his bed and in his life. As Erik drove them expertly down the narrow rutted lane, she stared out over the frost-nipped fields to the mountains beyond, unseeing.

"Hey." A pointy elbow jabbed her in the ribs. "Ye awake?" Florien lowered his voice. "I got somethin' t' say."

Mehcredi blinked at the boy's thin face. "Huh?"

But he didn't speak, only staring straight ahead, worrying at his lower lip. Slowly, a tide of red raced out of his collar until his face was beet red.

"Gods," said Mehcredi, alarmed. "What's wrong?"

"Nothin'." Florien swallowed. Then he said all in one breath, "Yesavedmylifean'Ithankye." He cast her a sidelong glance from under his fringe. "Why'd ye do it?"

"I didn't think," said Mehcredi, too startled for tact. "I didn't expect—Uh, why did you say that?"

"Cenda an' Gray sed I had ta," said Florien with brutal candor.

"Makes sense." Mehcredi settled back, and beside her, Florien blew out a breath.

"What ye goin' t' do now?" he asked.

"I think," said Mehcredi slowly. "I think I have to leave."

"Wit' Scrounge?" asked Florien, getting straight to the heart of the matter.

"I guess so. You think he'll follow me?" she asked softly.

"Yah." The boy blinked hard. "He likes me right enough, but it's ye he loves."

Gods, she didn't dare look up at the faces of the people in the wagon. She'd only just found them. They'd spoiled her dreadfully with their banter, their acceptance. Somehow, she'd got out of the way of being lonely. That wasn't clever, because already she could feel the ache of missing them. She drew in deep breaths of cold misty air. She'd learned a little of friendship, enough to know it took willingness and a certain skill. Once she was gone, she'd practice the craft of it with others and add to her friends—though she had the feeling it wouldn't be quite the same.

Walker didn't bear thinking of, though the closer they drew to Holdercroft, the more clearly she could feel him, as if the short absence had served merely to strengthen the link between them. The terrible tension had disappeared leaving him weary right to the bones, his exhaustion threaded through with wonder and joy. Yet underneath— she pressed her calf against the dog's small warm body—there was still a solid foundation of pain. Why was that?

"When are ye comin' back then?"

Mehcredi stared into the boy's dark eyes, thinking. "I'm not sure," she said. A fraction at a time, the stiffness bled out of her muscles. She rolled her shoulders, something warm and certain settling inside her. "When it's time. A year, six months?"

As a tiny baby, she'd fought to survive with the primeval instinct of a little animal. But now, she knew what she did, and why. She was a woman grown, with awareness and skills and . . . and confidence. The Sister knew what she could accomplish when she fought with purpose and guile, because this was a battle for the heart and soul of the man she loved more than life itself.

It would work. *It had to work.*

⁓

Walker stared at his sister. "*What* did you say?" He was so startled he forgot to speak in Shar.

Rhio chuckled and Amae smiled, the same mischievous quicksilver expression he remembered so vividly. Firelight lit red gleams in her black hair as she sat on the floor, toasting her toes before the blaze in a private parlor. Rhio lounged behind her in a big chair, one of her hands lost in his.

With the other, she gripped Walker's knee. She kept reaching for him, as if to ensure he was real and not the figment of a cruel dream. 'Cestors' bones, he knew how she felt.

"You thought you were the last of the Shar." Her smile very nearly blinded him with its brilliance. "I thought I was." She dropped back into the language, the words still awkward, unaccustomed on her lips. "We were both wrong, my brother."

She laid a protective hand on her flat belly. "I saw Ma Griddle last week. She says I'm three months along."

With a graceless *thump*, Walker fell to his knees beside her on the rug. He laid a shaking hand over hers. "You're sure?" he rasped.

Amae laughed. "I can't keep anything down 'til noon, and even then . . ." She pulled a face. "A summer child, Welderyn." Her lips trembled. "We will make a Song for the babe together, you and I."

"Yes." Walker bowed his head so his hair hid his face.

Amae glanced up at her man. "Rhio does his best," she said affectionately, "but his accent is terrible."

"Aye," said Rhio. "And I'm tone-deaf in the bargain."

"Thank you," rasped Walker. "She told me what you did. Thank you for setting her free."

"Aye, well." Rhio looked uncomfortable. "Once I saw her, my Dancer, it was all over for me. Anyway, you kept the diablomen off her, that time in the desert. We're even."

Rhio glanced from one face to the other. "I must be blind. Hell, I trained with you for years, Walker," he said. "Brother's balls, you're the spitting image of each other." Lifting Amae's hand, he pressed a kiss to her knuckles. "Warriors from a warrior tribe, the pair of you."

Raised voices and a clatter of boots announced the return of the party from the Lammas farm. Amae gave a watery chuckle. "I'd better see how Cook is doing with so many mouths to feed."

Oh gods, Mehcredi! Walking into the tavern, warm and lovely in his mind, filling the place that ached for her, filling him to the brim and beyond. "I have to be alone for a bit," Walker said.

Amae twinkled at him. "There's a lovely old cedderwood out the back if you need something green to talk to." When Rhio looked puzzled, she snorted with amusement.

Walker blinked hard. "You haven't changed, brat." 'Cestors be thanked. Carefully, he pulled his sister to her feet.

Rhio patted her bottom. "Find him a room, sweetheart. I'll go talk to Cook."

Amae took him up a set of narrow back stairs. "Here," she said, throwing open the door to a spacious chamber. "Best room in the whole place."

Walker shook his head. "Too big for one," he said. "Give it to Cenda and Gray, or Erik and Prue."

She shot him a shrewd glance. "What about that tall girl, the one with the bad hair?"

"Mehcredi?" Walker forced his lips into a curve. "No, nothing there."

"Hmm." Amae pursed her lips. "You look shifty, my brother," she said in Shar. "I must make this woman's acquaintance."

Before he had time to form a reply, she'd slipped down the stairs. He'd forgotten how quickly his little sister could move.

Supper lay like lead in Mehcredi's stomach, though it had been good country food, savory and hot. Walker sat farther down the table, next to his sister. In Amae, the hawkish profile was softer, more feminine, but unmistakably Shar. They'd been a handsome people. Mehcredi blinked down at the napkin she was pleating with her fingers. Sister be praised, Amae was pregnant. The Shar would live on.

Though his face retained its usual calm, the joy of that knowledge coursed through him, deep and steady. Beyond that—she frowned—it was difficult to tell, but he definitely wasn't as settled in his mind as she'd expected.

As chairs scraped back and people rose, Mehcredi sighed. *Sister give me strength.* Amid the general exodus to the taproom, she touched Walker's arm. "I need to talk to you."

Dark brows drew together. "Can't it wait?"

"No." Mehcredi raised her chin. "Your room in fifteen minutes?" Any longer and she'd lose her nerve.

He gave a curt nod. "Very well."

Shoving her hands in her pockets to control the trembling, she excused herself and climbed the stairs. Halfway up, she passed Amae on the way down. The other woman stopped and cocked her head. "You are Mehcredi, yes?"

"Yes. Congratulations. About the baby, I mean."

Walker's sister smiled. "Thank you," she said softly. "It is truly wonderful."

"Yes."

Silence fell. Mehcredi shifted uneasily under that penetrating gaze. *Say something,* she thought. *Anything.* "Uh, your accent isn't like his. Walker's."

Amae gave a fluid shrug. "I lived in Trinitaria from the age of fifteen."

"You were a dancer, weren't you?"

A flash of pain crossed the other woman's face. Mehcredi cursed her stupid tongue. "Gods, sorry," she said quickly. "I shouldn't—"

"I was a slave," said Amae flatly.

"I was an assassin." Mehcredi squeezed her eyes shut. Godsdammit, would she never learn?

"*Really?*" Amae's face lit with interest. An assessing look raked Mehcredi from top to toe. "Hmm. We should talk, you and I. Spar, perhaps."

"Can't. I'm leaving tomorrow," said Mehcredi, unable to prevent the misery from leaking out.

"Pity." Amae studied her face. "If you've come to say good-bye, his room is last on the right."

Mehcredi swallowed. "Thank you."

Ducking her head, she moved on, but the other woman took her arm in a gentle grip. "I don't know what's between you and Welderyn, but you are important to my brother. You could even be good for him."

Amae dropped her hand and stepped back. "'Cestors keep you, assassin," she said formally. "Know that you are always welcome in my house."

Mehcredi had to swallow again. "Thank you. That, ah, that means a lot."

"Mehcredi?"

She turned on the landing. "Yes?"

Amae shot her an impish grin, an expression that had nothing of Walker in it. "He was always deep, even when we were children. Don't give up."

Their eyes met. "I won't," said Mehcredi gravely. "I promise."

38

Walker's door was unlocked, so she let herself in and lit a fire. The first flames were racing over the kindling when the door swung silently open. She hadn't heard a thing.

She rose, dusting her hands. "You must teach me to walk like a Shar."

"No."

Long legs braced, the swordmaster stood motionless, studying her, his dark eyes fathomless, unknowable. Mehcredi watched the strong tanned fingers of one hand furl into a fist, then relax. He was so armored, so formidable—heart and soul, mind and body. The complete warrior.

Her throat dry, she searched for the comforting glow she'd felt on the way back from the farm, the knowledge that what she did was *right*. When it didn't come, she plowed on anyway, her heart knocking against her ribs.

"I came to say—" When she stopped to wet her lips, his gaze fastened on her mouth and something clenched hard inside him, she *felt* it. Gods, yes! Encouraged, she forced the words out. "I came to say g-good-bye."

Immediately, he pinned her with a glare. "No, you're going back to Caracole with us. Noblelady Izanami wants a live-in bodyguard for her daughters. I'll recommend you."

Mehcredi shook her head, hope fluttering to life in her breast.

"John Lammas and his brothers have grain wagons leaving for Ged tomorrow. It's all arranged." She managed a smile. "He'll even pay me."

"Is that what you want?" Walker stalked over to the bed, seized his pack and reefed it open. "Here." With a contemptuous flick of the wrist, he tossed her a small leather bag.

Mehcredi snagged it out of the air before it landed in the fire. "What—?" When she hefted it in her hand, it clinked. "Godsdammit!" Revolted, she flung it away from her. "What do you think I am?" Breathing hard, she gave him her back.

"Mehcredi." A long pause. A featherlight touch on her hair. "I'm sorry. This is the rest of Meck's money, earned fair and square." Firm hands grasped her shoulders and turned her around. Walker's smile was wry. "Did it never dawn on you to wonder what happened to your wages?"

"N-no."

"Of course not." He pressed the bag into her hands. "It's yours. Take it."

He stepped back, removing the warmth of his body, the scent, the presence, that was his alone, leaving her bereft. "You see?" he said. "You don't need to go to Ged. Another couple of days and we'll leave for Caracole. Home."

She lifted her gaze. "What about Amae?"

When he smiled, it reached his eyes. "She and Rhio are following, once they arrange for someone to take over the tavern. Just for a few weeks, then they'll return to Holdercroft. Amae wants the local midwife to deliver the baby. Their future is here." His eyes had softened to that rare rich shade like chocolat. "I'll be back for the birth though, to sing the baby's Song with my sister."

"That sounds . . . nice."

Mehcredi gathered her courage, leaving a horrible greasy space where her stomach used to be. It would have been easier to fling herself headlong from the high-pitched roof or face a hundred djinns. This was her life she gambled, her love—her everything.

"I'm still going to Ged."

"Listen, Mehcredi—"

"No! *You* listen!" She poked him in the chest for emphasis, then wheeled about to take a couple of hasty strides. "You can't have it both ways, Walker. Am I in your life or out of it?"

He pressed his lips together, color flushing up under the bronze of his cheeks.

Mehcredi let the silence stretch. The fire crackled and popped in the grate. "That's what I thought," she said at last. "I can't go on like this. It hurts too much . . . Every time I turn around, you're right there and I . . ."

She had the sensation the walls were closing in, the small cozy chamber fogged with grief and yearning. Hers? His? She couldn't untangle the knot.

Roughly, she cleared her throat. "I don't know a pretty way to put it." Squaring her shoulders, she looked him full in the face. "You lied to me."

Walker's features went stiff with offense. "Indeed? When?"

"You said you didn't want me."

She waited, but he didn't speak. "But you do. With the soul-link, even I can tell that."

He shrugged. "I'm only a man, Mehcredi. You're so very willing and really quite lovely." He favored her with a wolfish smile. "Enthusiastic."

She swallowed the hurt. "You doubt me. You think I don't know my own mind."

His expression softened very slightly. "I don't see how you can, not yet."

"Exactly. *Not yet*. So I'm going to fix that, once and for all." She put her hands on her hips. "Walker—*Welderyn*—I don't worship you. I don't think you're perfect." She gave a vulgar snort. "Godsdammit, you're not even close. But I . . ." For a moment, she faltered. "I need you like I need air to breathe. I can't explain it, I have no idea why, but—"

"I do. It's because—"

"No, you do *not*!" Mehcredi made a chopping motion with one hand. "You didn't make me, Walker. How dare you say you did?" The anger helped, she realized. It gave her strength, pushed her past her own boundaries. Gratefully, she gathered it around her like armor, used it to shore up her resolve.

He pinched the bridge of his nose between forefinger and thumb. "I didn't mean it quite the way it sounded, but you can't deny—"

"Yes, yes, I know. You taught me everything. So fucking what?" The growl that rumbled in her throat startled her. A wild tygre could have done no better. "I'm leaving though, just the way you want, you stupid bastard."

"Stop that." Walker grabbed her hands in a punishing grip. Oh. She'd been thumping his chest for emphasis.

"Let's see how we do, shall we?" she panted. "Because I'll be back." She rose on her toes to thrust her face into his. "I want your promise you won't run."

His eyes opened wide with shock and offense. "*Run?*"

The expression lasted for no more than a split second, but Mehcredi hugged it to herself with glee. *Got you!*

"You think I'm a coward?" he snarled.

"I don't know." A smile ghosted over her lips. "Are you? Swear on your Ancestors that you'll face me."

"No problem." He spoke a sentence in Shar, one that included her name.

"Translation?"

"I swear, on the bones of my Ancestors and on my Song, I will meet with Mehcredi of Lonefell when she returns." An aching pause. "If she returns."

"You don't believe me, do you?"

"Who knows what you will learn, who you will meet? There are men out there with clean hands and good hearts, just don't . . . don't take the first one who offers."

"I mean what I say. I will always mean it." Mehcredi stared, drinking him in, imprinting the proud features on her memory—the slashing cheekbones and imperious nose, the enigmatic long-lidded eyes. Those impossible lashes. As for his mouth—No, it wasn't possible for her to look at those firm lips without aching. Or his beautiful strong hands, or the set of his shoulders, or . . . or . . .

Not a single keepsake—beyond the alien stone he'd left inside her. She should have snipped a lock of his hair while he was sleeping. Mehcredi bit the inside of her cheek. Gods, she'd gone beyond besotted to mawkish.

Enough. Another second and she'd crumble.

Reaching behind her, she gripped the doorknob with trembling fingers and eased the door open. "Until next time," she said, tilting her chin and looking him steadily in the eye.

Then she ruined it. "Take c-care."

"Wait. I want—" His voice cracked. Before she could move, he'd swooped, pulled her back into the room and cradled her face between his palms. "No, *you* take care. Men can be—Don't believe everything—Oh, gods."

Walker hauled her up and took her mouth like a conqueror, angling her head for the best fit, exploring every recess of her mouth as if memorizing the heat, the wet, the texture. The soul-link burgeoned and the kiss exploded into a fiery darkness so intense it hurt. Mehcredi clung, moaning. She no longer knew where she began and he ended, she no longer cared.

Walker growled something and ripped his mouth away from hers. The world spun. The next moment, she was standing, shaking in the passageway, panting, her fingers pressed to her lips. The door still vibrated in her face, the slam echoing in the dark building.

After an eon, Mehcredi regained her breath. Slowly, trailing her fingertips along the wall, she stumbled back to the chamber she shared with Rose. Thankfully, there was no sign of the other woman save for a gown thrown across one of beds and her elusive perfume.

Zem and Topher Lammas would be bringing their wagons through Holdercroft in the hour before dawn. She might as well get ready now. There'd be little enough sleep as it was. The distress was so pervasive, so overwhelming, it was like a living thing gnawing at her vitals. She could no longer distinguish between Walker's feelings and her own. It was all awful. Moving like an old woman, she pulled off her shirt. By the Sister, she was fighting for her life, all over again. For her own sanity, she had to believe she was doing right. Gods, what if—? No, she refused to think it.

Tomorrow she'd be all day in the saddle. Might as well be comfortable. Mehcredi reached for the breastband, her lips curving with bittersweet memories. Glancing down as she shrugged into it, she froze.

What the—?

She angled her body toward the lamp, squinting. The merest whisper of a shadow showed beneath the pearly skin of her left breast.

Her lungs seized. The Mark. Barely there, so faint she had to peer in order to make it out. Wonderingly, she traced the swirling pattern with the tip of her finger and her nipple stiffened with a rush. Clutching the breastband, she sank back onto the bed, her head spinning.

She'd wanted a keepsake, hadn't she? A talisman she could look at every day.

A shaky smile bloomed on her lips.

When Rose came in a few hours later, Mehcredi was lying under the covers fully dressed, pretending to be asleep. It was still fully dark when she heard the distant creak of wheels, the jingle of tack. Shivering in the raw air, she threw the blankets back and crept to the door, pack in hand.

Rose sat up in bed. "Mehcredi."

She turned, caught the flash of Rose's smile in the gloom. "Yes?"

Rose held out her arms. "Come here."

Surprising herself, Mehcredi dropped the pack, crossed the room and bent to give the other woman an awkward hug.

Soft lips brushed her cheek. "Good luck, my dear."

Mehcredi straightened. "Tell the others I said good-bye . . . and thanks."

"I will." Rose settled back into the pillows. "The Sister keep you until we meet again."

"And you." A last look and Mehcredi closed the door softly behind her. Padding down the stairs, her head high, she went to meet her destiny.

FIVE MONTHS LATER

Walker reined his mount on the final approach to Holdercroft, something in him easing as he gazed across the open fields, golden with grain, to the village basking in the sun. He rubbed the heel of his hand over his heart, a gesture that had become habitual. Idly, he wondered if the child would have a Shar's black hair and eyes. But truly, it hardly mattered. His lips softened into an almost-smile. A new life to be celebrated, a new Song to be sung.

He nudged the horse with his heels, imagining Amae's face when he rode in, three weeks early. He hadn't been able to wait. 'Cestors' bones, he wouldn't miss the arrival of his nephew—or his niece—for the world. To be honest, he felt better today than at any time since the winter morning he'd stood at a tavern window and watched Mehcredi ride away into an icy dawn, out of his life. No, he had better things to think of than his assassin.

He snorted. And hadn't he told himself that a thousand, a hundred thousand, times? She lived. In fact, as far as he could tell from the distant glow of the soul-link, she thrived. Which was exactly what he'd intended when he'd made the bargain with his gods. Resolutely, he wrenched his thoughts away from visions of Mehcredi in another man's arms. He could never see the fellow's face, but he was young and tall and strong, and he'd better love her the way she deserved or—

Shit, not again!

Swearing under his breath, he dropped his hand from the sore spot on his chest. He knew full well there was nothing wrong with him physically. Only last week, he'd taken on Dai and Pounder together in an exhibition bout for his students and thrashed them both. On Yachi's recommendation, the queen had retained him to run advanced training for her guards. His House of Swords was turning a tidy profit.

His Magick was stronger than ever, honed by duels with Erik and Cenda, while Deiter looked on and swigged from a jug and barked instructions. A drunk he might be, but Walker had to admit the old bastard knew his stuff. Slowly, he was welding them into a unit, even devising strategies to include Gray's shadow sorcery and Prue's weird nullifying effect. Walker rolled his shoulders, feeling testy. Prue's non-Magick worked, but he didn't have to enjoy the sensations. A pity, because he was very fond of the little null witch. She had guts, Prue.

Gray had a background as a mercenary. He was ambidextrous, deadly with a short sword, plenty of potential there. Erik, on the other hand—Walker shook his head, his braids swinging. Fortunately, the big man was purely murderous with a quarterstaff and bruising with his fists.

Who'd have thought it? He was part of a godsbedamned *team*.

He wished the Necromancer joy of the icebergs. The Quintus had been nothing if not efficient. Every month, the Technomage sent Deiter reports inscribed on sheets of transplas. During the winter freeze, the djinn had slowly coalesced, repairing itself piece by piece. But after reading the most recent report, Deiter had thrown the transplas at the wall and gone on a week's bender. The djinn had vanished. The Technomages could find no trace of it, yet there had been no attacks, not even on Lonefell.

For a moment, Walker allowed himself the luxury of brooding. One day, if he accepted he was one of the *Sides* of Deiter's godsbedamned Pentacle—one day, he'd watch the Necromancer die, an inch at a time. In the process he'd destroy the man's demon. *Xotclic.* It was worthy work, and as near as he could come to completing his vengeance.

Ch'qui rolled off the waving expanse of grain in almost tangible waves. Walker lifted his face, breathing it in, letting the rage flow through him and away with a warrior's discipline. Pity he couldn't do as well with soothing the nagging ache. If it hadn't been for his garden, he would have lost his mind, he was sure of it. The emptiness, the godsbedamned misery wasn't acute—like a lump of cold dead flesh weighing him down—but it was constant, exacerbated by the fucking soul-link. He missed her, lovelorn as a boy with his first girl, that's all there was to it. Knowing he was being stupid, that he shouldn't need her, that what he'd done was necessary and right—none of it made any difference.

Every night, he woke from dreams of her. The darkly erotic ones were bad enough—her strong creamy body wrapped around him, her legs high on his hips, her throaty voice urging him on as he drove into wet satin heat, harder and harder, striving to bury himself inside her, make them one, indivisible. Gods, the ecstatic rush as his balls clenched and he spurted. She'd cry out, throwing her head back to expose the long beautiful line of her throat. And then he'd wake, sticky and disorientated, the cold jolt of disappointment as fresh the hundredth time as it was the first.

But the nightmares stripped all the courage from him. They drove him insane. In them, she was trapped, helpless and he couldn't find her, couldn't reach her, only hear her cries of agony, her hopeless sobs as she called his name, over and over and over . . .

Working in his garden helped—a little. And the *nea-kata*, but that was all. He set his teeth, breathed deep—and discovered he was rubbing his chest again. He'd never been a vain man, but he could no longer bear to meet his own eyes in a mirror. He looked . . . ill, haunted. 'Cestors be thanked, he didn't need to shave more than once a week, if that.

Lifting his face to the gentle breeze, he gazed out at the distant blue of the mountains. Ged, the second-largest city in the Queendom lay beyond the range. Like John, the younger Lammas brothers were tall, dark and well set up. Either of them would be a good match for her, Zem sunny and outgoing, Topher more reserved. Which had she chosen? Neither? Both? Of course, the pickings would be better in Ged, plenty of—

Grinding his teeth, he clattered into the market square of Holdercroft and headed for the tavern.

Rhio came forward from behind the bar. "Walker!" He grinned, pounding Walker on the back.

"How's Amae?" asked Walker, sidestepping.

"Fine." If anything, the grin widened. "Go on back and surprise her. She's in the parlor."

She was sitting in the big chair, smiling down at a little bundle wrapped in a light blanket. As he watched, the bundle heaved, squeaking like an angry kitten. A tiny pink fist waved, the fingers spread wide like an open flower.

Walker's mouth fell open.

"Welderyn!" Joy lit Amae's face. She leaned forward, stretching out a hand. "What are you doing here? We only sent the letter yesterday."

"I left early. Thought I'd get here in plenty of time," he said stupidly. "But you've had . . . it? The baby?"

Amae folded back the blanket to reveal a small pink face crowned with an absurd tuft of black hair. "Her," she said. "Your niece is nothing if not impatient."

Walker fell to his knees beside the chair. "Gods, is she all right? She's so small." The baby's whole head was about the size of his fist. With a shaking hand, he touched her cheek. Immediately, she turned, seeking, the rosebud mouth opening wide. The thin insistent squalls started up again.

"She's healthy?" Sudden terror seized him. "Amae, what about you? Was it very bad?"

"Oh, yes," said his sister serenely. "But I had people to help me." She looked up. "And Rhio was very brave. Weren't you, *carazadi*?"

Rhio smiled tiredly from the doorway. "Aye, love, that I was. Didn't pass out once." He walked forward. "She's beautiful," he murmured, his hand coming to rest lightly on Amae's dark head and Walker couldn't be sure if he referred to either or both of his females.

Awed, Walker stared down at the fussing baby. His eyes stung. A miracle, a true gift of the gods. "Can I see?" Gingerly, he parted the blanket.

The infant grasped his forefinger with surprising strength and the mewling trailed off into silence. Slate dark eyes locked on his, the baby's brow creasing with an expression of fierce concentration as if the secrets of the world were graven on his features. Walker froze.

The *ch'qui* coursed through his finger and up his arm, tingling beneath the skin, but nothing like the powerful surge he was used to. Instead, it scampered, like the lightest of footsteps, joyous and carefree. Trapped in the baby's cloudy purposeful gaze, Walker's breath hitched.

"What's her name?" he heard himself ask, as if from very far away.

"We thought . . . Gwin," said Amae, her voice cracking. It had been their mother's name. "Gwin'd'haraleen't'Rhiomard't'Lenquisquilirian."

"Yes," he said absently. *Welcome to the world, little one,* he thought. *When the time is right, come to me and I will teach you all you need to know of the Magick the gods have given you.*

Gwin blinked, her mouth opening on a heartbreaking wail. Released, Walker sat back on his heels.

Amae put the baby to the breast, hissing as Gwin fastened on and began to suck. "She might have come early," she said through gritted teeth, "but she's as fierce as any warrior." Gradually, she relaxed. "Perfect."

"You look a bit rattled," said Rhio. "Want a drink?"

When Walker shook his head, Amae chuckled. "Go talk to the cedderwood in the garden, brother mine," she said. "That should put you to rights."

"Amae, do you think—?" Rhio broke off, frowning.

"It's a beautiful day," said Amae firmly. "Go on, Welderyn. At least until your room is ready."

A few moments of solitude sounded good. "I'll start on Gwin's Song." He touched Rhio's shoulder as he passed. "Congratulations, my brother. You're a lucky man."

Walker brushed by before Rhio could collect himself sufficiently to respond. Stepping out of the tavern's back door, he took a deep breath of sweet summer-scented air. Amae was right, the cedderwood was a magnificent specimen, so ancient its gnarled trunk was broader than his arms' span.

A little dog trotted out from behind the stable and lifted its leg against a ticklewhisker bush.

The soul-link burst into life, filling his chest with delightful warmth. Walker stopped dead. No, it couldn't be—But the aching void he'd carried all the long lonely months was gone as if it had never been. Every nerve and cell tingled with the return of sensation, painful and wonderful all at once.

"W-Walker?"

Mehcredi stepped out from behind the cedderwood. The shaft of longing was so piercing, it nearly doubled him up. Grimly, he held himself steady, trying not to stare. Gods, she'd grown into herself, into her true beauty, settled in her skin like a warrior goddess. She wore the familiar shirt and trews, a short sword at her hip, but her hair fell in soft platinum waves almost to her shoulders and her ivory skin was flushed gold from the sun. As she walked slowly toward him, every muscle in that strong female body moved with the supple prowling grace only bestowed by perfect health.

She was Shiloh in the desert and he was thirsty unto death.

"Welderyn'd'haraleen't'Lenquisquilirian," she said in perfect Shar. She tilted her head, her silver eyes steady on his. "You swore you would not run, *carazadi*."

39

Walker wet his lips. "What are you doing here?" *Carazadi?* His brain spun. "Shar? You speak Shar now?"

Mehcredi favored him with a sunny smile, though her lips trembled with the effort. "I came back from Ged with the Lammas boys. It's been months now. And Amae taught me a few words."

He couldn't drag his eyes from the carnal glory of that lower lip, so pink and plump. He wanted to take it gently in his teeth, worry at it and kiss it better.

"Why?"

"I knew you would come," she said simply.

A strand of hair blew into his eye and he pushed it back with an impatient hand. "Godsdammit, you were supposed to learn, to grow."

Mehcredi's chin went up. "I've been working with Ma Griddle." Her face blazed with excitement and pride. "She's the healer here— and the apothecary too, because Holdercroft's only a village after all—and she says I'm doing very well, especially with the potions. I can read and write now—well, a little. Enough for the labels anyway, which is good because you have to be so careful not to—"

"*Mehcredi.*" Walker gripped his fists together behind his back lest he grab her and shake the answers loose. "A man." He gritted his teeth. "Did you find a decent man?"

"Oh, yes."

A giant hand gripped his chest and squeezed so hard he could barely breathe. "Good," he managed. "Who?"

Instead, she frowned. "Walker, you look terrible." She moved close enough to touch, so close he could smell the light perfume that rose from her skin and detect the female warmth beneath it.

"Your hair's got more gray in it now. Did you know? Just here."

Her fingertips fluttered over his temple, the touch bittersweet. Memory took him between one breath and the next. Because she'd touched him like this before. What had he said in his cold fury, a lifetime ago? *You are not my servant, nor my student. You are not my friend. Nor will you be, ever.* He winced.

"Are you all right?" Her brow furrowed with concern. "Have you been ill?"

Fuck, this was torture.

He gripped her wrist. "*Who is it?*"

Every vestige of softness died out of Mehcredi's face. "You know," she said. "You've always known." She stepped right into his arms, the tips of her breasts brushing his chest. "You, Walker." Her smile went crooked. "It's only ever been you."

Hope stripped him to the bone. He cupped her cheek in his hand, dimly aware he was shaking like a tree in a gale. "I left—" His throat was so dry. "A piece of my soul, my Magick, inside you. It could be you don't have a choice."

Her brows rose. "You mean this?" Fishing in her shirt, she produced a fine silver chain. Suspended from it was a small pearly globe encased in a network of fine wires.

"The itching drove me crazy for about a week, but thank the Sister, it worked its way out of the wound while I was in Ged. Didn't take long to heal either, though it bled a fair bit. I was going to throw it away and then I realized . . ."

Stroking a finger over the smooth opalescent surface, she glanced up from under her lashes. "This is your gift to me, freely given. Your life, your love. The most precious thing I'll ever have."

Walker closed his fingers over hers. "Be sure, Mehcredi. Be very sure." The words came out so raw and desperate he sounded like a stranger. "I can't do this again."

He watched her searching for words, his heartbeat thudding in his ears like a battle drum.

"No," she said at last, and his pulse jolted, hard and nasty. "Let me show you." Taking his hand, she drew him toward a rough bench in the shade of the cedderwood. "Sit down."

"Mehcredi—"

"I'm getting there. Just give me a minute, all right?" Her breasts rose and fell as if she'd been running. She wiped her forehead with one sleeve. "I've been practicing.

"Gods. Right. Don't laugh." Pulling in a huge breath, she clasped her hands before her at the waist like a little girl and opened her mouth.

"Welderyn'd'haraleen't'Lenquisquilirian, babe twice blessed with life and love," she sang in Shar, the notes breathy but true, the accent impeccable.

He'd never felt less like laughing. 'Cestors' bones, it was *his Song* she sang. How was that even possible?

"First Mother's breath to sing his Song, First Father's touch on his downy head."

She was midway through the next line by the time he'd recovered enough to speak. "Wait. Do you understand the words or did you learn the sounds by rote?"

Mehcredi sent him a long level look, implicit with a woman's challenge. His blood bubbled. "Judge for yourself."

Her voice rose again, soft and pure in the light summer air.

"Welderyn'd'haraleen't'Lenquisquilirian, last of the Shar, dealing death, swift hands, cold heart."

This was new, the lines unknown. Gods, had she—? No, surely not. Not possible. The strain was beginning to tell, the consonants slurring, yet the way she emphasized certain words, the emotion on her expressive face . . . She understood the import of every syllable.

"Yet his soul he gave me, never counting the cost. True son of the 'Cestors, First Father's courage, First Mother's heart."

Her voice wavered, dropping so he could hardly hear it. Desperate, he leaned forward.

"Mehcredi's beloved, two Songs twined like vine and tree, through all the years, 'til we lie as one in starfire's heart."

Completely incapable of speech, Walker grasped her hips, pulling her close and pressing his forehead into the resilient softness of her breasts. Tentatively at first, then with more assurance, Mehcredi's fingers stroked the length of his thick braid, picking at the ties that bound it, separating the strands, spreading it over his back and shoulders.

She sighed, letting it ripple through her fingers like water. "I've always wanted to do that."

Walker filled his hands with the firmness of her backside and let out a long breath. "Any time," he said. "Come here." He tugged her down into his lap, wrapped his arms around her and buried his face in her neck. There'd be time for kisses later, but right now, he was so rattled, all he could cope with was to hold her and never let her go.

The canopy of the cedderwood rustled overhead, fragments of shade shifting over her bright head, as light and loving as First Mother's gentle touch.

At last, Walker stirred. "You are without doubt the most amazing woman I have ever met. How did you do it?"

As she shifted, the pearl between her breasts rolled, glistening a delicate pink. "Amae tutored me." Smiling, she nuzzled the curve of his brow with her nose, drew back. "I've done nothing but work since I last saw you. You're going to be so proud of me, Walker."

His chuckle sounded rusty, disused. He cleared his throat. "*Carazada*, I already am." He considered for a moment. "I think I have been, for a very long time."

"*Carazada*." Mehcredi's lashes fluttered down, her lips trembling into a sweet knowing curve that was all woman. "I asked Amae what it means."

She turned her head, brushed her lips over one corner of his mouth and whispered, "Beloved, heart of my hearts, my world, my all. Mine." The huskiness of her tone, the pure temptation of her, coiled at the base of his spine, rippled over his balls. The point of her tongue crept out, asking for entry.

The soul-link bloomed with warmth and color and life, the energy of it pounding through him, blood and bone. With a deep growl of pleasure, Walker took over the kiss, hauling her into him and sinking into her mouth. Mehcredi met him stroke for stroke, humming deep in her throat, fingers tangled deep in his hair. She took his senses by storm, more intoxicating than the attar of his own dark roses.

Fabric ripped. Deliciously heavy and full, her breasts filled his hands, the stiff nipple burning into the center of his palms. Mehcredi made a breathless wanton sound, a delightful cross between a mewl and a wail. It went to his head like richest spicewine 'til he could barely breathe with the need to hear it again, to hear her scream in passion, his name spilling from her lips as she hit the peak and tumbled over.

He forced his eyes open. She was sprawled across him, her lips swollen, her thighs spread wide in a shameless display. Immediately, he clamped his hands on her hips, pulling her forward, notching his aching cock where it longed to go. Even through the trews, she scorched him. His groan split the air.

His shirt was hanging open. When had that happened? Mehcredi leaned forward, her breath scorching against his skin. She bit him, just above the nipple.

"Fuck!" Walker bucked. He knew there was a reason he couldn't throw her to the grass, rip her trews off and sink balls deep into the wet heat he craved, but he was having difficulty remembering what it was.

"Room." Mehcredi nipped his earlobe. "Upstairs." Her voice sank to a tortured whisper. "P-please."

He'd never felt such desperate urgency, not even in his adolescence. It took every scrap of warrior discipline he possessed to draw back. As he stared into his assassin's beautiful face, her pupils flared dark, almost eclipsing the pale irises. The creamy skin of her throat and cheeks flushed with gorgeous color.

"Yes." He cradled her cheek, his thumb tracing over her lower lip. "Ah, *carazada*, this is going to take a very long time." Gently, he helped her to her feet, rose and took her hand. "Hard and fast. Long and slow." Walking was a matter of breathing deep and taking care. He led her toward the tavern. "And everything in between."

At the whimper she couldn't repress, he chuckled, feeling lighter than he had in years, as if a weight had been lifted from his shoulders—a burden he hadn't known he carried.

"In there." Pausing at the top of the stairs, she pointed to a chamber at the back of the building. The inn drowsed in the warmth of the afternoon, business virtually nonexistent. 'Cestors be thanked, because the gods knew what they looked like, flushed and disheveled.

The moment the door closed behind them, Mehcredi dropped the bar across and set her back to it. "I want it all, for always. With you. Is that what you want too?" She fixed him with a serious silver gaze. "You know you have to tell me what you're thinking."

Mehcredi couldn't take her eyes from him. Walker gazed at her in silence, his hair falling across his forehead, his eyes the rich rare brown of chocolat. His shirt hung open, exposing a slice of smooth bronze chest, the dark crescent of one nipple. Helplessly, her gaze flickered down to the magnificent bulge in his trews and her breath hitched. From her fingertips to her aching nipples to the swollen liquid folds between her thighs, she throbbed and tingled, her skin too tight for her body.

Slowly, Walker's firmly cut lips curved into a smile, the tenderness warming his eyes beautifully, wonderfully, clear. "What does the soul-link say?"

Holy Sister, she'd been so caught up in him, she'd forgotten all about it. The moment she turned her attention inward, the floodgates opened. A great warm rush of love and tears and lust swept her away, tossing her this way and that, bearing her higher and higher, deeper and deeper.

"Gods!" She yelped with shock, reeling, her arms flying out in an instinctive grab for balance.

Strong arms banded around her. She was drawn up against the unyielding heat of his broad chest.

"I'm here," rumbled a deep voice in her ear. "I will never let you go." The grip tightened until her ribs creaked. "I love you, Mehcredi."

Oh, gods, it was true. Submerged in the soul-link, fathoms deep, she could see him with absolute clarity, immovable as the solid earth that gave him his Magick, steadfast as the ancient cedderwood in the yard. His soul was shot through with the exhilarating energy of the *ch'qui*, yes, but beneath it all lay the bedrock of him, so plain, so honest, it owed nothing to Magick—only to a great and giving heart.

What he gave her was the whole world, newly minted. She might stumble and fall as she explored it, but what he offered too was all of himself, a refuge that was hers and hers alone. Joy made her lighter than air. Laughing, she gathered up the love and the pleasure, magnified it and pushed it back at him through the link. Coherent thought was no longer possible, her mind had dissolved into a coruscating rainbow that danced and sang, *Yes, yes, yes!* with every beat of her heart.

Still bubbling, Mehcredi clung as the world shifted around her. Peripherally, she was aware of being lowered to the bed, of cooler air washing over her bare legs. Gladly, she spread, opening herself as Walker came down over her, his muscled flesh searingly hot and strong against hers. He murmured in Shar, the words so quick she couldn't catch them, but the link gave her the sense.

She was *his*—his life, his future, his *carazada*. And he'd die if he couldn't join his flesh with hers—right—now.

Her eyes flew open in shock, all the air punching out of her in an undignified grunt. Merciful Sister, she could *feel* the instinctive male urge to rut and thrust and spill, the way the soft wet heat of her drew him irresistibly forward, his hips already shifting with the urge to pump. Only his iron will held him back, because to give her a moment's discomfort would kill him.

"Gods, do it." Tilting her hips, she wrapped her legs around his waist. "I'm dying. Now, Walker, now!"

Almost before the words had left her lips, he surged forward, seating himself to the hilt in one smooth plunge. Her muted shriek stirred the silken curtain of his hair. Walker froze, holding his breath.

For a charged moment, he rested his forehead against hers. "Don't move."

"I won't," she whispered, licking into his mouth.

She tried, she really did, but the slick satin walls clamped around his girth throbbed to the beat of her pulse. Or was it his? She could no longer distinguish. Feminine nerves fluttered, impaled by an exquisitely brutal pressure that stretched and filled. But simultaneously, she had the amazing sensation of succulent woman-flesh, slippery and hot, sliding all along the length of his cock. Soft skin stretched over an engorged core, so sensitive that even the smallest movement was excruciatingly pleasurable. Her head spun as each sensation amplified the other in a dizzying, upward rush.

She dug her fingers into his shoulders, arching into the beautiful blessed pressure. "Walker, I'm—I can't—"

"Wait! Gods, fuck!" He dug his knees into the mattress, buttocks clenching with the force of each ramming thrust.

His climax triggered hers, so closely they were almost simultaneous. Mehcredi writhed and flailed, the double sensations hitting her from inside and out, so exquisitely powerful her vision clouded over. All she could do was cling while the world imploded. She could have sworn the building trembled as the earth shifted in its bed. The door rattled and something tumbled off the dresser to land with a dull thud.

Panting, she reached up to smooth the hair out of his eyes. "You didn't," she said. "Tell me you didn't."

Walker cleared his throat. "Didn't what?" His bronzed face was ruddy with color.

"Make the earth move."

"I may have . . . uh, let my control slip." He shot her a dark look, but his lips twitched. "Just for an instant. Gods, the soul-link . . ." The amusement faded from his expression.

"Amazing. Mmm." Her eyes half closed, Mehcredi undulated beneath him, her inner muscles rippling. He was still mostly hard, not far from the knife edge of full arousal. Erotic possibilities made her head swim. The muscles in her thighs tensed with near unbearable excitement as she recalled the musky, masculine taste of him, the smooth weight of hard cock against her tongue. She'd track his arousal, bring him to the brink over and over, drive him crazy. Gods, what delicious torture.

Walker swiveled his hips, slow and languid. "Whatever you're thinking, assassin, it works both ways." When she gasped, he grinned, smug and very male. "We've done hard and fast. I promised you slow and sweet. And just so you know, when I'm finished, I'm going to start all over again. With my mouth. Like this."

Mehcredi panted as he eased away, his lips traveling across the complex architecture of her collarbones, nibbling curves and licking hollows. When he nuzzled over one breast to take a pale pink nipple in his hot mouth, her spine arched clean off the bed. "Nngh! Walker, will you—Ah, gods!"

He spoke around his mouthful, the vibrations thrumming through nerve-rich flesh. "Will I what?"

She squirmed. "Your Mark never really went away. Mark me again. For good."

Seconds ticked by as he pulled back to stare down at the creamy swell of her flesh, the silk of his hair brushing her shoulder as he breathed. "Ah, *carazada*. It will be my very great pleasure."

Without warning, he lifted her legs and placed them over his shoulders. Mehcredi's scream degenerated into a whimper. Brows drawn with concentration, he flexed his hips, creating a leisurely rhythm of long gliding thrusts, interspersed with the hip swivels that hit nerves inside her she didn't know she had. Inexorably, he drove her back up, an increment at a time, exploiting the link. Gods, he was shameless.

Instinctively, she struggled against his control, thrashing beneath him. "Sshh. Sweetheart, trust me. I won't let you fall."

"Yes." She fumbled a hand behind his neck, his skin hot against her palm, his hair a cool slide against her knuckles. "Oh, W-Walker."

Smiling, he turned his head to press a kiss to the inside of her arm, never ceasing the strong gentle rocking.

Because of his size and the acute angle, it was an extraordinary sensation, so acutely pleasurable it almost hurt. Bracing himself on one arm, he spread a palm over her left breast. "I did this once in anger," he murmured, his voice very deep. "Now I do it with love."

He resumed thrusting, working to some pattern of his own, shallow strokes interspersed with longer ones, luxuriously deep. Floating on a sea of pleasure, Mehcredi felt the climax threaten like a far-off avalanche, building a pebble at a time, a series of tiny increments powerful enough to shake her world to its foundations. Gradually, she became aware of a bright thread, weaving a purposeful path through the soul-link, binding them together. It felt shiny and . . . *green*?

Magick, it had to be. Shaman's Magick, the—what did he call it?—the *ch'qui*. Panicking a little, she reached out, but he was there, solid as a mountain.

Where his palm cupped her breast, the skin prickled as the *ch'qui* bloomed, flowering in her flesh, the invasion satin soft, exquisite. Her clit throbbed in sympathy, a bud about to burst into full glorious blossom.

"Ah." She moaned, all the muscles in her neck going loose, her head rolling on the pillow.

"Good?" he whispered.

"Gods, yes." Mehcredi forced her eyes open. "Feel it. *Feel me.*" She thrust the sensations back at him.

"Fuck, you're amazing." Walker hung over her, his face stark, the skin drawn tight over strong bones. The Magick burned in him now, the sap of life boiling in his balls, rasping the length of his cock like a rough tongue, insisting and demanding. He groaned, deep in his chest. "Can't—Gods! Soon, love."

The thrusts came faster, the avalanche of sensation rumbling closer, the weight of it bearing down on her, the tension suddenly more than she could bear. Within seconds, the high, tight friction built to a pleasure point so fiery she could no longer breathe, let alone make a sound. Everything tangled together—the crushing pressure in his balls, the luscious tension in her pelvis.

Nothing was separate anymore. The *ch'qui* licked over her clitoris, hot and bright, and her climax flowered into full bloom. The avalanche trembled on the brink. With a roar, it swooped, thundering down to roll her under, obliterating all thought save one. Her fingers scrabbling at the quilt, Mehcredi hung suspended in ecstasy, conscious only that she was no longer separate. Everywhere she looked, Walker shone like a steady beacon, a candle lit for her in the window. He was there. He would always be there.

Dimly, she heard her name, his voice guttural, choked with passion, then so tender she could have wept. A hard breathing pause and he lowered her legs to the bed. Mehcredi turned her head into a sweaty shoulder as a big warm hand cupped her sex, gentling her through the aftershocks.

"Gods," she mumbled into his skin, pressing close. "That was—Gods."

"Yes."

They lay in silence, half dozing, legs tangled. At last, Walker said softly, "I've never done it like that before."

Mehcredi blushed. "In that position? I haven't either."

"No. With such joy." His lips took on a rueful curve. "I think I was a virgin."

Mehcredi murmured her pleasure, rolling over to lie half on his chest, half off. Staring into his face, she made a discovery. "You have the most beautiful smile."

Walker glowered. "Don't push your luck, woman." But he spoiled it by tucking a stray curl behind her ear. "Shar warriors do not smile. Ever."

"Do too." Untroubled, Mehcredi grinned. "And even when you don't, your eyes dance. You get little creases, just here at the corners." She sighed with satisfaction, smoothing them with her thumbs.

"I always thought that was silly. How can eyes dance? But yours do. And look at those eyelashes, that hair." She dropped light kisses on his eyelids, one after the other. "Sister in the sky, it's not fair. You're prettier than me."

Walker's expression hovered between outrage and amusement. "Shut up, assassin," he growled. "You talk too much."

Mehcredi giggled, unrepentant. "I think you like it. And don't call me—Mmpf."

Bending his head, he closed her mouth with his.

TURN THE PAGE FOR A PREVIEW
OF THE STUNNING CONCLUSION
TO DENISE ROSSETTI'S
FOUR-SIDED PENTACLE SERIES . . .

THE DARK ROSE

COMING SOON FROM BERKLEY SENSATION!

CARACOLE OF THE ISLES
PALIMPSEST

"I can't do it." When Rose opened her fingers, the crumpled sheet of paper fluttered down to the silk coverlet like a broken-backed bird. "I can't send another one to die."

"Rosarina." Noblelord Izanami's claw-like hand groped across the bed for the letter. "My dear."

"Don't 'my dear' me." Her skirts swishing with agitation, Rose crossed the elegant room to stand by the tall windows.

"Merciful gods." Her voice cracked as she rested her forehead on the cool glass. Below, blue wavelets kicked up in the light breeze and skiffs darted to and fro on the canal like improbable water beetles, bearing passengers and goods. Decked out with graceful bridges, fretted towers and pagoda roofs, the city of Caracole flirted with spring like the finest of courtesans.

Grimly, she turned her back on it and faced the long, gaunt figure in the bed. "For the gods' sakes, the man was torn to pieces! Gutted like a beast in an abattoir."

"I know. It means he got too close."

Unflinching, the queen's spymaster met Rose's anguished gaze. Did he have regrets? She suspected he did, but they could not compete with expediency, the greater good of the Queendom. Staring into those faded blue eyes, seeing the dispassionate intelligence there, the iron purpose, a wave of revulsion rose in her throat.

"How can you stand to look in the mirror?" She made a wild gesture. "Year after year, you've sent them out, knowing—" She squeezed her eyes shut for a moment. "Godsdammit."

"Three decades, to be exact. You forget, I am the Queen's Left Hand." Each word cost him dearly, but not even illness could rob Noblelord Izanami of his cool composure, his air of hauteur. "The responsibility is part of the office. All our agents know the risks." His gaze sharpened. "Just as you do, Rose."

He paused for a moment, gathering his strength. "There is no room for scruples in this business. And you cannot tell me you haven't always known it."

Rose pressed her lips together. "Not at first," she said. "Not for the first few years." She shot him a dark glance. "You were clever. You drew me in so slowly, so cleverly."

His thin lips had a blue tinge she didn't like, but he managed a smile. "Ah, you were perfect." He let out a sighing breath. "The best young mind I'd ever met, wonderfully subtle, incredibly devious, and yet—" Something sparked in his eyes. "In person, you were dazzling, more beautiful than the Sister Herself. Gods, what a combination. A courtesan and a spy without peer. Flawless."

Rose sighed. It wasn't flattery. Always a pretty child, then a lovely girl, she'd matured into a woman so breathtaking men stopped in the street to stare as she passed. The most sought-after courtesan in the Queendom, the Dark Rose.

It was the whole package she sold, the charm, the clever conversation, the music and the dancing. And in return? Rosarina of The Garden had always been discriminating in her choice of protectors, but she'd given good value. Her elegant presence on his arm gifted any noblelord with a certain cachet in public. In private, he gained an enchanted world in which he could be king or courtier as the whim took him, surcease from his troubles.

Always on display, always on stage, even in the most intimate moments. There'd been years she'd felt scraped hollow by the effort of giving and giving and giving, until there was only a tiny kernel of self left unsold, but godsdammit, in the end, she'd done it—escaped with the façade in place, her soul intact. And if the only person who knew the real Rosarina was a manipulative aristocrat old enough to be her father, well . . . that was the price she paid.

With a fluid shrug, she said, "I retired as a working courtesan years ago. When Prue and I bought The Garden."

"You are still my best intelligencer," the Left Hand said with quiet satisfaction. He cleared his throat. "And therefore best suited to succeed me."

"What?" For a second, she was sure she'd misheard, but before she could say more, the old man gasped for breath, his face first flushing, then going alarmingly pale. He clutched his chest, coughing.

Rose leaped for the bellpull, but a strangled grunt from the bed stopped her. "No . . . wait." The command was unmistakable.

Her heart hammering, Rose sank to her knees by the bed and took a long-fingered hand in hers. His flesh was cold and smooth, the bones brittle beneath the thin skin. Gradually, he grew calmer and a faint wash of color returned to his sunken cheeks, though his chest rattled with every breath.

"Noblelord," Rose said when she could force words through the lump in her throat. "This is nonsense. You're too godsbedamned mean to die."

"We all . . . die," he said acidly, but his fingers gripped hers with surprising strength. "This matter is not closed, Rosarina."

"If you mean the succession, yes, it is." Rose ripped her hands free. She stood, glaring down at Izanami. "I won't do it. I *couldn't.* Don't you see?" She whirled away, took a couple of hasty paces and turned. "I'm weak. I'll never be as . . . as cold-blooded as you. I know Green IV is a threat, I know we need information, but the thought of sending someone else makes me want to—I don't know—throw up. Scream out loud."

"You've been acting in my place for more than a month, since— Hand me that cordial, would you?" He drank, taking small, disdainful sips. "Every decision you've made thus far has been for the good of the Queendom." He closed his eyes, his breath still shallow and quick. "Give me . . . a moment."

Rose did so, disciplining her breathing. *In through the nose, out through the mouth. In through the nose, out through the mouth.* A solution existed for every problem—but only if you were prepared to accept the cost.

Disemboweled, the report had said. Body parts strewn about the room, the walls painted crimson with his blood. Gods!

The beautiful chamber was hushed in the warmth of the afternoon, bars of sunlight streaming in to spark on the jeweled tones in the carpet, to caress the thin hands folded on the old man's chest. When he died, they'd lay him out like that. Noblelady Izanami, small and dark and lively, would grieve for him sincerely, and his three daughters would be distraught.

And she? Rose blinked hard. She'd miss him dreadfully.

"I'll go myself," she said into the silence. "It's the only way."

The Left Hand's eyes opened slowly, as if the lids were weighted. He thought for a long time, his brow furrowed and his lips tight.

"Very well," he whispered at last. "I don't like it, but we must have someone on Green IV. I'll get Marot to step in here." He fixed her with an imperious gaze. "You will report frequently and you will do what I tell you. Do you hear?"

When she nodded, some of the tension left his long frame. "Come back . . . to me . . . my dear."

Rose bent to kiss his cold cheek, his gray stubble harsh against her lips. "Of course," she said steadily. "No one suspects the Dark Rose of anything deep. All she thinks about is parties and pleasure and whether to wear her hair up or down."

Carefully, she folded up the paper and placed it in her pocket. Then she slipped out of the door without looking back, heading for the music room where the Izanami daughters were waiting for their regular lesson in deportment.

THREE WEEKS LATER
BALLYNEWHAVEN, GREEN IV

Gravel crunched as the carriage swept down the long curved drive of the Lord-Scion Harte's town house. In the dim interior of the luxuriously appointed vehicle, Rose smoothed her long, trailing sleeves, conscious of a sense of trepidation so acute it approached exquisite. Every nerve tingled. Sister in the sky, how long had it been since she'd felt such a pure sensation?

Deliberately, she pulled in a long breath. She'd never been offworld before, but as the Technomage starship speared away from Palimpsest, she'd lain quietly in the safety webbing, staring out at the vastness of space. Tears of awe had sprung to her eyes. She and all those she cared for, they were no more than the merest specks, born alone, dying alone. It gave her mission a certain perspective.

She shivered, reaching up to rub the nape of her neck, but carefully. It wouldn't do to disturb the coiffure, not when it had taken the combined efforts of two maids to achieve it.

The carriage slowed, drawing to a halt. Hooves stamped, tack jingled. Rose's lips curved with pure pleasure. Four matched grays. Only the highest sticklers and the most wealthy on Green IV still used horse-drawn vehicles. Between them, Queen Sikara and the Left Hand had spared no expense. The rest was up to her.

She gathered serenity around her, shrugging into it the way she would have donned a cloak. This was her business, her profession— and by the Sister, she was very, very skilled. *A true courtesan creates a persona*, she told her apprentices again and again. *Achieve a certain mystique, make it look effortless, and you'll be irresistible.*

A bewigged footman opened the door and extended a gloved hand. Light from a myriad of glowglobes in fancy sconces washed into the carriage, a wave of sprightly music tinkled in the softly scented air. With considerable satisfaction, Rose observed the footman's eyes widen as he took in the picture she presented, but he was too well trained to do more than bow and murmur, "Scionelle?"

Hide in plain sight.

Tenderly, the man assisted her to alight. Together, the tips of her fingers resting on his serge-clad forearm, they climbed the imposing stairs, Rose's gem-studded heels rapping on the flagged stone like a delicate military tattoo.

The great house shone with light and music and laughter, its clean Palladian lines soaring up in a perfection of architectural rationality. As they passed through the columned portico, an impeccably suited majordomo appeared at Rose's elbow.

He bowed, betraying not a single flicker of surprise or censure. "Scionelle, what name shall I say?"

Rose gave him a contained smile. "I am the Noblelady Rosarina of Caracole." The queen had insisted on making the title real. Rose's mouth twisted a little. Ironic when she had a perfectly good title of her own, unused for twenty years and no more than a trifle tarnished.

"Thank you, Noblelady." Another bow. "I will announce you."

The ballroom glittered with the cream of the Sciony, the men wearing the pale breeches and fitted evening jackets dictated by convention, the women a bower of tropical flowers, each clad in yards of billowing silk. As they moved in the precise measures of a formal dance, all she could think of was the toy she'd had as a child, a tube filled with shards of colored glass. Shake it and everything shifted, but somehow the patterns always fell into a perfect symmetry. So pretty. So ephemeral.

The dance was drawing to its graceful conclusion, the musicians in the gallery slowing the pace of their plucking and fiddling. Already heads were turning.

Good. Standing at the top of the curving staircase, Rose lifted her chin.

As the last notes died away, so did the conversation. One by one, a hundred people turned to stare. Rose favored them with a tranquil smile, tilting her head as the majordomo pronounced her name. The man didn't even need to raise his voice. Truly, the acoustics were extraordinary.

The moment she took the first step, the murmurs began, as if a playful breeze had swept across a garden, setting all the flowers to nodding and swaying.

A middle-aged man with sandy hair detached himself from the throng and took the stairs two at a time, meeting Rose and her escort not far from the bottom.

Creases appeared at the corners of appreciative blue eyes. "I am Harte," he said in a soft brogue. Raising her hand, he brushed it with his lips and gave an exaggerated sigh. "Ah, the beautiful Dark Rose of Caracole. You are even more . . . spectacular than your reputation promised."

Rose gazed into those clever eyes. "Thank you, Lord-Scion. I am greatly in your debt for the invitation."

"I had no idea doing a favor for my old friend Purist Deiter would

be so delightful." Harte twinkled. "I am most thoroughly at your service, Scionelle."

This man had to be a wizard nearly as powerful as Deiter. What
sort of hold did the old reprobate have on the Lord-Scion? It must
be godsbedamned good, because Magick ran deep and strong in the
Harte blood. Aloud, she said, "Forgive me, Lord-Scion, but the cor-
rect form of address is Noblelady."

After an infinitesimal pause, he said, "Of course. And though
technically I'm entitled to be called Purist, I prefer Lord-Scion." She
caught a glimpse of teeth.

He offered his arm. "Come, Noblelady. Favor us with your delightful company."

It wasn't a request.

⁓∞⁓

"Will you attend the masque at Fitzgerald Court, good sir?" The little
blonde twined a shining ringlet around one finger.

The top of her head was about level with Quin's starched cravat.
Scowling, he subdued the impulse to rip the neck-cloth off so he
could breathe. For Science's sake, didn't these people have any concept of comfort in dress? The fitted jacket of dark green encased his
shoulders so tightly he could barely move, while the cream breeches
felt indecently snug. The only parts of him remotely happy were his
feet. He flexed his toes. The boots were a marvel of engineering, made
by hand, or so he'd been assured.

"But how silly of me! The Fitzgerald is your sponsor. Of course
you'll be there. You simply mustn't miss it, such fun, you know, all in
costume. It's a rural theme, so quaint."

He'd never liked the slick feel of the Technomage shoes that conformed automatically to the shape of the wearer's foot. They were
made of transplas, whereas real boots—made of real leather—weren't
that easy to come by, let alone in his size. He should order a couple
of pairs to take home to Palimpsest, but not in this over-the-knee
style. He glanced down. Made a man look ridiculous. Once the job
on Green IV was done, he could return to his familiar whites, to his
quiet lab and his prototypes. Ah, but the job . . . His pulse kicked up
a notch.

"I have a milkmaid gown, all in blue, very simple, very charming. If I wear my hair down, the effect . . ."

As the girl's voice tinkled on, Quin let his mind wander to the great Machine a mile beneath their feet, the beating, humming heart of Green IV. Now that was a marvel indeed, occupying most of the interior of the planet, drawing power from its molten core to create the atmosphere. Millennia ago, the Machine had been created to gift a barren rock with air and life, with fertile soil and pure water. Without it, none of this—his lips quirking in a cynical grin, Quin studied the silks and satins, the glowglobes sparkling in the chandeliers, the tables laden with elegant morsels and pale wines—none of this *frippery* would be possible. Did the Sciony understand the precarious nature of its existence?

The blonde had apparently run out of breath. Out of the corner of his eye, Quin watched her pretty tits rise and fall beneath the modestly cut bodice as she inhaled. He was bored, not dead.

"Blue's a good color for me, don't you think?" She swished her cobalt skirts in a meaningful sort of way.

"Mm," said Quin, leaning against the plinth of the statue behind him, the marble cold against his flesh even through the layers of garments. The perimeter of the ballroom was littered with the useless things, chilly maidens coyly covering their privates, proud warriors with stony chins and frozen genitalia.

"What's it like being a real Technomage?" The girl fluttered her lashes.

Quin grunted. He had no ear for music, and no time for it either, but he suspected the musicians were winding down. Good. "Ask a Fitzgerald or better yet, a Callaghan. Look, there's one over there." He gestured at a stocky youth hovering near the supper table, but the girl curled a pretty lip.

"Joey Callaghan?" she said with scorn. "I've known him all my life. He's like all the rest of them—such a bore, nothing like a real Scientist. What's it like to live in a Technomage Tower and have a number for a name? Wait a minute . . . Quintus . . ." Her brow creased. "That's a word. Didn't they give you a number?"

"Five." Was that a stir at the head of the stairs? Some aristocrat too lofty for punctuality.

"I'm sorry, I don't—"

"I am the Quintus, the fifth."

Two figures appeared at the head of the stairs, and though he wasn't an imaginative man, Quin had the strangest fancy that they stood in a frame, as if posed for an oil painting, the kind hanging in the gallery on the floor above.

Over the growing hush, the majordomo's voice rose clearly. "The Noblelady Rosarina of Caracole in the Queendom of the Isles."

Without quite intending to, Quin engaged the Augmentation in his left eye, and the Dark Rose sprang forward, filling his vision and his head.

He'd thought she looked lovely travel-worn and weary at Lonefell Keep months ago, her nose pink with cold. Here, in full plumage, gowned for battle, she stole the breath from his body.

His companion gasped. "Saints preserve us! What in heaven's name is she wearing? Who *is* she?"

"That," said Quin, "is the Dark Rose, the most famous courtesan in Caracole."

"But . . . her *gown!*" Now the girl sounded strangled.

"I like it."

Quin adjusted the magnification, focusing on the glorious bosom and shoulders rising unadorned from the deep scooped neckline like a flower from a calyx. The dark honey of her skin made all the Scionelles look pale and ill. He knew little of fashion and cared less, but he had no difficulty recognizing sheer nerve when he saw it. Rose's exotic garment was nothing like the billowing confections worn by every other female present. For a start, it was slimly fitted, the fabric richly textured in flowing patterns in every shade of warm red and soft pink with touches of gold and midnight blue. It looked both heavy and supple, hinting at the movement of shapely limbs beneath. Immediately below her breasts was a sort of broad belt, a band of darker gold-shot material, cinched tight. He could have spanned it with one hand, his thumb brushing the underside of a sweet curve, his smallest finger dipping toward the cup of her navel.

"And her *hair!*"

Blue black and glossy, it swept up to expose the slender nape of her neck, increasing the impression of vulnerability, making a man wonder whether she'd gasp when he ran a fingertip from the warm skin behind her ear all the way over the graceful struts of her collarbones and down into the fragrant shadow of her cleavage. She had the shining wealth of it gathered up in two large . . . knobs? Bunches? Something like that, anyway, and each was skewered with two slender jeweled shafts that winked in the light. A small golden headpiece with graceful upturned corners had been set a few inches back from her hairline.

Quin frowned, a vague resemblance niggling at his memory. Ah. The rooflines of Caracole, like pagodas. "It's meant to be national dress—I think." Turning, he blinked down at his companion, his vision filled with cavernous tunnels and hairs like tree trunks. It took him a couple of seconds of fierce concentration to pull the focus back to the blonde's retroussé little nose. Really, that was too slow. Augmentations required practice.

"Oh look, that's the Harte! Heavens, he just introduced her to his mother."

Ah, he loved it when life took a right-angled turn. Fighting to keep the hunter's grin on the inside, Quin closed his fingers over the cold toes of the stone maiden on her plinth. He knew for certain Rosarina of The Garden of Nocturnal Delights had never had a Technomage as a client or lover because from the moment of their brief meeting at Lonefell, he'd made it his business to uncover every fact about her. He might be a specialist engineer, but that didn't mean he'd forgotten how to research. Far from it. A night's work and Rose's history lay bare before him, every protector, every liaison, all the way back to the year she'd first appeared in Caracole—but no further. She'd been nineteen then and by all accounts, unbearably beautiful. The blank years, however, constituted a loose end. Quin did not approve of loose ends.

"Do you know her? She's dreadfully bold, but oh my goodness, she's lovely. I just adore those sleeves. So graceful."

The girl sighed in unabashed envy, and for the first time, Quin looked at her with real attention. No more than a child, really, trying her wings. Pity she was such an empty-headed piece.

"We've met," he said at last.

"Well of course you have, you're from the same place." She beamed up at him.

"Of course," Quin said. "There are no more than two billion people on Palimpsest."

She pouted. "Now you're making fun of me."

"On the contrary."

What color were Rose's eyes tonight? He remembered being fascinated with the way they'd changed with her emotions—from blue, to green, to gray, every hue on the spectrum. Stone toes creaked under the force of his grip, but he didn't notice. What shade would they be when she lay beneath him, lush and naked and panting? For a moment, he was tempted to use his visual Augmentation to check, but why rush? His mouth curved into a wolfish grin. He'd savor the discovery close-up.

Rose was the center of a laughing group, holding court with effortless charm. As if she felt the weight of his stare, she looked up. The world held its breath, then a dark brow arched in cool inquiry. Their gazes snagged, a salute like rapiers clashing. Quin's blood surged.

A small hand tugged at Quin's sleeve. "Will you introduce me?" the blonde girl asked, breathless with excitement.

"Mm?"

On the far side of the room Rose dismissed him, turning her head to converse with a young man wearing a waistcoat with huge silver buttons. The boy looked both poleaxed and delighted.

"No," Quin said.

"Oh." The hand fell away. A pause. "Why not?"

"I can't remember your name."

Ignoring the outraged gasp, Quin started across the floor. It wasn't until he drew level with the supper table that he realized he had a stone toe clenched in his left fist. Godsbedamned Augmentations. Irritably, he shoved the thing in a pocket. Didn't know his own strength anymore.

Oh yes, a blue dark as a midnight sea. Artfully outlined with something sooty.

Satisfied with the color of Rose's eyes, Quin wandered over to the food. A man his size took a power of feeding. The Dark Rose was busy right now. She'd keep.

✺

The sight of him stopped her heart. The boy with the regrettable waistcoat had been telling her where to find the most sought-after modistes and milliners, but her skin had prickled, a primitive, instinctive warning. With a shiver, she'd looked up—straight into hard hazel eyes.

Sister save her, *Quin*!

No, the Quintus, she corrected herself quickly. Only four ranks below the Technomage Primus of Palimpsest, and a member of the Tower's Council of Ten.

What in the gods' names was he doing on Green IV?

Calmly, she held his stare. He gave her a tight grin, no more than a baring of teeth. Standing between a vapid little blonde and a chilly marble statue, he was . . . well, startling, like some great tawny animal, his vitality forced into the constriction of evening dress. More bull-like than feline though, with those brutish shoulders and brawny thighs, his hair cropped short.

Something about his posture, the way he kept rubbing the fingertips of his left hand together, made her think he felt as out of place as he looked.

Her brain raced, sifting facts, arranging and discarding. In the secret drawer in her bedroom, back at The Garden, she had a sizeable dossier on Quin. Rose bit her lip. Sister, she wished she'd brought it with her, but who'd have thought he'd turn up here on Green IV?

Smiling, she accepted a glass of pale wine from the boy with the waistcoat. He cleared his throat, refusing to let his gaze drop below the level of her chin. Nice lad, well brought up.

Quin, on the other hand . . . No one in their right mind would ever refer to him as 'a nice lad,' not at any stage of his development and certainly not now. The Quintus was the brutal and calculated result of a Technomage charity program. Taken at an early age from the mean streets of the Caracole slums, his initial test results had been off the charts. The Technomage teachers had struggled to keep up with his thirst for knowledge. If he had family, he never mentioned them, or not that Rose could discover.

But he'd fulfilled that early promise in spectacular fashion, designing engines for starships and flitters. Apparently, he'd made amazing improvements to all kinds of devices, from glowglobes to laseguns.

The Quintus was not only a brilliant engineer, he was a Scientific maverick, creative, opinionated and moody.

He'd come to do something with or for the Machine. There could be no other conclusion.

Rose stiffened her spine. If she glanced over Waistcoat Boy's shoulder, she'd see Quin leaning against the wall with a plate loaded high, devouring delicate tidbits one after the other, using his fingers. Her lip curled. For the Sister's sake, he even ate like a machine, with extraordinary efficiency and dispatch. His eyes were very bright, and they never wavered from her face.

So strange. Rose knew all there was to know about men, how they thought, what they wanted, but she had no idea what was going on behind that level burning gaze, only that the heat bloomed in her cheeks as if she were sixteen and still a virgin. She stared down at her hands until the feeling passed and she could breathe again.

Very well. He obviously wanted to speak with her. She'd allow it, but she'd be on her guard, and so very cool his . . . interest . . . would shrivel to a nub.

"I declare, I simply *adore* those sleeves," said a girlish voice at her elbow. "You *must* tell me all about your modiste." With a smile, Rose turned to speak with a vapid blonde wearing a shade of blue too strong for her delicate complexion. When she looked up a few minutes later, Quin had disappeared.